W9-AFI-092

Tender Beasts

ALSO BY LISELLE SAMBURY

Blood Like Magic
Blood Like Fate
Delicious Monsters

LISELLE SAMBURY

MARGARET K. McELDERRY BOOKS
New York London Toronto Sydney New Delhi

MARGARET K. McELDERRY BOOKS

An imprint of Simon & Schuster Children's Publishing Division

1230 Avenue of the Americas, New York, New York 10020

Text © 2024 by Liselle Sambury

Jacket illustration © 2024 by Elena Masci

Jacket design by Greg Stadnyk © 2024 by Simon & Schuster, LLC

MARGARET K. McELDERRY BOOKS is a trademark of Simon & Schuster, LLC

Simon & Schuster: Celebrating 100 Years of Publishing in 2024

For information about special discounts for bulk purchases, please contact Simon & Schuster Special Sales at 1-866-506-1949 or business@simonandschuster.com.

The Simon & Schuster Speakers Bureau can bring authors to your live event. For more information or to book an event, contact the Simon & Schuster Speakers Bureau at 1-866-248-3049 or visit our website at www.simonspeakers.com.

Interior design by Lisa Vega

The text for this book was set in Urge.

Manufactured in the United States of America

First Edition

10 9 8 7 6 5 4 3 2 1

CIP data for this book is available from the Library of Congress.

ISBN 9781665903523

ISBN 9781665903547 (ebook)

AUTHOR NOTE

While this is a work of fiction, some of the topics discussed do exist in our real world. I've compiled a list of content warnings to help those who may need them. I've done my best to address everything here, but I keep an updated list on my website in case I am later informed of triggers that I may have missed. Please visit that site for the most updated information.

Readers who may be sensitive to any of these elements, please take note, or you may want to stop reading.

Content warnings: death of a parent/grief, animal death (on-page—cow and lizard; off-page, referenced but not described—cat; off-page, referenced and somewhat described—unspecified animals), mentions of self-harm/suicide, drinking and drug use, infidelity, discussions of toxic intimate relationships, detailed body horror/gore, violence, death (includes child death)

PROLOGUE

A insley Behre did not do lateness. She couldn't stand walking into a meeting after it had already started, a room of people turning to her with knowing smirks that said, "Black people are always late." It grated on her. Her dad regularly failed to be on time, and it didn't exactly endear him to the people who already hated him for what he had. And now that he was gone, what *she* had.

But, devoted as she was to punctuality, sometimes shit just hit the fan when you didn't expect it. Like the snowstorm that had suddenly swept across the East Coast. Her flight in from New York was supposed to land at Toronto Pearson Airport at 6:00 p.m. But the weather had caused delay after delay and when the aircraft finally bumped to a stop on the tarmac, she stared down at her phone and saw 11:05 p.m. staring back at her. Her lip curled.

When the seat belt sign clicked off and everyone scrambled from their seats, she rose slowly, unwilling to look like a panicked cockroach. She took her time retrieving her roller bag and slipped into the aisle. She'd been in the front row as was her preference, and so she was one of the first people off when they finally opened the boarding door.

As she departed, she checked her phone to see if Paris had sent her any messages, but there was nothing from the lawyer. For the sake of her retainer, the woman had better be working day and night on this case. Paris was calculating and meticulous, which was why Ainsley had taken her on in the first place. Also, she preferred to work with other Black professionals whenever possible. Paris was good, but she wasn't perfect. Though Ainsley's husband would say that no one would ever be perfect enough for her.

Ainsley attempted to ignore the blizzard still raging, which she could see out the giant windows as she stepped onto the moving sidewalk toward customs. Her shoulders cramped, and she took a moment to roll them back. The flight hadn't even been long, but that was the thing about getting older. Your body betrayed you more and more. Her heart rate accelerated against her will, and she immediately thought of the ranch. Of the suffocating stink of the blood. And that sour smell she couldn't escape. *No. Stop it*, she thought. *You're better than this.*

She forced herself to relax. It was fine. She was fine.

Ainsley made her way past the throngs of passengers heading to the long customs line and breezed forward through the mobile customs since she had the sense to arrange her affairs ahead of time. The same way she'd set her husband to the tasks that he needed to do today, but she wouldn't feel settled until she was home with him. Until she could ensure that everything was as it should be.

She was thankful that this business trip hadn't required more than a carry-on, so she didn't have to wait for baggage. Though she cursed herself when she nearly tripped over her feet rushing out of customs. She righted herself quickly, but not in time to avoid knocking into a little boy.

When she looked down to apologize to him, he stared up at her with a face she recognized, his lips pulled into a wide smile comically stretched from ear to ear.

"Excuse us," his mother said, tugging him away.

Ainsley squeezed her eyes shut, then opened them again. The boy was looking at her over his shoulder, but the familiarity was gone. She didn't know him.

She didn't have time for this.

The floor transitioned from carpet to tile, and the heels of her boots clicked as she strode across the space toward the parking garage. She checked her phone again as she waited for the elevator; it was only quarter past. She was going to make it.

"Ma'am?" someone called from behind her.

She turned and raised an eyebrow.

It was an airport staff member who pointed to a sign that she hadn't noticed. A sign noting that the parking garage could not currently be accessed by elevator. "You'll have to walk out and go down the stairs," he said. "The fastest way is those ones out door D. They're outside, but it's a bit of a trek otherwise."

She knew that he didn't deserve the look she threw at him, but she did it anyway. She couldn't bring herself to smile and be courteous. To thank him. To do any of the things that Ainsley Behre would usually do. This was not the day for it.

She considered texting her husband to tell him that he should prepare in case she was late. *No.* She couldn't be late. Jay had already messed things up last year. He could barely be counted on to tie his own shoes. The Jay she had grown up with had been so different. Confident. Assured. Calm under pressure. But the fire had changed that. Or rather, everything that came after had. She'd thought maybe he would grow out of it, like her. It was the worst gamble she'd ever made.

Instead, she walked to door D as she'd been directed. Outside she was immediately hit in the face with a torrent of hail and wind. Cars were lined up and slow moving, attempting to make pickups while passengers struggled with their luggage.

She yanked her suitcase behind her across the pedestrian walkway that led to the giant parking structure, searching for P3 signs. When she finally found them, she made a beeline to the set of outdoor steps leading down, which were covered in snow and ice. Because of course they hadn't salted them yet.

When she set her foot down on the first step, she felt the ground slip out from underneath her and clung to the metal railing, only just managing to keep herself upright. It worsened the pain in her shoulders, making it feel like someone had shoved their thumbs between the blades and dug in with their nails.

She was not going to be late.

She was not going to let Jay take over.

She was not going to let him fuck this up, *again*.

She walked, more carefully now, to the landing leading into the P3 garage. It was blissfully clear of ice because of the overhang of concrete from the upper floor.

Ainsley let out a sigh of relief when she spotted her black Cadillac Escalade and rushed down the rest of the stairs.

What she had failed to see, however, was the figure tucked into the shadows.

Half an hour later, an airport staff member would finally get a chance to go out and salt the area leading to the underground parking. That was where he found Ainsley lying on the steps with a key fob clutched in her manicured fingers. Her eyes were wide open with icicles forming on the lashes and a dark pool of blood spread around her head.

Meanwhile, the Escalade still sat innocently in its spot, waiting for her to get in.

Ainsley didn't make it home.

She wasn't able to take care of everything like she always did.

And as she'd died, she'd thought of one thing and one thing only.

Dom.

CHAPTER ONE

I t took Mom dying for me to realize that she had an excessive obsession with bears.

The tiny wooden carved bear on her key chain that they found in her frozen hand. The bear-shaped air freshener in her empty Escalade, just a few feet away from her. And the dozens of teddy bears that people brought to her funeral, that small detail being the most that the average person knew about her. The funeral we'd had all because of a patch of invisible black ice at the bottom of a staircase. One little slip and Mom was gone.

Now I looked to the handmade bowl on the coffee table with tiny bear ears on either side. The family was together on the main floor of our three-story lakeshore home. It was boxy and modern, and its design had been meticulously overseen by Mom. Every detail she'd insisted on had been carried out, from the open-concept main area, to the glass-enclosed pool attached to it that you could see into from the basement observation hall, to the precisely ten balconies—two of which were technically inaccessible but were needed for symmetry.

I tucked my feet up under me on the couch while our lawyer, Paris, explained to Dad how everything would go down today. She was a seemingly constant presence in our lives lately. A dark-skinned Black woman who I imagined white women might like to call strong. She looked at us out of the corner of her eye while she talked to Dad. Our living area included a giant U-shaped sectional, and yet we were all piled together in the middle.

I kept staring at the bear bowl. Now that I had time to think about it, it was wild how many things there were in our lives that fit the theme. Murals in our childhood bedrooms that ranged from cartoonish Winnie the Pooh–type designs to paintings so realistic that they reminded us of the real thing, which we often feared running into at our family-owned ranch in Oro. Our monogrammed towels in the washrooms with tiny bears embroidered beside the initials.

And then there were the songs she would sing to us.

She loved "Five Bear Cubs" the most.

> *One bear cub*
> *Feeling so blue*

She would point to Karter, the oldest, who would roll her eyes but have a smile tugging at the corners of her lips. Now Karter had on no makeup and stared intensely at Paris, her face looking oddly pale without her foundation.

> *Begged for a brother*
> *Now mama has two*

That was Mom's cue to point to Darren, who'd come next, kicking and screaming, though the song didn't mention that. He was the epitome of middle child syndrome before he even became the middle child. Now his eyes seemed hollowed out, and he picked at the chipping polish on his nails.

> *Two bear cubs*
> *On adventures at sea*
> *Wished for a third mate*
> *Now mama has three*

Kiley was next. The beauty of the family, which was so obvious that the rest of us couldn't even get mad about it. People of *multiple* genders had literally fought over her before. A lot of bad love poems had been delivered to our house over the years. She'd even incorporated them into a sculpture for a competition. She'd won it too. Now was the first time I'd ever seen her perfect skin dull.

As usual, she and Darren were huddled close together. They'd changed since Mom died. All of us had, I guess. But somehow I'd expected them to be less affected. Or maybe to bounce back faster. I always used to know they were home because of all their shouting and laughing and talking into the night. Now their rooms were quiet. They were the middles. That title felt like it should be some sort of armor. They were the ones who brought parties to life, even if they sometimes went too far. Though technically, they weren't the only middle children. I was too. Maybe I should have been mad to be left out. But I knew it wasn't me who they were ignoring.

Three bear cubs
Practicing their roars
They wanted to be louder
Now mama has four

That was my cue. I would pop up from wherever I was sitting and strike some sort of pose that would make Mom laugh and my siblings scoff. According to my parents, I'd come straight out the womb with a tiny, gummy smile on my face. It was why they'd abandoned their *K* and *D* naming pattern to call me Sunny. Because I came to them as a bright ray of sunshine. Now . . . well, now I look the same. I always do. A smile pasted on my face as I pretend to listen to Paris, feeling far away from the emotion that my expression would suggest.

Four bear cubs
Practicing their dives

Needed bigger splashes
Now mama has five

The song ended there, which I always thought was fitting. Dom didn't get his own verse, and when Mom finished the song, she wouldn't point at him. She'd just hold up five fingers and laugh, and we'd cheer and clap. Dom wouldn't say anything. He'd just sit in the corner, watching us.

The four of us were born in a row, one after the other. But Dom was born two years later. They'd broken their naming pattern with me, but when Dom came, they went back to it. Maybe that should have made him feel more like he belonged.

But it didn't.

I knew the middles weren't the middles because I didn't count.

They were the middles because we left out Dom.

And then he went and killed that girl.

Allegedly, anyway.

Now he was as separate from us as he could ever be.

I didn't think any of us really thought he did it. But at the same time, I also wasn't sure that any of us could say with complete confidence that he hadn't.

"That's everything. We're ready to go," Paris declared, apparently done with what she had to tell Dad, though I knew he hadn't actually taken it in. Paris talked to Dad because he was the "real" adult, but he was like a phone. He had the ability to do a lot of things, but he needed input. He needed someone to tell him exactly how to work his many functions.

That used to be Mom.

Now it was Karter.

But it should have been me.

It was our little secret, Mom and me. That I would be the one to lead our family when she was gone. But as it turned out, she'd hid this secret too well because I was the only person who seemed to know. Karter had just swept in like the controlling bitch she was, and what was I supposed to do now?

I had lived through things. I had perspective that Karter didn't. And I prioritized the family above all. I knew them better than anyone. That was what Mom had told me. She wanted me to lead, and I wanted to do that for her, so why hadn't it happened the way it was supposed to? Why was I sitting here like a spectator while Karter took the wheel?

I sucked in a deep, calming breath and disguised it as a "glad to have that all sorted out!" contented sigh, then stood up with a grin. "We should grab some McDonald's or something on the way. Dom would like that." He might. I knew he went there sometimes with his friend. I also knew that none of us wanted to endure a two- to three-hour sit-down meal with him.

I had that sort of attention to detail and understanding of the family. Karter didn't. And yet here we were.

My grin forced Dad to smile too. "Sure."

That was the point. I smiled when no one else wanted to, and it helped them do it. That was the Sunny effect. Even when I couldn't look at my oldest sister without wanting to glower at her, and despite the fact that Mom had promised me something she'd now failed to deliver and couldn't correct. I couldn't fix it either without breaking character. I did not create discord within the family. I soothed it. Accusing Karter of taking a role that didn't belong to her without proof was not very Sunny.

And I always lived up to my name.

The SUV stank of McDonald's.

We were packed into the Escalade and each had our own paper takeout bags in our laps. Probably, we should have waited for Dom and eaten together, but as usual, by the time we got him, he would be eating alone.

"She's not going to be there, right?" Karter asked. She was driving, seated next to Paris in the front seat while Dad sat in the second row with me and the middles were in the far back, dipping their fries into an Oreo McFlurry they were sharing.

Paris shook her head. "She'd better not be. She wasn't even supposed to know he was the one charged, but we can't do anything about that now. Either way, she's not going to talk, and no news source would publish his name even if she did, which she won't. Dom is a youth offender. Exposing his charge in any way would land her in serious shit. She could never pay back those fines. That's not even getting into the fact that she's got two boys at the academy. Ms. Allen will behave."

I remembered the courtroom from Dom's bail hearing. Remembered how we sat in those seats behind Dom and Paris, filling up an entire row. Dom had worn a perfectly tailored suit. It had fit him like a glove, but he'd still looked like a kid playing dress-up. The Crown had been on the other side—a plain-looking guy in his early forties who would be trying to prove beyond a reasonable doubt that our younger brother had murdered his girlfriend.

Despite how confident Paris had been going into it, bail was denied on the grounds of the seriousness of the crime. Dom's shoulders had slumped, but he hadn't said a word. Just quietly got up and followed the police out to where he would be transported to a juvenile facility.

When we'd walked outside, there she was. Ms. Allen. I only knew because Karter had let out this hiss between her teeth, and Paris had immediately turned to the Crown to snap at him that she shouldn't have been there.

But she was. Marsha Allen had stood next to a run-down red Honda Civic with her dark hair cut into a distinctly uneven bob. I'd looked over at her, and her face had twisted into this expression of perfect fury. Lips peeled back, crow's feet at maximum crease, eyes narrowed so hard they were watering.

Then Karter had snapped at me to keep moving, so I'd turned away and headed for the SUV with my family. Ignoring, as usual, my instinct to snap back at her.

We left together, knowing that we would see Dom soon enough, assuming that Paris would come through like she was supposed to.

Ms. Allen stood alone.

I could feel her eyes on my back even when I was inside the vehicle. They'd followed us as we drove away. And when I'd lain in bed that night, I'd thought about them.

Now we pulled into the parking lot of the juvenile detention center where Dom had spent the last couple months, and Dad went inside with Paris. I smothered the smile that my lips attempted to peel into when Paris told Karter that they only needed his legal guardian and she should stay in the car. That wouldn't have been the right sort of smile for me to have on my face.

"Well, Paris came through," Darren said from the third row, pitching forward, playing with his septum piercing. "She got him out."

Karter frowned at him. "Of course she did. Aside from the obvious, he's got a clean record. People accused of worse have been able to go back to their normal lives until trial."

"What's worse than murder?"

"Uh, serial murder. And first-degree murder. Premeditated shit. Which would be obvious if you used your own brain for two seconds."

"Even Paris said the evidence was largely circumstantial," I added. Most of the details had been kept from us between Mom, Dad, Paris, and Karter. And it's not like I casually talked with Dom to ask him about it. But that was the line our lawyer kept using, so I assumed it held some weight.

"But *should* he be out?" Kiley mumbled. We all looked at her, but she was staring at where Dad and Paris had disappeared, chewing on the same fry for so long that it must have turned to mush in her mouth by now.

"Dom is innocent," Karter insisted, her voice firm. "And I don't care if you have a dissenting opinion, but keep it inside."

I could have rolled my eyes. Jesus. She really couldn't find a way to put everyone at ease instead of just telling us to keep our mouths shut?

Darren actually rolled his eyes. "We know that."

Kiley chose to stay quiet.

Before Mom died, I would have said we were close. All of us. Not Dom. But the rest of us. Now there was something fractured. Split and cracked like the ice that'd taken her from us.

"We're getting our brother back," I said. "That's what matters. That's what's the most important. We'll be together again."

Even if we're together without Mom.

Dad, Paris, and Dom walked out of the building toward us a while later.

It was a shock briefly to see my younger brother. He seemed older even though it had only been a couple months. Not a man, though the Crown had at every turn referred to him that way. Like he was grown. But he wasn't.

I forced myself to get out of the car and slapped on a smile for him. I opened my mouth but couldn't quite figure out what to say, so I settled for launching myself at my brother and tugging him into a hug. He smelled like antiseptic. Like they didn't have detergent in the center, only bleach.

"We're so happy to have you back," I gushed as I held him.

He snorted. "Are you?"

I froze for a moment and resisted digging my nails into his

shoulders. No, that wouldn't be very nice, would it? I laughed and stepped back. "Of course we are."

His expression was blank. Like he wasn't even remotely happy about getting out of juvie.

His locs were gone. He looked so much like Darren now. The same dark skin and shaved head. But he was different from our older brother. I hugged Darren and felt happy. Comforted. Hugging Dom was a chore. And I felt like he knew it.

Ms. Allen and Dom were both familiar with being alone. It was what I felt when she glared at me. The heat of her eyes that followed me home. They were like my brother's. A deep sense of solitude that was catching. Like an infection. I suppressed a shudder.

I thought of Mom's note, handed to me by Paris in a private meeting after the will reading. We all had one because of things she wanted to say to us. Instructions left. At mine, Paris had just handed me a sticky note that read, *Take care of Dom.*

It was a slap in the face.

After everything she'd told me, all the time we'd spent preparing me for this role, and her *promise* that she would leave something that made it clear that I was to take over, all I'd gotten was a pink Post-it note.

About *Dom* of all people.

He stared back at me, his face devoid of anything.

Exactly how I remembered him.

Take care of Dom.

I didn't often feel anything about Dom. But in that moment, I wanted to strangle him. Instead, I held up the greasy paper bag in my hand. "We got you McDonald's!"

CHAPTER TWO

O n the first day of school, I cut across the track field with Dom and tried not to think about if people would find out he was charged with murder.

Every single one of our siblings had attended Behre Academy. It was Mom's invention. A scholarship-based private high school that only accepted students who were considered in need. It was her way to empower kids who wouldn't otherwise have access to even the tiniest bit of what her own children had. We, as students, obviously weren't needy, but it was important that we attend the same school for solidarity. It showed how much she believed in the quality of education at Behre Academy that she would send her children there too, instead of to any one of the other elite Toronto private schools.

Though it clearly stood apart from those other institutions. For one, the building wasn't what you might call beautiful. It was a functional brick box that spanned three floors with the addition of a basement and rooftop. I'd asked Mom why we didn't upgrade the design of the school once, when I was younger and didn't know any better, and she said, "We're not trying to compete with Toronto French School or Upper Canada College, or any of them. This is a high-quality institution for underprivileged youth that relies on donations. What do you think would happen if investors visited an absolutely gorgeous campus that their privileged children were denied?"

I didn't know. So I'd just shaken my head.

She'd continued, "They would be upset. They would feel . . . short-changed. We want them to see our academy as quaint and cute. Lovely to toss some money at but ultimately subpar for their own precious angels." She'd smiled at me then. "At the end of the day, all that matters is that these kids get a quality education and enough of a boost to be given a chance. That's a lot more important than what the school looks like. And it's crucial that you be a good ambassador for the family while you attend, especially because you'll be the one running things when I'm gone. Be humble and open-minded, and check your privilege at the door every day you walk into that school."

And now, here was my brother, walking toward the building without a single care despite the fact that he could destroy everything she'd created.

It had been two weeks since we picked him up, which he had mostly spent in his room. Including Karter's birthday the week before, when the rest of us went out for dinner.

He kicked at the ground as he walked, his backpack sliding off the single shoulder where he'd slung it. It wasn't cold, but he had a bright orange knit hat pulled over his shaved head that reminded me of prison jumpsuits. His jeans hung low on his hips, and he had pulled on a T-shirt with a portrait of some anime-looking girl whose face was distorted, the fabric punctured with safety pins.

We were supposed to be in uniform.

He had done this *deliberately*.

Technically, I couldn't know that, but I felt it. It seemed natural that Dom, once again, had to find a way to stand apart from this school. Mom's school. Because even though we pulled back from him, he kept his distance too.

I, of course, had my uniform on. The green-and-white plaid skirt that fell just above my knees, crisp white socks, black shoes, and a matching white polo with the school logo on it. A roaring bear. Mom's touch. I even accessorized with a matching headband placed on the fresh silk press I got done yesterday. On her way out the door Karter told me that my level of matching made me look desperate and sad. Then she treated me to a lecture about watching Dom at school.

She was trying her best to replace Mom. Something none of us asked for. She even carried around a journal with all her notes and appointments like Mom had.

I couldn't wait until it came out that I was actually the one meant to be in charge. I pictured the expression on her face, and it brought me an immense amount of joy. It wasn't that I hated her. I loved Karter. She was family. It was just that she was so unbearably smug about a title she'd just taken for herself that Mom had never wanted for her. She wasn't even executor of the will—Dad was. There was nothing proving she deserved the role she'd assumed. But Karter was the sort of person who, once she'd decided to do something, pursued it relentlessly. Out of all the Behres left, she had the sharpest teeth. And she was the most willing to bite.

I gnawed on the inside of my cheek. Grinding my teeth along the flesh, trapping the smallest amount between them and pressing down. When the pain had calmed me enough to speak, I said to Dom, "You'll have to change when you get in."

Uniforms, Mom said, were the great equalizer. Kids didn't have to worry about having the latest brand-name clothes, shoes, or accessories they couldn't afford because they weren't allowed. There was a set dress code. The uniforms at Behre Academy were given free of charge. A set of three summer and winter uniforms plus one accessory and a standard shoe.

This way, when we walked in, no one could tell us apart from the other students who attended based on need. The ones who weren't living in mansions by the lake. It was our duty not to shove our wealth in their faces.

"I'll go in the back," Dom said. "I have anatomy first after home-room anyway."

"Anatomy? That's a grade-twelve class."

My brother shuffled in place. "Yeah, Mr. Balmer said I could take it if I do my grade-ten bio in the summer. It's self-guided and super easy. All my bio classes are easy. That's why he's letting me do the anatomy. I like it. And he said that in grade eleven he can help me take the university-level exam so I can—whatever. I have anat-omy." He abruptly cut himself off, almost like he was embarrassed by everything he'd said.

I had no idea that Dom was doing so well in biology, and defi-nitely didn't know that he was passionate about anatomy of all things. "Okay . . ."

"Cool." Dom veered away from me toward the southeast end of the building.

My hand reached out automatically and snapped onto his wrist.

He paused and stared at me.

My fingers shook. "I—just don't leave the house without a uni-form again. Okay? That'll save you having to do any of this." I paused before forcing myself to add, "Why don't we go in together?"

"Afraid to have me out of your sight?"

Yes.

"No," I said. "I just thought it would be nice."

He looked down at where I was gripping his arm, then back up to my eyes.

I let go.

"I'll be fine," he said. "I'm supposed to meet Jer."

I held my face still so I wouldn't frown. Jer, aka Jeremy Lidell, was Dom's best and only friend. He used to live a few blocks away from us, and the two of them had basically been besties since they were seven. He was a permanent fixture at our house until he and his dad moved a few years ago when their apartment complex renovated and raised the rent. They'd lived there since Jeremy was born and had spent the whole time being slowly but surely priced out as the neighborhood evolved. They'd been forced farther east between where we were and Mimico.

Jeremy was annoying, mostly, but all right. The real problem was that he'd also been in and out of juvie several times, which wasn't exactly great for Dom's public image.

"Do you think that's a good idea?"

His eyes narrowed. "You're not going to tell me who to hang out with. You're not Mom."

No. Mom was six feet under. He knew that. He'd been there when we buried her. It was the first time I'd seen him cry in years. He'd had more tears for Mom than his dead girlfriend. Though the latter hadn't gotten any that I'd seen, so there wasn't much competition.

I trapped the air that rose in my throat and swallowed it down. I didn't need to huff a breath out. I was calm. I wasn't going to try to physically shake intelligence into my brother.

Dom continued, "I'm not going to say anything to anyone. I already promised Paris and Dad that I wouldn't. Jer already knows, so too late on him, but he won't say anything either. There's no one else I would tell."

I swallowed and tried not to look worried. The strain squeezed at my neck like someone was gripping the back of it with meaty fingers. "I'm sure you won't. You remember what you're supposed to say, right?"

During the summer, we'd needed to continue attending public functions without our brother. It helped that he usually didn't come anyway, but it wasn't foolproof. Paris's suggestion was to say that Dom was suffering with depression and had a mental breakdown under the pressure to perform in his schoolwork. When Paris announced this as the cover, Darren had left the room, Kiley going with him.

I remembered a time when we had to take all the knives out of the house. All the pills. Anything with a sharp edge. How Darren had to stay home because Mom and Dad were afraid to let him go out.

They told everyone he went on an artist retreat.

We never said the D-word.

But we could say it with Dom because it was a lie.

I thought of that rhyme, *Secrets secrets are no fun, secrets secrets hurt someone*. Everything was so much nicer in a nursery rhyme. But in reality, truth was a luxury. One that we, even with all our money, couldn't afford.

Dom shrugged. "Yeah, whatever." He didn't wait for me to say anything else before he left.

I turned away from him so I didn't shout that he was being an entitled brat. That the rest of us had swallowed the lie for the sake of the family, but he always thought he was an exception.

That was when I spotted a white woman standing near the hedge by the corner of the school, beckoning to me. She was wearing a black hoodie with the hood pulled up over her face and it was clearly several sizes too big for her. She kept looking around even as she tried to get me to come over.

Well, that was creepy. And of course, now I had to go deal with this.

I made my way over to her. "Ma'am, are you a parent? You need to check in with the office. Otherwise, you can't be on school property." I did carry a small amount of spare change for homeless people, and I dug out a toonie and offered it to her. "Did you want some change for coffee?" That was usually enough to get strangers off campus.

She refused the change, which was not at all how this usually went. Her eyes were a dull blue and her hair was hidden by the hood. "Do you know the Milk Man?" she said, her voice low and urgent.

It was too early for this shit. "Ma'am, you can't be here. Would you like money for the streetcar or . . . ?"

She grabbed my arm, and I stopped myself from jerking away, but the smile slid from my face. "Please, I need to know. I can't tell you any more until I know what you know. You might be in danger, but I might be too if I say anything. The Milk Man wants ruination. He wants to spoil the milk. He—" The woman cut herself off abruptly. "I'm sorry . . . I don't know if I can do this . . . I need to go." She dropped my arm and ducked her head, rushing across the track field.

I could still feel her hand on my arm. It hadn't been gentle.

I sighed but then perked up when I saw Destiny Mable, who I had history with last year. She was the most boring person I'd ever met and always seemed to have something stuck in her teeth that I was forced to helpfully tell her about, but I needed an easy win. I grinned at her. "Happy first day of school!"

She smiled back, and the tension in my neck finally let go.

CHAPTER THREE

School was a delicate dance. A ballet. You had to be careful and there were a lot of things to balance as you moved. There were eyes watching your every bend and leap. And in my case, a lot of people in the audience hoping that I would fall.

I never did.

I was a master at it.

I could confidently remember the name of anyone in my grade, where they lived, and something about them. Ju-Eun lived in North York and had the longest commute to school; she liked golden retrievers. Lauren was from Jane and Finch; she wanted to be an elementary school teacher. Ian lived in a set of older apartment buildings in Mimico; their brother died last year.

It wasn't interesting, but it was necessary.

When I entered the lunchroom, every face that turned to me had a smile, and I had a smile for them. The cafeteria was loud with the sounds of students collecting lunches and the staff banging pots and pans in the kitchens. The academy provided free hot lunch for every student every day, and some were sent home with leftovers after school too.

I collected my tray and stood in line to be served the vegetable lasagna with a side salad, milk, and a couple of oatmeal cookies.

Scanning the space, I saw Dom in the corner with Jeremy, thankfully in uniform like he was supposed to be.

Next, I looked for a spot to sit. I never sat with the same people twice in the same week. I didn't like what it said. That I was picking groups. And you couldn't really be friendly with everyone if you had a group. Cliques were exclusionary by principle.

But I did like to start the week off strong, so I headed toward Craig's table. The people who I guess would be my core friend group if I didn't avoid having one.

Craig grinned when he saw me. His brown curls were perfectly arranged, and his skin had a golden sheen to it. Dewy, almost. Last year, he was a lot more normal-looking. But during the summer he'd suddenly discovered hair and facial products, courtesy of Darren off-loading a bunch of his old stuff onto him. Now all Craig's socials were just thirst traps on different platforms. He had also discovered tanning, and now looked more racially ambiguous, and less like your run-of-the-mill white boy. Darren called it Blackfishing. Which seemed a little extreme to me. Lots of white people got tans. It wasn't surprising to me that my boyfriend, who was sensitive to what people thought of him, wanted to improve his appearance. He liked to control how he was perceived. Though he was bad at it.

He scooted over, and I slipped into the seat beside him. He immediately wove our fingers together, and I smothered a sigh. How would I eat now?

I dealt with the inconvenience of only having one free hand and leaned over for the kiss I knew he would want.

There were five of us at the table: me, Craig, Mercy, Shyanne, and Duane. I felt the worst for Duane, who was a constant fifth wheel. More so because he had nursed a crush on Mercy for an entire year and hadn't been smart enough to put together that the offhand comments she made about girls she thought were hot and constant reiterating of not being interested in guys meant she was a lesbian. He had weirdly thought the things she'd said were jokes. He'd also thought she and Shyanne were just really close friends for months before I finally, in what I thought was a generous show of compassion, clued him in to the fact that they were dating. Something they were so open about that he really had to be in active denial to miss it. It was his own fault, but when he broke down crying in the back room of a party, reeking of beer, had I told him that? No. I'd given him a hug and reassured him he would find someone someday.

And I was rewarded with him deciding to crush on me instead. Something Duane thought he hid well.

He didn't.

Craig had noticed and now just barely tolerated the boy who had previously been his best friend. Shyanne and Mercy didn't seem to like him much either, to be honest. Though they also sometimes seemed to not like Craig, too. But we all still hung out like this.

I was so over high school drama.

Craig had gotten a text and was staring down at his phone. I was tempted to peek before I realized that I truly didn't care. Probably looking at memes.

"How was everyone's summer?" I asked.

"Fine," Shyanne said with a shrug. "Just chilled mostly." She fingered the fresh cornrows on top of her otherwise shaved head. They were just long enough for her to pull the braids at the end into a tiny ponytail.

It was a shame because Shyanne was actually cool and seemed like she would have done something interesting. Now the conversation had stalled, and an awkwardness settled around the table.

I obviously wasn't going to mention the Dom stuff. I also wasn't going to talk about our family vacation to the Maldives. Partially because it was kind of shit. And partially because most of my peers had never been on a family vacation, period. I'd already preplanned to talk about going with the middles to that ice cream place that sold waffles shaped like dicks. It was just edgy enough for this particular group of friends to enjoy. And affordable, so as not to be isolating or too much of a reminder that I had money and they didn't.

Next year, I would escape all of this.

I was an ambassador of the school. Of Mom's legacy. And a future owner of the academy. It was important that I be liked. Important that I make friends with as many kids as possible and leave a positive impression on them.

But it was also exhausting.

Next year, I would be at university. I would still be a representative of my family, of course, but the visibility would be gone. I could turn the "sunny" dial down a little and try less. I had also assumed that I would be too busy working with Mom on our plans for me once I graduated to even have time for friends. And I didn't care because I would have rather spent the time with Mom anyway. Though I wasn't sure how that would work out anymore.

Mostly I was looking forward to the inevitable breakup with Craig. There was nothing wrong with him. I had liked him in the beginning. But that had waned, and now he just bored me. He wasn't exactly exciting. He kept his nose clean. Potentially because both his brothers were in and out of trouble with the law. This school was his ticket to avoiding the same future, and he was doing well. I'd thought that was what I wanted. But it wasn't. It was just what looked good given how I presented myself.

But if I broke up with him over something as inoffensive as losing interest, I would look like a bitch. Which was not helpful to my image. So I was stuck waiting for the relationship to play itself out. I envied my siblings. They got together with and broke up with whoever they wanted, whenever they wanted, for whatever reason they wanted. Darren had multiple ex-boyfriends he'd just gotten bored of. Kiley had both an ex-boyfriend and ex-girlfriend who she'd dumped because they picked bad restaurants for dates. And Karter had broken up with her last boyfriend because they were supposed to wear matching outfits to an event and he'd chosen the wrong shade of black.

"Hey," Craig interjected. "Where is everyone applying? We're going to do U of T." He grasped our joined hands and smiled at me.

What. The. Fuck?

"I thought you were going to do McGill?" I pressed. Craig was supposed to go to school in Montreal next year, five hours away. He had the grades for it and schools *loved* accepting academy students. Otherwise, the University of British Columbia was the backup, which was even farther. There was no way our relationship could keep working at that distance. We could fade away amicably in a way that wouldn't make me the villain.

But if he went to U of T, that wouldn't happen.

The University of Toronto was where *I* was going. It was Mom and Dad's alma mater, and we already had a separate house downtown where the middles and Karter lived so they wouldn't have to commute to school from our lakeshore house. There was an empty room in the downtown house for me.

There was no *we*.

He shrugged. "I don't even speak French."

"You don't need to speak French in Montreal. Besides that, you shouldn't give up on your dreams." I forced my voice to be light. Encouraging. Hopeful. I stomped down on the panic rising in my chest. "What about UBC?"

"They're both far." His smile had fallen some.

"We can make it work."

"Don't . . . don't you want to go to school together?"

Shit. His voice had taken on an unsure quality that I had learned to identify as insecurity. I didn't want to be consoling him right now. "Of course! I just didn't want you to miss applying because you're a little doubtful. You never know until you try."

"If you both go to U of T, then we can still hang out," Duane piped up.

Hanging out every day with the dude harboring a crush on me was the last thing I wanted to continue doing in university. I tilted my head and smiled at him. "I mean, we're not *all* going there, are we?"

Mercy played with her braids. Hers, unlike Shyanne's, covered her entire head and she'd made little space buns in the front with some of them. "We kind of have to, don't we?"

"I thought you wanted to go to Queen's."

"I do. But, like, how would I get two and a half hours away to Kingston? Who's going to pay for me to stay in residence? How will I get home during holidays? The scholarships we would be up for even with the academy's edge won't cover everything. I want to go to Queen's, but it's not possible." Finally she mumbled under her breath, "We can't just go to school wherever we want."

"Right," I said. "Sorry." She was right, I knew that. But the way they'd all talked about their dream schools last year, I just assumed they were going to work something out. I shifted in my seat. So much for checking my privilege at the door. I could picture the way Mom would look at me if she'd heard this conversation, her eyes intense and her lips frowning.

Maybe I'd been thinking about this wrong. Maybe Mom hadn't left anything for me because she'd changed her mind. Maybe I had done something that made her think I couldn't take on the role after all.

Shyanne jumped to the rescue, always prepared to defuse even the slightest hint of conflict. "She didn't mean it like that."

"No, no, it's okay. I appreciate her being up-front with me." I smiled, but it was too tight and uncomfortable, so I had to relax it. Smile too hard and you just grimace. No one likes a grimace. "Duane is right. It'll be fun to go to the same school."

The others jumped in with ideas about what we would do at university. Craig even brought up that he and I could have the same major and go to our classes together.

I smiled and nodded along with everything.

I was fucked. I didn't want to leave Toronto. But if we all went to U of T, this would never end.

This would be it. Exactly this moment. Over and over, for the rest of my life.

My eyes drifted over the cafeteria to land on Dom laughing with his friend.

Even when he was shackled with a criminal charge, he was still freer than me.

CHAPTER FOUR

'd been diligent about checking in on Dom. Not because Karter told me to—which was laughable—but because it was what Mom would have done. And for a month, everything had been fine.

Until today.

I watched the group of students who'd stayed after school to play basketball at the outdoor courts. It was fall now, but not cold enough that they couldn't manage once they'd worked up a sweat. It was a scheduled activity, and the school provided the equipment that was now being put away.

The problem was that Dom was supposed to be here.

My eyes tracked over the court, darting between the people cleaning up, looking for my brother's face. I'd found an excuse to stay after school in the library so I could check for him—watching his small form from the third floor. When I'd seen the game finishing, I'd come downstairs. Somewhere in between he'd disappeared.

I licked my lips and searched for Jeremy, heading straight toward him. I made my voice sweet and unconcerned, all while resisting the urge to ball my hands into fists. "Did Dom leave?" I asked. "He said he would be playing today. I figured we could head home together."

Jeremy stared at me, a little grin on his face with his signature red headphones around his neck, dressed in a now sweat-soaked

T-shirt and basketball shorts halfway down his bright orange underwear. He had the same shoulder-length locs that Dom used to have. His face said, "Since when do you two walk home together?" Then his mouth said, "You don't have to do the high-pitched voice thing with me. I know what your actual voice sounds like."

This was what I disliked the most about Jeremy. When we were younger, he'd developed a crush on me, which I had noticed too late. Apparently, I had a habit of attracting annoying boys. Anyway, he'd spent an ungodly amount of time watching me. And one day he came over to me and said, "How come you act different than you are?" I knew then that I'd made a mistake in not paying attention to him. But nothing had ever come of it. My family treated me the same. Even Dom. But being "sunny" with Jeremy was no longer possible. Still, habit always made me try.

"Where is he?" I said, keeping a pleasant expression on my face for any onlookers but not bothering with the sweet voice.

Jeremy shrugged, tucking his hands into his pockets. "I thought he went to take a leak, but he probably went to get snacks from the breakfast room. He usually does that on basketball days." Jeremy raised his eyebrows at me in a way that was maybe supposed to be suggestive but was just comically awkward. "You should have just played ball with us; then he would have never left your sight. Or you could have—and this will be shocking—just asked him to text you so you could walk home together."

I checked to see if anyone was watching before rolling my eyes at him, which in turn made him roll his eyes at me. "You're not cute and you're not funny," I said.

Jeremy beamed. "I know you're only lying because our love is forbidden. I could never do my boy like that. Sisters are off-limits."

"Goodbye, Jeremy," I droned, and turned to go back into the school. Now I had to go to the breakfast club room to search for Dom.

The breakfast club was a program Mom was proud of. Had been proud of. Kids who couldn't get a reliable breakfast at home—which was a lot of our students—could get a full meal as long as they came to school early. It was important to Mom that a Behre family member volunteered at least once a week. You went into the room, unlocked it, and helped get everything ready.

Dom and I were supposed to be trading off shifts, but he had skipped all of his, so I had been taking them.

But he still had a key to the room.

He wasn't supposed to be casually grabbing food from there for his little friends, but of course the rules meant nothing to him.

Inside, the halls were abandoned. All the after-school activities had finished, and the only reason I was allowed to continue in the library was because I was a Behre. Mom didn't approve of us using our privilege like that but I figured she would allow it given what I was doing.

I stepped into the second-floor hallway and paused. There was a sound. A scuffing noise. The auto lights were on where I was but dim in the other areas of the hall, making me feel strangely illuminated in the fluorescents. Singled out. Like a deer in headlights before the crash of glass, metal, and bodies.

Just as I was about to open my mouth to call for my brother, I shut it. I kept my lips pressed together in a frown. And then I crept toward the one hallway with its light on that I knew led to the breakfast club room. I pressed myself against the wall and tried not to feel ridiculous. What was I even doing? What did I think *he* was doing?

But I was committed now. I peeked around the corner and froze.

Goose pimples rose along my skin and pricked at the back of my neck. My teeth clenched together, and my jaw cracked and ached. Sweat broke out on my palms, and I gripped them into fists.

There, in the hallway, was a boy, lying on his back with his head toward me, and he wasn't moving.

I could barely feel myself stepping forward.

My eyes were glued to his flesh.

And it was only when I got close that I could see the real damage.

Saying his throat was cut felt like a clear understatement. His throat was severed. It was butchered. It had been decimated. The cut was so deep that I could see through to a line of bone, slick with blood that was still oozing from the wound. It had a shine to it that was mesmerizing. And all the skin around it was so pale now. Washed out. Turning the deep ebony brown into an ashy version of itself. Soft and limp and empty. His eyes stared up at the ceiling. Unblinking and brown.

Eyes that I'd seen at lunch earlier.

And there was a scent. It was familiar in a way that I couldn't place, something thick and sour that coated my tongue.

I threw up in my mouth, and it spilled onto my lips. I pressed my hands to my face to hold it in, trembling. I swallowed with a gasp, and my stomach roiled in protest.

When I looked up at the door to the breakfast room, Dom was standing there with blood on his hands, unmoving.

Sweat washed over my body and chilled in the same moment, casting a thin, cooling layer across my skin that made me shiver.

I needed to go.

I needed to run.

I needed to get away from him.

But I couldn't push my body into action. Instead, a dry wheeze passed through my lips, tasting of sick.

"I didn't do it," Dom said finally, his lower lip trembling. Like a child who'd gotten in trouble, begging for forgiveness. "You have to believe me. I just . . . I found him, and I tried to help, and I just . . . I don't know what to do."

I had to move. I had to *move. Move. Move. Move.*

I remembered the forest. How I had felt so much smaller than I already was at seven. I kept calling for Mom. Only for Mom. My voice echoing off the trees, and it kept getting darker. I knew the hide-and-seek game was over, but I couldn't find anyone. It was so dark and cold. Freezing. I was desperate to get warm. And then I saw a tent and crept toward it. The lady inside was still, and her blood coated my knees. But I'd had no choice. People could freeze to death. I'd seen it on TV. And I didn't know where else to go.

Now I pressed my fingers against my mouth so hard that my nails dug into the softness of my cheeks, and I panted through them. Fighting the overwhelming urge to scream.

Then I remembered Mom. I remembered her arms around me. I'd cried so much at first, until I realized how much my pain was hurting everyone around me. That was when I put on a smile and pretended that I was okay. I remembered how strong Mom said I was later. How proud she was that I'd taken that horrible thing that happened to me and shoved it down, all for the sake of the family. So they wouldn't feel bad about the way the game had gone. About losing me. So they wouldn't worry. I put them first at my own expense. That made me strong. Stronger than anyone else in the family. Strong enough to lead.

And all at once, I calmed.

My breathing evened out, I pulled my hands away from my face, and I wiped the dregs of vomit off my lips. Quickly and quietly I gave my brother instructions.

I made him wipe the blood off on the inside of his pants where it could be hidden on the walk home. I would burn them later. I had him text Jeremy that he was going home with me so he wouldn't be waiting around for us. We took the gloves from under the sink used for hygienic food prep, and we cleaned everywhere that my brother said he had touched.

And when we were done, I stared down at the boy.

I stared down at *Duane*.

My head felt like it was floating. Like I was watching this scene from underwater. My body moving without me.

And somehow through that haze, I noticed the piece of paper held loosely in Duane's hand. I reached down and retrieved it. I felt the soft flesh of his palm. Smelled the scent of shit and decay as I got closer to him. And I tucked it all away in the back of my mind.

The note said:

> *Take your teddy and put him on your nose*
> *Take your teddy and put him on your toes*
> *Watch the teddy shake*
> *Make the teddy cry*
> *Let the teddy bleed*
> *That's how the teddy dies*

"Sunny?" Dom whispered, and my neck snapped up and away from the note. And suddenly everything flooded back.

I was standing over a dead body. I was standing over the dead body of a boy I knew. Of a boy who liked me. Of a boy who my brother had almost definitely killed. And Dom was staring at me with that kicked puppy expression, his eyes wide and his cheeks tearstained.

I wanted to scream at him to stop making it worse. Couldn't he see that I was trying to fix this? Didn't he care that what he had done could destroy our already fragile family? Didn't he know that Mom told me to take care of him, and I had apparently already spat in the face of her final wish?

I crushed the note in my gloved hands and, shaking, put it back under Duane's fingers.

It took everything I had to grind out, "Let's go home."

As we left the school, I saw the woman again. That Milk Man

freak. In her same hoodie. I stopped and swallowed as she stared at me and then at Dom. But before I could say anything, she turned and ran away.

I stared up at the ceiling in my bedroom, the lights off, covered in darkness. It had been hours since Dom and I got home. I'd taken his pants to the shed beside our house. Mercy had burst into giggles the first time she heard me say that. "You mean the second house?" I laughed along with her and corrected myself. Though I still called it a shed in my head.

The middles used it for their art projects because Mom was tired of messes in the house. I'd put the pants into one of the sinks, doused it with paint thinner, and set it aflame with the lighter Darren kept in a drawer with his weed that he didn't think anyone knew about. But of course, we all did.

That was the thing about families. They knew even the things you wanted to keep secret.

But I had done my best to hold everything together. I'd made it through getting Dom home. He'd retreated to his room. I had dinner with Dad and Karter. I'd even done my homework. Though I hadn't been able to bring myself to respond to Craig's usual barrage of texts. I would save those for tomorrow.

And now here I was, finally alone.

I rolled over, stuffed my face into my pillow, and sobbed. Tears fell down my face and pooled onto the silk of my pillowcase. My body shook.

Duane was dead.

Dom had killed him.

What the fuck was I supposed to do now?

Anxiety crept up my body. It had wound between my toes and slinked up my ankles and thighs. Pressed itself against the soft small of my back. And it was sliding between my shoulder blades, making them shudder.

I jerked up and threw myself out of bed. I trudged into the bathroom, and the light flicked on automatically. I splashed water on my face. It wasn't exactly smart because now I felt more awake than before.

Did Mom know this would happen? Is that why she'd left me that note?

I gripped the edges of the sink and tried to calm down.

Dom said he didn't do it. Did I believe him? No. But Mom told me to take care of him. I couldn't just do nothing. You always need a plan. And another plan for if that plan goes wrong. That was what she taught me.

And even if no one else knew it, Mom wanted me to lead this family. She would never just let this sit. She would fix it.

I exhaled hard and squeezed my eyes shut. On the back of my lids, I was looking into Duane's empty eyes, and they mingled with the woman's. That woman, sprawled out in that nasty tent that I'd found while lost in the woods on our first family camping trip. Karter said we should play hide-and-seek, and I hadn't been smart enough to realize that she'd just wanted to ditch me. But I'd gone too far into the trees. I wasn't familiar with the area like I was at the ranch. It got dark and cold, and I thought of that show I watched with the middles about people surviving in the wilderness. They always talked about how if you didn't find warmth and shelter, you could die. There was nowhere else to go. So I'd crawled into the tent and sat beside her, and zipped us up to keep the cold out. I slept huddled into a ball. That was how they found me in the morning—lying next to a dead body.

Everyone thought I would fall apart. I'd wanted to. I had a bit, honestly. But then I saw my parents fight. Saw my siblings who were supposed to be watching me wracked with guilt, compounded by our parents blaming them too, and Karter most of all because she'd told me to hide but hadn't done any seeking until it was too late. And I knew if everyone saw I was okay, it would stop. So I'd put a smile on my face and acted like everything was fine.

It worked. The fighting stopped. I still had nightmares until I was twelve, but as long as I pretended everything was fine, I could keep the peace in my family. I had helped them with nothing more than a smile.

Mom said that was the moment she realized that I was resilient. I had the motivation to prioritize the family over myself. That was what was needed to lead.

I tried to remember that as I stared at myself in the mirror.

I could shove it down. Just like everything else. Bury it and put on a smile instead.

I left the bathroom and headed to the mini fridge in the corner. Outside the balcony doors, the night was quiet. The cold of the fridge blasted me, and I scanned the shelves, noting that the pitcher of water was empty.

Right. Maisey and her team came in on Wednesdays. Tomorrow. They cleaned everything and did other stuff like replenish the drinks and snacks in my mini fridge.

I shut the door and sighed again, leaving my bedroom for the kitchen. Thankfully, I was only on the second floor, so it's not like I had far to go. The hallway was silent. Darren and Kiley probably weren't in their rooms. I paused before the stairs, looking down the hall where Dom slept.

Where a *killer* slept.

I continued downstairs. The kitchen was right at the foot of them, and as I turned the corner, the automatic lights flashed on.

Illuminating Dom, standing in the dark.

I slapped my hand over my mouth to stop from screaming.

He was wearing a pair of loose shorts and no shirt. Standing by the island with a glass of water in his hand that he wasn't drinking.

"Sorry," he said. "They went off."

I wanted to ask why he was standing so perfectly still that the autos went off, but sucked the question in.

I forced out a laugh. "It's okay, you just . . ."

"Scared you?" His voice was quiet, but his gaze was penetrating.

"Startled me."

I moved past him to the cupboard, grabbing my own glass and pressing it to the fridge's dispenser. Ice then water chugged into the cup, and I brought it to my lips.

"Sunny," he whispered. "You believe me, don't you?"

"Please don't talk about it," I said back, working hard to keep my tone even. I didn't want to discuss this right now. I needed time to figure things out. I was still trying to get the image of Duane's corpse out of my mind. "We'll talk about it later."

Footsteps padded on the stairs, and we both looked as Karter came down in a pair of silk purple pajamas. Without makeup, it was easy to see the dark smudges under her eyes. I guess she hadn't planned to spend her junior year of university looking after the family. She was supposed to be in the UK on exchange, but that had been canceled once Mom passed.

"Why are you awake?" she snapped at us. "It's a school night."

Karter was pretending to be Mom without any of her bedside manner. It was clear to me now, especially given everything, that I needed to find what Mom was supposed to have left me. I needed to prove that if anyone was going to step into Mom's shoes, it should be me.

Dom wordlessly put his still-full glass in the sink and walked away.

Karter's eyes followed him and then settled back on mine. "How's he doing?"

"Fine. Adjusting." I didn't need a smile to sell it. Just a pleasant quirk of my lips.

"You want an Ambien?"

Fuck, yes, I wanted one. "Sure. Thank you."

This was a time when I was glad Karter wasn't like Mom, who never would have casually given me an addictive sleep aid. Karter might not be a good leader, but she'd always been a good sister. Had brought me soup when I was sick and cuddled up to watch cartoons until Mom came home. She'd taken me to get birth control without our parents knowing and taught me how to use condoms. She showed me how to properly make a fist in case I needed to hit someone, though she assumed that I never would because I was me. I missed that Karter.

But she was gone now, just like Mom. It was like we'd all been on an island together, and Mom was at the center. But she'd broken away and left cracks in the foundations. Now all my siblings were drifting away too. And I kept trying to drag them back, but it wasn't working.

Karter brought out the Ambien bottle from the pocket of her pants and handed it to me. I took it, staring. I looked up at her but didn't ask how she knew to bring it downstairs. She answered my wordless question anyway. "You're not the only one watching him."

Clearly, she wasn't watching close enough. Or she would have been the one to find him with a dead body instead of me.

I opened the bottle, popped the pill in my mouth, and drained my water glass.

CHAPTER FIVE

I woke to screaming.

For a moment, all I did was lie in bed, halfway in a dream I couldn't remember and halfway out, listening to Karter's shrillest octave.

Normally I would have thought that she was being an inconsiderate bitch because some of us were sleeping. Something that I would never say to her face. Not unless I wanted to be on the receiving end of years of boxing classes. But today of all days, I suspected that her behavior was warranted. And still, I didn't move, hoping somehow that it wasn't what I thought it would be.

I crawled out of bed, tore off my silk bonnet, grabbed my phone, and went into the hallway. At the bottom of the stairs, Karter was shrieking into her phone.

"What's happening?" I asked, walking to the living room.

She paused to glare at me and pointed to the phone as if to say, "Quiet, can't you see I'm on the phone?" Like she hadn't just been screaming at the top of her lungs.

I spotted Dad on the couch, lying with his arm over his face. He looked hollowed out. Like everything inside him had been scooped dry and laid at his feet.

I put a hand on his shoulder. "Are you okay?" I asked, instead of "What the fuck is happening?"

He moved his arm from his face and smiled wearily. "Sunny," he said, reaching out for me, and I joined him on the couch, snuggling underneath his armpit like I did when I was little.

This was what Dad was good for. Comforting. Sometimes him to you. But mostly you to him. I liked it anyway. He needed me. He needed all of us.

"How can I help?" I asked.

"Can you unmake a dead body?"

I stiffened against him. There it was. Exactly what I'd been hoping against.

After a moment, I figured that I should say something, and muttered, "What?"

Too late, Dad seemed to realize that maybe that wasn't the sort of thing he should burden his youngest daughter with. Because, of course, he wasn't aware that I already knew. That I had helped cover it up. That I was an accessory.

He looked around for a second, and I knew he was looking for Mom. For someone to say, "You can tell her," or "Don't tell her, she's a child!" Even though he was the literal principal of the school now and should have some leadership ability. I wondered if, before Mom, he had been the sort of person who could make those decisions. He must have been. Otherwise, I couldn't see her having the patience for him.

He'd degraded.

Karter clocked us and snapped her fingers at Dad. "She doesn't need to know," she said, and waved her hand at me. "No school today. I already texted Dom. And I don't know, eat breakfast or something. Go away."

I didn't know where I was supposed to go while also cooking

when our entire main floor was open concept. If anything, she should be the one leaving. Her bedroom was on the third floor and had plenty of privacy.

"I can make breakfast," I said to her. "Do you want anything? Eggs? Bacon?"

"Actually, yeah, please. Coffee, too."

I wanted to say, "You know how to say please?" but, as usual, refrained.

I started to cook a full meal of eggs, bacon, toast, and some of the fruit we had ready in the fridge. Meanwhile, Karter stalked off to the pool room, the doors whooshing shut behind her because they were all soft-close. Though high-pitched shrieking still happened, and glass wasn't a great sound barrier. I finally got the gist that she was talking to press.

My hand trembled as I flipped the bacon.

Some incoherent thought in my brain wanted to scream that it was Dom. To let everything fall out of my mouth. Like when we were kids at the ranch, and he'd wanted to go farther away from our property. I had run home and told Mom, and she'd looked at the spot where he'd disappeared and said, "It's fine, let him go." And we'd gone into the tree house that was just for me and her and eaten lunch. I sat in the space between her legs, my back pressed against her chest, her arms encircling me.

I clenched my fingers around the spatula in my hand.

No.

I couldn't just "let him go," not this time. That would be me off-loading him. And no doubt, Karter would swoop in like she could fix it. There was a reason Mom left that note for me. And yes, at first, it felt like she was shafting me. But now I could see this for what it was: a trial. A way for me to protect the family and prove that I was supposed to lead it, exactly the way Mom and I had always planned.

By the time I finished making breakfast, I had calmed down a bit. And I had a plan. Once Karter was done screaming and filled with food and coffee, I could ask her if she was okay because that conversation seemed stressful. Yes. That was the nice thing to do. Considerate. Making it about her instead of making it about me.

That was the secret to being nice. You made everything about everyone else, and you shoved yourself down, deeper and deeper.

I would help get her settled, then Dad, and I could deal with Dom when he came down. I would quietly put out the fires around me, and then I would get my brother alone, and we would make another plan for fixing this. And I would not get distracted by thinking about Duane's empty eyes staring up at me.

"You want pepper on your eggs?" I asked Dad.

"Yes, please!"

I got out a bottle of pepper sauce and shook it onto his eggs, wetly scrambled. Karter had sunny-side up. And Dom had a well-done scramble with chunks of ham in it. Mine was a mix of Dom's and Dad's leftovers, because I had made too much.

"Breakfast is done!" I shouted.

Dad got up from the couch right away and came to get his, kissing me on the forehead. "Thanks, baby girl."

"No problem."

A few minutes later Dom snuck down the stairs into the kitchen and sat down.

I purposely turned away from him, observing instead out of the corner of my eye.

There was something empty about the way he stared at his meal and crammed forkfuls into his mouth.

I took my phone off Do Not Disturb and saw the dozens of messages from the group chat with Craig, Mercy, Shyanne, and Duane. I was in something like fifteen chats between all the different friend groups and the things I was involved in with school. It was exhausting to keep up with them, but I worried about someone asking something of me specifically and me missing it, which would be seen as rude or stuck up, so I did my best. Suddenly all of them had active conversations.

Mercy: holy shit, holy shit, holy shit!
(Link to article: GRUESOME DEATH AT FAMOUS TORONTO PRIVATE ACADEMY)

I stared at the link preview unblinking. The group chat was blowing up. Craig, Mercy, and Shyanne, all chiming in to freak out. And to talk about Duane, and how this could have happened to him.

Finally I opened the link and was greeted by images of police rolling out a body bag in front of the school, the name BEHRE ACADEMY on the building in full view.

Karter walked into the room at the same moment and narrowed her eyes at me. "What?"

I held out my phone to her though I hadn't even had a chance to read the piece. She would find out one way or another.

She strode over and snatched the phone from me. The instant she saw the screen she screamed, "Fucking goddammit!!" Karter threw my phone at the wall, where it cracked and slid to the ground, then stormed up the stairs.

This was the difference between us. That was her reaction. Meanwhile, I was calm in a way that felt unnerving. But I had to act like I would if I'd only just learned this. Which was fine. I was good at that. I did it all the time.

My hand shaking, I picked up my phone with its cracked screen as the group chat kept going.

Mercy: Sydney was the one who found him
when she went to open breakfast club
She said his throat was cut so deep that his
head was almost coming off!!!

Shyanne: I just can't believe that's him
Why would anyone do that?

Craig: people are fucked up!

Mercy: that's not even the only thing
Sydney said they found a paper in his hand?
But she didn't see what it was
But she said the cop looked really
concerned

Shyanne: and he's his mom's only kid

I closed the chat and squeezed my eyes shut.

He was an only child. I'd forgotten that. I'd met his mom once.
She was sweet.

When I looked up from my phone, Dom was staring at me.

I nodded to him, and his eyes got shiny. I wanted to tell him to
cut it out before anyone noticed, but he managed to gather himself,
staring down at his plate.

I made myself believe in the possibility that he hadn't done it.
Thought about it objectively. His ongoing charge was one thing.
Torri Allen had been his girlfriend. They'd dated for six months,
though none of us had known that until the police came knocking.
But there was no motive when it came to Duane. Then again, maybe

he was just like that. Craving violence. When I looked at him this way, though, his eyes downcast, that was harder to believe.

No matter how much money we had, how much good our family did, how much acclaim, people would look at Dom and see a guilty dark-skinned Black man—not an innocent fifteen-year-old boy. Because at the end of the day, he was an easy and familiar target.

It didn't matter if Dom had done it or not. He wasn't going to get a fair shot.

Even what he'd managed so far was only because we had the money to make it happen. And it was still nowhere near how things would be if he were white.

The police knew my brother's history. Chances were, they were already knee-deep in looking into him. They were going to try to pin him.

So we had to find the right person. Quietly. Without giving any hint that he was even slightly involved. And if the right person *was* Dom . . . we would cross that bridge when we came to it.

I was going to do what Mom wanted. I was going to protect my little brother, which would also protect the entire family. Because if Dom went down for this and it got out to the public, we would all go down for it.

And I was not going to be the one who let the Behres die not even a year after Mom did.

CHAPTER SIX

I took a deep breath and knocked as gently as possible on Dom's bedroom door. I couldn't help glancing over my shoulder at the middles' bedrooms across the hall. They were home for the weekend. And I didn't want either of them to poke their heads out and ask me why I was speaking to the brother we all usually avoided.

I looked at Dom's door and knocked again, a bit louder.

The door opened, and I stepped back. "Morning," I said, trying to not make it obvious that I was attempting to be quiet.

Dom rolled his eyes and moved aside to let me in. I closed the door behind me. In the days since Duane's death, he'd moved away from that scared and shaken boy back to his aloof, standoffish self. It was now harder to buy that I'd seen him at rock bottom at all.

Or maybe that was the act, to make sure I believed him, and this was the truth.

My brother's bedroom had so many posters and prints on the wall that I could barely see the paint underneath. Mostly it was anime stuff. Some of it more sexual than I think Mom would have been okay with, but I guess she didn't come into Dom's room much either. I stared with a frown at a blond character whose chest was barely covered.

"So . . . ?" Dom asked, playing with his hands and looking from me to the poster I'd been examining. Maybe he also hadn't expected anyone to be coming inside and judging his stuff.

I stepped over a pile of clothes and settled for sitting on the violently orange gaming chair in the corner by his desk, which was crowded with monitors and opened chip packages.

"I thought that we should start making plans about what to do." And it was best if those plans didn't have a digital trail, so I had to talk to him in person. "Even if you didn't do it, someone did. And you're an easy suspect for the police. I think we need to look into finding the real murderer."

Dom's face slipped into obvious relief. "Yeah, okay, uh . . . what do we do?"

This was a point in his favor. If he'd done this, why would he want to investigate? He should want the opposite. "Well, there was that note Duane was holding, for one." I told Dom what it had said. "I think considering our last name, it means this is probably about us. So we should start in Mom's office and see if there's anything there. Notes about problem students or enemies or something." There was also that woman in the street, Milk Man lady. She was already super creepy and had been there the day Duane had been killed. I couldn't discount that. But she might also just be a random woman. Better to focus on one thing at a time.

Dom nodded. He opened his mouth and then shut it.

"Something you want to say?"

He shook his head. "No. That's a good idea. Checking Mom's office."

This wasn't going to work if Dom was going to keep secrets from me, but I couldn't pry them out of him. This needed delicacy. It needed the Sunny touch. There was a reason people liked to share things with me. I just needed time to have Dom trust me that way.

The door to Dom's room opened, and Darren walked in. I was apparently the only sibling polite enough to knock. "Karter says to— Oh, hey." His eyes locked on mine, and I forced myself not to stiffen. "You two are . . . hanging out?"

I stood. "I just wanted to see if Dom was okay, given everything that happened at school."

"Wasn't Duane *your* friend? Why wouldn't Dom be okay?"

"Yes, but I've gone to the grief counseling and Dom hasn't." I'd attended the multiple sessions held on Thursday and Friday to look supportive. They were agony. We'd sat in a circle, and it was as if his body was lying in the middle of it, his empty eyes locked with mine, blood seeping from his mangled neck. So when I cried with the others, it was real—it just wasn't for the same reasons.

"What does Karter want?" Dom said, deciding to ignore everything I'd said.

"Police are here."

I busied myself with placing my hands just so on my lap. "Why?" I said, pitching my voice to sound curious, but cautiously so, and concerned, but not guilty.

Darren shrugged. "No idea. Paris is here too. We're all supposed to go downstairs and show a united front or whatever. Not how I wanted to spend my Saturday, but it's happening." My older brother waved us out the door, and I felt him questioning my reason for being with Dom as his eyes lingered on me.

He wasn't buying the lie.

I needed to do better.

We went downstairs together where the rest of the family was seated on the couch. There was a Black woman in a pair of loose dress pants and a cheap blouse. Plain clothes, meaning she was a detective. She sat on one side of the giant sectional while the family sat on the other side, and Paris toward the middle.

"You must be Sunny, Darren, and Dom," the woman said. She reached out her hand for us to shake. Darren and I did; Dom just sat down. Karter narrowed her eyes at our youngest brother. To her credit, though, the detective took Dom's snub in stride. "I'm Detective Chambers. I'm just following up on what happened at the school."

Paris was wearing the same pieces as the detective, dress pants and a blouse, but her combo was impeccable. Designer with a tailored fit. The blouse had the sheen of real silk, and I had seen the pants last year at Toronto Fashion Week. She also had a sleek, short, boss-bitch haircut compared to Chambers's functional bun. "The detective just wants to ask if you saw or heard anything. And this is, of course, strictly related to Mr. Mathers's death. She's aware of Dom's preexisting charges, but they are unrelated to this discussion."

The explanation was plainly a warning to the detective. It wasn't subtle, and it wasn't supposed to be.

Detective Chambers smiled at Paris and then looked at the rest of us. "Exactly. You are all in the unique position of being not only owners of the school, but in some cases, students and staff." She waved between me and Dom, though I noticed the way her eyes stayed on him just a beat longer. "Did you two notice anything after school on Tuesday? Or did you come straight home?"

"I don't think their whereabouts are strictly relevant," Paris said, her gaze sticking to us. "But absolutely, if you noticed anything, please say so."

Damn, we really were getting our money's worth with Paris. I had already put together a story of where we'd been that day and when, repetitively drilling it to Dom as we walked home, but it remained a weakness. Especially since that Milk Man woman had seen us. Though I knew that if it was my word against hers, I would win. But Paris had saved us from even touching upon it.

"I really wish I had," I said, slipping a pained smile on my face. "I would love to be able to help find out what happened to Duane." I wondered if I should add a little sob or something, then decided that was excessive. Besides, I worried that even a tiny bit of sincere emotion might break the dam open. If I full-on bawled over a boy who I had barely tolerated, it would raise red flags. "But there wasn't anything I noticed."

Karter brushed invisible lint off her leggings. "If anyone in this family had seen something important, they would have told me right away. None of us want a dead body in the halls. However, it's more possible that a student witnessed something, and so we'll be offering an anonymous tip line that they can access."

Chambers pulled her eyes away from Dom, where they had strayed more than once. Dom simply lay back into the couch cushions, staring vacantly at the bear-shaped bowl on the coffee table. "It would be ideal if we could interview them."

"We're not letting police interact with our students unless it is legally enforced," Karter said, her voice iron. Honestly, I felt a bit proud of her. I still didn't think she was ideal for this role in our family, but she had her strengths. "Perhaps you're unaware, but many of our students come from backgrounds in which they've had traumatic experiences interacting with law enforcement. Your very presence is triggering." She met Chambers's eyes and held them, daring this Black woman to push back about something she must already be very well aware of. I wondered if they assigned her to us because we were a Black family. Like we might trust her more because of it.

"Maybe we could access your security footage? I realize that the Behres have worked with Linet Security for quite some time, and they power the systems for both your home and farm property.

We made a call just to confirm, and it seems there's a system for the school, too, though we'd need your permission to access it."

I glanced sidelong at Karter, who, like the rest of us, had twitched at Chambers incorrectly identifying the ranch as a farm—we raised cows, not crops. But really I cared about this cameras-in-the-school thing. Mom would have never done something like that. And if there were cameras, then Karter would have footage of us cleaning up the crime scene. No way she would have seen that and said nothing.

Karter said, "The academy was listed because it was a consideration, but ultimately my mother decided against it. We run a school, not a prison, and cameras suggest the opposite. Since she's passed, returning the security equipment hasn't been a priority. And as I'm sure you know, Linet doesn't do any monitoring. We keep a closed system and handle this ourselves. So they wouldn't actually know whether or not a system is active. They just know they provided us the equipment. I'm sorry if they misled you on that point. Is there anything else you need, Detective Chambers?" It confirmed what I'd suspected, though I was more surprised than I wanted to be that Mom had ever considered it. She hadn't even liked having cameras on the outside of the house.

I watched as Chambers smiled tightly, holding in a breath. I could almost see the moment she realized that she wasn't going to get anything useful out of this conversation. "No, no more questions. I'll leave my card for you in case you think of anything." She put it on the coffee table and pushed it toward Karter, who glanced down at it without moving. Paris reached out and took it, slipping it into her purse.

Detective Chambers was escorted out of the house, and as the door shut behind her, we all stood and waited for a moment.

I realized after a minute that we were waiting for direction. That was what Mom would have done. Turned to us and debriefed, outlined a plan, created a strategy, and reassured us that everything would be fine. It was exactly what she'd done when we'd had a different detective visit to ask how Dom knew Torri Allen, and were we aware that the girl had been missing and her mother was very worried about her? That they'd heard she and Dom were "close" and would love to chat.

I looked at Paris, but she was typing something on her phone.

Dad sighed and collapsed into the couch cushions.

Karter looked around at us. "If you saw something and you don't tell me right now, you'll wish you were the one with your throat cut open."

Tactful as always. Good job, big sis.

"So what are we doing about this?" Kiley asked, unfazed by the threat. "Besides grief sessions?"

Her curls were messily bundled onto her head, which on her looked effortlessly stylish, an effect only increased by the faded denim coveralls she wore. She'd bought them from a plus-size brand in the UK and custom painted the colorful designs on the pockets. There was something on her fingers, paint or cement or glue. I couldn't tell. My sister had never held impressive grades but she made up for it with award-winning art. Sometimes she would be holed up in the shed for days, barely sleeping or eating, and then she would drag herself into the house and do nothing but sleep and eat for an equivalent amount of time. Clearly, this family meeting had interrupted that cycle. Her fingers twitched, like she was mentally still working on her piece.

Karter said, "We're not the police. They'll handle the investigation, and I'll look into some discreet security measures in the meantime. You don't need to worry about it."

Darren added, "I heard there was, like, a note from the killer or something. Is that true? They didn't report on it, and the detective didn't ask about it." He also had unidentifiable art supplies on his hands, but he was relaxed. He created at his own pace and had never actually sought out the accolades that came to him. He certainly had never missed sleep or a meal for creation.

Karter narrowed her eyes at him. "Where did you hear that?"

"Twitter."

"Really?!"

He shrugged.

The police probably wouldn't ever publicize the rhyme. It was too creepy. It would make people panic. But now they would also know that this had something to do with us. This likely wouldn't be the last time we saw Detective Chambers.

"It doesn't matter," Karter continued. "Let the police do the digging. Paris, anything to add?"

The woman looked up from her phone. "Do not speak to the authorities without me present. And, I'll be frank with you, they can't add anything to Dom's initial charge, but any implication or involvement in this could damage my ability to poke holes in what they have."

"But Dom hasn't done anything," I said, less as a show of support, and more because I wanted to hear her opinion on it. But it would come across as the former, which I liked.

Paris shifted her gaze to me. "It doesn't matter. If they want him for it, they'll find something. So let's avoid giving them anything."

It was confirmation of what I'd already surmised. Made worse because Dom *had* been involved. We both had.

I could feel him standing behind me. I pictured the blood on his hands, and that panicked expression on his face, still lined with baby fat.

Paris nodded to Karter. "I have to go, but text me if anything comes up."

"I'll walk you out," Karter said. The two of them headed toward the garage and the middles went upstairs to their rooms.

I approached Dad, who had transitioned to lying down. I took a moment to grip his hand in mine and kneel next to the couch to press my cheek to his. "It'll be okay, right?" I frankly wasn't sure it would be, but the words were for him, not me.

"Yeah," he intoned without feeling.

I squeezed his hand one last time and stood, glancing at the door to see if Karter was on her way back. "I was looking for my stapler. Have you seen it?"

"No. Buy a new one."

"Can I just grab Mom's from her office?"

"Sure."

I smiled. "Her door code?"

"6293."

"Thank you."

When I looked over my shoulder, Dom was standing there. I fought the shudder that wanted to roll over my body. There was something about the expression on his face, the sort of detached calm as he'd watched me, that made me feel like he was seeing beyond my carefully designed facade. But now, he needed me, which meant accepting a little deceit.

CHAPTER SEVEN

I wasn't prepared for the mental assault of entering Mom's office. She was everywhere here. There were her favorite pens, meticulously ordered alongside everything else on top of her desk, which included a tiny carved wooden bear and a portrait of the family—everyone on a white sand beach dressed in linen.

When I turned, I jumped. Dom was leaning over my shoulder, looking at the picture. Even though I knew it wasn't possible, I swore that I could smell the blood just from him being near me. I remembered the way it dug into the soft grooves of his palms and tucked under his nails.

I held the frame tighter but didn't move. In the photo, he was strangely off to the side. The photographer had instructed us to put our arms around each other. But Dom hadn't. He was like that.

"Surprised she didn't have me photoshopped out," he said, and stepped back.

I tried not to let my shoulders drop in relief and frowned at him. "Why would she do that?"

"I think she kept it as is because she did virtual meetings in here," he said, ignoring me. "Would have looked bad."

"You're her kid, just like the rest of us." He'd even been given an equal portion in the will; she obviously cared in some way. He'd also had a private meeting like the rest of us. I wondered what he'd gotten in his. If he had his own sticky note. Still, I knew there was too much accusation in my tone. I needed to reel it back. "She loved us all."

He leveled his gaze at me. "Said like the favorite."

Yeah, okay, I was the favorite, what did he want me to do? Pretend otherwise? Apologize for whatever had made Mom hate him? I sucked at the inside of my cheeks because it helped me look embarrassed and shy. "She didn't pick—"

"Bullshit. You were her favorite, and I was . . ."

Her least favorite. Though saying "favorite" at all was generous. But I was also tired of trying to encourage him, and if we took too long, it would cause problems. The door to Mom's office was through our parents' bedroom, and if Dad came back and found not just me but Dom here, *still*, for a task that should have taken seconds, it would be bad. "Let's just look for anything that might be helpful. Okay?" Hike up on the last word to sound optimistic.

"What about her journals?" Dom asked.

"They're just dates and appointments. We're looking for something with more information."

For as long as I could remember, Mom kept journals. They were spartan and focused. Neatly lined-up dates and checklists. We'd had multiple sessions in which she'd taught me her organizational key and noted how I should record information. Paper, she'd emphasized, didn't die of uncharged batteries and couldn't be hacked. It was versatile, and it was private.

That was how I knew that if there was something to be discovered, something that might explain someone murdering Duane in a weird, targeted attempt to harm our family, it would be written down. Just not in the same place where she recorded appointments.

We searched through the room in silence, pulling open drawers and putting things back as neatly and exactly as possible.

"Ranch was up and down," Dom muttered, casually sitting in Mom's chair. A muscle in my neck twitched, and I ignored it.

Our ranch in Oro-Medonte, north of Toronto, was a calf-cow operation, meaning that we raised up the cattle and sold them off to slaughterhouses. We didn't do it ourselves. Not commercially, anyway. In the nineties, a rich white man gave his now multimillion-dollar business to Grandpa, one of his few Black workers, and suddenly his and Mom's lives had changed. He'd died when I was really young. Stroke. I barely knew him. But after Mom took over, she'd added a bunch of businesses to the mix, and our wealth increased. Though the ranch had always contributed the most to our fortune.

Good money in meat, apparently.

He put down the file, which showed the costs and revenue for the ranch over several years. There were a bunch of highs and lows from the mid-nineties, then steady growth around the time ownership transferred to Grandpa, and now a recent decline and frantic ups and downs. Probably because Dad started trying to get more involved in the businesses. I'd only ever heard him and Mom argue about it once, but it was enough. I assumed they thought I hadn't. Just like Mom probably thought I hadn't heard her arguing on the phone with someone about the ranch. At the time I hadn't thought much about it, but she'd mentioned accounts. Now I wondered if it had been the bank.

"The ranch will bounce back," I said.

"Oh, it's not just the ranch." Dom flipped over several pages, which showed similar information for our family's other businesses. Sharp declines and unsteady numbers as of the last couple years.

I swallowed. "I think we would have noticed if we were going broke."

"Would we? Most wealthy people end up in serious debt situations before anyone else in the family realizes that something has gone wrong. Rich people are good at hiding their descent into"— he dramatically pressed a hand against his chest and looked at me—"*upper middle class.*"

I didn't know why he was acting like that wasn't a big deal. He would lose just as much as the rest of us if our cash flow dried up. "I'm sure it's fine."

"You would think that."

"I'm not sure what that means."

He leaned back in the chair. "It means that you're used to the lie that everything in this family is fine. You like it. But me? No one bothers to hide the ugliness that goes on here from me. After all, it's gotta go to someone."

"I think I've seen enough ugliness."

Dom had the decency to look away. He'd only been five when the incident in the woods happened, but it didn't matter. It hung over the family. I knew that I was handled with more care as a result. And yes, maybe Mom and Dad gave me more attention because of it too. But it wasn't like that made me immune to noticing the unsavory things that happened in this family, including helping my brother hide the evidence of his involvement in a murder.

"What did Mom give you? In your will meeting?" I asked, voicing what I'd wondered earlier.

He shrugged. "Money. I don't even know why we needed private meetings for that."

I couldn't tell if he was lying or not. But assuming the truth, maybe Mom gave us all meetings to disguise the fact that she'd left me something special. Which wasn't ideal, because if I'd been the only one with a private will meeting, it would have lent some legitimacy to the fact that she wanted me to take over. Her method had equalized us. The alternative was that my brother was lying, and I wasn't the only one Mom left instructions for.

The gentle whooshing sound of the bedroom door opening reached my ears.

Dom and I looked at each other. I rushed to put the financial records back and scrambled around the room, searching for somewhere to hide. Fucking auto lights. Even if I physically turned them off, when I moved to hide, they would just turn on again.

My brother opened one of the cabinets. It had shelves on the bottom, but the open cupboard up top was big enough for us both to fit. He pushed Mom's chair over and motioned for me to step on it to get inside. I did. Behind me, he struggled to shove himself in while the wheels of the chair made it unstable.

I gripped his upper arm and tugged him inside. The force of it sent the chair spinning back toward the desk. I closed the doors and tried to stop myself from trembling.

What was I even doing?! It was Dad and Karter. I should have just thought of an excuse, but I didn't know what to say. Besides, more family members seeing me casually hanging out with Dom twice in one day? It would ring major alarm bells.

Calm. Down.

I heard Karter say, "What did Sunny need from the office?"

"Stapler," Dad replied. "She's probably already been in and out. What did Paris say?"

The door to the room swung open, and Karter made a sound in the back of her throat. "She thinks it's fine. Dom is basically being accused of going drunk swimming with some girl who passed out, and they think he left her there to die. They wanna say he drugged her or actively drowned her, but they don't have enough. The bruises on her body aren't consistent with that. It's why they didn't try charging him as an adult. They need more. So now they want to catch him on this and do everything they wanted to do with Torri's case. First-degree as an adult. But the crimes are nowhere near the same, and they have nothing on him."

I peeked over at Dom, whose face was stoic while our sister off-handedly discussed his murder charge. We were shoved up against each other, and that scent, that invisible smell of blood, snuck into my nose again. *No.* Hadn't I just said today that he had no motive? That if he had done it, he wouldn't be helping?

Either way, Dad was at least somewhat concerned. Whether some of that concern was for Dom was its own question. Unlike Mom, Dad didn't actively ignore his younger son, but their interactions had a sort of businesslike perfunctory nature to them. Like Dom was an acquaintance he was forced to be polite to. He didn't get the fun and warm version of Dad that the rest of us did.

There was the sound of drawers opening and closing. "Looking for something?" Dad asked.

"Just curious," Karter mused.

"About?"

"What she left behind." She'd said it so quietly that I almost didn't hear.

"She already gave you everything she felt you'd need."

"I know."

My breath started to come faster, and I had to fight to keep it regulated. What did that mean? What had Mom given Karter? A sticky note like I'd gotten? Or was this some metaphorical bullshit? No. Karter would never buy into that. If it wasn't something physical, she would be complaining about it.

A drawer slammed closed, and then Karter said, "The stapler . . ."

I froze. *Shit. Shit. Shit.*

Dom lightly touched my arm, and I jerked my head toward him. He held up the stapler with a smile. He'd taken it. I'd been so panicked that I hadn't even noticed. I found myself smiling back, nearly beaming.

"What about it?"

"It's the bear one, right? She'd better put it back when she's done."

Did she really have to micromanage everything?

Finally the door to the room closed, and I didn't let out a sigh until I heard the second door, the one to the bedroom, close too.

Dom and I climbed out of the cupboard, jumping the small distance. I stumbled and fell awkwardly. I went to push myself up, then paused. There was a little yellow piece of paper peeking out from underneath the cupboard. "Can you hand me a ruler?"

Dom did, and I used it to fish the thing out. It was a Post-it note. Innocent enough, except on top it said, *Sunny—this should help explain everything.* I blinked at it. I flipped it over but there wasn't anything else. I tried to remember if maybe I'd seen it before, but I hadn't.

"What is it?" Dom asked.

I had no idea. But then . . . Mom said she was going to leave me something, hadn't she? About leading the family. What if this had been attached to it and had fallen off? Did that mean the thing still existed? And what had Karter gotten from Mom?

After a moment, I stood up from the floor and looked over at Dom. "What else happened with Duane?" This note could wait. But searching this room had been a bust, and I knew that my brother was holding something back. "What happened before I got there?"

"I told you. I tried to help. To do CPR, but it was too late."

I hoped that he never had to tell this story to the police because it was so weak. Who saw someone with their head nearly decapitated and thought CPR would revive them?

All I wanted to do was snap at him to spit it out already. But I forced patience. We'd just gotten through this hide-and-seek bullshit together. If there was a time to show him he could trust me, it was now. "Dom . . . we need to be honest with each other. This is to help you. Anything, even a tiny detail, could be a huge clue."

He bit his lip.

"I'm all you have right now," I added.

That did it. His shoulders hunched. "After I realized that CPR wasn't going to work, I panicked, looking for something to get the blood off my hands. That's when I saw a symbol drawn on the corner of a countertop . . . I wiped it away."

Amazing. Even more tampering with evidence. But some random symbol didn't seem relevant enough to bother with. "Why?"

"Because it was the same symbol I saw carved into Torri's headboard the last time I saw her alive."

Well . . . fuck.

To be read in the event of my death.

These journal entries are leftovers from my teenage self. I include these because I think it's necessary to experience this the way I did in order to understand where we are today. If there is one lesson you take away from this experience, it's that history is important. My father, your grandfather, didn't know much about where he came from, and I never knew my mother, and so my history began on that ranch. Your father's did too, in a way. And certainly you know a version of it. But you don't know all of it. That is why I've compiled these entries for you.

With all my love,
Mom

January 6, 1995

Something changed the day that Shirley Feeney nailed that squirming lizard to the tree and lit it on fire. We all watched it burn. ~~At the time, I was just happy to be included.~~* I expected it to stink. But it wasn't much different from hot dogs on a fire. Though the smoke got in my eyes and stung.

According to Shirley, this was our first sacrifice to the Milk Man.

---

* This was crossed out in the original text. I used to be a little more needy than I liked to admit. Though I grew out of it. Contrary to what your father might suggest, you <u>can</u> outgrow unwanted habits.

That was days ago now, but I still have a feeling something bad will come of it. Dad always says that if I would feel ashamed for him to see me do it, then it's probably something I shouldn't do. He's always been like that. He lives his own way no matter what anyone else thinks. And I wouldn't have wanted him to see me like that, in that circle of girls.

But I wasn't going to tell Dad about it, obviously, so I told Jay instead. I don't know why I thought that would be better. He thought it was really messed up. He didn't get why I'd watch, and I didn't have a good way to explain it. His dark skin was dusty from helping toss hay into the cow shed, and I could smell the sweat on him. It stunk on the other boys, and it stunk on him, too, but I didn't mind as much with Jay. Maybe because ours are the only black families on the ranch. Or maybe just because we're friends. He's always nice to me. His brother Jonas, too. Which is hard, because sometimes I think other boys notice when one of them is nice and they try to stamp it out. And it's one thing to be nice to a girl because you want to be with her, and another thing just to be nice to her for the sake of it, like Jay is. I told him that whole theory once, boys being nice and stuff, and he said he thought that I was thinking about it too much.

Jay, in general, isn't a deep thinker. He's smart. He reads more books than anyone else I know. But he doesn't sit with his thoughts. Me, I think about things a lot. It's why I started writing the thoughts down, just to get them out of my head.

Mr. Owens always says, "This isn't just a ranch, it's a family." But he doesn't get it because he's white. There are at least eight families living and working on the property, and if they don't like us, it doesn't matter what Mr. Owens says. And sure, they love Whitney Houston and Michael Jordan, but that doesn't translate to liking us. And we need that. I need that. So Dad can get better shifts and a better position and pay for me to go to university in Toronto. 'Cause right now, a service technician's salary isn't cutting it. It's only one step above being a general laborer.

And so I work my ass off too, though it never seems to amount to anything.

Meanwhile, Shirley's dad is the ranch operations manager, second only to Mr. Owens.

That's why I hang out with those girls and play their Milk Man game. I don't actually believe some invisible guy is going to fix my life, no matter what Shirley thinks. But being friends with her means that she'll mention me, and maybe her dad will get to know my name, and when a promotion comes up, he'll think, "Behre. Oh yeah, Shirley's little friend," and it'll matter. It probably won't. But at least this feels like doing something.

And so I stood and watched that lizard burn with the other girls. But inside, I knew that someday this would come back at us. I hoped Shirley the most.

And when it does, I can look back here and know that I called it.*

Because in here, I don't have to pretend.

This is the only place I get to be Ainsley, exactly the way I am.

January 12, 1995

Dad has this idea that I can go away for school no matter how much money he makes. He talked about loans and scholarships

---

* I would like you to know that I didn't feel much satisfaction in being right. Not about things going wrong. Though I did in being right about Shirley. She always took things too far. Restraint is an important skill—make note of that.

and all this stuff. He acts like I'm not half of his workforce. Sixteen is old enough for me to get paid my own wage, and I always give it straight to him because we need it. If I leave, that's just gone. And then what, go to the city without anything?

He always says, "Bears are strong enough to weather any storm. And we take care of our own as fiercely as we can." He carries a teddy bear on his key chain and has all these bear-themed things around the house that he says remind him that he's a Behre.*

But I don't want to be weathering storms. I'm tired of this struggle shit. I want to be like Will. Whisked away to live with rich relatives, all the opportunities to make something of myself and help my family. But real life isn't like that. Nothing good is going to just fall into my lap. Not a black girl living on a ranch in Oro. I have to *make* it happen. That's why I have to hang around Shirley all the time now even though she's hella annoying.

She's saying the Milk Man has new requests coming, and soon he's going to visit our bodies, and we should accept him into our hearts if we want the ranch to prosper. But until then, we're supposed to burn more lizards. We stand around her, watching the flames flicker while she preaches at us, the smoke billowing around her face.

The weather's been bad this year, which means the grass is suffering and the herd isn't getting enough food to keep their weights up, and Mr. Owens can't afford to buy feed elsewhere.

For Shirley, I know this is just about the attention. If she really wanted to help, she would tell her dad to do something.

---

* Yes and no, if you were wondering if this is the reason for my decor tastes. But I will also say that my father had a much better understanding of what it meant to be a Behre than I did at this age.

He's a bad operations head, pure and simple, and he only got that position in the first place because he talked crap about my dad. I <u>know</u> that's why. Mr. Owens was dropping all sorts of hints about Dad being up for that position, and then suddenly Mack Feeney is the one getting it!

I keep all those feelings to myself, of course, because I want Shirley to like me. So I pretend to prepare to accept the Milk Man into my heart. I figure as long as I fake it well enough, she'll be happy. I wish I had a better plan, but I don't know what else I can do. Dad is already such a good worker. And the guys like him. The ones that aren't racist anyway.

Jay still doesn't get it, even though I've explained it multiple times and suggested he try the same with the boys. After all, even his sister runs in Shirley's group. Though she never talks to me. Feeney's older son has a few years on Jay, but it could be worth a shot. He said me and his sister can do that if we like, but he isn't interested in that shit. I told him that I wasn't interested either, but I have to help my dad. Then he asks how far I'm gonna go with it. What wouldn't I do? What does that even mean? So I asked him if he wouldn't do anything for his dreams, and all dramatic he says that he wouldn't kill someone.

We both laughed, but I didn't say that I wouldn't. ~~I don't know why.~~

Jay said it's like the TLC song. Don't go chasing waterfalls. That sometimes you reach too far and you get burned.

I wasn't sure that was what the song was actually about. I thought it was just about not acting like something you're not. Which, technically, supported what he was saying. Though I didn't tell Jay that.

January 27, 1995

Something is changing on the ranch. I really didn't think much of it at first. People were talking about Mack Feeney. Even if he wasn't good at his job, it was important. But now it's different. It's like people are all about him. I keep hearing talk about how he's the best operations head we've ever had.

Can you believe that shit? Since when?!

Even Dad thinks it's weird. His shifts are different now because Mack proposed this new working schedule, and everyone just agreed. Dad said he almost did too, but then he thought about it more and realized that maybe it wasn't the best plan. But when he spoke up, no one wanted to listen. They were all on Mack's side.

And it's gone straight to Shirley's head. She's been strutting around and calling us the milk maidens. <u>Openly.</u> We're way too old to be playing pretend, but she doesn't see any issue with it. Says the Milk Man is going to change everything for the better.

The Feeneys go to church regularly, and I sometimes feel like she's just copying what she hears there. Turning God into the Milk Man so she can guide us instead of the Lord. We never go to church. I tried to tell Dad that we should, since so many families on the ranch do, but he said he would rather use the time working.

Sometimes I feel like he doesn't even want to get promoted. He's like Jay. He never tries for more than he's already got.

I am the only one working for our family.*

---

* You may often feel like this during the process of caring for this family. It will be frustrating. I wish I could tell you to lean on others. But I don't know that that's ever actually worked for me.

February 9, 1995

The Milk Man has performed his first miracle.

According to Shirley, anyway.

I think it's a lot more obvious that the weather has just improved. It's still cold, but it's not as harsh, and a lot of the snow has melted early.

Everything in the field is shooting up. The cattle are reaching higher weights even earlier than usual. Dad is pretty sure we're going to hit a record. But . . . he said it strangely. It should have sounded like, "I'm pretty sure we're going to hit a record!" With a smile and a wink or something. But that wasn't how he said it. His face was hard and near expressionless, and he said it with less emotion than I've heard him use to talk about what we're going to eat for dinner. I asked if anything was wrong, but he denied it. It felt weird to even ask. The ranch was doing better. How could that be bad?

But he's been off ever since the ranch meeting they had a few nights ago. Mack Feeney was the one who called it, and I don't think Dad wanted to go, but he did anyway. Everyone is still wild about Mack. I don't get it at all. He's just as shit as he was before. I think they were supposed to talk about the state of the farm, though it was already doing better by then. When I asked him about it afterward, Dad just shook his head and said it wasn't much of anything, more of the Mack Feeney show. I asked if shifts were going to change again and if Dad had said anything against it. But all he did was shake his head one more time and say that no one would listen to him anyway.

Even though a bunch of us kids work on the ranch too, we weren't invited. Adults only. Which was fine. I didn't care much, but it annoyed Jay.

And so, when we were supposed to be cleaning the cow shed together, he was mostly stomping around and muttering under his breath. Jonas was with us and tried to calm him down, saying the meeting was probably boring. Jonas is good like that. He's tall and dark-skinned, and he puts on muscle without even trying, so a lot of people assume he's some rough aggressive guy. I know some of the kids on the ranch are scared of him too. If they talked to him for two seconds, they'd know they were wrong. His voice is soft, and he's always trying to help people. I've never even seen him squish a bug. He's the only one Jay actually listens to. At least he got him to stop throwing hay around like he was having a tantrum.

It's funny because Jonas and Jay are pretty much the same age. Jonas was born in February and Jay in December. But Jonas is a lot more mature. Like years more. Not that I would ever say that to Jay.

Either way, meeting or no meeting, the ranch is finally doing better, which is great for us. Because I know if money got tight and people needed to be let go, we would be in trouble. Mr. Owens seems to love Dad, but you never know. Sometimes when it comes down to it, white folks stick together, even if they made room for you before.

And of course now everyone is praising Mack Feeney even more. Like the ranch doing better is actually because of him. I can't roll my eyes hard enough. But on the bright side, he knows me now. Passed by and thanked me for helping Shirley and the girls with our prayers for the ranch. I wonder if that's how she's selling that whole Milk Man thing to him.

It may be bittersweet, but it's still a win.

February 13, 1995

I hope I can read this later. My hands are shaking so much. My heartbeat is loud in my ears, and I keep thinking that somehow Dad will hear it in the bed next to mine. We only have the one bedroom, so there's not a lot of space to hide myself. Thankfully, he's already asleep. He's been going to bed earlier these days. Sometimes I find him there in the afternoon, lying on his back and staring up at the ceiling.

When I asked what he was doing, he said he was "concentrating." When I asked what that meant, he walked back on it, saying it was nothing. Then denied ever having said it when I brought it up later.

Something is going on with Dad. I don't know what he did, but it feels like something's changed between him and the others on the ranch.

But everything tonight started all because Shirley kicked me out of her little club. It feels so ridiculous to realize that's why now. Anyway, I saw her heading into the forest with the other girls and realized they hadn't come by. So I went over and asked to come with them. I didn't want to, but I was trying to make this Shirley thing work.

This fucking girl looked down her nose at me and said I was out. Not only had I not let the Milk Man into my heart and could therefore not be either a milk maiden or a little calf (since when did she add calves into this?) but also my daddy had apparently offended the Milk Man. When I asked how, she just turned and marched off with the girls following after her. I tried to lock eyes with Jay's sister, thinking maybe she might stand up for me, but she wouldn't even look my way.

I'm sure it had nothing to do with Shirley's game and everything to do with Dad somehow pissing off Mack Feeney. Everyone on the ranch was so obsessed with the guy lately. And Shirley was his daughter. It would also explain why Dad had been so strange, but I couldn't figure out what he'd done.

In the moment I was too shocked to do anything, but later on while Dad was asleep, I snuck over to the Feeney house. I figured if I could talk to Shirley, I could find out what was happening.

But as I came around the back of the house, I noticed Donald. He's her older brother. The one I wanted Jay to be friends with. He was squatting down by the shed where they keep garbage so bears and other animals can't get at it.

I was about to say hello when I heard the sounds.

Soft purring.

Dad was allergic so I couldn't have anything furry in the house. But there were a few cats who wandered around the property that I liked to pet. I was going to walk over to do just that, figuring I could ask Donald if Shirley was around at the same time.

But then . . . it started to cry.

And then scream.

I stumbled backward and went home.

Sat on our couch. Quietly. Not knowing what to do. And that's how I got here. Writing everything down, letting the thoughts pour out.

I just . . . Why would he do that? I know Shirley is weird, okay, and she's done worse to lizards, but that's basically just a giant bug, and what he was doing was different. It crosses a line.

Something is wrong with him.

CHAPTER EIGHT

Spirit Halloween locations across the city had already been open for a month by the time we were able to go in October. The Stockyards District store was farther away than the one in Mississauga, but Craig insisted that it was the better one. His face was practically split open with a smile as we entered the Spirit hand in hand, with Shyanne and Mercy following behind us—the two of them just as excited as he was.

We were immediately greeted by a plastic clown with sharp bloody teeth in an outfit that was somehow pristine despite the gore on its face. The masked eyes were black and empty. Another clown held a motorized chainsaw that made revving sounds, though the chains didn't move. They were also colorfully decorated with blood splatter.

It looked so fake in comparison. Real blood was darker. But maybe that was the point. For it to look fake. Fake was safe.

It had slowly begun to dawn on me that there was a murderer running free with access to the school. One who wasn't a fan of my family and was also potentially associated with Torri's murder. What was the plan? How many bodies were going to end up involved in this?

Craig nudged my shoulder at the same time that my phone

buzzed. I checked, and it was Dom agreeing to talk after I was done with my friends. Good. We needed to figure out this connected-murders-via-symbol thing.

My boyfriend loudly cleared his throat.

I looked up. "Sorry, my brother texted."

He had an expectant look on his face. Shit. He'd said something, and I'd missed it reading the text.

"I think you two should go as zombie Ariel and Prince-what's-his-face," Shyanne suggested, widening her eyes at me. Mercy had already left us to run through the store.

I threw Shyanne a grateful look before turning to Craig and saying, "That could be cool. I could get red crochet locs put in."

He nodded, but his smile had dimmed significantly. Great. Now he was going to mope. It was the same way when we watched movies and I didn't like them as much as him. Or he wanted to do something and I wasn't enthusiastic enough. If the guy needed his girlfriend to love everything he did, then why wouldn't he just break up with me and find someone else? It would do us both a favor.

Mercy rushed around the corner in a melting human face mask and screamed, "Boo!"

Shyanne cried out dramatically and pretended to run away so her girlfriend could chase her, cackling while she did.

A clerk up front lazily said, "No running."

Shyanne and Mercy liked the same things and had fun together. Whenever Craig and I went out, it was like being with a friend who you didn't know very well and occasionally had sex with. It wasn't a good time, but you didn't hate each other, so why not?

The girls came back over to us, Mercy pulling off the mask with a sigh. No one said anything for a moment.

There was an absence. A gaping wide-open space that none of us had addressed. I cleared my throat and said, "How is everyone doing, given everything?" It seemed like someone should mention it. Wednesday's classes had been canceled, but we'd gone back to the academy on Thursday. Dad had, poorly, conducted an assembly to mourn Duane, and we'd had our grief sessions. Then it was Friday, more sessions, and then we were leaving school. We hadn't actually talked about the person missing from our lunch table with just us since that initial group chat.

Shyanne shrugged. "It's sad, but it is what it is."

Craig nodded, shoving his hands in his pockets.

I said, "Yeah . . . I've been surprised, honestly, by how normal everyone seems to be." It wasn't like students were crying in the halls or anything. Outside of the emotional grief sessions, it had almost been like nothing had happened.

"What else can we do?" Mercy said, meeting my eyes. "Some of us are used to shitty circumstances, you know? You have to keep it pushing. There's no time to like, go destress at a spa or whatever."

Was that seriously how little she thought of me?

My mom *died* this year.

I lost the most important person to me and then had to come to school with a smile on my face like everything was fine because we had an image to uphold. An image that was necessary for the school my mom devoted her entire life to.

If Mercy thought I was so disconnected that I couldn't even be slightly sympathetic to people outside of my tax bracket, why did she even hang out with me?

Shyanne glanced between the two of us and rubbed her head. "You probably get that though, right? Since you lost your mom this year. And she was, like, a real one. But you're here still, moving on."

For the second time that day, I was grateful to Shyanne. I gave her a small smile. It almost felt weird on my face. An expression that genuine. "Yeah," I said.

"Right, sorry." Mercy at least had the decency to look sheepish. "I just mean that most of us have a lot of practice in picking up and carrying on after things go wrong. Doesn't mean we're not still upset. We can't, like, take days off, is all."

I tried to stop being annoyed. I got it. When I was having a rough time, if I really needed it, I could take a month off and know everything would be fine, but a lot of them couldn't. They weren't just students. They were part-time parents helping to look after their younger siblings or part-time workers contributing after-school job money to their families.

"So . . . ," Craig said in an obvious attempt to cut the tension. "I actually like that zombie Eric and Ariel idea. We should look for a tail." He squeezed my hand and started dragging me toward a separate section of the store, and I let myself be led.

Several minutes later, we'd found what Craig deemed to be the perfect tail and he insisted that I try it on. The same bored clerk pointed out the changerooms at the back of the store.

They were makeshift, like everything else in the pop-up, located down a long hall with dark cloth drapes. I followed Craig as we made our way along and came to a split with signs pointing left for girls and right for boys.

"Take lots of pictures of what yours looks like, okay?" he said.

I nodded and left him, going to my own section. It was a lot quieter than I thought it would be. But it was a Sunday, and we had to come at the ass crack of dawn because Craig was worried about all the good costumes being gone.

The changerooms were unsupervised and seemed like they hadn't been cleaned from yesterday. There were discarded neon-green tights, bright wigs, ruby-red slippers with their buckles loose, and a stray eyelash. I picked one of the stalls and pulled the flimsy curtain over the opening.

I sighed and shimmied out of my jeans, tugging up the sequined mermaid-style skirt that had a cheap chiffon burst at the bottom meant to mimic the end of a tail.

I looked into the mirrors on the sides of the stall to check it out. I was turning to see from a side angle when out of the corner of my eye, I noticed a hand sneaking around the privacy curtain. It was cloaked in a black leather glove, like the person was already in costume.

The hair on my arms slowly lifted off my skin, joining the goose pimples peppering the area.

"Someone's in here," I said, my voice more snappish than I wanted it to be. It was fine. Just a random person without enough common sense to realize if the curtain was closed, someone was inside.

The hand immediately pulled back, and my shoulders dropped.

Then it came back, faster than I could track, and tore the cloth aside, exposing me to the open changeroom. I tried to rush forward but was restricted by the tightness of the skirt and nearly fell attempting to waddle out of the stall. When I finally got out, I looked up and down the aisle, but no one was there.

My lower lip trembled, and I bit down on it savagely. *Calm down, Sunny. It's just someone trying to freak you out.* I couldn't stand Halloween. All these bullshit pranks. It was probably Mercy trying to scare me. I could imagine them, her and Craig, giggling at their joke. Though I liked to think that Shyanne wasn't that mean-spirited.

I was about to head back inside my stall when I noticed the black boots under one of the other stalls. Their shiny leather matched the gloved hand.

"Hello?" I called. What I really wanted to say was, "What is your problem?" but I refrained. I shuffled closer to the stall. "Hello? Was that you just now?" I forced out a laugh. "So funny, you really got me."

The person didn't answer. They just stood there. Unmoving.

"I thought you were supposed to save the pranks for Halloween night," I tried, pushing good humor into my voice.

I could feel the pounding in my chest the closer I got. This was so ridiculous. I bet the instant I got close, Craig and Mercy would pop out and scream or something. I was just playing right into their hands. But still, I kept creeping forward until I was right in front of the stall.

My hand shook as I reached for the curtain. "Last chance . . . ," I said, though my voice wobbled in a way I despised.

I ripped the curtain aside to . . . nothing.

I looked down and rolled my eyes.

There was a pair of leather boots. Empty and abandoned.

A laugh escaped from my lips. Fuck, this was embarrassing.

I turned around, convinced that I would see my friends behind me with their phones held up, laughing at my reaction. But no one was there.

What I *did* notice was that the curtain was closed around the stall I'd just come out of.

I rushed back to it, not giving myself time to panic more, and opened the curtain. I stepped in front of the mirror and stared at the words that streaked across my reflected face, written hastily in fake red blood.

I KNOW WHAT YOU'RE HIDING, BEAR CUB.

"Sunny?"

I screamed and whipped around to see a shocked Craig in a white button up and blue pants.

"You scared me," I ground out from between my teeth, trying without much success to pitch my voice high enough to seem normal.

Craig looked me up and down before reading the message on the mirror. "What's up with that?"

"I thought that was you, pranking me. I guess it was Shyanne and Mercy?"

He shook his head. "They left. They wanted to check out the Value Village down the road. It's cheaper."

"Oh." I didn't know what else to say.

"Are you . . . okay?" He looked over at the message again. "That's super weird."

"Yeah, it's fine. Just a random prank. I'll meet you outside in a minute."

Craig nodded, though he still seemed unsettled, and walked away to his changeroom.

I looked back at the mirror.

I knew this couldn't be random because this person, whoever had written this, knew me. They knew my name. My family name.

I thought of the message that had been in Duane's hand and shuddered.

No. No one knew. If they did, we would have already been arrested on suspicion of murder. And if this was the same person who had slaughtered Duane like that, surely they would do something a bit more serious than a note in obviously fake blood. Someone was just messing with me, that was all.

But I was Sunny Behre. I was nice to *everyone.* How had I managed to make an enemy?

I pushed the thoughts out of my head, and Craig and I cashed out and left the store. We'd barely walked outside when we were cut off by a woman. *The* woman. Milk Man lady.

This bitch. First she'd come to school to freak me out, then she'd been there when Dom and I had found the body, and now she was showing up just after I'd dealt with that bullshit in the changerooms.

"I'm sure you're a very nice person," I lied, stepping toward her. "But I am going to report you if you continue to follow me." Also a lie. I wouldn't sic police on a vulnerable woman when private security could be just as intimidating with fewer consequences and a lot more discretion.

Craig looked between me and the lady and went from zero to a hundred. "Wait, she's stalking you?"

The woman cringed, shaking her head. "I didn't know how else to get in touch after Ainsley died. I just . . . I wanted to warn you about the Milk Man. I just want to know what you know."

I did not like the way this woman had my mom's name in her mouth. "I really don't appreciate you trying to scare me."

"No!" she shouted. "No, I would never want to frighten you, I—"

I didn't get to hear what else she was going to say because Craig had puffed himself up and was getting in her face. "Why are you following her around?!"

Holy shit, I kind of wanted to cheer for Craig. The intimidation was a bit too alpha male but he was asking the questions I wanted to ask with the aggression I wanted to bring.

The woman shrank in on herself. It was weird. She did actually seem terrified of Craig. Was it an act?

"Beware of the yew branches," she said, before turning on her heel and running away.

Craig shook his head. "What was that?"

"I don't know. I think maybe she needs help." That was not actually what I thought. She was saying gibberish, but she was strangely coherent. And *consistent*. This Milk Man shit. She didn't seem to have what it took to be the murderer . . . but she might know something about who the murderer was.

And suddenly I wished that Craig hadn't scared her off.

CHAPTER NINE

When I stepped into Dom's room that afternoon, I was both confused and dismayed to see Jeremy flopped on a giant plush floor pouf, grinning at me. My brother must have bought it recently, potentially specifically for Jeremy, because I hadn't noticed it the last time I was in his room. Meanwhile, Dom was on his bed, lying on his stomach, playing some game on his Nintendo Switch.

"That's my girl!" Jeremy said, jumping up and throwing out his arms for a hug. He'd dyed the tips of his locs neon green. He was wearing a puffy jacket that I was pretty sure used to belong to Dom. "Bring it in, Prez!"

I hated that nickname.

I was *not* the student body president. It wouldn't be fair to participate given that I was the daughter of the school's owner. But Jeremy, despite being corrected many times, insisted that I had been robbed and had dubbed me "Prez" because, according to him, everyone needed a nickname.

"Jeremy!" I said with mock enthusiasm, though I didn't hug him. "I didn't realize you were coming over." I threw Dom a look that was pleasant enough but clearly held a question in it. The question being, what was Jeremy doing here?

We were supposed to be discussing the details of this symbol he'd mentioned. I wasn't sure how we were going to do that with someone who should definitely not know that we'd interacted with Duane's dead body.

Dom put down his game and sat up. "Jer already knows every-thing about my case, and he's good at researching, so I figured he could help us with this symbol thing. You know, since it has to do with Torri and may come up in the trial."

Sometimes I forgot that Dom was still a Behre, even excluded like he was. He could still put together a good lie. And somehow, even though Jeremy had caught on to some of *my* lies, he was totally igno-rant when it came to his best friend.

So Jeremy didn't know anything about Duane, thankfully, but he knew about the symbol being present at Torri's murder scene. We were going to talk about this like that was what we were really interested in. And I would consider whether the woman who had been following me was something I wanted to share.

I took a seat in Dom's gaming chair. My phone buzzed with texts from Craig about Halloween plans that I responded to quickly before putting it on silent.

"Tell me about this symbol," I said, cutting straight to the chase. The rest of our siblings were out of the house, and I wanted to get this done before anyone came back and caught me in Dom's room again.

Dom tucked his legs into a crossed position. "Like I said, I was hanging out with Torri that night and she showed it to me. Said she found it. It was kind of hidden, like by her pillow. She thought it was cool. It's, like, this circle with these slashes through it that kind of look like a *V.*"

I did not under any circumstances want to dissect what my brother meant when he said he was "hanging out" with his girlfriend.

I really didn't want to think about any of my family members' extra-curricular activities. It was bad enough to be in the bedroom facing the hot tub on the balcony that each sibling—minus Dom—seemed to think was a perfect make-out spot. Occasionally more. Meaning I ended up sleeping in the spare room upstairs instead.

"And this is the same night she went missing last year?"

"Yeah."

"What happened after that?" I asked.

Jeremy raised an eyebrow. "You don't know the whole story?"

I didn't. Mom and Paris were exceedingly tight-lipped about the whole thing, and it wasn't like I casually talked to Dom. All I knew was that he had apparently been dating some random white girl who lived nearby, and she'd gone missing. Despite her brothers attending, she hadn't even applied to the academy. She seemed to be the rebellious type, so I assumed she'd avoided it because her mom wanted her to go. Instead, she'd gone to the local public high school, so I hadn't known her. She and Dom had met because he was hanging out in the park near her apartment. And he'd kept their relationship a secret from the family. Then she was found dead. Initially they ruled it an accidental drowning because she was under the influence.

The news said they had a wide window on the time of death because damage from the water and some animals getting to her body had made it hard to nail down. But they knew the last day she'd been seen alive. It was the same day that Mom had died a year later. It was eerie as far as coincidences went. And sure, I wasn't 100 percent on Dom's innocence, but I doubted he was working up to be a serial killer. No matter how he felt about Mom, he'd cried real tears at her funeral. I just couldn't picture it. Torri was another situation altogether. Boyfriend of a murdered girl was a classic, after all. What mattered was that the Crown figured Dom was the last person to see her alive. That in combination with being the boyfriend had made him the perfect suspect. I learned a lot more from what we'd over-heard Karter say, but I'd definitely never heard my brother's version.

Though now that we were looking into this murderer targeting our family, I wondered if the similar dates did mean something after all. If this went back as far as Torri . . . could it also involve Mom's death? Or maybe I was just wasting time speculating. Hoping for something more sinister so there'd be someone to blame for why she wasn't still with us.

Dom played with the toe of his left sock. They were also anime themed. Some guy with white hair and a blindfold. "Yeah, so, like, we hung out for a bit. She showed me the symbol. Then her mom came home, so she said we should meet later at the lake. You know the park along Lake Prom?"

"Yeah." Lake Promenade was the street our house was on because Mom had wanted the view. To the east, there was a small waterfront park. I assumed the same park where Dom had first met Torri.

"But then she took forever to actually text me, so me and Jeremy hung out at 7-Eleven."

God, they were truly inseparable. Even after Jeremy moved, he still came to our neighborhood to hang out. And, as far as I knew, Dom went out to his area pretty often too.

Dom continued, "Then she finally texted me, and Jeremy went to visit his cousin. But when I got to the lake, she was gone. So I went home."

That's it? "I'm . . . confused. You weren't swimming with her?"

"Nope," Jeremy said, turning onto his back and looking over at me. "The cops said they could place him at the scene because he was technically there that night even though they have shoddy evidence for time of death, and her mom—"

"—doesn't really like me," Dom cut in.

Jeremy rolled his eyes. "She's a racist. But, like, in a polite way. As in, 'The Lord doesn't foster hate, but I don't agree with anything that isn't straight and white.' So of course, she was all like, 'He did it!'"

And so that was it. They had his texts, too, so they would have known that he was supposed to meet her.

"And now it showed up again at the school?" Jeremy asked.

I froze. *Wait, what?* I turned to look at Jeremy. Now I had no idea what he did or didn't know.

"Yeah," Dom said, looking over at me. "When I went inside, I saw it."

"I'm sorry," I cut in. "You saw it where exactly?"

Jeremy decided that he was the perfect person to answer this question. "Oh shit, Prez, you don't know anything, eh?"

Apparently not.

Jeremy continued, "It was, like, on the staircase, in Duane's *blood.*"

I turned with strained precision toward my brother. I took it back. He wasn't a Behre. He'd told some weird lie that didn't even make sense and now connected him to the crime at the school. What was he thinking?!

"I think!" Dom said. "I don't know. It was red."

"And then what happened?" I said. "To the symbol . . . ?"

"I wiped it away. I freaked out. I don't know what's in the disclosure or whatever materials they have, but I worried they would know about the symbol being at Torri's place and connect it to me, and I didn't do any of that shit, and . . . yeah."

So he had essentially told a version of the truth that separated him from the body but still admitted to tampering with possible evidence. Wonderful.

"This means the murders are connected, right?" Jeremy said,

finally sitting up straight. "Like someone is obviously trying to frame Dom."

It wasn't a terrible leap, but Jeremy made it without effort. The earnestness in his face told me that he 100 percent believed Dom. He had no doubts about the story his friend had told him and had already moved on to investigating.

That easy.

And he almost had a passable theory. That symbol being in both places did connect the crimes, both of which Dom did not commit— assuming his innocence, which I was trying very hard to do. But then there was also what had happened to me today. In the moment, I hadn't believed they were connected. But I'd had a whole Uber ride to think about it. That message on the mirror and the one in Duane's hand both had to do with bears. Maybe this was about Dom, but I thought it was a better theory to assume that it was about our family. Not personal grudges, but some vendetta against the Behres as a whole.

But why?

And how had that woman on the street known to warn me? I had no idea who the Milk Man was or who she thought he was, anyway, but it was logical to figure this was about the murderer. Someone she was scared of. And that person had something against us. Why hadn't this lady warned us way back when the shit with Torri went down? Why would she wait until now?

I didn't know enough about the stuff with this woman to bring it up. So we might as well start with the symbol. "This is a good start," I said finally. "Dad did a bunch of stuff about theology and symbols at university. He may have something to help since I assume you already looked on the internet and found nothing."

Dom and Jeremy both nodded. I made a mental note to try by myself later tonight.

I'd never had a lot of interest in what Dad had studied. I thought it was history for the longest time since that was what he taught at the academy, but then I heard him chatting with a guest at an event and he said it was theology and symbology. Surprising, because he wasn't religious. We'd never once stepped into a church outside the context of a wedding or charity event, but he *was* superstitious. He threw salt over his shoulder and knocked on wood and carried rabbits' feet. I figured that was where the interest came from. It wasn't exactly a one-to-one, but it was the only thing that made sense. I wasn't excited about having to look through his books, but we needed somewhere to begin.

"I'll do my best to keep looking into it," Dom said, and shifted on the spot. "But . . . I feel like Karter is watching everything I do. So I don't know how subtle I can be. Might be better if whatever books Dad tells us to get, we look at outside the house where she's not around."

He wasn't wrong. If Karter wasn't watching him herself, she was enlisting me and probably everyone else in surveillance. I didn't think she was expecting him to run out and stab someone. She just thought if she obsessively watched him, she could control the situation. It was a bad strategy because now he was hyperaware of her.

I wish I knew what Mom had attached that sticky note with my name to, but we hadn't found anything in her office that fit. I would have to check our tree house the next time we went to the ranch, see if there was anything there.

Jeremy grinned. "So we'll keep our noses clean and investigate, cool."

"Shouldn't be too hard, right?" I asked. "To stay out of trouble."

Jeremy's smile dimmed a little. "Yeah, for sure, Prez."

"Sometimes trouble follows you, even when you're not doing anything," Dom mumbled and we both looked at him.

He wasn't wrong. After all, he'd stumbled into not one but two murder cases.

Dom mentioned having to pee, and I decided to make my exit then. I didn't want to be left alone with Jeremy, who I suspected would just try to irritate me into revealing how much of what I'd said was true and how much was bullshit.

I'd avoided the conversation, but I felt Jeremy's eyes on my back as I left.

The next morning, I woke up at the perfect time to catch Dad downstairs with his cup of coffee. Both the middles and Karter had left and were presumably at the house downtown. Meaning I could get him alone.

I grinned as I came down the steps. "Morning, Daddy!" Too thick. I needed to turn it down.

Dad didn't seem to notice anything off. He smiled back at me, his hands wrapped around his mug. It was a bear made of carved, fired clay. "Morning," he said. There were extra wrinkles around his eyes that I had gotten used to seeing since Mom died.

I let the conversation flow naturally as I poured myself a cup of coffee from what was left in the pot. We had a proper espresso machine, but Dad couldn't figure out how to use it. He relaxed against the island. It wasn't like he had a guard to let down in the first place. He was an open book. But still, I wanted to ease into it.

"Oh, I wanted to ask you!" I said, like the thought had just struck me. "I saw this video online that was talking about these hidden symbols in ads and stuff, super weird. Anyway, I ended up in a research spiral, but there was this one that didn't have a lot of info on it. I wondered if you had ever seen it? I know you did this stuff in school." I'd drawn the symbol based on Dom's description, and I pulled it up on my phone to show Dad.

He looked over at it, and then his eyes immediately slid away. "Sorry, baby girl, I don't know that one." He chugged the rest of his cup and smiled again. "We should head out, eh?"

I grinned back.

Takes a liar to know a liar.

Dad was a straight-up nerd about this shit. Anytime I showed him something he was interested in, he was always like, "Let's look into this together!" And we would end up doing an impromptu library visit or a bunch of searches through academic journals. He never just brushed something off.

Which meant he knew exactly what the symbol was and was pretending not to.

And I needed to know why.

CHAPTER TEN

n the last two weeks, helping organize the academy's annual charity gala had taken over my life, the media coverage of Duane's death had died off, and there'd been zero progress on this mysterious symbol. Dom and Jeremy had made no headway, as expected, but I at least meant to get into Dad's office at school to check out his books. But anytime I went anywhere, a committee member had some emergency. Between that and schoolwork, it had fallen by the wayside. And I'd spent every single one of those days looking over my shoulder for the mysterious woman, who had stopped appearing. I didn't know if that meant Craig had scared her off for good, if the Milk Man she was so terrified of had gotten her, or if she'd simply given up on trying to help me.

I felt . . . watched now. As if someone was just over my shoulder, staring. But when I turned around, no one was there. Now I knew that the family was being targeted, and the more time passed, the more it felt like eventually a shot had to be taken.

I brushed my hands down the front of my dress as I entered the academy. The gown had long sleeves and a hem that brushed the floor. It had a floral pattern and cutouts on the top that suggested skin and sheerness but was opaque fabric. It had come from a place downtown that specialized in high-quality rentals that the academy used to provide formal clothes for students to attend events. That way, they didn't need to stress about having something to wear for special occasions. And it was Mom's rule that we do the same.

I took the stairs to the third-floor assembly hall where the event would be held. A man in a black suit brushed by me, and I smiled and acted like I didn't know that he was our low-key security. Karter had hired a company that knew how to be discreet and blend in. They would be wandering around during the event posing as guests, caterers, chefs, valets, and other staff.

It was smart. Smart enough that I was annoyed she'd thought of it, even if it benefitted us. I hadn't had any time to look into something to validate my claim to family leadership because I was too busy with this event and trying to preemptively prove the innocence of our brother. It was less satisfying doing things for the family under the radar. I tried to remember that Mom always said leading was a thankless job and that searching for praise would only make you bitter.

I entered the hall, which the committee members and I had completely transformed that afternoon. Gold and white balloons were strung together across the ceiling and around the stage. There were twenty tables draped with soft cream cloths and matching chair covers, gold chargers sitting below porcelain plates. Each center-piece was a three-foot-tall arrangement of flowers made up of autumnal hues—dusty pinks, reds, and off-white accented by stalks of palm leaves and bunny tails. A mix of fresh and dried. Heavily suggested by me and technically chosen by the group.

"Looks amazing," a voice whispered in my ear. I jerked around to see a grinning Craig behind me. He wore a maroon suit jacket paired with matching pants and a white dress shirt. "Which table am I at?"

"One," I replied automatically. I'd memorized the seating

arrangements. Not on purpose. Just because I was looking at them for so long. "The NDP leader is at your table." I said it casually, as if having a major political party leader eat dinner with him was a fun footnote. When really it signaled that he was at the best table. Special students were selected for this event, whether that meant academic excellence, athletic achievement, or some sort of talent worth showing off. They were put at tables with prominent Torontonians who they would spend a dinner hour trying to impress and influence to donate to whatever school improvement they'd proposed.

Last year, Gregory Hayes had schmoozed his way into getting a rooftop garden project funded so that students could eventually grow their own fruits and vegetables.

"Hey, so, once this whole thing is over, should we do a dry run of our costumes? See how they look together?" Craig asked, sticking his hands in his pockets. "You don't have weekend plans, right?"

"What?" I said, distracted watching a student test the mics onstage. "Costumes?"

"For Halloween . . . ?"

It took me too long to realize what he was talking about. The only thing that had stuck in my mind from that day was the message on the mirror and that woman. I was supposed to have booked a hair appointment to get the red locs installed too, which I hadn't done yet.

Craig's smile dropped. "What is up with you? It's like you're not even excited for it."

I wasn't. Halloween was *his* favorite holiday. Him, Shyanne, and Mercy. I was just along for the ride. I didn't even understand why he was freaking out. I was still going to dress up. Why did I need to love it just because he did?

"I *am* excited!" I tried to look earnest. Like I cared. "It's just with all the event stuff and my brother—"

"You didn't give a shit about your brother until like this year. Now it's always, 'I have to do this with Dom' or 'I have to look after Dom.'"

My mouth dropped open, and it wasn't the least bit fake. Craig did not get angry with me. Not *ever*. I struggled to figure out what to say, but I couldn't get over the shock fast enough.

"Forget it. You and your fucking family." He spun on his heel and stalked away.

I still hadn't figured out what to say. Had he seriously just lost it on me?

"What's his problem?" Karter said, walking over to stand next to me. I'd missed her coming in. Her hair was piled on top of her head in a sleek updo with wisps of pressed and then curled hair falling into her face. She wore a black silk dress that clung to the jutting bones of her hips and had a slit that ran down her right thigh. The neckline dipped low on the chest but looked high class instead of inappropriate. Unsurprisingly, the dress was almost definitely not from the rental place. For one, it fit her like a glove, so it was clearly tailored. And for two, it didn't have so much as a stray thread or hint of a stain.

"Nothing, he's just nervous." The excuse sounded shitty even to me but, for once, Karter let me off the hook with it.

"As long as you're fine," she said, reaching out and fixing my hair.

I nodded. "I'm good."

She gave me one last long look as if to make sure I was really okay before she left. Times like this, it made me feel bad that I spent so much mental energy critiquing her. Even if she wasn't who Mom wanted, she'd always done her best to look out for us.

I shook the guilt off and dove headfirst into helping run the event I had spent so much time organizing. Guests filtered into the academy, and I greeted them alongside Karter and Dad, and escorted them to their seats. I checked in to make sure the food came out as it was supposed to and helped with testing the equipment for the evening entertainment.

Despite the earlier Craig hiccup, everything was running as it should. Even Dom was helping. He was at the donation booth, cashing funds through the system with an iPad and at least making his best attempt to be pleasant.

I spotted Dad talking with the NDP leader and Karter deep in conversation with a well-known socialite. I muttered to the girl next to me that I needed to go to the bathroom and left the assembly hall. It wasn't ideal, but this would be a good time to get to Dad's office without anyone around. The hallways were quiet since everyone had already arrived, though I noticed a few stragglers on my way down the stairs who were heading outside to smoke.

I checked over my shoulder twice and mentally reassured myself that no one was following me. I was fine. Yes, there was a murderer running around with a vendetta against my family. Yes, the woman who'd tried to warn me about it had suddenly disappeared. Yes, I was a target. But I also needed to figure this out before it got worse, and so I had to find out about his symbol. The leader who Mom thought I was would push aside her feelings and focus on the task at hand. I could do that.

When I got to the first floor, I was surprised to see Craig there talking in a low voice to Shyanne, who was running the greeting station in a pink neon pantsuit. There was something urgent in his tone, though I couldn't hear the specific words.

I tried to slow down so I could catch what they were saying, but the click of my heels gave me away. Craig's neck snapped up and he looked at me, forcing a smile. "Hey . . ."

"Hey . . . ," I echoed, looking at Shyanne, who shrugged before she got busy grabbing a coat for a guest. "Why aren't you upstairs?" I asked him.

"Just, like . . . wanted some air." The latter part of the sentence rushed out of his mouth. "Taking a break from, like, being *on*, you know?"

"Yeah."

"How about you?"

I straightened. "I needed to get my dad something from his office."

"I'll come with you!" Craig brightened as if this was the perfect idea.

I didn't need this right now. But admittedly, it didn't really matter if he came along. And a small part of me was screaming that I didn't want to be wandering the hallways alone anyway. "Okay."

He grinned, and we both headed off with a quick nod to Shyanne, whose lips couldn't quite make it into a smile. It was weird, but I didn't think it was something I needed to get involved in. Shyanne and Craig could deal with their own stuff. I slipped between the white curtains put up to stop people roaming the halls, taking a left to Dad's office. His door had a code just like every other room except the breakfast club one. Because of course that was the room they missed. Mom was in the process of arranging for them to update the lock when . . . yeah. After that, changing a lock was at the bottom of the priority list.

But I didn't need a key for Dad's office, and I'd had to grab things from him before, so I knew the code. I punched it in, and we slipped inside. The walls were packed with bookshelves, and even still, half his desk was covered by more stray books and papers, and the couch that was supposed to be for guests was also blocked by books.

Craig took the liberty of pushing some of the stacks aside and settling on the cushions. "Hey . . . I'm sorry for before. That wasn't fair."

"It's fine," I said, searching along the spines for anything that hinted at symbols, pulling books off and riffling through them quickly. It wasn't fine, really, but if he wanted to sweep the whole thing under the rug with a single "sorry," I was willing to do it. I didn't need the conflict.

"What are you looking for?" Craig said, standing. "I could help."

"Um . . . it's just one of my dad's symbology books. One of the guests was interested in it." I hoped that my boyfriend wouldn't decide to chat about this with Dad at any point. "What were you talking about with Shyanne?" I didn't need to be involved, but I was curious.

"Oh, nothing really. I was just saying that I was stressed about having to impress people, you know?"

"She seemed uncomfortable."

I paused searching to look at him. He rubbed the back of his neck. "Yeah . . . well, you know. She wasn't invited—like, as a guest, I mean. And I think she was kind of annoyed that I was complaining about it."

"Oh."

"Yeah."

He sat back down, and I returned to my search without asking him for the help he'd offered. Honestly, that didn't really sound like Shyanne. She was usually the one most understanding of the perspectives of other people. Mercy was more likely to call Craig out for ignoring his privilege in being involved tonight. But all thoughts of Craig left my mind when I saw a piece of paper tucked under several others with what looked like the symbol on it.

As I reached for it, the room went dark.

I didn't move for a moment, expecting the lights to come back on right away, but they didn't.

Something brushed against my arm, and I jerked away with a shriek.

"Sorry," Craig said. "Was just trying to find you."

"It's fine." Fine. Fine. Fine. Everything was fine.

But in my head, I was hearing that woman talking about the Milk Man and ruination.

I stumbled my way to the door and ripped it open. A flashlight shone directly in my eyes, and I whipped my hand up to block it.

"Sunny?!" Karter lowered her phone, and I had to blink a few times to get my vision back. Before I could open my mouth to ask what was going on, she said, "Where is he?"

I didn't need to ask who she meant. "He was upstairs with Dad last time I saw him, but then again, that was the last time I saw you, and now you're down here."

Karter swore under her breath. "Came down to take one quick vape and shit hits the fan." She then paused like she'd just noticed Craig and raised her brow. "Wow, Sunny, in Dad's office?"

What was she— Oh. *Ohhhh.* She thought Craig and I had snuck down here to hook up. He'd clearly caught on and was spluttering, trying to think of an excuse. Honestly, I preferred her assumption to the truth. "Let's just find Dom," I said, turning away like I was embarrassed.

I rushed up the stairs as fast as I could in heels, in the dark, which wasn't very fast at all. We got to the third floor but couldn't see him in the crowd of people shining their phone lights around.

Dad came over to us. "I'm going to check the breakers."

I wanted to ask if he even knew where those were. Karter seemed to have the same thought because she said, "I'll go with you."

"I can check the roof," I offered. It was the last place I wanted to be, but I knew Dom liked to hang out up there with Jeremy during school.

Dad shook his head. "You just stay put, Sunny. Besides, I think we decided to lock the roof access for this event, didn't we?" He looked to Karter for confirmation, and she nodded.

"Just keep an eye out for Dom," Karter said.

With that, she and Dad headed back downstairs.

I attempted to compose myself and noticed that I'd lost Craig at some point. Which, honestly, was ideal. The longer I was forced to stay in this relationship, the more I wanted to avoid him. I would just look around for Dom. It wasn't exactly easy given that it was pitch black and people kept stopping me to ask what was going on. I finally picked out some volunteers to help in going around and explaining the situation to people. Though I really wished that Karter and Dad would hurry up.

Finally I decided to go check the roof anyway. Even if the door was locked, it was tucked away in an alcove that was still pretty private. Maybe Dom had tried the door and then decided to stay in that space to play his games or something. I knew that he'd brought his Switch tonight despite being told not to.

I went up the darkened staircase, holding my phone in front of me until I reached the double doors leading to the roof. No Dom. I did an experimental push on the bars and was shocked when they opened.

Well, shit.

The locks were digitally controlled. I wondered if they'd opened when the power went off. I stepped outside, and the doors banged shut behind me. The night air was chilled, and I shivered, rubbing my hands against my arms. Late October was not a good time to be outside in a dress.

The rooftop was surrounded on all sides by black wrought-iron rails and included the odd bench for sitting, and the beginnings of the greenhouse that was supposed to go here. Usually it was open to students and guests. It was decorated nicely and was often a feature during events. I guess Dad and Karter must have been trying to be extra careful given that we had a murderer running around. Though it's not like there was anywhere to escape to up here. It just made it inconvenient since now everyone had to go all the way back downstairs if they wanted to smoke.

"Dom!" I shouted, looking around the area. You could easily see the whole space with a single glance, and it was clear that my brother wasn't up here. Not unless he was hiding behind the giant ducts and vents, which would be a whole other conversation. And I was not going to go searching behind them. Not alone. I would go find Craig and come back.

I turned back toward the doors, pushing on them.

They didn't budge.

I shoved again, harder now.

Again, they didn't move.

"Are you fucking kidding me?" I hissed.

The doors weren't supposed to lock like that.

I stepped away, looking around, and that was when I saw her, peeking out from behind one of the ducts. The Milk Man woman. But instead of her hoodie, she'd dressed formally. She was in a pale pink slip dress with her dark hair tied up. She'd blended in and gotten inside the school. Which made me wonder how easy it would be for someone else to do the same.

Now we were alone together. Me and this creepy woman. If she didn't seem so pathetic, I would be more scared. It was hard to be intimidated by a woman shivering on a rooftop in a dress. Meaning I probably didn't look very threatening either.

It's not that I wanted to talk to her, but now that I knew she might actually have information I needed, I couldn't pass up the chance to learn more. I made my way over to her, slowly, like I was approaching a wild animal.

She looked over my shoulder, maybe checking for Craig, but he wasn't here. She stayed pressed against the duct as if it were supporting her.

I stayed a few feet away, but even from there, I could see that her shivering was a lot more violent than mine was. It was more than just the cold.

"You saw my note?" she asked.

"Note?"

Her brow furrowed. "Asking you to meet me here. I left it—"

"Who is the Milk Man?" I said, cutting to the chase. It was worth being a bit rude to get any information she had faster. But I made my voice gentle to soften the blow. I didn't care that I'd missed her note. I was here now, and I needed answers.

She shook her head. "He's . . . I don't know how to describe him. He has his milk maidens, and he ruins the little calves. He tricks you. He's never satisfied no matter how much you give him. He'll always want more. When you find him, you have to kill him. It's the only way to st—"

The woman suddenly stopped speaking, and it took me a few blinks to figure out why.

She had a knife sticking out of her throat.

It hadn't been there. And now it was. Blood spurted onto the concrete between us. She gurgled.

There was a knife. In her throat.

I repeated it to myself because I was having trouble understanding what was happening.

There was a knife in her throat. There was a knife in her throat. There was a *knife* in her *throat*.

I couldn't tell if I had started screaming right away or if there had been a pause while I deciphered what I was looking at, but I was screaming. I could feel that it was happening though the sound was muffled.

The woman fell to the ground, still trying to speak through the wound and revealing someone clad in all black from head to foot standing behind her. The size of the duct and shadows had hidden them. Their face was covered by a ski mask.

I stopped screaming as they looked at me. Like they'd cut off the sound with a button click.

And it was only when they stepped forward that I finally ran. I clip-clopped faster than I had ever moved in heels and yanked on the doors, which remained locked.

No. No. No. No.

"Somebody help me!" I screamed. "Help me! Open the doors! Help me!" I couldn't make myself look back to see if they were coming. I couldn't. I didn't want to.

I squeezed my eyes shut and screamed as loud as I could.

It was only when I was being shoved backward that I realized the doors were opening. Craig was there. Craig was opening the doors.

I rushed inside and then pulled the doors closed behind me. "We need to keep them shut. We have to keep them shut." I couldn't stop saying it, over and over and over.

Craig was trying to explain something to me, but I still had my hands on the doors, trying to hold them closed. He was saying something about calling someone for help. But I didn't want him to take his hands off the doors.

It felt like it was a long while before I finally allowed him to let the doors go. My fingers trembled. They were cramped and sore from how hard I'd been gripping the push bars. I slipped to the ground as Craig took my phone, turning it toward me to unlock it with my Face ID. Then he was talking to someone.

He was trying to get me to say what happened, but I couldn't make the words come out.

Eventually Karter appeared, kneeling on the ground in front of me and holding my face between her hands. Her grip was surprisingly gentle as she asked me what'd happened, even as her words were harsh.

"We told you to stay put," she hissed. But she and Dad went out onto the roof to check out whatever had put me in this state.

When they came back, she, Dad, and Craig all looked at me strangely.

I stumbled to my feet, and after I was assured that Craig was holding open the double doors, I went outside.

To find absolutely nothing.

The person in black and the Milk Man woman were gone. No traces of blood, either. Not on the ground where it had spurted out as the knife went in, nor where she'd fallen.

It was as if everything I'd seen hadn't happened at all.

CHAPTER ELEVEN

Saturday mornings were for family time. It was something that Mom insisted on every single weekend. And something that had been barely kept up since her death. But this morning, Karter loudly stomped through the house, waking each of us up and telling us to get our asses downstairs. As I went to my door to follow her crudely communicated instructions, I heard angry whispers. I paused, listening. I couldn't make out what was being said, though. They were talking too fast and too low. When I pushed the door open, Darren abruptly stopped speaking, turning away from Karter and stomping down the stairs. I threw a questioning look at my sister, injecting some concern so it would look more like worry than curiosity, and she waved me off. It wasn't necessarily uncommon for them to fight, but it was strange for Darren to just let it drop like that.

Now we sat at the dining table, which was loaded with what was clearly a catered spread. It had perfectly sliced and glistening mango, still-hot croissants and pastries, platters of eggs, and bacon, and sausage, and stacks of pancakes and French toast. The TV played one of Mom's infinite roster of cartoons that made up the background noise. I remembered sitting with my plate in front of the TV, cuddled up to her side. She'd smelled like roasted coffee beans and the sweet maple syrup she poured over her pancakes. We would cry out at big action moments and laugh at funny ones.

As far as everyone was concerned, it was a normal Saturday.

But yesterday, I'd watched a woman die, and there was no proof that she even existed.

And so I had done what I knew Mom would have thought was best. I'd shoved it down. Pretended I had seen a shadow and gotten spooked. At first, Dad and Karter had looked skeptical, but then I'd brought up the incident. The woman in the tent. The blood. And they'd shut up.

Our school did not need another body. Our *family* did not need another body.

It was in our best interests to pretend it never happened. I knew that was the right move. The move that would have made Mom proud.

I had the sudden urge to cry, though I didn't.

Karter, like Mom used to do, served drinks, alternating between the pitcher of already mixed mimosas, a thermos of coffee, and a jug of plain orange juice. Mom would have cared about who was and wasn't of legal drinking age, but Karter didn't bat an eye when Kiley requested a mimosa. Kiley looked tired, her hands seemingly permanently splattered with paints. She was always focused when she prepped for a contest, but now she just looked worn out.

I eyed the mimosa pitcher, but underage drinking wasn't exactly model citizen behavior, so I asked for coffee.

"Thanks for putting this together, Karter," I said, smiling at my older sister and wondering what her angle was. Usually I would have tried for a more peppy grin, but on account of seeing a murder last night, I couldn't work myself up to it.

She swallowed the chunk of watermelon in her mouth. "You're welcome."

It must have been nice. To be accepted as the leader when I'd just single-handedly saved us from another PR disaster. More nightmares for me now, Duane and the Milk Man woman mingling in my mind. I'd done it for us, and I had nothing to show for it. But I couldn't expect rewards for good leadership. I needed to remember that.

Karter gave everyone the courtesy of a few more bites before she said, "We're going downtown with Dom to have a meeting with Paris today." She nodded to Dad to make clear who "we" referred to.

"On a weekend?" Darren asked, chewing on a piece of bacon. "Doesn't she charge extra for that?"

"I'm sorry, are we suddenly in the struggle?"

"No, but why be wasteful? Mom would have never wasted money like th—"

"It's an emergency meeting," Karter ground out between her teeth. "The disclosure is ongoing, as you know. Meaning they're sharing all the evidence. Paris has been trying to comb through everything as fast as possible, and there is now something of note that she has some follow-up questions about. We're just trying to resolve it quickly."

I looked to Dad for a hint of what she might be talking about, but he was tight-lipped.

"But there is good news," Karter said with a smile. "There's video footage of Dom at the 7-Eleven at the time of the murder. Which Paris thinks is amazing evidence in our favor."

"I thought they weren't sure about time of death," Kiley said, staring down at her plate.

Karter rolled her eyes. "They weren't and then suddenly they were so they could charge Dom. But now we have this footage."

Darren said, "Damn, that is actually good news."

"I know. That's why I said it."

Kiley asked, "What time?"

"Why?"

"Curious." Though the intensity in Kiley's eyes was a lot more than simple curiosity warranted.

"Around midnight." Karter nodded to Dom. "You'll be ready to go after breakfast?"

"Yeah," Dom replied.

If they had such great evidence for his case, what was this other stuff they needed to talk about so urgently? It must be something that could derail things, right?

I subtly glanced at my younger brother, but he didn't seem bothered at all, just kept eating bits of mango—from the sucked-clean skin on his plate, he was already on his second one. I wished I could be that unbothered. After all that frantic searching for him at the gala, he'd just been in the bathroom.

When he got back later today, I would 100 percent be grilling him on what was going on. Moreover, I needed to find a way to ask if Dom had noticed anyone following him without raising any alarm. I didn't know if the murderer had been stalking me or that woman or both of us, but we were in danger. And I had to signal it to him and the rest of the family somehow.

Though I couldn't help but wonder why the person in black hadn't come after me, too.

It had been hours since Dom, Dad, and Karter went to go meet with Paris. They'd left shortly after breakfast, and it was already well past dinnertime. Meanwhile, I'd been catching up on my homework, but now I was done with that for the day. There was no way the meeting could possibly be that long. Were they just hanging around downtown now? At this hour, they would probably stay at the house there, meaning I wouldn't learn what happened until tomorrow.

The door to my bedroom banged open, and Darren and Kiley

walked in. "Get dressed, we're going out!" My brother was wearing a pair of designer ripped jeans, a deep V-neck white shirt, and an extremely sparkly black suit jacket. Kiley had on a bright yellow jumpsuit and had styled her curls into a sort of mohawk.

I knew by now not to ask questions and honestly, I was kind of desperate to do or think about something else. I'd already snuck into our parents' bedroom to look through Dad's bookshelf there without any luck. And I couldn't go to back to his office at school during the weekend without tripping an alarm that would bring up a lot of questions. There was no way I would be going back there alone anyway.

Besides, from the strain at the edges of my sister's eyes, I kind of wondered if she needed this break. And I hadn't hung out with the middles in what felt like forever. I missed them.

I let my siblings riffle through my closet and choose an outfit for me. Considering that they refused to say where we were going, it was better for them to decide.

"All your clothes are shit," Darren grumbled.

"Thank you," I said, letting the bit of sarcasm out. I could with the middles sometimes.

Kiley yanked out a dress and smiled as she thrust it at me. "This one." It was a blush-colored puff dress that fell to my knees with huge billowing sleeves. I'd worn it last year as part of my Halloween costume because we were supposed to be fantasy creatures and I picked a fairy. *Shit, Halloween.* The party we were supposed to go to was next weekend, and I still hadn't made a hair appointment. Low-key, I was entertaining the idea of feigning sick the day of.

The middles rushed me out of the house into an Uber, and forty minutes later, I understood exactly where we were going. The Suburban we were in pulled up alongside the Royal Ontario Museum with its brick Gothic aesthetic mixed with the explosion of sharp angles and glass attached to the front. People were lined up around the block waiting to get in, though the middles didn't even glance at the queue, instead bringing us to a back door, where they knocked twice.

The door opened to reveal a white guy in all black: suit pants and a matching jacket and shirt. He ushered us in and brought out a bunch of orange wristbands, handing one to Darren, then to Kiley. He looked at me, then Darren. "Her too?"

My brother shrugged. "She looks nineteen, doesn't she?"

I was about to protest but Kiley shot me an exasperated look, so I shut my mouth.

And so, one was slapped on my wrist too. Meanwhile, Darren unfolded a few bills and handed them off. "You're the beeeessst."

The guy blushed. "Yeah, yeah. Just go fast, okay?"

"But not too fast," Darren said with a grin, and the guy got even redder.

Kiley laughed and gave our brother a shove. "Let's go."

We left out of a side door that led directly into the ROM. Inside the normal lighting was dimmed and the air was filled with the pumping thrum of bass from the club music being played throughout the museum. I'd never actually been to ROM After Dark, though I knew about it. It was a strictly adults-only event where they opened the museum after hours and threw a party that was part culinary experience, part art appreciation, and part club night.

I looked at the band around my wrist. I couldn't wait to drink something and forget about it all. Forget about the woman with a knife through her neck and the murderer pursuing our family. Forget about everything with Dom and the fact that Karter was parading around like she was Mom. But I was me, so I had to protest a little. "I really shouldn't drink."

"Why? You're nineteen, aren't you?" Darren said, his voice completely serious.

I didn't even bother to conceal my smile.

"It's fine, Sunny," Kiley said. "It's not like you of all people are going to get sloppy. At least have one."

I made a show of acting like I was really struggling with this decision. "Okay, just one." I could sneak a couple more while they weren't paying attention and pass them off as nonalcoholic.

Kiley hooked her arm around mine and Darren took the other one, and we strode forward, a weird three-headed huddle making our way onto the main floor. Darren bought us an obscene amount of food and drink tickets, and we stopped at our first station, having a noodle dish paired with a bright green cocktail.

We were in the ancient China section, surrounded by gilded pots, stone statues of long-dead people of renown, and intricate pottery. The lighting here was more like the normal brightness of the museum, so you could actually appreciate the pieces.

Darren pointed out the display of snuffboxes. "I like those. People in ancient times were classy with their drugs."

"A girl in my psychology class does coke out of a pendant on a chain around her neck," Kiley said. "She saw it in a nineties movie."

"See, somehow, I don't like that. That feels very contrived."

I smiled, letting their conversation wash over me as I sipped my cocktail. Sometimes I just liked listening to the two of them going back and forth. It was so easy between them. I used to be a lot more jealous of it. After all, it wasn't like Dom and I were like that. And I wouldn't even attempt that sort of closeness with Karter. She was too hot and cold. But Darren and Kiley have always found their own way to include me. And I'd had Mom. She was, as cheesy as it sounded, my best friend.

This was the first time since she'd died that it felt like how it used to be. Me and the middles spending time together instead of us all orbiting around one another, this invisible distance keeping us apart.

Kiley brushed her fingers against my hand, and I jumped. "Where did you go?"

"Sorry. Was just thinking."

"About Mom?"

I blinked at her, shocked that she'd guessed.

Kiley shrugged. "We're all thinking about her, aren't we? She's our mom, and she hasn't even been gone for a year." She picked at the stubborn bits of paint on her fingers.

"It's easier without her," Darren muttered.

Kiley made a sound in the back of her throat, and my eyes widened.

Darren swirled the liquid of his drink in the glass. "I'm not saying that I wished she was dead. I miss her. I wish she were here. But, like, don't you think it's easier? Aren't some things just simple now? I feel like I can breathe finally." He gave our sister a pointed look. "And you can relax too. You don't have to win every art contest or be featured in every show to impress her anymore."

"You don't mean that," Kiley bit out, tapping her ringed fingers against her glass.

"I *do* mean it," Darren insisted. Her jerked his head to me. "Do you think you would just be casually hanging out with Dom if she were here? Like, I dunno, whatever if you're figuring out how to bond with him. But she would have broken that shit up so fast."

I shook my head. "We're not hanging out. I was just checking in on him."

"That! See! Why are you being weird about it? He's our brother. Why wouldn't you spend time with him?"

"Because he murdered a girl," Kiley breathed, her voice so light it was almost lost in the thrumming bass beat.

"Allegedly," Darren added. "And even then, that's a recent thing. What about every time we went to the ranch and played without him? What about when we fucked up and blamed it on him and he just took the heat? What about when Mom would take us out some-where and 'forget' to bring him along? What happened then? Like, if he's done something, maybe we drove him to it."

I didn't like this, seeing the two of them argue. Clearly, this was one of the few things they didn't agree on. And I didn't like to think about how so much of our childhood had been purposely excluding Dom. I especially didn't want to think about the times when he was actively treated like shit.

"And why did we do that?" Darren pressed. "Because we knew Mom wanted us to. She never liked him, and when we showed that we didn't either, she liked us more. And my God, didn't we all just *need* her to like us?"

"Mom loved all of us," I said, but my voice was quiet.

"I don't think she did."

He was wrong. Because otherwise, why would she have left that note for me about Dom? She wanted someone to take care of him. He meant *something* to her.

"You're really the best of us, Sunny." Darren nodded to me. "You went and visited him in juvie, and you've found a way to connect with him. Honestly, that's what we should all be doing."

Yes, I'd visited Dom when no one else had. And sure, I hadn't done it because I wanted to, but I had done it because it was the kind thing to do. Karter hadn't. I remembered once, I must have been eleven or twelve, I asked Mom if Karter wasn't a better fit for leader. She was strong and assertive like Mom was. I'd asked because we'd been at some event and these boys were making fun of my outfit. I'd just smiled at them. But Karter had come over and told them to fuck off or she'd make them regret it. She'd been more effective. Mom had her own pleasant manner, but she was cutting like that when she needed to be. She could bring out the claws. I was all soft and supple honey. Tame.

We'd been at the beach at the time, and Mom had stroked the scars on her stomach. The ones she'd had from surgery to reclaim some of her old body, since having us had changed it so much. Whenever she brushed her fingers against them like that, I felt that she must have been thinking of us, her children. She'd told me that strong was great in the short term, but kindness won out in the end. That she'd burned a lot of bridges being too assertive. So I'd have to be tough on the inside and lead with a smile.

I wondered if she ever thought about Dom in that way. If she regretted not giving him more kindness. But then again, it wasn't like she'd given him strength, either. She'd given him nothing.

"Then why aren't you?" Kiley said, and she looked over at Darren. "You could buddy up with Dom anytime, but you're not."

They just stared at each other for a long moment. There was something being exchanged between them, but I couldn't read it and I wasn't supposed to.

"Hey," I said. "Speaking of Mom, did she leave you two anything? At the will reading."

Darren's eyes flicked to Kiley before he answered, "No. Just money."

"Yeah," I mumbled. It was the same answer that Dom had given and somehow, I didn't believe Darren, either. But I also didn't know why he'd lie.

"Why?" he asked. "What did you get?"

"The same," I said because keeping the pattern seemed safe. "I guess I just wished she'd left more."

The silence held in that moment and neither of my siblings commented on it. Finally Kiley downed her drink in a quick gulp and said, "Let's go dance." I took my sister's hand, chugging my own cocktail and following her onto the dance floor.

We left Darren standing posed by the statue, bathed in the harsh museum lighting.

The next day I woke up in the middle of the afternoon with dry mouth and a headache. Darren and Kiley had somehow made up by the time she and I finished dancing. It wasn't like they talked it out or anything. It was just over. And so we got more drinks and headed up the stairs to look at the gemstones.

Now I made my way downstairs to the kitchen and living area, but it was empty. No one was in the pool, either. I went into the basement to an equally abandoned movie room and finally found Dom in the game room next to it, firing a video game gun at zombies while he sat in a beanbag chair.

"Where is everyone?" I asked.

He didn't even glance back at me. "Upstairs. I think they're having some sort of family meeting."

". . . Shouldn't we be there too?"

He laughed.

Right.

Our family meetings regularly didn't include him, so why would now be any different?

But it was. It was different for *me*. Now *I* was being left out. The middles had obviously noticed me spending more time with my brother, and so it made sense that everyone else would. And who else would they be talking about but Dom? Maybe they thought I would tell him.

Since we were so close now.

I stretched my fingers until they cracked to stop myself from gripping them into fists.

The sooner this was done with, the better.

And I'd decided that once I'd fixed this entire mess, I could let the whole family know that I'd saved us from ruin. I would play it humble, of course. But they would realize that I'd done something a lot more significant than Karter had managed. I wouldn't need whatever Mom left me to make the shift into the role I should have always had. They would see that I was the better protector of this family.

And that was worth the nightmares.

"Something happened at the ranch," Dom said, pausing his game and turning around to look at me.

I blinked at him. "You guys went to the ranch? I thought you were going downtown."

"Yeah, but then Dad said he had to go check on some stuff. And, like, this guy was on the property, and Dad was super pissed about it, and he never gets mad about anything. Maybe it's nothing, but it was weird."

I frowned but didn't say anything. I didn't know what that would have to do with what was happening at the school. But then again, someone creepy suddenly appearing wasn't a move that was wholly unfamiliar anymore.

"Have you noticed anything like that? Someone weird showing up? Threatening you?" I asked.

He frowned. "No. Have you?"

I gave him an abridged version of the truth, which included the threatening message I'd found at Spirit and the Milk Man woman but skipped over the weird shit she'd said and everything that happened at the gala. I also stressed the importance of being vigilant. I added, "Just keep an eye out. I saw something in Dad's office during the gala that seemed related to the symbol. I'm gonna check on it again tomorrow." I eyed him on the chair. "What about this emergency meeting? Anything to worry about?"

"No."

I waited for him to elaborate, but he didn't.

I took in a deep breath through my nose and blew it out my mouth. I told myself that if it were relevant to what we were doing, he would say something. After all, this was for his benefit. And so I left Dom to his games and planned out the best time to check Dad's office again.

But on Monday, when I snuck back in to look for the paper with the symbol, it was gone. I wondered if it had ever been there in the first place. But I remembered it. I had seen it. Which meant that somehow, he'd known to move it.

CHAPTER TWELVE

I tugged my coat closed and weaved around the people walking along Yonge Street, with Dom barely making any effort to keep up behind me. Accompanied, of course, by Jeremy. Probably I should be grateful for the help since Dad's office was a bust and it would be better to have more people to sift through library books instead. It had already been over two weeks since the gala without any progress, and I was eager for a win.

As usual, I scanned over my shoulder for signs of anyone in dark clothes and, as usual, I saw no one. Which meant nothing. I felt watched even while I slept, the image of a knife going through that woman's throat playing behind my eyelids.

We rounded the corner and came up to the Toronto Reference Library, a massive building made of glass and brick that housed an extensive collection of research materials and a place that I knew Dad visited on the regular. His office didn't have that scrap of paper anymore, but I knew what I'd seen. And I had a way to confirm it too.

We walked in through the doors and were immediately surrounded by a large area where you could see all five floors stretching up to ceiling. The upper levels had open balconies with people browsing the stacks or gathered at tables with laptops. And everywhere you looked, there were racks upon racks of books. We scanned our library cards to get in, and I walked over to the map to see where we needed to go.

"You want the fourth floor," Jeremy supplied.

I blinked at him.

He grinned. "I come here a lot after school."

It was kind of a trek to get here from the academy, but I guess he liked it enough to do it. "Okay . . . lead the way."

We followed Jeremy into the glass elevator and watched as we rose up to the fourth level before exiting. We weaved around a mix of working adults and stressed students as Jeremy brought us to the stacks. "Symbology stuff should be over here in the languages section. If not, we can check the third floor in humanities and social sciences."

"Actually," I said, "let's go to a table for a second."

Dom gave me a look. "Shouldn't we, you know, go look at the books?" he asked.

"In a minute." Without waiting for them to agree, I found a free table and sat down. I pulled out my phone and opened up Facebook Messenger.

Dom laughed. "Holy shit, you use that?"

"No. I just need it for this."

"What's 'this'?"

I navigated to my message chain with Henley Forrester.

Jeremy squished nearer to peer at my phone along with Dom. "Who's that dude?" He gave me a serious look. "Prez, I think that guy is too old for you."

"Gross," Dom said, making a face.

I resisted the urge to roll my eyes. "Dr. Forrester went to school with Dad. I'm pretty sure, anyway. They're mutual friends with the same graduation year and they both studied theology, and this guy is a professor at U of T now. I figured he might know something, so I sent him a picture of the symbol."

I had messaged him explaining that I was Jay Behre's daughter and wanted information on a symbol I had seen, and my dad had suggested that I ask him about it. So far, he'd said that the reference library would probably have the best material and gave me a short list of books, but he needed to check his sources and get back to me after school about any scholarly articles. But it was well after three thirty p.m. and there wasn't a new message yet.

I bit my lip. "Okay, well, I guess until he messages me, we can look for the books he mentioned. I'll text you the list."

Dom held up his phone, and Jeremy scanned it and nodded. "I know where to go!" he said, talking too loud, and a few people glared at us, but he wasn't bothered. He and Dom went off to search, and I pulled out my laptop to do homework while I waited.

Finally my phone dinged with a message from Dr. Forrester.

Sorry for the delay! I thought I recognized that symbol. I'm confused about why Jay would tell you to ask me about it . . . But I'm sending you a link to an article that should help. You'll probably find more from those books at the reference library.

Thank you so much for your help! I replied.

Yeah . . . , he typed back. Though you really didn't need it if you have Jay haha.

I frowned at the screen. What did he mean? I clicked the link and it came up with a scholarly article entitled, "Examining the Effects of Symbolic Worship on Fringe and Alternative Teen Culture." And it was written by James Robinson.

Dad.

I asked him once why he'd taken Mom's last name instead of the other way around, and he'd grinned and said, "May as well switch it up." And Robinson was, technically, his maiden name.

I scanned the appendices and there it was, the exact symbol we were looking for, which was apparently called, "unknown name and origin, referred to in this paper as a 'V circle.'"

My phone dinged with another message from Dr. Forrester.

> I know your mom didn't really like this line of research and so he ended up switching to more of a historical theology focus, so maybe that's why he preferred that you talked to me about it? Honor her memory, you know? I'm so sorry for your loss.

Yes, that's likely why, I responded. And thank you.

It wasn't a terrible explanation. Usually, when Mom didn't like something Dad was doing, he dropped it, and they moved on from there. I guess I always figured that she knew best. It made sense that she would have done that even back when they were in school together. After all, he'd been on track to be a professor and dropped that to teach at her school instead.

I thought of what Dom said about Mom not loving us all, and even what Darren said about it feeling easier without her. I wondered what Dad thought. If he also felt that things were better with her gone. Even though he was still honoring her wishes.

Dom sat heavily into the seat beside me, and I jumped, whipping my head around. His brow was furrowed, and Jeremy slinked behind him, dropping his bag down. A security guard who seemed to materialize out of nowhere was now eyeing our table.

"What happened?" I asked, looking between Dom and Jeremy.

Jeremy let out a hiss from between his teeth. "Man, don't even worry. Just regular bullshit. You know, I come here like every week, they know me, and still . . ."

None of that clarified anything for me. I looked over at Dom, who sighed.

"Those books we were looking for, they weren't in the right spots. But Jer said books from that section aren't allowed to be checked out. People have to read them inside the library." He glanced over at the security guard with narrowed eyes. The man had stopped staring, but he'd also taken up a permanent position with us in sight. "So we went to ask the librarian, and she said they were stolen. And then wanted to ask all these questions and, like, it was obvious she was blaming us. So Jer cussed her out, and then the security guy was all, like, 'What's going on here?' Like, why would we ask about books we'd stolen?"

"It's bullshit," Jeremy said, again too loud, because people looked over at us once more.

"It's okay," I said, softening my own voice, trying to get them to calm down. "We know you didn't steal them."

Jeremy ducked his head and smiled. It wasn't like he usually smiled. It was tight and stretched. "Yeah, you know what, you steal it or you don't, it doesn't even matter. If you look like you did, you still get busted."

It was . . . unsettling to see a kid like Jeremy, who was usually talking at the top of his lungs and grinning from ear to ear, like this.

I shook my head. "Forget them. So someone—not either of you, obviously—stole the books?"

"Yeah," Dom said.

I couldn't tell if that was a coincidence, but the alternative seemed unnecessarily sinister. I showed the boys the Facebook messages and the article. "Dr. Forrester sent me this paper that Dad wrote."

Dom's eyes went wide. "But he said he had never seen the symbol?"

"That's shady," Jeremy said, shaking his head.

I nodded. "Has the symbol come up in the evidence against you? Has Paris ever mentioned it?"

"No," Dom said. "I didn't say anything to her about it. At first because I didn't think much of it. I kind of even thought Torri might have done it herself just to freak me out. As, like, a joke. It was only when I saw it for the second time that I realized it might matter."

That meant Dad didn't know the symbol had anything to do with Dom's case. If he had, that might have been a reason to avoid telling me about it and having me get involved. Unless it *had* come up in the disclosure and Paris had told Dad and Karter about it but not Dom. "What about that emergency meeting?"

Dom swallowed and stared down at his lap. "That was for something else. It's not really relevant."

"What was it?" I looked at Jeremy, but he suddenly developed a fascination with his hands.

I looked back at Dom, who mumbled, "Just . . . like . . . me and her used to, like . . . you know. Have sex and stuff."

I resisted the immediate urge to shut this conversation down. I did not, under any circumstances, want to hear about my brother's sex life. She was a sophomore like me when they started dating, and he was in his last year of middle school. It's not like it was illegal but it felt weird. "Can we create a shorter version of this with as few details as possible?"

"There were bite marks on her body . . . and that's what it was from. Not, like, me attacking her. But Paris thinks that's what the Crown is gonna say."

I massaged my temples. I had so many questions now, and I didn't actually want any of them answered.

He picked at the peeling laminate on the table. "It's what she wanted me to do. I dunno. It wasn't my thing. I don't even think she liked it, but I guess she wanted to? Like, it was edgy and that meant we should be into it. It's not like I knew what I was doing anyway. I wasn't an expert."

"Okay so, maybe she didn't actually like it, but she asked you to do that. What about you? When you say it wasn't your thing, like, you didn't want to do it?"

Dom shrugged.

"You know that if you don't like a thing during sex, you can say no, right?" Which, yes, was hypocritical considering that I liked almost nothing Craig did and never said shit, but it rubbed me the wrong way to think of my younger brother having to deal with that.

"Sure," he said, clearly uncomfortable. "But yeah, it wasn't anything about the symbol."

I let the subject drop for his sake and suggested we read the article. I scrolled to the part about the symbol and turned the laptop so we could all see it.

But by the time we finished, the only information we gleaned from Dad's article was that the symbol had become popular among some teenagers who were using it as a hipster version of a pentagram. Just something they thought meant they worshipped the devil or some version thereof, completely divorced from any understanding of pagan traditions or Wicca. Though Dad had also confirmed that no one seemed to claim this symbol. It wasn't part of any existing religious tradition.

Jeremy said, "So . . . basically he had no idea where the symbol came from?"

"That's what it seems like," I said.

Most of the paper revolved around actual known symbols. This "V circle" was just a short part of the research. "Based on what he wrote, do you think the killer is one of these kids grown up? Or, like, someone our age that's bringing it back? Sequel-style."

"Boruto for murder," Dom added.

"Yes!" Jeremy said, holding his fist against his mouth like Dom had dropped some sort of mind-blowing revelation.

"Is this an anime thing?" I asked.

"Maybe," Jeremy responded.

Wow, this was so unserious. And yet it was also actually my real life.

But he did have a point. It could be a person who was older now, but someone our age would have easier access to the school. I avoided mentioning that Dom and Jeremy looked exactly like the sort of people who would be into this given the macabre shirts they liked to wear, which didn't exactly help his case. But there was no way that Jeremy was setting his best friend up. It just didn't stick. Besides, even though he was annoying, he was overall a sweet kid. Always had been. I remembered him picking dandelion bouquets for me. Yeah, he screwed up sometimes. All kids did. It was just that some got punished for it more than others.

Jeremy sighed. "Maybe if one of Torri's friends went to the academy, I might say they were a good prospect."

Dom glared at his friend.

"What? I didn't say her." He mumbled under his breath, "Though she wasn't great either."

"Stop," Dom said, his voice low.

I looked between the two of them. "Am I missing something?"

"No," Dom insisted.

Jeremy said, "I just think it's weird when a white girl says she specifically likes Black guys. And, like, she thought you'd already had sex with tons of people. Don't you think that's messed up? And the shit with her mom . . ."

I turned to Dom for confirmation and tried not to be judgmental. I knew almost nothing about Torri, but so far nothing I'd learned had made me like her.

Dom crossed his arms over his chest. "Torri was better than a lot of people, you know? I've gone to cons and cosplayed—" He paused, catching my confused expression. "Like, you dress up as characters in anime and shows and stuff. Anyway, I had a guy come up and tell me that my costume was good but too bad it wasn't ever going to be 'accurate.' And Torri shut it down, asking how accurate the guy was with his own character who's supposed to be Japanese. That cosplaying is about having fun. She stood up for me. It's a lot to ask for her to stand up to her mom, too. We know that better than anyone."

I clenched and unclenched my jaw.

"Whatever," Dom said. "So, the symbol means that it's either older people who used to do this when they were our age, or actual people our age, right?"

"Maybe," I said, letting him switch the subject again. But it bothered me. Poked at me that this girl had just had unfettered access to my brother and none of us had known about it. Because we hadn't cared. "I don't think we have enough to say anything definitively, but it gives us a couple directions to go in."

I tried to think of the build and height of the person I'd seen on the roof. Did they look like a student or an adult? I couldn't tell.

Dom mumbled something about going to the bathroom, leaving me alone with Jeremy.

I waited until I knew for sure that my brother was gone before saying, "It is bullshit." I nodded to the security guard. "We could probably get him fired. If you wanted."

Jeremy shook his head. "Nah, I don't want to put anyone out of a job. Though it's kind of twisted that you thought of that right away." It was supposed to be admonishing, but Jeremy smiled as he said it.

I shrugged. "Torri was bad, wasn't she?" I asked. "Don't lie."

"I'm not the one who lies. And yeah, she was bad, not that y'all cared."

That was the flip side to this agreement that Jeremy and I had. I no longer had to bother pretending, but he had the same privilege. "I know."

Jeremy leaned forward on his elbows and examined my face. "What's up with you? You're all jumpy and shit these days."

"I'm fine."

He rolled his eyes.

I sighed and slouched in my chair. "Just . . . watch out for Dom, okay? This person, whoever it is, has something against us, and they're using him to punish the family. There's nothing to stop them from deciding to do that more directly." Though what we were being punished for, I didn't know.

Jeremy took a moment to soak in my words before he said, "I always have Dom's back. You know that. But the only people I see watching him are his own family. Like he's about to stab someone any second."

I wasn't worried about my family paying extra attention to Dom. I already knew Karter was. "First we don't care, and now we care too much?"

"I just wish you guys were watching him for the right reasons, is all." He shrugged. "No shade to you, though, Prez. You've been cool lately."

"Don't call me that."

"Oh, I'm not going to stop now." His grin was wide and shit-eating.

"Brat."

Dom rounded the corner, and I sat back up straight in my chair and smiled.

"Damn, just like that. You flip back quick," Jeremy mumbled.

I shot him a look, and he made a comically innocent face complete with his fists under his chin and rapid wide-eyed blinking. I suggested to Dom that we'd done all we could for the day and should leave. Jeremy, however, stayed where he was and waved goodbye.

As we left the building, I looked over at Dom. "He's not going home?"

"No. His dad got a new job around here a few months ago. So sometimes Jer comes here and stays in the library until his dad is finished, then they drive home together. He says it's better than being alone in the apartment and the Wi-Fi is faster. He just does homework and stuff. I've been showing him my advanced anatomy assignments and he's been studying it. I think he wants to take the class."

"Oh, okay." I guess that explained why he was so familiar with the library. "Are you okay? Like, with the Torri stuff?" I couldn't make myself drop it.

He hiked up his shoulders. "Yeah. Jeremy never liked her. It's whatever now anyway."

The quiet part was that she was dead now. It was over. And neither of us were going to say that aloud.

But I still said, "You would tell me if you were dating someone new, right?"

"I'm not."

"But if you were?"

Dom stared over at me. "Why?"

"Just . . . I don't know, to tell me."

"In case I might kill her?"

I stopped in the street, and my brother stopped along with me. We stared at each other. I wanted to make sure he didn't end up in a relationship like that again. With some girl who treated him like a stereotype and asked him to do things he wasn't comfortable with. But he was already so sensitive about the topic that I didn't know how to say so without making him mad. "No," I said, settling on that single word.

My brother looked down at his sneakers, scuffing the toe on the sidewalk. "Okay."

And that was enough.

February 26, 1995

It's been a while since I saw Donald Feeney kill that cat. I avoid him whenever I see him. I avoid Shirley, too. I avoid the entire Feeney clan.

At first, I wished that I'd never witnessed it. But now, ~~I'm glad~~ I'm seeing the silver lining. This is my chance to get the Feeneys out of favor and get my dad where he's supposed to be. Where <u>we're</u> supposed to be. If people on the ranch knew that the son of their manager was doing that, they would drive the whole family right off the property. All I need to figure out is how to prove it.

Today, I saw the Feeneys going out for church looking like a normal family: Donald and Shirley and little Mack Jr. dressed up along with their folks. Though it wasn't quite the same. Usually Mrs. Feeney is hanging off Mack's arm, but this time she didn't even look at him when he was talking to her. And he had this sour look on his face too.

I went to see Jay later that day since I know the Turners go to the same church, and I asked him if he noticed anything weird about the Feeneys. But Jay was being weird himself. Usually, when he's not working or running around with Jonas or his friend Andy (he says he has lots of friends, but I'm pretty sure it's just Andy and Jonas), he's in his room, poring over dozens of books from the library. This time, he was just staring at the words without flipping the pages. But when I asked him what was wrong, he had nothing to say.

Honestly, everyone is strange these days. We keep having accidents because people aren't paying enough attention or are distracted.*

Meanwhile, Shirley Feeney is acting like she's the second coming of Christ, parading around the ranch with her milk maidens. I guess when she mentioned the calves before, she'd just meant the actual herd.

I don't care anymore. I wouldn't join them even if they asked to have me back, which they haven't. I can't stop thinking about seeing her brother, crouched down, and that terrible screaming.

Everything feels off somehow. Tilted at the wrong angle, and I keep trying to stay level by myself. I'm focusing more on school and doing as much work as I can at the ranch. Taking whatever extra shifts they'll give me. I don't know if it'll be enough to afford school in the city, but I have to try something.

Still, I keep thinking about what I can do to show everyone who the Feeneys really are. Until then, work it is.

I can only do what I can do, even if it feels like I'm doing nothing at all.

April 15, 1995

When I decided to keep my head down and wait on a chance to expose the Feeneys, I didn't think I would be waiting this long. We're already into spring now, and Donald's stopped coming to school. He doesn't go outside anymore either. Not even on a Saturday like today.

---

* This is a good lesson in observation. I was always great at noticing things, but I couldn't put the pieces together yet. That's an important skill for you to learn. If something feels off, dig deeper.

I'm getting impatient. I've thought of trying to lure him somewhere where people can see what's wrong with him, but I don't want to be near him myself.

The Feeneys are saying he's caught the flu. There are a few kids who have been sick lately. So I've got lots of extra shifts to pick up. Me, Jay, and Jonas usually work together. The two of them are quiet a lot of the time now when usually we'd all talk about something.

I finally got Jay alone to ask what's going on. He gnawed on his lip like it was something sweet and juicy. He talked about how his parents seemed to be having trouble. They were arguing all the time. And they were being strange around Jonas. He'd even heard his dad talking about sending his older brother away. Jay didn't understand why they were acting like this when Jonas was the same as he'd ever been. He was scared that he'd lose his brother. And then Jay started to cry. Right then and there.

I didn't really know what to do. So I kind of held out my arms and let him fall into them. ~~He smelled like~~ He was shaking and so I held on tighter.

It doesn't make any sense to me, either. Jonas is great. Why were their parents suddenly turning on him? What were they seeing that we weren't?

Jay said that family helps family. That they don't abandon one another. If something is going on with Jonas, his parents should be trying to do something. Not sending him away.*

I don't know about that. My mom sure didn't think so. She left so early that I wouldn't have known what she looked like if

---

* I still remember when he said this. It was my guiding light for a long time, even if I didn't realize it. Family is the most important thing. But you already know that better than anyone. It's why I chose you for this task. And it is that. A task. It requires effort and commitment.

Dad didn't have a picture. She hated the ranch, apparently. Met a rich guy and took off with him. I guess she's living a nice life now. And she's got no interest in giving me a taste of it. So here I am, having to try and make it myself.

What Jay said next, though, made me feel a little better. His mom is no longer a fan of Mack Feeney. His dad's even talked about what they can do to get the Feeneys kicked out. Since he told me that, I've been watching and listening, and they're not the only adults saying it. I don't know what he did, but Feeney hasn't just become unpopular with his wife, he's pissing off the whole ranch.

I let myself brushed Jay's head and stayed with him until he felt better. Then I finally went home.

I was sad for Jay and Jonas, but I was also happy for me. For what it meant if Feeney was losing traction.

This was it. This was my way to get them out. I didn't have to prove anything about Donald. I just needed to give a little push in the right direction.

I told Dad that if Feeney is making trouble, he should stand up to him. That's what a Behre would do. People believe in him, and maybe he should be in charge if Feeney isn't doing the job right. This was a real opportunity to turn the tide. But Dad got this look on his face like he was terrified worried about what I was talking about. I just said I'd heard that people were upset with Feeney, and he relaxed. They hadn't listened when he'd challenged Feeney before, but maybe they would now. After a moment of silence, Dad nodded and looked more like the man I've always known—straight-backed and ready to go.

This could change our lives. Get Dad a better job and make everything we've wanted possible.

April 22, 1995

I've ruined everything. Yesterday, the adults had another meeting, and now it seems like everywhere I turn, every conversation I listen in on, they're talking shit about Dad. They're calling him high and mighty. They're saying that he's acting like he's better than them. That at least Mack Feeney pretends he's the same as the rest.

I'm the one who told Dad to stand up to them, but whatever he said, it's had the opposite effect.

I saw Dad going over to Jay's place, and I trailed him. Ducking behind trucks and sheds to make my way to the Turners' house. Except as I did, Jay came around the back with Andy. I put a finger to my lips to keep them quiet and motioned to the window. Andy looked kind of excited by the prospect. Sometimes white people get excited over weird things. But Jay didn't seem like he wanted to be doing it, even though he came over and listened with us.

Mrs. Turner was screaming at Dad. Saying stuff like he didn't know what they were going through, and that he was making it worse, and her family was already suffering enough.

Dad kept telling her that they had to stop this. Though he didn't say what "this" was. Then he put the nail in the coffin and told Mrs. Turner that her family would always just be another set of blacks and nothing they did was going to make the other families see them any different.

Mrs. Turner looked him dead in the eyes and told him that they didn't need to belong, they just needed to survive. Then she told him to get out of her fucking house.

I'd never heard her cuss. And at Dad of all people. I didn't like the way that felt. As if she was shutting us out. And what would that mean for me and Jay if his mom hated my dad?

Jay tugged me away from the window, pointing at the cover of trees near the house. He seemed as rattled as I was to hear his mom talk like that. So I went with him into the forest, with Andy following behind us.

Andy, for all his excitement before, was quiet after. He mumbled that something was up with everyone lately.

I felt that too, but I didn't know what it was. We all stood there for a moment, breathing hard though we had barely run. That was when I noticed that Jay and I were holding hands. He must have grabbed mine to pull me away. I kept looking at our fingers. Then he noticed, so I yanked my hand away. I shouldn't have

I confessed that everyone hated my dad now. I didn't want to sound desperate, but I knew I did. I asked them what would happen if everyone hated him so much that he lost his job and we had to leave the ranch.

Andy piped up that he didn't think his parents hated my dad, that they were just annoyed with him.

That didn't help, but I didn't snap at Andy because I knew he was trying to make me feel better.

Jay reminded me that Mr. Owens loved my dad and he was the owner, and that had to matter.

I nodded, though I hadn't seen Mr. Owens in a while. He used to always be around somewhere. He would walk the grounds and check in with us or even do work. His kids would play on the property, and his wife would visit with them. But I hadn't seen them, either.

Jay reached out and grabbed my hand again.

And this time, I didn't pull away.

October 14, 1995

I haven't wanted to write, though I kept thinking that I should. After their argument, Mrs. Turner put her foot down. Got Mr. Owens to fix our shifts so I don't get any with Jay or Jonas. She's keeping them inside more too. I barely saw them the entire summer. I thought when school started, I could sneak over to Jay's class. But he wasn't there. They'd been switched over to homeschooling. Lots of people on the ranch are homeschooling now. Not as many kids working either.

People are sticking to their own these days. I never thought we were the family Mr. Owens wanted us to be, but now we feel like a bunch of little islands. Isolated and alone. When I walk around the property, it's like it's abandoned.

Today, the Poirers left the ranch with their boy in a casket. He was one of the kids who'd caught whatever started going around way back in April and hadn't gotten better. Though the couple times I'd seen him around, he hadn't looked sick. But I guess he must have been, since he's dead now.

There's a cemetery nearby, but they don't want him buried there for some reason. Dad said it's because they're originally from Quebec and they want him there. That's where they're moving back to. But the way he said it . . . his voice was so empty and small.

Sam was too young for me to know him well, just twelve. But I would have wanted to say goodbye to him anyway. His sister and I had classes together. We didn't talk anymore since she was part of Shirley's group, but I'd liked her. I was able to catch her just before they left, to say I was sorry for her loss. But when she looked at me, her lips were twisted in a near snarl. I even stepped back because it was such a shock. She said I didn't know how lucky I was. That my daddy had looked after me, and her daddy had had to . . . something? She never finished the sentence, she just started bawling. I never learned what her dad had been forced to do.

She got into their car, and the Poirers left.

They weren't a popular family, but everyone seems touched by the death. I saw Mrs. Feeney on her back stoop, huddled over their patio table, sobbing. I guess maybe she thought no one would be around. What was it she was crying about? Her husband's unpopularity or her son being sick knowing that Sam had died from the illness? I couldn't know.

It was awkward to see, so I turned away. I haven't told anyone about it either. It feels private.

But there is a bright side.

Mr. Owens came by tonight to say he's giving us the Poirers' house and that Dad has been promoted to Mr. Poirer's job of technician supervisor. Meaning he won't be the grunt guy working on the machines. Instead, he'll oversee those workers and report directly to Mack Feeney. Better pay, for sure. And the house is bigger than ours. I'll get my own bedroom, even. Mr. Owens came by to tell us personally, and he smiled, but there was something off about it. Like he was trying really hard to keep it on.

It's amazing news! And I feel bad for the Poirers but finally something is working out for us. Jay was right. No matter what the others think, Mr. Owens does love Dad. I can tell. He's looking out for us.

Before Mr. Owens left, he said that Dad was the best of us. That he'd fought when the rest of them hadn't even realized they needed to be fighting.

But when I looked at Dad, he was just staring down at the mug in his hands, eyes blank, not even the tiniest upward quirk of his lips.*

---

* You didn't get much of a chance to know him, but my father was a kind man. And that was exactly what ruined him. He was too kind, and people knew it, and they walked all over him. He couldn't get the right balance. Neither could I, to be honest. But you can. Be sweet on the outside, but on the inside, you have to be ready to strike back.

CHAPTER THIRTEEN

I was doing my absolute best to pay attention to Harriet's unnecessarily long speech about why we should have "cool down" rooms for the winter dance. She was, like me, part of at least a dozen different clubs and societies, and even led a book club specifically devoted to reading memoirs by powerful and successful Black women, as she aspired to be. Her ideas were actually good; I just didn't have the focus for it today. I'd forgotten that we would have to stay after school for this. Alone and unsupervised.

While a murderer was running around targeting my family.

But we would be done soon. I would be okay.

We were in the assembly hall doing a walk-through to discuss the layout. The room was currently in its usual state with the rows of benches in place, but we had our imaginations and an iPad so we could draw things out.

"That sounds good," I said once she was done talking, and she beamed at me.

She turned to Ziggy. "How about you?"

The girl shrugged and adjusted her glasses, which had gotten tangled in her red hair. She nonchalantly ripped the knotted strand right off her head. "I'm fine with that. It'll be good for people who just want to chill without loud music blasting in their ears."

The two of them started talking about something else, and though I tried to pay attention, I could feel my mind wandering.

After yesterday's library trip, Dom and I knew what the symbol represented, but it had changed the possible murderer from some faceless stranger to potentially a student—someone our age who we might know. Someone who could easily have access to the school. If we stuck with that theory, anyway.

And I couldn't shake the fact that Dad had lied to my face about the symbol. Something that shouldn't have even mattered enough for him to hide it from me. Which was making me think that it had, in fact, come up in the disclosure but Dom hadn't been told about it. That wasn't great either. Because what did that mean if parts of Dom's case were being hidden even from him?

Harriet cleared her throat, and I blinked, snapping my neck toward her. She pointed to the tablet in my hands. "Are you drawing the layout?"

"Yes! Sorry."

Great, now I looked inattentive. I focused on making notes and drew out diagrams as we talked about how everything for the dance would be organized. I made a note in the margin to double-check that the rooftop doors were properly locked. All the doors, really. Just the main entrance would be open and looked after the whole night.

My phone buzzed, and I took it out and checked the message from Karter. The girls paused and looked at me. "My sister is texting me, hold on." I handed them the tablet and its pen and walked into the hallway to read Karter's text.

Where are you?

I sighed. We all had to sign into online logs for after-school activities now to keep better track of students. She could have taken two seconds of her time to look and discovered where I was.

> At school. I have a winter dance planning meeting.

> Does anyone live near us? Who are you walking home with?

> No, they both live in Mississauga.

Truthfully, I had planned to walk with Harriet and Ziggy to the main street and take the streetcar home. Public transport would be safer than just walking like I usually did. But I wasn't about to let Karter know that I'd changed my routine. She'd know it was because I was scared even if I didn't say it. She'd scent the weakness and be on it like a feral cat. Digging in with sharp claws. She'd be able to use it against me if I ever found a way to properly challenge her position as leader.

This didn't please Karter, who texted, You don't need to be involved in everything, you know that right? Maybe you should think a little more about your own well-being.

I texted back, I'll be fine. We're almost done.

Karter didn't seem to feel the need to respond to that one.

I knew that she cared about me, but it was awkward for her to actually express it. Though I guess I shouldn't have been surprised. I knew even she had leftover guilt about when I'd gone missing. She was, technically, the reason why I'd been wandering around in the first place. Something that both Mom and Dad didn't see any problem with communicating to her directly.

I turned back toward the assembly hall but stopped when I realized the girls' voices had dropped. I moved out of the view of the
windows in the doors and kept my steps light, creeping toward the
room.

"—she literally left him alone on Halloween," Ziggy said. "Poor
boy was walking around in his zombie Prince Eric costume saying
Ariel was seasick."

"That's too cheesy. He's always doing the most," Harriet replied.
"But if she was sick, she was sick, right?"

Ziggy added, clearly excited to spill the tea, "But, like, Thandie
said she heard Mercy and Shyanne talking, and apparently Sunny
and Craig were supposed to get together and do their costume stuff,
but she kept blowing him off."

"Do we trust Thandie, though?"

"I don't know. I mean, Sunny is way too *nice* to do stuff like that,
right?" There was a way that Ziggy said "nice." A specific emphasis
that made her and Harriet dissolve into giggles.

Harriet stopped herself. "Okay, okay, don't be bitchy. She really
is nice. She literally sent my family this gift basket thing when my
mom was having complications from her surgery."

"Yeah, but you're not even friends. When has she ever actually
cared about you? Don't you feel like sometimes she does stuff more
to look nice than because she actually gives a shit? It's like PR for the
school."

"No, she's just like that. I mean, I couldn't be friends with her, so
annoying, but I think she's genuinely sweet."

I turned away, walking back across the hall and giving myself a
minute to take a deep breath and soak into a fantasy where I pushed
open the double doors and made it very clear that I'd heard their
conversation. Where I said absolutely nothing, just stood and made
my eyes watery like I was actually hurt by their opinion of me. I

would luxuriate in how they'd shift and twitch on the spot, talking over each other to apologize.

I wasn't bothered. I didn't care. Yes, I had spent hours picking out Harriet's mom's gift basket. Yes, I had cried because her mom was still alive and mine was gone. And yes, I had done it anyway, because it *was* nice, and because her mom probably didn't get things like that a lot.

But fuck all that, right? Because my boyfriend was mad at me over his Halloween costume that I never cared about. And I hadn't wanted to go out, so I'd followed through on my pretending-to-be-sick plan. I drank a smoothie of raw eggs and banana, both of which made me gag, and threw up in the kitchen sink. Karter was the one who had to text him that I couldn't come. It sold the story more. And admittedly, she had seemed worried and ordered me soup, and that I had felt bad about.

Which, sure, saved my reputation, but it hadn't mattered. Now I knew that people could also hate you for being too nice. Besides, they weren't wrong, were they? I *was* fake. I knew that. It didn't matter what they thought. It mattered that I'd ruined my image without even realizing.

Mom had been loved by so many students in the school. That was the way the leader of the family should be. It was part of the reason Karter was such a bad fit, but apparently I wasn't any better.

I opened my eyes, composed myself, and walked back to the assembly hall. I pushed open the door and smiled at the girls. "All good, my sister just wanted to know where I was."

They grinned back like they hadn't just been dunking on me.

The rest of the meeting went smoothly, and we finished up just as Ziggy looked at her phone and swore, "Shit! The streetcar is literally coming right now."

"Now?!" Harriet said, eyes going wide.

"You two can go, I'll close up," I offered. "I live close."

This was the last thing I wanted. I didn't want to be alone in the school. I didn't want them to leave me. I wanted them to say no. But I also knew that this offer might help fix things. Maybe they would think twice about secretly hating me if I did more for them. I could make this right. Locking up would take five minutes max. *Don't be such a little bitch, Sunny.*

"Are you sure? Alone?" Harriet's eyes darted to Ziggy, to me, and then to the staircase. They wanted to go. I could feel it.

Stay. Please stay.

I made myself smile harder. It was a grimace now, but I couldn't do any better. "I'm good," I said. "School is locked up. No one's here. Go ahead."

"Thank you!" they both shouted, and sprinted for the stairs, rushing to make it to the streetcar stop in time.

I exhaled long and slow.

Now I was alone.

Had they really heard Mercy and Shyanne saying that stuff? How many other people didn't like me for being nice? It was bullshit. I was like this *for* them.

I closed the assembly hall doors and pushed the button to lock them. My fingers shook, and I gnawed on my lip.

I went back to the open classroom and did the same.

The lights clicked off, and I held back a scream.

The trees were dark and closing in, and I didn't know where I was. I was stumbling and cold. I missed Mom.

No. This wasn't happening. No. No. *No.*

I pulled out my phone, and the screen lit up. Six p.m. A small laugh escaped my lips. The lights auto-shut-off by that time. I waved my arms around, trying to trigger the sensors. They were supposed to turn back on.

But they didn't.

I was in the tent, curling myself around an already cool body, trying to stay warm.

No, I wasn't. I was here. I was in the school. And I was better than this.

I stood in the darkness and considered stomping my feet and screaming, just to let something out. Instead, I flicked on the flashlight on my phone.

A creak sounded, and I whipped around, shining the light on the assembly hall door. The door that I'd *just* closed, which was now ajar.

I locked that. I did. *I did*. Right? I wracked my brain for it, but the memory was gone. It was easy to forget things that you did automatically like that.

I went to the door, meaning to close it, but paused when a shadow moved inside. I held myself perfectly still, my phone clutched in my hand.

And then the shadow moved again.

I stumbled back and, quick as I could, flicked the controls on my screen and shut the flashlight off, plunging us both back into darkness.

If I couldn't see them, they couldn't see me.

I moved quietly, just like I had when I'd eavesdropped on the girls, slowly making my way backward toward the stairs. I knew this school. I could easily navigate it in the dark. But if this was the same person who'd been on the roof at the gala . . . they seemed to know the school well too.

Then light flooded the space as the person flicked on their own flashlight, pointed straight at me.

"Why are you doing this?" I managed to croak.

For a moment, they said nothing. We just stood across from one another in silence. Then, they looked down at their phone, tapping something.

A computer-distorted voice poured out from the phone's speaker. "Run, little bear cub. Run, run, run!"

My legs wouldn't move. My bottom lip trembled. This wasn't happening. It wasn't.

But the instant the stranger stepped forward, the words registered in my brain, and I turned and ran.

I sprinted down the hallway toward the stairs, footsteps thumping behind me. I barely made it down the first flight before they managed to gather my shirt in their fist. I shrieked and thrust my elbow back as hard as I could, the way Karter taught me to do if I was ever in trouble.

The assailant grunted and let go.

I rushed to the last set of stairs. If I could get down there, I could get outside, and the security camera would see me. I could scream and the neighbors in the houses across the street would come out.

My head was filled with the pounding tempo of my heart as I rushed to the next set of stairs—and my ankle rolled underneath me.

And then I was falling.

I fell head over heels, and the landing came up to meet me, my head slamming into the wall. I gasped and crumpled at the bottom.

Shit. Fuck. Shit.

Breathing heavy, I pushed at the floor, trying to get up, but I wasn't fast enough.

The person grabbed a handful of my hair, tugging on the strands in a way that got my attention but was almost gentle at the same time. That made it worse.

Pleas fell from my mouth. "Please don't. Please, please don't." My head was throbbing, and I couldn't think straight. I didn't know any more of Karter's moves. I didn't even know what I was begging them not to do. This wasn't like the other times. This wasn't just to creep me out. This was serious.

I thought of a knife plunging into a woman's neck. I thought of Duane's spine barely connected to his body. I thought of the woman in the tent covered in blood and her open, lifeless eyes.

Their phone screen lit up as they put it near my face. A pathetic mewl I'd never heard from myself before came out of my mouth. They pressed a button on the phone, and the same computer-distorted voice said, with a sickly sweet tone, "Bears who dig too hard lose claws. So quit while you still have all your paws."

They knew we were looking into the murder. Looking into *them*. This person, who had me at their mercy.

"I w-w-will. I'm sorry," I croaked. Tears were falling from my eyes, and I couldn't stop shaking.

And all at once, they let go of my hair, my head thumping back to the ground, and left.

I stayed where I was. Unable to move.

I was in the tent.

I was cold and scared and alone.

I wanted my mom to come and save me.

CHAPTER FOURTEEN

Harriet was getting tears all over my sheets, and I wasn't even in the mood to feel vindictive about it. She was kneeling at the side of the bed, blubbering about how they shouldn't have left me alone while Ziggy stood awkwardly behind her. The latter girl's face was flushed, making her white skin look blotchy. The middles were sitting on the couch by the balcony windows, watching the entire scene after having let the girls into my bedroom. Honestly, I would have been touched by them sacrificing their free period to come see me if they hadn't been talking shit about me right before everything went down.

Though Harriet at least seemed remorseful. She was probably remembering her petty conversation with Ziggy. Because I was so nice. And they'd been bitchy about it, and I'd ended up attacked.

My fingers twitched in the folds of the bedspread, and I tried pushing the scene out of my head. I didn't want to remember the way my mind had emptied when faced with a threat. How pathetic my voice had sounded as I pleaded for my life. Didn't want to think about how I should have seen the escalation coming a mile away. I should have prepared for every eventuality like Mom would have.

But whoever that was, they'd planned to spare me from the start. They didn't even have a weapon on them as far as I could see. I wasn't a target. Because there was no way that Duane hadn't begged for his life too. And the Milk Man woman hadn't gotten to beg at all. For some reason, this person wanted me alive. I remembered the way they'd been almost *gentle* while grabbing my hair. How could that same person have committed the other brutal murders I'd witnessed?

The girls left with promises to get me my missed schoolwork as if my dad weren't the principal and could easily organize that for me. Or maybe not. Dad already had his hands full trying to avoid panic among the students.

Last night, Harriet and Ziggy had missed their streetcar and come back to see if they could get into the school and wait there instead since the next one wouldn't be by for half an hour. That was when they saw me on the stair landing through the window. The school doors had auto locked, so I had to get up and let them in so they could call Karter and get me home. The two of them were asked to keep quiet about it. I wondered if that was actually going to work. Maybe if they felt like telling anyone about it would jeopardize their place at the school. Which was fucked up, and I knew Dad wouldn't do that, but they might not know that.

Now, while the middles walked the girls out, I checked my phone. As far as anyone else knew, I was sick again. Even though, physically, I was fine. The doctor had said several times that I was lucky to have walked away without even a concussion. Shyanne had texted to ask if I was okay. Mercy and Craig hadn't. I didn't expect Mercy to, but my boyfriend should at least check in.

I should be happy. Maybe Craig was finally getting tired of us, and I could expect to be cut loose soon.

The door creaked open, and I looked over, expecting to see the middles coming back, but instead, it was Dom. He was in a pair of worn yellow basketball shorts and another oversized T-shirt.

"Shouldn't you be in school?" I asked.

He shrugged. "I wanted to make sure you were okay. No one is going to care if I miss a day." He came inside and sat at the edge of my bed. He looked uncomfortable there, which made sense because I wasn't sure if he had ever been in my room before.

It was a lot different from his. For one, my clothes were neatly stacked in my hamper, and I didn't have any posters on the walls. I had just let the interior decorator choose a bunch of artwork to stick up and memorized the artist names and blurbs about the pieces in case I was ever asked about them.

"Are you?" Dom asked. "Okay?"

I smiled.

"For real. Don't just say you are if you aren't."

The smile dimmed. I didn't know how I felt. I wanted to stay in bed for an amount of time that I hadn't decided on yet, but it could be forever. But I also didn't want to be alone. One comfort was that I definitely didn't think this was Dom. Why threaten me to stop digging when he was the one benefiting from it? Unless the entire point was just to torture me.

And then here he was again, coming to my room to check on me. How many times had I seen him upset and just left him to it? I was a bad sister. I was a bad sister to Dom, specifically.

The middles came back into the room before I could say anything, clocking Dom on the bed. My younger brother awkwardly stood up and shuffled to the side.

To his credit, Darren didn't mention it. "Why don't we go skating? Just to get out." There was something tense about his voice. I guess him trying to sell it. Trying to make things better.

I didn't want to go anywhere.

Kiley came over and brushed my hair with her hands. She hadn't shaken off the strain that seemed to be slowly drowning her the last little while. But she was still here for me. "Might be a good distraction instead of sitting with your thoughts. But if you really don't want to, we can do something here. Watch a movie in the basement." I leaned into my sister, letting her squish next to me on the bed and laying my head on her chest.

I wanted my mom.

"Sure," I choked out. "Skating sounds all right."

Kiley smiled. "Good. And you have to have fun with us. Anything otherwise would be homophobic."

I let out a dry laugh, and she tucked my hair behind my ear, fussing with the strands.

Darren nodded several times like he hadn't actually expected me to agree. "Cool, cool. Let's get you dressed then."

Dom gave me a little smile. "Hope the skating helps." He was moving to leave the room when Darren spoke again.

"You may as well come. We'll rent skates."

Dom blinked at our older brother.

Kiley's hand paused in its petting of my head.

"Yeah . . . okay," Dom said. He looked at me as if for permission, and I nodded. I wanted him to come. He'd been here for me, just like the middles had.

Once Dom had left the room to get changed, Kiley looked over at Darren. "You think that's a good idea?"

"Yes." Darren's voice was resolute.

Kiley frowned but didn't push it. Instead, she stood and started picking out clothes for me.

Long Branch Arena was a short walk away from our house, tucked into the neighborhood and decorated with white, navy, and sky-blue tiles on the outside. It wasn't exactly the nicest skating rink. It was old and creaky. But the academy still regularly brought students during the winter season as part of gym classes. I suspected this was why Darren was able to get us in this casually for a place that didn't usually do public skate times.

The rink was empty, and our voices echoed in the space. Not to mention that the ice wasn't exactly as fresh as it could be, but it would work.

I found myself looking into dark corners and checking that doors were locked after we went through them. Were we safe here? Or were we fooling ourselves into thinking that we were?

"Look what I found!" Darren exclaimed, and I jumped. His smile slipped for a moment when he noticed me startle before it bounced back. He produced a chair with tennis balls attached to the bottom. He slapped it onto the ice and waved me forward. "Your chariot awaits." His voice was too loud. Too forced.

Usually this would be Mom's job. She would have done it naturally. It wouldn't have been this hard.

I went over and sat in the chair.

Darren immediately started pushing me as fast as he could. Despite myself, I let out a squeal. He paused, worried maybe, and so I added a laugh so he would know I was okay. Then he was laughing too. And then I started laughing for real.

My brother pushed me around in a circle, then did donuts. When he got tired, Kiley decided to take over, but we went a lot slower until Dom came up beside her and offered to help. She gave him a look for a few seconds before nodding. And then it was the three of us, spinning around.

We eventually abandoned the chair because I wanted to move on my own. My ankle had rolled, but it was fine, just a bit sore. I would rather use and strengthen it. With Darren's encouragement, we linked arms and skated all together in a row. It was graceless, but when one of us stumbled, the rest of us helped hold everyone up.

And when we fell, we all fell together in a heap of limbs and skates and puffy jackets.

We ended up taking a break like that. Just sitting on the ice.

I looked over and saw Dom's face split with a grin. It was so weird to see on him—that sort of wide-open smile—that I ended up staring.

He caught me, and his lips flattened and his cheeked puffed up in a way that I suspected was embarrassment as he looked away.

If Darren hadn't made sure to invite him, Dom wouldn't be here right now. He'd already been on his way out. He'd assumed that he wouldn't be involved. And I hadn't even questioned it. And Kiley had basically been against it.

"We should have invited Karter," Kiley said quietly.

Darren's expression changed. He looked annoyed suddenly. "Why? She didn't even come to check on Sunny. Clearly, she's too busy 'running the family' to actually take care of the family."

"She's trying her best."

"Is she? Or is she just on a power trip?" Darren snapped back.

The middles didn't fight like this. Didn't disagree like this. But it felt like I kept seeing this happen more and more over the last few months. They used to be so similar that they would sometimes feel like the same person. Now it was like they were splintering, and I didn't know why.

"She's trying to fill a hole," Dom said, and the middles both turned to him. Like they were shocked out of a trance. Broken away from their own private argument. Dom shifted in place and shrugged. "Karter, I mean. And I just think . . . it's too big of a space for her."

She shouldn't have been the one trying to fill it in the first place.

Darren sighed. "She should have come down, anyway. Mom would have found time."

"But that's what Dom means," Kiley said. "She's *not* Mom. It's too much for any of us to try to be Mom."

I suppressed the frown that started to pull itself onto my face. "I don't mind," I said. "I know Karter's busy."

"You never mind!" the middles snapped at the same time.

I blinked at them.

"Sorry," Darren muttered. "This was fun anyway, right?" he said, changing the topic.

I nodded.

Dom opened his mouth and then shut it. Looking down at his skates.

Kiley noticed. "What were you going to say?" she asked him.

My little brother shrugged and kept looking down. "I was just wondering if we could have always been like this. But I know we couldn't have. We always had that distance between us, and she would stand in the space. Now she's gone, and it feels like we can finally move toward one another. You know?" He peeked up then. "I dunno, I guess this is the sort of stuff I wished we could have always done . . . but you all never seemed to want to."

I thought suddenly of that day at the ranch, when Dom had gone too far into the forest. I had left him. Run back to Mom. I'd thought he wanted to be by himself. Wanted to be alone. I never wondered if he was hoping I would go with him. After all, if it had been anyone else, I would have.

Kiley got to her feet and held her hand out, helping Dom up from the ice while Darren helped me. They stood there for a moment, Kiley with her hands wrapped around Dom's. Finally she let go. "Well, let's get our hour's worth."

And so we linked arms again and finished our skate.

On the way back home, I checked my texts and noticed a bunch from Craig. Apparently, Harriet and Ziggy had decided that he deserved to know the truth as my boyfriend, and now my phone was filled with all the concern that he hadn't bothered with when he just thought I was sick.

I'm fine, I replied.

If Craig really knew me, he would have seen it for the dismissal it was. But he didn't, so he sent back a row of heart emojis.

In the evening, I went to the shed to go call the middles in for dinner. When I opened the door, I saw a sculpture broken into pieces on the floor. Clay and bent bits of metal, half-painted pieces scattered among wet spots of fresh material. And in the middle of the mess, Kiley sat, her eyes vacant and her hands covered in drying paint. It looked like a piece itself. Her sitting in the chaos. A part of it.

Until she looked up and saw me. Her eyes widened, and she smiled sheepishly. "Had to scrap it."

I saw myself in the expression. The gesture. The tone.

The performance.

"Isn't the contest soon?" I asked, my voice tentative.

She nodded, and nodded, and kept nodding. "Yeah, I'll figure it out."

I looked toward the back of the room, where Darren was facing away from her, bowed over something on a table. I thought maybe paper, but when I craned my neck, it wasn't anything. He was just sitting there. Hunched over.

Kiley followed my gaze. "Dinner, right? We'll be there in a minute."

"Okay . . ." I backed out of the shed because she seemed to want me to leave.

We were falling apart, and I didn't know how to fix it. I only knew that I had to.

CHAPTER FIFTEEN

I felt myself coming awake long before I actually opened my eyes. It was like that sometimes. Sounds or thoughts infiltrated my sleeping mind, and I would slowly find myself becoming more and more conscious. Usually because it was time to wake up. Only a few days after the incident at school, I was back to my normal routine. And it wasn't strange to get up before my alarm.

But when I finally peeled my eyes open, it was dark.

It was a deep, penetrating sort of night. I'd started to close my curtains before I went to sleep, blocking out even the light from the moon. I kept thinking that I would look over at the exposed window and see the person who attacked me against the glass.

I blinked, waiting for my eyes to adjust when I slowly came to realize that I wasn't alone.

I meant to gasp, but it came out as a shocked inhale instead.

Someone loomed, standing at an awkward, sloping angle directly above me. Not doing anything but standing there, swaying slightly like they were being pushed in a breeze that I couldn't feel.

As my eyes adjusted more, I recognized the shape of a long loose T-shirt and shorts that dropped to the knees. The shaved head and the shorter height.

Dom.

I swallowed. My heart was speeding up but felt dull in my chest, like the muted thud of shoes on carpet. I gripped the sheets between my fingers, not sure what else to do.

"I know you're awake," he whispered. His voice crawled across my skin in a lazy wave, and I shuddered.

Sleepwalking. He must be sleepwalking. That was all. I had no memory of that ever being a problem for him, but I also knew very little about the brother I'd ignored for most of my life.

"Go back to bed, Dom." It didn't come out right—high-pitched and breathy. It reminded me of being huddled on a stair landing, pleading for my life.

He didn't respond.

I swallowed and crept my fingers toward my phone on my bedside. When they got close, the screen lit up, illuminating Dom's wide-open eyes and the smile stretched across his lips.

I jerked back and slapped my hands over my mouth to keep from screaming.

The sound of whispers and footsteps reached us from the hallway. Dom stepped back and looked at my bedroom door.

In that moment, I launched myself off the bed and tugged the door open, stumbling into the hall and slamming it shut behind me, the wood pressed to my back, chest heaving, my forehead covered in a thin sheen of sweat.

Kiley and Darren were there in the hall, frozen. Clutching each other.

It was a Tuesday. They shouldn't even be here. They should have been downtown.

My older brother was sobbing, tear tracks running down his face as he attempted to keep quiet.

"What are you doing?" Kiley whispered, staring at me.

"I . . ." I considered talking about Dom in my room, but it seemed ridiculous to bother them with that when Kiley was basically dragging my brother along with her. "What's . . . Is he okay? Are you okay?" I directed the last question to Darren.

My older brother shook his head.

He broke away from Kiley to wrap his arms around himself. "I'm taking him to the hospital," she whispered, looking at the staircase and then back to me.

I knew immediately that she was checking for Karter.

"I'll come too," I said.

Kiley furrowed her brow, and I knew it wasn't what she wanted, but she nodded. "Yeah, fine. Let's go."

I followed my siblings downstairs and gave my bedroom one last look. Somehow during the course of our conversation, the door had opened, just the tiniest bit. Enough for someone to peek out. I suppressed a shudder and rushed down the stairs.

We crowded into the back seat of the Uber with Darren between us, and I noticed belatedly that it was an Escalade. The same SUV that Mom had. The one that currently sat in our garage that only Karter drove. *Great.* The middles did have their own car, an electric Mercedes, but I figured that neither of them felt like driving right now.

Meanwhile, the Uber guy took one look at the three of us stumbling into the vehicle and turned to the front, wisely avoiding any small talk.

I had the sense to take off my bonnet and shove it into my pocket before we got in the car. Though I was still in my pajamas underneath my winter jacket.

"I'm sorry," Darren mumbled.

Kiley shook her head and gripped his hands. "Don't be sorry. Nothing to be sorry about."

"Your sculpture didn't come out right 'cause you keep spending time on me instead—"

"That's not why. It wasn't working. That's a me-thing." She shook her head. "There's not even any point," she mumbled.

Darren acted like he hadn't heard her. "Sunny . . ." He trailed off and looked at me. There was an intensity there that I didn't understand. "I'm so sorry, Sunny."

"You don't have to be sorry to me, either," I said, shifting closer to Darren.

Like when Kiley spoke to him, he didn't seem to register it. He kept muttering that he was sorry. I thought he also said something about just wanting to help, but that didn't even make sense.

I locked eyes with my sister over him and she bit her lip, tears gathering in her eyes. She took a hand away from Darren to swipe at them.

I should have said something the other day when I saw them like that in the shed. I should have done something. But I hadn't known what to do.

Fifteen or so minutes later, we pulled into the driveway of Etobicoke General Hospital, the name spelled out in big block illuminated letters on the side of the massive rectangular building. Or, I suppose I should have said, set of buildings. Kiley directed the driver to an entrance that wasn't the main one or the emergency.

We got out, and she kept her hands clutched around Darren, leading him through the entrance. It was an indistinct hallway. No waiting room or anything. Just a starkly lit expanse of gray tile flooring marked with arrows that meant nothing to me, and four chairs seemingly placed at random.

Kiley sat us down but stayed standing, texting on her phone. I held on to my brother's hands instead while she walked down the hallway. Hunching as she gave up texting and called someone despite the signage asking that we not use cell phones.

I didn't know what to say to Darren. What could I say? He didn't look like he was doing well and by his own admission wasn't fine. I didn't know how to make this situation better. It felt wrong to just smile and act like everything was fine. That wouldn't work here. It wouldn't help him.

". . . least Mom isn't here," Darren said under his breath. "Would probably just call me a failure too."

I swallowed and said nothing, though I wondered who would say something like that to him.

"I'm a bad brother," Darren said, and looked up, so I knew he was talking to me.

I shook my head. "What are you talking about? You're the best brother. You always bring me Starbucks when I ask, and I don't even have to tell you what to order."

The corner of his lip quirked a bit before it fell again. "I'm not a good person."

"You are."

"No . . . *you* are. But I'm not. None of us, really. But you, always you. You're the only good one. The things I've done . . ."

I kept shaking my head. But I also wanted to say, "What have you done?" It probably wasn't anything. He wasn't exactly in his normal state of mind, after all.

Kiley let out a gasp of relief, and I jerked my head toward her. A Black woman came down the hallway in a pair of scrubs that were a deep plum purple, wearing New Balance sneakers, and with her hair pressed and pulled into a tight bun.

She came right up to us with a smile and said, "Hey, Darren. I hear you're not doing so well?"

He shook his head.

"Come on back with me. We've got a room for you. And we'll have a chat and see how we feel, all right?"

Darren nodded and disentangled his hands from mine, standing and following the woman, who put a reassuring hand on the small of his back.

She knows him.

This nondescript hallway and this woman, this had happened before. Happened enough for familiarity.

As Darren and the woman disappeared behind swinging doors, Kiley slouched over and sighed, pressing her hands to her eyes. Then her breaths got heavier and she started to cry. I rubbed her back.

"What's going on?" I said, looking at her curls since her face was hidden behind her fingers. "How many times has this happened?"

"Don't worry about it. I shouldn't have let you come."

"I wanted to come. I wanted to help."

Kiley jerked her head up and glared at me. "Help how? With a smile and the power of positive thinking?"

I had nothing to say to that.

My sister sighed. "Sorry, that was bitchy."

It was. But I wouldn't say so. "Is this why you keep being home at these weird days and hours? Because you come to this hospital, and it's closer to get to from the house than downtown?"

"Mom set it up. That woman, her kid went to the academy. Mom felt this would be a *discreet* way for Darren to get care in emergencies." Kiley rolled her eyes. "But nothing wrong with publicly saying Dom, who doesn't have depression, had to be inpatient for the summer, right? Suddenly that's okay. But Karter wants us to keep doing this cloak-and-dagger shit for the sibling who actually needs help. 'Cause that makes sense."

It didn't. I knew that. I think we all knew that, but we went along with it. We were used to following instructions.

"I didn't realize it was this bad," I said. "Or this often."

"It wasn't . . . but now . . ." Kiley stared at the floor tiles. "It's just one of those things no one tells you. Another shit show that you get to skip out on because no one wants to saddle Sunny with the bad things."

It was an unpleasant echo of what Dom had said to me at the beginning of the school year when we searched through Mom's office. "I didn't ask anyone to do that for me," I said, voice low.

"We have to, though. Because we already messed up. We were supposed to protect you. We could have lost you, but we didn't, and you still came out like you. Somehow, you're the only one that's not fucked up."

"That wasn't anyone's fault," I whispered. Though I hadn't always thought that. In that tent, huddled against the cold, I'd wondered why no one had noticed I was gone. Why they hadn't looked out for me. I wondered if Dom felt like that all the time. But it was different, because the truth was, they had. My family had done everything they could to get me back. And even now, a decade later, they still felt bad about it.

A wry smile formed on Kiley's lips as she turned to me. "It doesn't matter now. All I know is that I look at you and I see this happy girl, and I want to keep seeing it. It's just . . . at times like this, it doesn't really work."

I thought of Harriet and Ziggy's conversation about me. Too nice. And apparently, that extended to my family. I thought that I was making things better by maintaining this whole "sunny" thing. It was even what had helped Mom realize I was best to lead. I thought that was what people wanted from me. And according to Kiley, they did. But only when they needed it.

I wasn't the one they wanted to call when they were struggling. That was when I would get left behind.

And I hadn't even noticed.

And yet, I'd thought that I would do so much better than Karter with this family. I curled my shoulders forward and stared at the floor.

In that way, I was more like Dom than I thought. The difference was we were leaving him out to protect ourselves because we didn't want Mom to associate us with the child she didn't love, and they were leaving me out to protect me from them.

And here we were, in this hallway, hiding Darren to protect the image of the family. Because it was apparently only in danger from the truth.

When we got back home hours later, it was still dark outside, but the sun was starting to make its way up. Darren was quiet. They'd given him something to help, and it was making him sleepy. His eyes kept dropping closed. Kiley helped support him as we walked inside. The lights were on, and Karter was sitting at the kitchen island with her head in her hands. I felt Kiley flinch beside me.

Our older sister pulled her face from the cradle of her fingers to look at us. "Sunny. Come sit with me for a minute." Karter's voice was mild, but I understood the command in it.

I rubbed Darren's back, though I didn't know if he noticed, and smiled at Kiley, who nodded back before continuing on with him up the stairs to their rooms.

I went to the island and sat down across from my sister. She winced and pressed a palm against her head. "Headache?" I asked.

"Yeah. Kept me up. I already took something." Karter frowned as she watched the middles leave. "How is he?"

"Um . . . I don't know, honestly. All right for now."

My sister blinked at me. "That's . . . surprisingly realistic for you. A constant optimist."

I shrugged, playing with my fingers. "How come we can say

Dom went to inpatient but we're so quiet about Darren?" The words came out before I could stop them.

Karter narrowed her eyes at me. "Don't talk like you have any idea how this family works."

I held myself still so I wouldn't snap back that she didn't know any better than I did.

"What do you want me to do? He's getting the help, isn't he? He's got medication. He's got therapy several times a week. And you're mad because we're not shouting it from the rooftops?"

"I—"

"Is that even what he actually wants? No, it's not. What he wanted was for Mom to act like she wasn't ashamed of him, and it's too late for that because she's dead. And nothing I say is going to change that. I am doing the best I can do. And if you think I'm fucking up, cool, that's your opinion."

"I didn't say—"

"Do you know how ridiculously privileged you are? Do you? We've got this trial hanging over our heads, and we're hemorrhaging money. We cannot handle any more losses."

I swallowed. Now I had somehow gotten Karter on a rampage, and I didn't know how to escape from this. I didn't want to be here. I didn't want to be yelled at. I didn't want another family member telling me how easy my life was, like I hadn't been attacked a few days ago.

And now she was on about our money. I thought of the ledger we'd seen in Mom's office with the up and down figures. "We have the ranch . . ." I regretted speaking almost the instant it happened. The best way to deal with an angry Karter was to keep quiet while she did her thing. I *knew* that.

"The ranch is nothing but trouble, and if we just sold it, we could fix a lot of our problems."

"Mom always said the ranch was her legacy." Now that I'd started talking back, I couldn't stop it. I blamed the lack of sleep.

"Not everything Mom loved is worth keeping." She met my eyes then, steely and stoic. There were bags underneath her own. No concealer to hide them. My sister sighed and leaned back in her chair. "Go to sleep." As I stood, Karter watched me and bit her lip. "Sorry for yelling," she mumbled.

Karter always apologized too late. She'd blow up at you and then try to smooth it over after instead of just learning not to freak out in the first place. I knew she felt sorry. I could see it in the way her eyes shifted away and her shoulders hunched.

It made me think of that day. After the police had cleared us and Mom had washed off all the blood. The first thing Karter had done when we were alone was scream at me for wandering too far. Then she'd tugged me to her chest and held me. She'd cried and pressed her favorite stuffed animal into my hands. My homecoming gift. She'd apologized for yelling and kissed my forehead.

She was always sorry in the end.

But it didn't make me feel forgiving. Not today.

I went upstairs and stood in front of my door for a moment before pushing it open. I flicked on the lights and moved around the room, searching for Dom, but he was gone.

I tiptoed over to his bedroom, inching open the door, bit by bit. But when I looked inside, his bed was empty. The sheets thrown off.

When I went back to my room, I locked the door behind me.

CHAPTER SIXTEEN

was starting to understand why police investigations took so long. I tugged up the material of the insulated leggings I wore under my skirt as Dom and I made our way to school. It'd been three weeks since Darren's emergency, and it was hard to tell if he was doing better or if things were being hidden from me again. Though, on the positive side, Dom hadn't come into my room at night again. Couldn't, since I locked it now.

Otherwise, our sleuthing had stalled. We'd learned nothing new about the symbol or the killer. I'd done my own private searches on the Milk Man and his maidens and calves, which produced nothing. Later I'd remembered what the woman had said about yew branches when Craig and I were at Spirit, but that just led to learning that it was a poisonous branch. Some people apparently would use them to warn off others. But I think I would have noticed if someone was sending us cautionary poison plants. Or had the woman simply meant that she was signaling impending danger? None of it made any sense, and I didn't know where to go next.

Now I always made sure to walk to and from school with some-one and avoided being alone in the halls. Dad had offered to buy me a car and hire a driver since my license wasn't advanced enough to let me drive alone. But there was no way I could deal with the fallout of that. Coming to a needs-based school with a private driver felt like the opposite of checking my privilege at the door. At worst, I could take the streetcar if no one was around to walk with me and have the comfort of being in public with strangers.

Precautions aside, I hadn't even seen a hint that the murderer was lurking around. I wondered if maybe they felt like I was following their instructions and not digging anymore. I told myself that I hadn't subconsciously failed to discover any new leads in order to listen to the threat. We just didn't have any more clues. Mom wouldn't have been scared into submission, and neither would I.

I gave Dom a sidelong look. The knit hat pulled over his head was predictably black, though his winter jacket was an alarming shade of neon green splattered with some additional bright print. It was like walking next to space vomit, but I was managing. My younger brother, on the other hand, looked tired. Weary. Or maybe I was projecting.

Every once in a while I would peek into his room if I happened to be up late at night, and more often than not, he wasn't in there.

"How did you sleep?" I asked him. I hadn't brought up the sleepwalking incident because it seemed like it would be an awkward conversation. Besides, it's not like he could help sleepwalking. But I was curious if he was aware of his involuntary nighttime activities.

He shrugged. "Fine."

"You don't have any trouble with it?"

"Sometimes. I'll wake up in the middle of the night and just be like, alert. So I go to the basement and read manga or watch TV. Better than lying awake staring at the ceiling."

Or you walk into your sister's bedroom and creepily stand over her.

He looked over at me. "Why?"

"Nothing. You just looked tired. I was concerned." He seemed skeptical about that but didn't push it. "Have you always had trouble sleeping?"

He shook his head. "No . . . it's been mostly since Mom died. I don't know. It's not like I'm awake thinking of her, I'm just . . . up. So, like . . . you don't have to check in on me."

"Just wanted to ask and see if you were okay, that's all."

Dom stopped walking. "No," he said. "At night, I mean. You don't have to check if I'm awake or not."

The air felt colder suddenly and I fought the shiver that rolled down my arms. I hadn't realized that he'd noticed. But then . . . he hadn't said anything about it until now. I was concerned, yeah, but it was a mixture of *Is Dom okay?* and *What the fuck is Dom doing?*, and the latter bit was what I didn't want him to notice.

"I'm sorry if it's been too much. I was attacked the other day and I'm feeling paranoid. I just want to make sure you're okay." I injected a healthy dose of anxiety and worry into the sentence to make sure it didn't come out abrupt or bitchy. *I'm sorry if it's been too much* (said quietly, avoiding his gaze because I was embarrassed). *I was attacked* (up-pitched with a note of desperate anxiety, extra emphasis on the word "attacked") *the other day* (it was nearly a month ago, but a bit of shake in the voice because it still felt like yesterday, which wasn't a total lie) *and I'm feeling paranoid* (a slightly lower volume again as if I was afraid to admit it, followed by a sheepish smile, because it was so totally silly to be worried about being murdered by someone who stalked and attacked me and had slaughtered multiple people). *I just want to make sure you're okay* (this called for direct eye contact because it was important to me for him to know I cared).

The entire time I went through the motion, I was aware of the way I'd started gripping the straps of my backpack. Holding tight enough that my palms felt warm despite the cool winter air. Because every time I looked in on him, he either wasn't there or he was asleep.

So when had he noticed me? Had he been on the staircase? Watching my back? Eyes following me as I tiptoed to his door?

But, as intended, Dom ducked his head. Shame. Yes, that was perfect. "Right, yeah, no, it's fine. Just didn't want you worrying," he said. He hesitated for a moment before saying, "Maybe you need to spend some time doing something fun? To get your mind off it?"

"I have fun," I said, whip quick and defensive.

"Like, I appreciate it, but if you're not spending time on school or event planning, you're trying to figure out this murder stuff, and honestly we haven't made any progress. And it's kind of dying down now anyway. Maybe everything will be okay?"

It was true. The police had seemingly given up on Duane's murder. It was grisly and terrible, but also quickly became old news. Shockingly, news outlets weren't very invested in the loss of Black boys. Though of course it wasn't a shock at all. We knew they would lose interest. And no one else knew about that woman. I kept expecting a report about her to come up, but it never did. She'd been killed, and no one cared but me.

I hadn't expected the murderer to just stop after that. It didn't make sense. If they wanted to take down our family, shouldn't they have kept going until the job was done?

"You'll be pleased to know that I am going to do something fun today," I said to Dom with a bright smile. "We're going on a double date in the afternoon while the teachers do their afternoon PD."

Craig was the one who suggested going to the pop-up sugar shack at Exhibition, and in an attempt to be a better girlfriend, I said I knew someone who could get us free tickets. Meaning that I bought them online and pretended someone gave us free tickets.

We walked in through the back doors of the academy and Dom nodded approvingly. "Good." As he moved to leave, I grabbed on to his sleeve. He turned back with his brow raised.

"Hey . . . if something bad happens, you can tell me, you know? I'm not too delicate or untainted or whatever. Just tell me." I didn't want any surprises, and honestly, how could I ever lead this family if they hid things from me? I couldn't help Dom if he held back.

He stared at me for a moment before nodding. "Okay."

I watched him as he walked away.

We stepped off the GO Train at Exhibition Station with a rush of teenagers who clearly had the same idea. I recognized some of the uniforms of the other students since most high schools in the neighborhood tended to do their PD, or professional development days for teachers, around the same time.

I was still in my uniform, but Mercy, Shyanne, and Craig had changed into new sets of clothes. When I checked the group chat, I realized that they had talked about ditching uniforms, but I'd missed it. I'd started slacking with my group chats lately. I needed to get it together.

Though I didn't mind wearing my uniform. We had on jackets anyway so you could barely see the outfits underneath.

We went up to the ticket booth, and I had the guy at the front scan my phone for entry and collected the tokens we'd need for food and drinks that I'd prebought. On the other side of the turnstile, I handed them out. "They sent us a bunch of these, so we'll have like ten each."

"They probably thought your whole family would go," Mercy said, shoving her tokens into her jacket pocket.

"Probably," I echoed. It was the exact excuse I had ready to give if they asked why there were so many coins.

Craig jerked his head toward the exhibition grounds. "They have a bouncy castle."

He and Mercy looked at each other and she said, "You want to go?"

"Yes!"

The two of them turned to us, and I shook my head. Shyanne said, "Yeah, I'm with Sunny."

Craig and Mercy ran off, leaving me and Shyanne alone. She smiled and turned to me. "Thanks, by the way, for the tickets and stuff."

"Oh, well, I didn't have to pay—"

Shyanne rolled her eyes. "For real? Just as Craig suggests it, suddenly someone is offering you free tickets?" She laughed. "Besides, usually when that happens, you begrudgingly have Craig take a picture of you right away and post it so you can be done. Saying some stuff like, 'Omg thank you SO much to Suzy's Sugar Shack for sending me to this awesome event.'"

Well, shit.

She cracked up watching me. "Your face! You really thought you were so slick." She shrugged, digging her hands into the pockets of her coat. "I get it. You're trying to be nice. But you know, it's not that bad. All of our parents could give us twenty dollars to go to something. It's just a big difference between that and paying to drive us two hours away to go to university and stay in a ten-thousand-dollar-a-year dorm room."

I could feel my entire face heating up. Was I really that transparent? "Sorry . . ."

"Honestly, that used to annoy me about you. I joke about being poor, but, like, I can still go to the movies and shit. And you always magically have all these coupons ready like we couldn't afford *anything*. Then I googled your family's net worth—"

My eyes went wide.

"I know, but when I realized what your family was making, I was like, 'No wonder she thinks we're so poor.'" She snorted into her fist. "I don't really have anything against you. And I'm sorry if this is outta pocket or whatever, but, like, you're so disconnected sometimes. If you don't know if we can afford something, just ask us. We're right here. I get that money is embarrassing and shit, but it's also embarrassing to have you act like we don't have two pennies to rub together."

I tried not to feel annoyed. Not at Shyanne, but at myself. Once again, this image that I'd thought was so ironclad had holes. Ones people had seen through. More people than just Jeremy, who I at least knew about and had an understanding with. "Sorry," I said again, for a lack of anything else to say.

"Don't say sorry again! You're making me feel bad for you, and this shit is about us."

I opened my mouth and then closed it because "sorry" was the only thing I could think to say.

Shyanne said, "Anyway. Now that we've chatted about this, you should know that Craig is probably going to use some of that money he saved from his summer job to get you a corsage or some other fancy bullshit for the winter dance next week."

Why was he doing all that? "It's not prom."

"Try telling him that." She paused for a moment, then said, "You two *are* going together, right?"

"I . . . thought that was obvious."

Shyanne nodded over at Mercy and Craig, who were screaming and shouting as they bounced around like they weren't ten years above the intended bouncy castle audience. "Maybe it's because we went to middle school together and I'm more used to him, but Craig, is, like . . ."

Deeply insecure? Needy? Clingy?

"He doesn't have the highest self-esteem. And usually I wouldn't entertain it. I've literally told him multiple times that this tanning crap is not cute. But, like, even that is this desperate plea to fit in.

Though I'm not giving him any free passes for that. My point is, I don't think you should assume that *he* assumes that stuff."

I knew she had a point. After all, he should have just texted me and mentioned the Halloween costume thing again, but he was probably embarrassed after all the times I ignored it. "Yeah, thanks for reminding me."

"No problem. As long as you also remind him that tanning is supposed to complement your natural shade, not trick people into thinking that you're not white."

"But . . . that's not what he's trying to do, right?"

"I don't know, but it looks a certain way. Especially hanging out with us. I already told him if he comes back from winter break and isn't several shades lighter, I'm not associating with him." She looked over at me. "I'm not gonna tell you what to do, but, like, it's a problem."

I winced. The more people mentioned it, the less I was able to ignore it. I just didn't want to have to be the one to get into this confrontation. There didn't seem to be any way to add the Sunny touch to "you're doing some racist shit." "Yeah, I'll say something."

Shyanne grinned at me. "Cool. Now let's go get those fools."

We met back up with our respective partners and went onto the real sugar shack portion. It featured an open-faced cabin, like something that belonged in a showroom for outdoorsy people but was instead dropped in the middle of Exhibition Place.

We lined up in front of the giant wooden trough that was filled with snow and watched as workers in red-and-black flannel jackets spread pure maple syrup onto the ice flakes and then put a popsicle stick at the bottom, slowly rolling up and gathering the sweetness until they created a maple syrup lollipop. We handed off three tokens and took our sticks.

"We're gonna go take pictures." Mercy pointed to a standee that was made up exactly like the sugar shack that you could poke your head into.

Craig moved to follow them, but I hung on to him. "Can we go watch the ice carving?" I pointed to a small crowd gathered around a guy with a chainsaw ripping into a giant block of ice.

"Yeah, sure."

We made our way over, and Craig was immediately enraptured by the performance. I took a lick of my maple syrup and enjoyed the crisp chill from the cold. It was nice because they used a thinner syrup than what you got from the bottle. Fresh, so it wasn't too sweet.

I said, "Hey, we're going to the dance together, right? Did you want to do something beforehand? Get dinner together?"

Craig whipped toward me, eyes wide. "Oh. Yeah. I mean, yeah! That would be great." He nodded again as if confirming. "Yeah, absolutely." He grinned, and I smiled back.

I'd thought it would be easy to bring up what Shyanne and I talked about but I felt the words sticking in my mouth. What if he got annoyed with me? What if he talked behind my back like Harriet and Ziggy, telling people I was overly sensitive or critical of his looks? Mom made being loved look so effortless, but even she hadn't covered all her bases. To the public and for the business, she'd been perfect, but for her family, opinions varied.

But I knew that I wasn't being seen the way I wanted to already. And this was something I actually wanted to say. So I pushed the words out. "And maybe . . . let's maybe ease up on the self-tanner. Not just for the dance, but like, in general."

His eyes widened again, and I wondered if he was suddenly going to snap at me, but he just smiled sheepishly. "Yeah, yeah, Shy and Mercy are on me about that. For sure, I'll tone it down."

That was it. Easy. Just like that.

I mean, it wasn't exactly a perfect admission of everything that went into the tanning, but it was good enough for now. Which was the epitome of Craig, I guess. Good enough for now.

He returned to watching the ice carver, and I let the smile melt from my face. I'd confronted him on something uncomfortable but also made him happy with the dance stuff. Shyanne was kind of an icon.

The only problem was that I didn't want to go to the dance with Craig. I didn't want to go at all. But what I wanted in the moment didn't matter as much as what I would achieve in the long run. I just had to hope that everything I did would pay off one day.

CHAPTER SEVENTEEN

There was too much blue, but I couldn't do anything about it now. I watched the gauzy white and cerulean swaths of fabric decorating the bannisters as Craig and I walked up the stairs. It also made me regret my dress choice, which was the same color combination. It had a semitransparent white corset top and an A-line skirt thick with layers of white organza, lace, and tulle. There were delicate little blue flowers embroidered along the off-shoulder sleeves and down the ribs, trailing onto the top of the skirt. Karter had said that I could get something new if I wanted, but I stuck to Mom's rule of renting through the usual place.

I looked at mine and Craig's tangled fingers and the corsage on my wrist. It was a small bundle of white roses and blue ribbon, a match to the boutonniere he had pinned to his jacket. He grinned at me, dressed in a suit similar to what he'd worn to the gala but in a deep indigo with a dress shirt in a lighter blue that matched the flowers on my dress. I didn't remember telling him that, but he figured it out somehow. Probably because it was a winter dance and tons of people were wearing the exact same colors. Which I knew would happen and was why I picked it. So I could, once again, do my best to blend in with the students instead of standing out. Before, I'd wanted them to like me. And now that I knew some of them didn't,

I wanted it more. Whatever I could do to shift my image closer to what I'd intended was worth it.

"Let's go take our picture!" Craig tugged me toward the backdrop decorated with fake snow falling on a Toronto city background including the CN Tower. Cringey, but well received by the rest of the organizing crew.

He tucked his arm around my back, and I leaned into him, placing one hand on his chest and smiling. I did a few additional poses around Craig, who stood in the same position the entire time.

Finally we could walk into the assembly hall, where music pumped so loudly from the speakers that we'd heard it all the way on the first floor. The stage was occupied by a DJ, and the space in front of it was filled with dancing students, since it was already thirty minutes into the event. I'd wanted to come early, but I'd promised Craig that dinner, and Harriet and Ziggy must have still felt guilty, because when I asked if it would be okay to come later, they practically fell over themselves to assure me that it was.

"There's Mercy and Shyanne," Craig said, dragging me directly over to our friends. What I should have done was make my rounds, greeting all sorts of people, but I was attempting to repair things with Craig, so I went along with it.

Mercy was dressed in a black one-shoulder dress with a cutout that exposed a bit of her stomach and a slit up the side that showed the perfectly moisturized sheen of her leg and the silver heels she'd paired with it. Meanwhile, Shyanne had decided to wear a white lace suit—the palazzo-style pants, the sleeves of her suit jacket, and the entire back of the ensemble was a mesh of geometric lace with a flesh-toned liner.

"You both look amazing," I gushed, which I would have said to anyone, but it was the truth with them.

Mercy shrugged, though I could tell she enjoyed the compliment. "Same to you."

"We were gonna grab a table." Shyanne pointed to one of the open spots, and we headed over to the table, which also had white and blue linens. God, the matching was suffocating. But I wasn't about to say that in meetings.

Just as we sat down, I noticed Dom and Jeremy ducking out of the room in a duo of black and neon. The last thing I wanted was for Dom to go missing during an event again. I narrowed my eyes and looked around, noticing that Dad was engrossed in a conversation with one of the other teachers, and Karter wasn't even in the room.

"I'm just going to check on my brother real quick . . ." It was out of my mouth before I could stop it.

Craig turned to me, the excited smile he had worn all night dropping off his face. "We just got here. He's fine."

"I'll just take five minutes to check on him and then be back, and we'll have the rest of the night." I pitched my voice to be as pleasant as possible, smiling like I wasn't noticing Craig's mood plummet. I'd just spent an hour and a half at dinner with him. I couldn't go for five minutes?

Shyanne cut in. "Why don't we dance for a bit, and then Sunny can go check on her brother after that and come back?"

I knew she was creating a compromise. "Does that work?" I asked Craig.

"Sure." He didn't say it with any amount of enthusiasm but led the way to the dance floor.

I prayed that Karter didn't decide to make an appearance right then. Every time she saw me dance, she would make a point to be like, "Okay, white girl, I see you!" And I had to laugh indulgently at the joke instead of snapping back that I was sorry that I couldn't distract people from my lack of rhythm with aggressive twerking the way she could. To be fair, Darren also made fun of my dancing, but it was more tolerable from him.

I suffered through the upbeat song, eyes darting to the door in case Dom came back. Maybe they'd just gone to the bathroom. They would be fine together anyway. I had only ever been targeted when I was alone. But I couldn't help but think that they'd been gone for too long.

The annoying thing was that I would know how they were doing if I didn't have to play babysitter to my clingy boyfriend. He was so hot and cold lately too. One moment he was ignoring my texts, and the next he was sending more heart emojis than I needed in a lifetime.

Mercy body-rolled close to me and whispered in my ear, "Can you at least pretend you're enjoying this instead of acting like you can't wait to leave?" She jerked her head a bit to Craig, who was grinding his teeth.

Shit. I hadn't even noticed.

"What's up with you lately?" she asked.

"Nothing, sorry," I said, forcing a grin onto my face so hard that I could feel my lips twitching.

The song ended, and Craig muttered something about the bathroom before storming off. I sighed. Great. Now he was mad.

"Guess I'll go find my brother," I said, following him out.

While Craig went to the bathroom to, presumably, calm down, I walked through the hallway and toward the library, which was now the designated chilling room. I hoped they would be in there. I hoped Dom had the sense to know that he shouldn't be wandering off to floors without chaperones.

I entered the library, which, for once, was not at all quiet. Students lounged on the furniture with drinks in their hands, talking to one another, while the librarian stood pressed against the wall with her arms crossed. She had not been a fan of this idea.

I wandered through the stacks and aisles, glancing down them and checking in corners. I was about to move on when I heard a giggle from a supply closet. I narrowed my eyes and yanked the door open, revealing Dom, Jeremy, and a giant puff of smoke with a distinct skunky odor.

Jeremy had a vape pen clutched in his hand. He smiled at me. "Would you believe me if I said this isn't what you think it is?"

I looked around quickly before stepping into the room and closing the door.

"Yo, Prez, are you gonna chill with us?"

I was trying to remind myself of why I'd decided Jeremy was actually a sweet kid and struggling with the recollection. I said, "I don't want to 'kill your vibe' or whatever, but smoking underage is the sort of thing that goes against bail conditions, you know that, right?" I looked pointedly at Dom. He had either abandoned his suit jacket or hadn't brought it, leaving him in only a bright red dress shirt and black ripped jeans.

He gestured to himself. "I'm not the one with the vape. I'm just here."

I rolled my eyes. "Please finish up and get back out there."

"Wait, wait, but, Prez, we came here for a reason," Jeremy chimed in. He had on an offensively neon green suit and his signature red headphones around his neck.

"Yes. I can see the reason." I waved at the vapor in the air.

"A *real* reason," Dom insisted.

I looked between the two of them. "What?"

Jeremy grinned. "I found something out about the symbol!"

"Something new?" I tried to sound nice and not like I was skeptical of how he could have discovered something I couldn't.

But I was clearly losing my touch because Jeremy smiled wider, like he could tell I was annoyed. "See, this is where your nature fails you, because you're such a good girl. But me . . ." He pressed his hand to his chest and wiggled his eyebrows. "I'm a bad boy."

I couldn't help it, I rolled my eyes.

Dom blinked at me in surprise, and I attempted to play it off like there was a hair in my eye that I was trying to get out. I couldn't believe I'd done that while Dom was here. Meanwhile, Jeremy's face lit up with unrestrained glee.

My brother said, "Jer, just tell her."

"Okay, okay. So at my last juvie stay, I met this kid that was, like, all about the dark web. Real underground. And the other day, I had a thought that maybe he could find something we couldn't. So I hit him up."

I looked at Dom for some sort of clue as to where this was going. He shrugged. "He hadn't actually gotten around to telling me yet. This is new to me, too."

"So what did you find?" I asked.

"So apparently, the symbol isn't just like a knockoff pentagram. It's the symbol of a thing that this group of people worshipped. It's, like, this entity? They called him the Yew Man."

"The Yew Man," I cut in, thinking of what the woman had said. "Not any other name?"

"They named him that cause the symbol is actually an arrangement of yew branches. People used to set it out in this shape to warn other villages and shit that he was coming. 'Cause yew is poisonous. But then I guess his followers adopted using it?"

Was this what the woman had meant? Beware the yew branches meaning beware this symbol. Because it was the symbol of the Yew Man or the Milk Man or whatever. "Okay, what else?"

"Yeah, so these followers, they're not really affiliated with any other religions or practices. It's kind of their own thing. They were just a random bunch of people, so maybe they were fakes, but they said when they sacrificed to him that he, like, fulfilled their dark desires." Jeremy's eyes had gotten progressively wider as he shared the information. "Messed up, right? And the sacrifices were, like, animals and even"—he paused for dramatic effect—"*people*."

"And the Yew Man is, what? Some kind of demon?" I had no idea why I was entertaining this. But it fit with what that woman had said, and she'd literally died to get me that information, which had to count for something. I wasn't believing it was supernatural or anything. But she'd been scared of this figure. It wasn't a terrible hypothesis to think that maybe the murderer was buying into this stuff too.

Jeremy shrugged. "I dunno, he's something. Apparently, he's, like, all about ruination. Other signs of his influence are, like, the spoiling of crops and stuff."

The Milk Man wants ruination. He wants to spoil the milk. Another thing the woman had said.

Suddenly I remembered that smell. The scent that had lingered over Duane's body. Why it was familiar.

It was spoiled milk.

Okay, so the killer was clearly playing into something and must have hidden rotting milk somewhere to keep in this gruesome theme. But either way, the Yew Man and the Milk Man were likely one and the same. "Was there anything else about him?" I asked.

Jeremy shook his head. "That was it."

This had done nothing but show that the person we were looking for was more deranged than we already thought they were, and that they and that woman were clearly sharing a delusion. But someone real was killing people. And I did feel like a student was still our best bet because of the school access. They would have an easier time blending in than an adult, too. Which was also unhelpful because again, the only students who seemed like they might be worshipping fake "entities" were the ones I was standing with. And I wasn't actually ignorant enough to think that clothing styles dictated people's hobbies, but not everyone thought that way. That was the problem in the first place. Why we had to look into this at all. Because people loved to assume criminal activity based off appearance.

The door to the room was pulled open, and we turned to the doorway, where Darren was standing. He raised an eyebrow at me. "Wow. Sunny. I didn't know you had it in you." Kiley giggled from behind him.

My jaw dropped. "I wasn't smoking!" I scrambled out of the closet along with Dom and Jeremy.

"Karter's looking for you, come on," Darren said to me as we walked out of the library and into the hallway.

"Why?"

Before my older brother could answer, a shrill scream echoed through the building. Then two. Then an undetermined amount.

Darren froze. Kiley pasted on a smile that didn't look right. She said, "Just kids messing around, probably."

Except now students were running down the stairs.

Dom was faster than any of us, making his way toward them. I followed after him, hiking up my skirt as I ran down the stairs. There was a group coming up at us, girls screaming, mascara running. And some of them were half-naked, dresses falling down to their waists and bikini tops underneath.

I looked back over my shoulder at the middles. "The pool," Kiley said.

We raced down the four flights of stairs to the basement door, which was supposed to be locked. But when Dom went for the knob, it turned easily.

"Look," Darren said, pointing at a piece of tape over the hole in the doorjamb where the lock was meant to slot in.

I swallowed. Someone had done that. Someone had *planned* that.

We sprinted down the hallway and threw open the doors to the boys' pool changeroom, marching through them toward the actual pool area.

Dom was still in front but stopped abruptly. I almost slammed into his back before I stepped aside to see. And once I could, I stopped too, and slapped my hands over my mouth.

I could remember each and every time I'd seen a dead body.

The first, that woman in the tent. Left to bleed out.

The second, Mom. Lying in her casket, makeup done, wearing a designer dress.

The third, Duane. Throat cut to the spine, wide eyes staring up at me.

The fourth, another woman, but one who'd tried to help. The knife protruding from her throat, in a pool of her own blood.

And now the fifth, *Ziggy*.

She was upside down, her head a foot off the floor, her legs splayed apart and her hands at her sides. Dressed in her bathing suit. A black one-piece with cutouts. Encircled by blood, drawn around her body, which was nailed to the wall. Bolts puncturing her feet and hands to keep her in place. Her throat slashed wide open and leaking blood that made a trail from her neck and dripped into the pool. And laid over it all was that faint lingering scent of spoiled milk. It clung to the back of my throat, and I had to cough to clear it.

It was so much blood.

But it was also the right amount. I knew how much blood should come out of a body. I'd sat in that dark red puddle when I was a kid. And I'd seen it again recently.

But Duane hadn't had that much around him. He'd had too little.

Harriet was huddled in a corner with her knees tucked up to her chest. Bawling while another girl tried to make her get up, sobbing herself.

I was walking over to her and kneeling down before I'd even consciously decided to do it. "Harriet? Harriet? What happened?"

She shook her head. Her fists were balled so tightly that they trembled. And between the fingers, I saw a bit of white poking out.

"Harriet . . . what's in your hand?"

"She . . . she was holding it," she whispered.

"Harriet, can I see the paper? Please?" I didn't know why I kept saying her name. I guess to keep her with me. It was what they'd said to me when they found me.

"Sunny, are you hurt anywhere?"

"Sunny, can you let us know if you're all right?"

"Sunny, please let go of the lady's hand. You need to let go, Sunny."

For a moment, I thought Harriet wouldn't do anything, then slowly she let her fist unfurl, and I took the piece of paper, smoothing it out so I could read it.

> *These bears have no claws*
> *These bears have no claws*
> *They can't fight back*
> *but when they scream*
> *they really stretch their jaws*
> *'Cause these bears have no claws*

I pressed my fist against my mouth, crumpling the note in my hand. I gave it back to Harriet, and she resumed clutching it and hiding her head in her knees.

I looked back at my siblings. Darren stumbled on the spot, stepping back and shaking his head. It was all the warning given before he threw up, the fluid slapping against the tiles.

Kiley, meanwhile, wasn't looking at him or me. She was staring at Dom, whose eyes were glued to the body. Her lip was curled, and she was stepping away.

No.

It wasn't him.

It couldn't be him.

But I could tell. Could *feel* that she thought it was.

After all, he'd been at the front of the pack. Almost leading the way.

She turned away and tended to Darren, who was dry heaving now.

"It looks like . . . ," Dom said, trailing off. "It looks like—"

"I know," I cut in. I didn't want him to say it. I looked over at Ziggy. At the way her legs were positioned and the ring of blood that stopped at her hips instead of going around her entire body. A circle with a V-shape.

The symbol.

Beware of the yew branches.

Looked like our killer was back from their break.

CHAPTER EIGHTEEN

The next day, I stood in front of Dom's bedroom door, staring at the whitewashed wood, willing myself to knock. I couldn't get Ziggy's body out of my mind. It wasn't just the gruesomeness, it was the staging. It was the way someone had used her as material in their fucked-up art project.

And Kiley. She'd looked at our brother like she couldn't believe he would do something like that, and yet, somehow, she could. I couldn't help but wonder if she knew something I didn't. Or if the difference was just that I had spent time with and gotten to know Dom over the past few months.

Finally I forced myself to reach out and turn the doorknob, slowly inching it open. I expected to be waking my brother up, but he was already awake, sitting on his bed, staring at the wall across from it. I pulled the door shut behind me.

He looked at me. "You're up early. We're on vacation." He said "vacation" with a flat voice, which felt appropriate given everything.

By design, the winter dance was held on the last day of classes before the holiday break. Something that came in handy when someone had brutally murdered a student at your school and you didn't want any of them to be inside it anymore. Dad had rushed us out to the ranch that same night, death gripping the steering wheel as he sped down the highway to Oro. Meanwhile, Karter had stayed behind to sort everything out with the police.

Now we were at the ranch, which was usually where we spent Christmas anyway. The workers who managed the operation were gone for their break too. We'd go back to Toronto in time for New Year's. Though I doubted we'd be attending any parties this year.

I settled on the bed next to Dom just as we heard a door shut somewhere else.

It was easy to hear everything in this house. It was only two stories. And it was so quiet out here with several acres surrounding the property and no one else around. The original owner who'd gifted the ranch to Grandpa had his house in the same spot, but it had burned down a long time ago. It had to be rebuilt a lot smaller than the original more mansionlike structure, and then Mom gutted it again so it could be customized to fit us all. But unlike our house in Toronto, she hadn't upgraded it. She liked that it was smaller. Humble beginnings, she'd said.

Dom and I left the room, purposely being as silent as possible. I crept close to the staircase that led directly to the front door, crouching in the corner and listening.

Mom and Dad's room was the only bedroom downstairs.

Dom kneeled behind me. He whispered, "Is it Karter coming in?"

"I don't know." Conceivably, Karter could have talked with the police all night and then headed over in the morning. But she'd seemed so exhausted lately, I couldn't see her putting herself through that just to get here for vacation. Besides, she hated the ranch. If anything, I expected her to spend as much time as possible alone at the house. But as we listened, there were murmurs that sounded male. "I think he's talking to someone outside . . ."

I tiptoed down the stairs and was thankful that they didn't creak. As I got to the bottom of the staircase, I could hear Dad moving around on the front porch, and his voice became a lot clearer.

I waved Dom down behind me, and we got close to the door.

Dad's voice filtered in from outside. ". . . How am I supposed to deal with this? Ainsley could barely deal with it, and Ainsley was . . ."

"Damn near perfect," said a man's voice. I didn't recognize it. It was gruff, but not in a way that sounded rough or unfriendly, just like it came from a big guy. "I really am sorry for you losing her. For a lot of reasons. I know what it's like to lose family. Though I know back then, well, it was a good and bad thing, I suppose, but it still hurt."

"Yeah . . . I just . . . It's a lot."

Who was this guy that just casually said his family member dying was good and bad? But then again, Darren had said the same thing about Mom.

"I honestly don't know what else I can do for you, bud. Just getting that report for Ainsley was a big ask. Wife's upset about me being involved and risking my job. But I'm here for you every other way. I never forgot you and Ainsley looking out for me. You just need to figure out what to do. Make a plan. You got kids to think about."

Dad didn't say anything for a moment. Meanwhile, I wondered what they could be talking about. It must be Dad worried about what was happening at the school. But why would he be getting advice from this random guy? Though if I was honest, it wasn't like I knew anything about Dad's friends. I didn't even think he had any. But this guy and he were talking like they went way back. He'd even gotten some sort of report for Mom that could have cost him his job.

Finally Dad said, "Mack Junior's been showing up on the security cameras. Skulking around the property. He would have never done that when Ainsley was . . . when she was here."

I searched my memory for the name and came up blank. We had cameras around the property. Mostly they were just monitoring tools. Made it easier for the operations manager to check on the herd, but they were also a just-in-case for theft or breaking and entering.

"You're damn right he didn't try this shit with Ainsley. Pretty sure he was terrified of her." The man sighed. "Fucking Feeneys. This is on them, you know? They cursed this ranch. Now Mack is always half in the bag, wandering off his skid mark piece of property next door. Wife's had to call the cops on him more than once for trespassing, which I suggest you do too. Even Shirley's given up on checking in on him. Though she's no better. She should have been locked up. Everything that happened was her fault. God knows where she is now."

"They had it rough too. And we don't know that it was her fault."

"Don't we? And who cares about them having it rough? You had it harder. You and Ainsley. Bless her soul, but my mom said some foul things about your families when she was still kicking. You all deserved that ranch after everything. Mr. Owens knew it too. Still think it should have gone to your family, but it came to you in the end."

Dad let out a little laugh. "I couldn't have handled it. After Jonas . . ."

"Yeah . . . Shit, wife is texting me about breakfast. I gotta go. But call me, okay? I don't know what to do either, but I'll listen if you want to talk."

"Thanks, Andy."

I didn't know of any Andys, Jonases, or Shirleys. I think Mr. Owens was the guy who gave the ranch to Grandpa, but that was it. Either way, I didn't have time to contemplate it all right now. I gave Dom a small shove into the kitchen and started making noise. Lifting the kettle from its perch and filling it with water.

The front door clattered behind him, and Dad peeked in on us. "Morning."

"Morning!" I chirped, all happy Sunny cheer.

Dad smiled at me and nodded to Dom. We discussed what we would do for the day and Dad helped me make breakfast. He brushed his hand over my hair, smiling at me as he did. I grinned back and chatted inanely about whatever came into my head.

But really, I wanted to know what Dad and Andy had been talking about.

Andy was right—Mack Feeney Jr.'s ranch was a dump.

It only took a few minutes of thinking back on their conversation for me to figure out where he lived. Andy said Mack was next door, and it reasoned that he was also pretty close to us if he was wandering over. Meaning he was probably one of the properties past the forested area that separated our land. And I knew the one to the right was an orchard, so he must be on the left. A property I'd never actually been near since I didn't wander far.

Dom and I tracked a path through the forest, hoping that if we started from the tree line where our house was, maybe we could end up close to where his was. Snow crunched under our feet, and I tucked my hands into my jacket pockets. The ground was littered with roots and sticks hidden under the ice, and it's not like we were following any sort of set path.

Dom was quiet beside me, his brow furrowed as he looked down at his feet. He'd been like that pretty much since yesterday, which I didn't blame him for.

I distracted myself trying to connect the dots between Mack Feeney Jr. and what was happening at the school. Our working theory was that it was a student doing this, and they clearly had something against our family. And now here was this guy who had some history with us too. I just didn't know how they could go together. Maybe Mack Jr. had nothing to do with this, or maybe he and the student were both tied into the murders somehow? Was he one of the kids Dad had written his paper about who'd bought into this symbol and had passed the torch down to some other kid who now went to our school?

"I think that's the barn? Or a shack?" Dom pointed out a structure slowly becoming visible to us through the trees. It was wooden with a barn roof and maybe once was painted white but now looked like a sad, peeling beige on top of rotting wood. "I used to wander out here sometimes. It's shittier than it used to look, but I never thought anyone lived there."

"I think that's his house . . ."

Dom jerked his head toward me. "Stop the cap! No one could live in that. Right?"

I looked around the property and saw a larger structure a little ways away. It could maybe be a cow shed or something, but there weren't any signs of life otherwise. It didn't even smell like livestock the way our property did. Otherwise, there were only a couple other collapsed outbuildings. As unfortunate as this place seemed, it was the most livable structure.

We crept closer, and I noticed the tire tracks in the snow. Which meant he had a vehicle. You needed one out here. But I couldn't see anything. I said, "I think he's out."

"And so we're . . . what?" Dom asked. "Breaking into his house?"

Was breaking and entering good-girl behavior? No. But I didn't expect anyone but Dom to catch me at this. And in his case, it could be seen as being for the good of the investigation. "No, *you're* staying here. Because breaking and entering is very much against your bail conditions. *I* am going to sneak into his house. The murderer has a grudge against the family, and it seems like Mack Junior might have some history with us too. It's a connection worth exploring. So while I do that, you keep a lookout and text me if he comes back."

Dom scowled.

"I'm sorry, would you like to go back to jail?"

His eyes widened.

Goddammit, Sunny. "I'm just worried for you," I tacked on, though even I knew it sounded insincere.

My brother smiled at me. "No, no, it's cool. I mean, I don't."

"I was just *concerned*."

"Yeah, okay."

I took a moment to steel myself. Yes, I was going into a potentially dangerous situation alone, but it was a small house that I could quickly get out of, and Dom would be on standby, so I wasn't really alone. Moreover, Mom would not have been this much of a little bitch. So neither would I.

I left Dom at the tree line and took off for the house. There were security cameras, but they were hanging with their wires exposed and clearly out of commission. I went around the back of the house and turned the knob. I was almost shocked that it was locked.

I lifted the back rug, cringing at the mess of frozen bugs underneath, and shoved the toe of my boot around until I unearthed a key. It was rusty, but it would work. I unlocked the door, then put the key back, sliding the mat over it and slipping inside.

The back door led directly into the kitchen, where dozens of dirty dishes and beer bottles were stacked in the sink and had a distinct odor to them. I wrinkled my nose. Not just at the smell, but at the peeling stick-on tile serving as a backsplash. The flooring was parquet and had clearly been there for a very long time.

I followed the hallway into a living room with sagging leather couches with stuffing peeking out and even more beer bottles. On the left were two doors. One led to a bedroom with a mattress on the floor, and the other led to some sort of office. It was filled to the brim with boxes upon boxes of papers. I stepped inside and quietly closed the door behind me.

There was a small photo on the desk that I looked at briefly featuring a white family: father and mother with three young children, two boys and a girl. I turned away and started rifling through the papers until I found a stack of newspaper articles about the ranch. And one about us, too. From the *Toronto Star* about the opening of the academy. I started taking pictures of whatever seemed relevant. A bunch of them were from the nineties about ranches in the area doing poorly. I remembered the ledger we'd found in Mom's office. Apparently, our ranch wasn't the only one having a hard time back then. I pushed aside the thoughts about the Milk Man ruining crops and scanned the other articles, looking for something that stood out.

And then I found it.

MASSACRE AT JIM OWENS'S FAMILY RANCH. 29 DEAD AND 5 INJURED.

What. The. Fuck.

I went to dig in the box for more and jostled the desk. A few items on it fell over. When I was arranging them, I noticed a different framed photo, this one of a white man and woman. And . . . I knew the woman. I gripped the frame in my hands.

Her hair was blond instead of the brunette I'd come to know her by, but it was her.

It was *the* woman. The Milk Man woman.

I fumbled my phone, making sure to take a picture of this too.

I was still reeling from finding a trace of that woman in this place when the office door creaked open. I whipped around with a gasp to find a man standing there. The man in the photo I was holding.

He was wearing a flannel jacket and a matching hat with flaps pulled onto his head. He looked like he was maybe a few years younger than Dad. But his face was more lined—they were etched onto his forehead, the corners of his eyes, and around his mouth.

"You're in my house," he said plainly.

I struggled for words. What could I even say? Why hadn't Dom texted me?!

"Do you know that your grandpa stole that ranch from us? I lost both my parents. My older brother, killed. And my sister was never the same. She can't even bring herself to live on this land. You people *destroyed* her." He practically spat the word "destroyed." And as he spoke of her, he stared at the photo in my hands. "If Owens felt bad for somebody, it should have been me."

The woman in the photo was Mack Jr.'s sister. *Shirley.* Shirley had come to warn me of the Milk Man. Shirley was *dead*, and no one but me and the murderer knew.

I swallowed. Mack had recognized me instantly. No hesitation. Meaning he'd been very recently keeping track of our family. And apparently wasn't afraid to share that he didn't like us much. "I'm ... sorry." It felt like the only appropriate response. And I *was* sorry. Just not for breaking and entering. I was sorry because actually this man had lost his entire family and he didn't even know it.

"You're not," he said simply. "But you might be one day. My family was. Maybe your mom was too. Your uncle definitely was."

What did that mean? "I don't have an uncle." Mom and Dad were both only children.

Mack Jr. broke into a laugh suddenly. It was higher-pitched than I thought it would be, and I found myself looking around for somewhere to escape. "That's funny. That's very, very funny."

What was he trying to say? That I *did* have an uncle? Why would my parents lie about something like that?

"You know, the girls all used to play a game. Go out to the woods together and talk to the trees. But only my sister stayed all fucked up over it, how's that?"

I didn't know what he meant, only that for however much he hated our family, his sister had tried to help me. "I . . . don't know."

"No . . . you don't know much of anything, do you?" He stepped closer to me, and I flinched. "Get out."

I nodded, edging past him. He hadn't quite moved out of the doorway, so I had to get close to pass. The fronts of our jackets pressing together as he stared down at me, the stale scent of alcohol wafting from his mouth.

And then I ran.

CHAPTER NINETEEN

I dove back into the trees where Dom was waiting, waving his hands like he was imitating a helicopter. I suppressed the urge to immediately scream at him that he'd done a shit job at being lookout. Except he really did look stressed. The second I was within talking distance of him, he said, "I texted you a million times! What happened?"

I pulled out my phone to check for these supposed texts and realized it was on Do Not Disturb. The setting I usually put on to go to sleep. I'd been too caught up in sneaking onto Feeney's property to turn it off. I saw a ton of texts from Dom telling me to get out of there alongside a message from Craig asking how I was doing.

I sighed. "It was still on Do Not Disturb." I waved toward the house. "Let's go."

Dom's jaw dropped. "Are you serious?"

With my phone, I double-checked the photos I'd taken and looked up the article about the massacre, and began walking toward home, glancing over my shoulder to see if Mack Jr. was coming after us.

"Hello?" Dom said, following behind me. "What happened in there?"

"He had all these articles about the ranch. Some about our family, too, who he doesn't seem to like very much."

"Okay . . . so he's been, like, researching us?"

"Or just keeping tabs on us?" I scanned over the article. "It says that on our ranch, back when Mom and Dad were kids, there was this huge fire. You know that guy who used to own the ranch whose house burned down? It was that fire. And apparently a bunch of workers were inside when it happened. They say it was set by a seventeen-year-old boy who also murdered his mother in front of witnesses. But he was a minor at the time of printing, so they don't say his name." The article did however, helpfully mention that he was suspected to be African-American.

"If you get tried as an adult, they can publish your name later," Dom said. "See if there are any more articles."

I didn't like that my brother almost definitely knew about that because it'd come up in relation to his own case.

I looked back over my shoulder, convinced that Mack Jr. was going to run out at any moment. "I'll search more at the house. Let's just get out of here first."

Dom nodded and quickened his pace alongside me. "Did he say anything?"

"Yeah, he was talking about his family being killed and his sister not being the same after."

"What does that have to do with us?"

"He's mad that we got the ranch. He says that it should have gone to him because of what his family went through." Actually, Andy had said the same thing about Dad's family. That *he* should have gotten the ranch instead of Grandpa and Mom. I knew Dad's parents had died young, and it was starting to seem like this fire was what had done it.

Dom tucked his hands into his pockets. "Isn't that a little cliché? The creepy guy in his shack killing people in the school to ruin our family's academy as revenge for us getting a business he thought he should have?"

"It's also cliché for it to be the boyfriend or husband, but that's exactly who it is most of the time." It was out of my mouth before I could think about it properly. "I mean, obviously not all the time—"

"It's fine, Sunny," Dom cut in, looking down at his shoes again.

Shit. This Mack Jr. stuff had scattered my brain. I had spent so much of my life ignoring Dom, but I couldn't stand seeing him like this. With his shoulders hunched and eyes downcast. I didn't want to be the reason for that.

Dom said, "So what about that Jonas guy Dad mentioned? How does he fit in?"

"No idea . . . Dom, I'm sorry. You know I didn't mean that you—"

"It's *fine.* Just let it go."

I let the subject drop.

And even though I'd said that, I also had trouble seeing Mack Jr. as a suspect. Sure, he gave me the ick, but that would also mean that he'd killed his own sister. But even Andy had said that she was done with Mack. Had their falling-out been that bad? Or had she just not believed in exposing him? It would make sense why she would say something like the "Milk Man" if she'd wanted me to be safe but also hadn't necessarily wanted to send her brother to jail. It would also explain how she knew this stuff was about to go down even before it started.

We broke out through the trees onto the property just as Karter was climbing out of the Escalade. She was, ridiculously, wearing red bottoms. She scowled at the snow as it touched her heels, then looked at us and her scowl deepened. "What were you two doing?"

"Just taking a walk," I said brightly, plastering a smile on my face like I hadn't just been running away from someone.

Karter frowned and jerked her head toward the house. "Dad's looking for you, Dom."

Dom blinked before nodding and heading inside.

My sister gave me a look that said she wanted to chat, so I stopped in front of her.

"How are you doing? After everything?" she asked.

"As well as I can be," I said, deciding on a tortured but brave answer. I wasn't going to tell Karter that I'd started dreaming about Ziggy hanging on the wall, Duane and Shirley underneath her, and all their eyes open and staring at me. Blaming me. Because this was about our family, and they were just collateral damage. "Did the police find anything?"

"If they did, they won't tell me. But concerned parent calls are flooding in, so we might have to delay coming back after break. I don't know." She sighed and picked at her nails. "Everything is fucked up. Was the dance fun, at least? I saw you and Craig together for a bit."

"Yeah, it was fun up until that point."

She gave me a long, searching look. "High school boyfriends are temporary, you know? I get that Mom and Dad were together since they were teenagers, but it's not the nineties anymore. A fresh start next year would be good."

Yes, that was exactly what I wanted, but thank you, Karter, for another piece of unnecessary advice. I decided to feign confusion and a tiny bit of sadness. Probably a better bit would have been to declare that Craig and I were in love, but I couldn't stomach it. Best to look unsure so I didn't have to act too broken up when we drifted apart.

Karter seemed to take the reaction as acceptance enough. She rolled back her shoulders, the cracking of them audible. "We're gonna do the thing in fifteen, so get prepped."

"The thing" wasn't the official name of our annual tradition at the ranch during holiday time, but it was close enough. We had interchangeable euphemisms that we used to describe the tradition

Mom had done with her own dad from eighteen and continued on her own into adulthood, and finally included us when Karter turned fourteen.

Our cows were sold at auction after we got them to the right weight. We never saw them die. But Mom didn't like us being that separated from the process. She felt that we should understand exactly where our money was coming from. That was the point of doing this when we were young. Usually, after weaning, when the moms were no longer needed to care for the calves, we'd sell off a bunch. Keep a few for breeding and one set aside just for this tradition. To be killed. Skinned, drained, and butchered. Then we'd eat part of it for Christmas dinner. The rest was usually frozen and used throughout the year.

We rotated through the duty as each of us turned fourteen.

"We're still doing it?" I mumbled. We'd never done it without Mom. She was the one who guided you through the process. Taught you how to work the bolt gun. Showed you how to get the carcass strung up. Stood by you when you threw up into the grass or cried with blood up to your elbows.

Who would do that now? *Karter?*

"Yeah," Karter said. "Dad said it's Dom's turn."

My eyes went wide.

It was a family tradition. But Dom never participated. Even though he was old enough to do it last year.

It felt too soon after seeing Ziggy like that. Hung like an animal. It felt like we should skip it. But this was another one of Mom's things. If we skipped it now that she was gone, would we just never do it again? Would everything she did with us just fade away?

In seventeen years, I would have been without her just as long as I was with her. And I would only be in my thirties. Not even Dad's age yet.

I didn't notice my eyes were filling with tears until they were slipping down my face.

Karter's eyes softened. "Sunny . . ."

She reached for me, but I stepped back. "I . . . I'll be there. I promise. I just need . . . to be alone for a bit." I didn't wait for her before stumbling off around the side of the property, heading straight for the tree house.

When I was ten, I decided that I wanted a tree house. I described it at length to Mom. It was going to be a small space because if it was too big, my siblings could come in. It needed to be large enough for just the two of us, Mom and me. And so it was built for my eleventh birthday.

Now I sat huddled on a floor cushion with my knees tucked up to my chest, staring at the dancing bears painted along the top edge of the walls. I didn't even understand why I was crying. I hated killing the cow. But that moment belonged to Mom. And somehow I had just realized that she wasn't ever going to help with it again. She wasn't going to be here again. Not anywhere, and definitely not in our private tree house.

Looking around the room, I noticed it was perfectly preserved, save for the slushy footprints that I'd now left. It had a set of two floor cushions and a desk tucked in the corner in case I wanted to use the space to study. And everything was clean because Mom had it built like it was a real house. No holes or cracks for animals and bugs to get in. There was even a coded lock on the door because I'd wanted privacy, and I got it.

I rose from the floor and went over to the desk. There were childhood drawings stuck to the walls alongside posters of celebrities. I didn't come in here much anymore. But Mom did. I would see her sometimes climbing up here, and then I would go join her.

Now no one had been in here for months.

On top of the desk were bear-decorated notepads and empty notebooks. I opened the drawers, looking for more memories, and found a journal. I opened it, fully expecting the pages to be filled with boring dates and times. I just wanted to see her handwriting.

I flipped back to the first entry, and the date was from late 2013. I'd been seven. It was the same year the camping incident happened. And, just as expected, there were dates and appointments and to-do lists. I sat back down on the cushion, propping it on my knees, staring at the precise black ink.

But then there was an entry that wasn't like Mom's usual. It deviated from her meticulous style and it had a sticky note attached to it that said, *Include for Sunny.* I pressed myself closer to the page, as if I needed to be less than an inch away from the paper to understand what I was reading.

05/25/2013

Karter, 10—found slicing lizards in half. Reprimanded her and she seemed to feel bad. Next week, neighborhood girl accuses Karter of biting her. Same girl's cat is also missing.

Darren, 9—saw him holding something underwater in the backyard pond. Couldn't see what it was, but it was thrashing.

Kiley, 8—found collection of dried items in her dresser drawer. Expert confirmed these were severed tongues from several types of small animals.

Sunny, 7—n/a

Dom, 5—no instances

And then below that Dom entry, in a new pen, in ink that was clearly fresher, Mom had noted:

Dom, 14—brought in for questioning regarding the murder of a girl. Andy was able to get copy of autopsy for me. Need to be vigilant to avoid another Jonas situation.

What was this? This list . . . I didn't remember ever seeing my siblings do stuff like this, and definitely not all in the same year. It was unsettling. Why would she mention the cat missing alongside Karter? Did she think Karter had killed a cat when she was ten? And that Darren was drowning something? And those tongues! Kiley couldn't even watch movies with dogs because she cried too much.

And Dom . . . Did Mom really think he did it? That he killed Torri?

But then there was also that date she'd crossed out. It was the day I'd gotten lost. . . . Why had Mom included it with all these other notes?

I turned to the next page and saw a piece of paper glued inside. I opened it to reveal a diagram of a woman, the front and back, and pen marks all over the page marking the different regions. An autopsy report. I wondered if this was the report that the guy who Dad was talking to, Andy, had risked his job to get. My eyes scanned the paper, cringing at the notes on bite marks and bruises.

But worse was what was drawn over the diagram.

It was in the same pen Mom used in the rest of the journal.

She'd played connect-the-dots with the injuries, linking one with a line to the next and the next and the next.

And the final image was a symbol. A circle and a V-shape across it.

I clasped my hands over my mouth and leaned back, letting the journal topple to the ground.

This wasn't happening. This couldn't be happening.

Why would she address this to me? Why had she wanted me to see this?

I stumbled out of the tree house. Slamming the door closed and nearly falling down the ladder.

I went into the house, but no one was there. Then I remembered. I swallowed and looked across the property to the barn several feet away. My thoughts were scattered as I made my way toward it and stepped inside the huge structure with its towering roof.

There, my family was gathered in one of the pens where a cow kept apart from the others was tied off.

"Finally," Karter said as she saw me walk inside.

I couldn't make myself say anything. I just watched.

Watched as my dad and siblings gathered around my younger brother. As he pulled the cattle bolt off its holder and checked that it was loaded before clicking the safety off. Watched as he held it between the animal's eyes. As he pulled the trigger.

I wondered then if Mom hadn't let Dom do this ritual not because she was trying to exclude him but because she was worried that he would like it too much.

Because it was clear to me now. Mom thought he'd done it.

And that he'd done it in service to a symbol that was now linked to multiple homicides. Murders that would destroy the things Mom loved the most, by a boy Mom loved the least.

Mom, who'd died a year to the day after Torri was killed.

And she'd wanted me to know.

Take care of Dom.

CHAPTER TWENTY

I had a dream about Dom butchering the cow. He was in the small wooden shed we'd designated for slaughter, and the door was just the tiniest bit open. Enough for me to see his boots and a sliver of the left side of his body, wearing gloves that went up to his elbows, colored a teal green that reminded me of hospitals. The squelching sound of blood and viscera reached my ears, and I heard the wet plop of a discarded organ being thrown in a bucket. I kept creeping closer. I was trying to be quiet, though I didn't know why. And as I got nearer, I noticed he was singing something under his breath, though I couldn't make it out yet. The sounds were too loud—the slap of organs in the bucket and the squish of blood against vinyl gloves. I was almost to the door. Now I could smell it. The scent was part manure and part thick and heady copper, like pennies stuffed in your mouth until you were gagging on them. And finally I could hear what he was singing.

> *These bears have no claws*
> *These bears have no claws*
> *They can't fight back*
> *but when they scream*

they really stretch their jaws
'Cause these bears have no claws

And then I peeked through the crack in the door, and it wasn't a cow on the table. It was Ziggy. Her bright red hair matted with blood, her eyes wide, glasses askew, and her skin so pale I could see the snaking of green veins underneath. Her ribs were cracked open, and Dom was throwing her innards into the bucket.

I pressed my hands over my mouth and backed away, and all the while, my brother sang that nursery rhyme. And I ran with it drumming in my head.

Then I woke up. And that was almost worse.

Now I stared down at my breakfast plate. Perfectly poached eggs, crisp thick-cut bacon, fresh homemade hollandaise, and neat slices of avocado and lightly sugared grapefruit on the side. Courtesy of Jerri, a Black woman a couple years older than Karter who used to go to the academy and now ran a private chef operation. Mom had hired her the last couple years to come out to the ranch and cook our meals for Christmas Eve, Christmas, and today, the seventeenth, Dad's birthday. He was forty-five.

Mom, on the other hand, would be forty-four forever.

I sliced into the egg, put it in my mouth, chewed, and smiled at Dad, who was happily cutting into his stack of French toast. I fought the sensation of the food trying to make its way back up my throat.

I hadn't looked at Dom yet. I needed time to fix my face just right.

The rest of my siblings actually seemed to be fine. Or maybe they were just making the same effort that I was. Kiley and Darren were asking Dad what he was going to buy himself now that he was old enough to be allowed a midlife-crisis purchase. Karter was making suggestions of boats, sports cars, and vacations, and hadn't even glanced at her phone once.

And finally I risked a peek at Dom. He looked . . . at ease some-how instead of sullen.

I turned away from him just as a knock sounded at the door.

We stared at it.

No one should have been coming by. Jerri'd already gone to get fresh ingredients for whatever she planned to cook for dinner and had left us with more than enough charcuterie boards and fresh pastries to last until then.

Dad started to rise from his chair, and Karter waved him back down. "I'll get it."

With how small and open concept the ranch house was, we could all see as my oldest sister walked to the front door and opened it to reveal Detective Chambers.

The food came straight up my throat into my mouth. I swallowed it back down with a choking cough.

"Sorry to interrupt," the detective said, adjusting yet another cheap blouse tucked into dress pants. The same dress pants, it looked like. "But I think we need to have a conversation."

Karter angled herself in front of the detective as if to block the rest of the family off from the officer. "It's my dad's birthday," she said, and I could hear the strain of her pushing it out between her teeth. "And it's the holidays."

"All the more reason for it." Detective Chambers was apparently not going to back down. "I've been very patient in trying to get in touch with you, Ms. Behre, but I'm afraid it's become urgent now. I would love to come in, if you don't mind."

I wished suddenly that I could see my sister's expression. I'd thought we hadn't heard from the police because they'd given up on the investigation. But the detective was talking like she'd been trying to reach Karter this whole time.

Karter stood her ground. "Well then, I'm afraid you'll have to wait while we contact Paris. Because we won't be talking without her. And please spare me the 'innocent people don't need lawyers' spiel."

"We know Dominic had access to the breakfast club room, and we're about to place him at the scene."

I stiffened. How were they going to do that? We'd been so careful. I had triple-, quadruple-checked everything. Had I missed something, or was she bluffing?

I glanced not at Dom's face but his hands. They were casual and loose around his cutlery, which he set down before his hands disappeared into his lap.

Dad got up from his chair.

"Sit down," Karter hissed without so much as a twitch of her head in our direction. "You're 'about to,' meaning you haven't, meaning you have nothing."

Dad didn't sit. But he didn't move toward Karter, either. He sort of stood in limbo, staring at the detective without moving. I wanted him to do something but I didn't know what. And then again . . . should he? Because the detective was right. Dom *was* at the scene. So was I. I'd seen him.

He said he didn't do it.

I thought of that autopsy drawing. The bruises and bite marks. How Dom had sheepishly shared that Paris had wanted to talk about those being brought up in the disclosure. How he'd dismissed that evidence. And yet the injuries culminated in the symbol the killer had been leaving at the crime scenes. The same one on Torri's headboard.

The yew branches.

I wanted to scream. It didn't make sense. Sure, in the heat of the moment yesterday I'd connected the date of Torri's death to Mom's, but there was no way. He didn't hate Mom like that. And why would he do this whole weird Milk Man thing? Why would he make me investigate this if he'd done it?

Or . . . maybe that was part of it. Getting perfect little Sunny, Mom's favorite, involved in protecting the person trying to destroy everything she'd built. Including the family who'd shunned him his entire life. And I'd helped him cover it up. I was an accomplice.

Detective Chambers's gaze shifted to me for a moment, and I tried to make myself smile but failed.

Karter stepped into the detective's sightline, blocking me from view.

Chambers said, "We have a fingerprint in the lab right now. Are you confident that it won't be his?"

"If he had access to the room, it could be a fingerprint from literally any other time."

"A fingerprint covered in Duane Mathers's blood?"

My sister stayed silent.

Detective Chambers drew herself up. "Look, let's be honest with each other, okay? I've been given a lot of shit cases over the years, and this one, it's high profile. It's easily the most important of my career. But we all know that the reason I'm standing here is because I'm seen as someone who you all might 'relate to and trust' for reasons that we know have nothing to do with me being a fantastic people person."

Karter's fingers flexed at her sides.

Chambers continued, "I want to see your family do well. Your mother did wonderful—"

"Do not talk about my mom!" Karter shrieked, and it startled me so much that I dropped my fork. A utensil that I wasn't even aware I was holding.

And then Dad was there, his hand on her shoulder, gently pushing her back toward the table. Karter's face slipped into a strange sort of shock, like even she hadn't believed it. And she actually stepped aside, hovering awkwardly between the table and the door.

Dad faced the detective. "My family and I are just trying to celebrate my birthday. Maybe it's a bit selfish to make that out as more important than the work you're attempting to do here, but it's the first I've had in a very long time without Ainsley, and I would like to enjoy it without a police officer accusing my son of murder."

Out of the corner of my eye, Dom didn't move. Not even a twitch.

"I'm not making an accusation. I'm just trying to let you know that they're closing in on him for this, and if there was ever a time to cooperate with me, it's now."

"I like that," Dad said with a chuckle. "I like how you say 'they're' closing in on us, as if you aren't the head of this investigation. You are, aren't you?"

Detective Chambers pressed her lips together and said nothing.

"'You' and 'they' are one and the same. Let's settle that first. And secondly, my daughter told you that we won't be talking without our lawyer present. So if you like, you can wait in your car while we see if she's up to traveling during the holidays. If she isn't, unfortunately, we won't be speaking at this time. And if she is, well, great luck for you, isn't it? But either way, you'll be getting off our front porch now unless you have a warrant to enter the home."

"You're going to regret this," the detective said, her voice low. "I could help you."

"Don't worry, I'm very familiar with regret. And yet I've always managed to get through it. Now, please do not make me ask again."

The detective stepped back, and Dad shut the door in her face.

I'd never been more proud of him.

Finally I looked full-on at Dom, only to find his gaze locked on his plate.

"Holy shit, Dad," Darren breathed from the table, a little laugh coming out alongside it.

Dad reached for Karter, tugging her to his side and pressing a kiss into her hair while he rubbed her back. "Don't worry about Chambers. Let's eat!" He pulled away from my sister, who shuffled back to the table in a daze.

"You okay?" I asked her, my voice a whisper, though I didn't know why. I'd never once thought of Karter as fragile, but she looked it now.

She pushed out a long breath and pressed her fingers to her temple, wincing like a headache was starting. "Yeah, fine."

Dad clapped a hand on Dom's back in that reassuring fatherly way I'd seen him do to Darren a hundred times but never my younger brother. Finally Dom's head rose. He transformed under the small gesture, his eyes crinkling and the hint of a smile coming through before he spotted me watching and twisted his lips into something more neutral.

I wondered suddenly if Dad and Karter believed Dom. If that was why they were fighting for him like this. Or if they weren't sure either.

From the way Kiley shot side glances at him, I knew she wasn't exactly sitting pretty on team "innocent," but she also wasn't saying anything about it.

Was my brother a killer? Yes or no?

And more importantly, if my goal was to protect this family, did it matter?

November 26, 1995

I feel like I'm being watched. I'm not used to having my own
bedroom. I sit in here, and it's like at any moment, the Feeneys
could come through my window. Donald. Or Mack. I want to
sneak into Dad's room, but I don't want him to realize anything
is wrong either.

I'm not making sense. I know that. I need to write down
what happened first.

We live closer to the Feeneys now, since taking over the
Poirers' place. We're nearly neighbors. I can see their house from
my bedroom. I sleep right under the window. Sometimes, I look
out and see the shadows of Mack and Mrs. Feeney arguing on
their second floor. Him shaking his hands at the heavens and her
getting in his face. Donald's window is always dark.

I was sitting on my bed when I saw Donald's window light
up for the first time and his dad went into his room. It was late,
and my dad was in bed, though he'd already been there for a
while. I watched as Mack dragged Donald out of the house, and
in his free hand was a coffee thermos.

I knew it was a bad idea, but I was hungry for something to
use against them. Something concrete to hold up as evidence.
So I pulled on my shoes and followed them into the forest.*

---

* This is what I would call good instincts. It might not be scientific, but following
your gut is not always wrong. As long as you, unlike what I did here, actually create
a plan to follow.

Donald was like an animal. Snapping at his dad with his teeth and muttering how he would tear him apart and gnaw on his bones. It was like something out of a horror movie. I half expected Mack to pull out a cross or something to keep his son at bay. Instead, he just snapped that he didn't want his wife to see her son like this.

I wondered if that was what they kept arguing about. About whatever was wrong with Donald.

Mack kept dragging Donald along, and I had to weave around the trees while staying back a safe distance.

He finally got his son into a clearing and pushed him down. And then he took out the thermos and forced Donald's mouth open and started pouring this stuff in. He was muttering something about how he "couldn't keep waiting" and this would "tide him over," whatever that means. Some of the liquid splashed onto Donald's lips, and I squinted at it. It was too thick and dark to be water. On God, it was blood. I know it was.

That was also when I knew I had made a mistake. I shouldn't have been there. What if they found me? I stepped back, and a twig broke under my foot.

They'd heard it. I knew from the way their heads snapped up and turned. Like wolves sniffing at the air.

I panicked and ran, darting through the trees, hearing Mack yelling about who was there.

And Donald, I swore that he growled. Like some sort of beast. Something inhuman.

I ran faster.

The trees weren't familiar anymore. I started to feel like I wasn't going the right way somehow, even though I'd grown up on this land. I tripped and fell, and as I scrambled to get up, someone tugged me by the back of my jacket and slapped their hand over my mouth.

Instinctively I bit down and heard a voice I recognized swearing and asking me to stop.

It was Jay.

Apparently, he'd been coming back from hanging out with Andy and saw me following Mack and Donald into the forest. I was about to tell him that I didn't need his help when we heard a crack of branches.

We ducked down, trying to keep still.

Donald wandered out of the trees, licking his lips lazily and chuckling. Practically singing for us to come out, come out, wherever we were. I'd never seen him like that. He was ... different. He'd been different for a while. He said that he could smell our sweat, could tell we were shaking.

And the worst part was that I <u>was</u> shaking.

I didn't notice until Jay pulled me closer to him, against his solid unmoving chest.

As Donald got closer, I started to notice a scent. Thick and ripe. I pressed my hand against my lips so I wouldn't gag. We didn't run a dairy ranch, but I knew it all the same. Rotting milk. Sour. I wondered how long he'd gone without bathing that he smelled like that.

I didn't know Donald anymore. I couldn't predict what he would do if he found us. He was practically on top of us, he was so close. I found Jay's hand and squeezed it. Meanwhile, he began to push me to the side, getting in front of me like he was really planning to fight Donald. Jay, who was maybe half his size.*

Then Mack broke through the trees and hauled his son back

---

* Your father used to be brave.

by his collar. Donald really bit his dad that time. Like, actually closed his mouth down on his hand. Without any hesitation, either.

Mack backhanded his son with his free hand so hard that I flinched.

Donald dropped to the ground and started moaning, and then crying. Sobbing. He'd gone from a beast to a baby in an instant.

His dad pulled him over and thrust the rest of thermos his way and commanded him to drink it.

Donald took it in both hands and chugged it down until it was empty.

Mack nodded, satisfied. He pulled Donald back toward their house, but not before looking around once more.

It took another few minutes for me to calm down, and a nudge from Jay that we needed to bounce before I finally got moving toward home. Jay made sure to walk me right to the door and watch me go in. It felt colder now that I wasn't pressed up against him. I said good night and thanked him.

And then, once I was alone in my room, I cried.

November 27, 1995

Today, I dragged Jay to my house as soon as I could. Andy wiggled his eyebrows and made a big thing out of us going to hang out together, which I ignored. He's always doing shit like that with us. I hate it because I can tell it makes Jay feel embarrassed. I guess the idea of being with me is embarrassing. Though before we left, Jonas said he would come with us too, which at least shut Andy up. I'm glad he had to help in the fields so he couldn't tag along.

Dad was out working, so he wasn't home when the boys came over. It was weird for a moment because they hadn't been allowed to see me for so long. Still weren't allowed, technically. Jay seemed the same but maybe a bit weighed down, but Jonas acted like he had a boulder on his shoulders. He hunched them and stared at his feet. But he'd still wanted to help, whatever helping meant.

We sat down in our now much larger living room. Jay jumped right in to tell me that I shouldn't have been out there. ~~I wanted to ask Jay why he hadn't worked harder to keep me in his life.~~ I caught Jonas up on what was going on. How I'd been observing the Feeneys, specifically Donald. Then I told them both that Donald had been drinking blood.

I wanted them to understand that there was something wrong with these people we were living with. Who were in charge of the ranch. But all I got back were skeptical looks. I suggested reporting them to the police.

Jay questioned why they would believe some black girl who didn't even have real proof. No samples. And it also wasn't illegal to drink blood, it was just . . . though he didn't have the words to complete his own sentence.

I knew he had a point. And so then I decided that we would get the evidence. After all, what if it was human blood? What if they'd hurt someone? <u>That</u> was illegal. The police would be able to figure it out if they had a sample. Even so, being charged with breaking and entering wasn't something I thought universities appreciated about their applicants. But I knew what I'd seen and what I needed to do.

Jonas was frowning, so I told him that he didn't need to come, Jay either. But it was obvious that they weren't going to let me do it alone.

We waited until we were sure no one was inside the house. Mrs. Feeney was off taking Mack Jr. on a walk, the Feeney kids had after-school jobs on the ranch, and Mack was still working.

I pulled on a pair of my winter gloves, checked that the plastic bag I brought was still in my pocket, and crept toward the house. Jay stayed a ways back on lookout, ready to make warning noises if needed, and Jonas came along with me to help search. Jay would attract less attention than his older brother as a lookout, so it was the better arrangement.

The back door was unlocked. None of us locked them. Lots of people thought it would be rude. On Mr. Owens's ranch, we were all family, and you didn't lock doors to family.

The first place I checked was the sink in case they'd already washed the thermos. Which actually doesn't matter. I saw on Cops that when people try to clean up blood, it leaves traces. You need the right kind of bleach to get it off. And it's not like the Feeneys would be washing their dishes with that. So I could still send it to the police.

But it wasn't there. I frowned and looked around, backtracking.

When I turned, Jonas was still standing by the back door, holding a thermos.

I immediately got excited, telling him that was the one.

He peered inside, and then something strange happened. His eyes went wide. Bigger than I'd ever seen them stretch. I had to ask him what was wrong three times before he finally looked at me.

Jay poked his head in the door to tell us to hurry up.

I reached out my hand to Jonas. He swallowed before handing the thermos to me. I made sure to rub the outside with my gloves to get any of his fingerprints off. I wasn't sure that would work but I'd tried. I tossed it into the plastic bag and we left, running away as fast as we could.

When we got back to my house, Jonas sat heavily in a chair, staring at his lap.

I opened the thermos, expecting blood. What else could have shaken him up like that? But instead of redness, it had a thin white coating that I would know anywhere. Milk. Though I swore that it was a little pink.

I threw a questioning look at Jonas. He asked me if this had anything to do with the Milk Man.

I didn't get it. Why was he asking about Shirley's little game? But when I said that, Jonas just shook his head and said he needed to go. Jay offered to come with him, but he waved his brother off, saying he wanted to be alone.

Jay and Jonas were basically attached at the hip. Best friends more than brothers. But from the way Jay looked at Jonas's back, I got the feeling that Jonas had wanted to be alone a lot lately. When I asked Jay what was wrong with Jonas, he'd said nothing. Absolutely nothing. Only he couldn't say the same for his parents. They were still being strange with him. Their dad . . . and that was when Jay cut himself off.

Their dad had done something to Jonas, but Jay didn't want to say what it was. Not even to me. Instead, he turned my attention back to the thermos.

Writing this now, I still don't get it. I don't know if I was wrong and it was never blood, or if Mack emptied it out, then had a big ol' serving of milk inside instead. Maybe that's why it was kinda pink?

Either way, I still packaged it up with a note that I wrote with my left hand so my handwriting wouldn't be detected. I had to take one of the big mailers Dad had lying around, but he wouldn't notice. He was so out of it these days. I didn't put a name or return address on the package either. It needed to be anonymous.

Jay gave me a long look as I put it in the mailbox, asking if this was really about everyone's safety or if it was about my dad getting Mack's job.

I didn't appreciate the suggestion. Instead, I asked if he wasn't worried about the way Donald was acting, and all the kids who had been getting sick after him. What if he was spreading something? What if it was catching?

Everything seemed to start with him.

But actually, everything had started with Shirley. I'd never forgotten that lizard. And now I was remembering how Jonas had mentioned her game like it meant something. It had felt like something was starting then, and now here we were. And yes, I had no love for the Feeneys, and even though Dad has a better job now, he deserves the one Mack has. But I know there's something rotten about that family.

I asked Jay if something was wrong, because he just kept staring at his shoes. He shook it off and went home.

It was only after he'd left that I wondered if he was still thinking about Jonas.

But when I tried to bring it up again, Jay didn't want to talk about it.

~~At least he was talking to me at all.~~

CHAPTER TWENTY-ONE

Dad standing up to Detective Chambers had felt like a high, but things only went downhill from there. Something had gotten into the shed where the cow carcass hung and left the door open, and other animals had taken advantage and torn it apart. There were bite marks and gouges in the flesh that reminded me of Torri's autopsy report.

Following that, Christmas Eve and Day had been its own waking nightmare of pretending to be cheerful while Mom wasn't there. We'd all gone to bed at six just to avoid one another. And then New Year's Eve came. Usually we went back home to Toronto and attended several events. It was our big start to the year. But this time, we stayed at the ranch in our rooms, gathering briefly for the countdown, where I exhausted myself shouting down the numbers and waving my noisemaker alone.

The next day, Karter announced to academy parents via email that the school would be opening, as usual, next Monday, and for the first time, there would be visible safety measures. Backpacks would be searched upon entry, private security would be on-site, only one entrance/exit would be operational, and after-school programs would be canceled until further notice. And then we packed up our things and started the drive home.

So when, an hour or so later, the Escalade pulled around the corner and our house came into view surrounded by police cars, somewhere in the back of my mind, I wondered if I'd expected it. It was just icing on the shit cake that had been building since the dance.

"What the fuck?" Darren breathed, leaning forward in his seat to get a better look.

Karter didn't even take a second before she started barking at Dad to text Paris, slowing our approach to a crawl.

I glanced over at Dom, who stared silently out the window. It had been weird for us on our vacation. Ever since I discovered what was in Mom's journal, I hadn't been able to act normal around him. In fact, I'd been avoiding the entire investigation altogether, feigning sickness or running off to the tree house. I got the impression that Dom had picked up on my energy, because he'd gone back to existing how we normally did. He didn't smile or nod at me when I entered the room. Didn't knock on my door to try to chat. He barely looked at me at all.

Now I thought about reaching over and holding his hand. Or patting his arm. Doing something reassuring. I should do it. Not just because it was the Sunny thing to do, but because I wanted to.

But instead I was thinking about those bite marks on Torri's body.

The first police car in our driveway flared their siren. That quick burst of sound that was meant to be a warning.

Karter stopped the SUV alongside the curb in front of the house. She took a deep breath and said, "Stay inside. Hands visible. Keep quiet unless spoken to. If you're asked to get out, do so slowly. But remember, we are not criminals."

With that, she rolled down the window and smiled as an officer came over. "Happy New Year. What can we help you with?"

The guy wasn't having any of the pleasantries. "We have an

arrest warrant for Dominic Behre." He peered into the vehicle and spotted Dom. "Please step out of the vehicle, son."

I resented the use of the word "son," like this guy gave a shit about us. Like he would ever treat us like family.

"Stay put for now," Karter said to Dom as his hand inched to the car door. To the officer she said, "Under arrest for what?"

"For murder in the first degree of Duane Mathers."

To her credit, Karter moved on without a single pause. "You're taking him to the Division Twenty-Two station?"

"Yes. Get out of the car, Dominic."

Dom looked at our older sister, who nodded. Slowly he opened the door and leaned away.

Before I could stop myself, my hand reached out and clasped onto his fingers. The quick movement made the cop jerk, and I flinched. But I didn't let go. I kept hold of my brother.

"Sunny," Karter said, her voice gentle when I expected her to snap. "Let go of him."

I looked into my brother's eyes and felt tears flooding into my own.

No. I didn't want him to go there. He should be home with us. I didn't know what I thought anymore. If he'd done it or not. But I didn't want them to have him. I didn't want him alone in a cell.

"It's okay," he said. "I'll be okay."

I gripped his fingers harder, and then . . . I let go.

Dom got out of the car, and the police swarmed, telling him to put his hands up and turn around. They pressed him against our vehicle while they read his rights and put cuffs around his wrists.

And we watched, for the second time in our lives, as my brother was put into the back of a police car and driven away.

Karter and Dad hadn't even gotten out of the Escalade. Dad had just told me and the middles to go inside, and that they would text when they had more information. We'd listened and watched out of the glass windows as they took off to the station, where they would probably meet Paris.

Kiley had ordered us Vietnamese for lunch, and the three of us sat in the living room, waiting for the order to come. In silence. When it did finally arrive, Kiley methodically unpacked the dishes and laid them out on the coffee table instead of the dining table, moving the bear bowl to the floor.

I wanted to shove everything off and put the bear back in its spot.

"I can't take it anymore," Darren said, turning on the TV.

Kiley snapped at him. "Don't."

"We have to know what's going on."

I put a fresh roll in my mouth and chewed, trying to distract myself with the flavors. Meanwhile, my brother selected YouTube on the TV and started playing a news report. The headline read: POLICE FINALLY MAKE AN ARREST FOR A SERIES OF GRISLY PRIVATE SCHOOL MURDERS.

The newscaster was out in front of the school. Our school. And with him was a group of women holding signs that said, DON'T LET HIM COME BACK! And PROTECT OUR CHILDREN! And TIME TO BEHRE THE TRUTH!

"Really? A pun?" Darren grumbled.

But I was barely listening to him because I recognized one of the women. Her dark hair was still cut in the same short bob style. I remembered her stare that had followed us from Dom's first bail hearing. Marsha Allen. Torri's mom. She was clearly the leader of the group of mostly white women, though I did spot a couple women of color, specifically Duane's mom. Ziggy's mom was there too, marked by the same red hair her daughter'd had, tears running down her face.

The newscaster said, "I'm here at Behre Academy, a private

school located in the Etobicoke region that only accepts needs-based scholarship students. Every year, hundreds of teens apply to get into one of the city's highest-ranked secondary schools. However, this year has been overshadowed by fear and tragedy. In early October, young Duane Mathers was found brutally slaughtered in a hallway, and only weeks ago, Penelope "Ziggy" Moore was also found dead at a school dance. And now a suspect has been arrested in connection with Duane Mathers's murder." I noticed that he was carefully dancing around mentioning who had been arrested because, legally, he wasn't allowed to.

He gestured to Ms. Allen. "I'm here with Marsha Allen, a concerned mother with two children at the school, who lost her own daughter not too long ago. Ms. Allen, why are you out here today?"

"I'm here to protest the administration of this school. They have not done nearly enough to protect the students. You won't say it, but I will: the boy who was charged attends this school and is already on trial for the murder of my daughter, and they let him attend knowing he was dangerous because it's their own son!"

The middles and I turned to each other at the exact same time. Apparently, this shit cake needed a cherry on top. Dom and I were the only Behres who were currently students. She may as well have just said his name. "They shouldn't have broadcasted that," I said.

Kiley bit her lip. "It was live."

"I'm texting Paris," Darren said.

I turned back to the screen, where the newscaster appeared nervous about what Marsha had declared but didn't say anything in opposition.

Ms. Allen sucked in a deep breath, holding back tears. "These are very powerful people. And my sons need this school. There was an implication that if I was vocal, my kids would lose their spot. But no more! There's been too much death. They need to be stopped!"

"I'm sorry, did I miss something?" Darren snapped. "Who was implying that?"

"No one," I said. I had to believe that. I had to believe that even Karter wouldn't have weaponized the academy just to keep Marsha quiet. The *law* was supposed to keep her quiet. Though apparently that wasn't enough.

The clip cut back to the newsroom, where they said some spiel about Marsha's statements being allegations that have yet to be proven.

"Thank you!" Darren shouted. "But too fucking late!"

The newscaster continued by saying police would only confirm that they had a suspect in custody and that the suspect was a minor. Which basically confirmed it without confirming it.

"So much for unbiased reporting," Kiley said, staring at the screen. "And that's defamation, isn't it? We could sue her. Honestly, that's already enough identifiable information to show she's broken the law anyway."

We both looked over at Darren, expecting him to say something, but he was staring at his phone. He said, "Oh, she's done a lot more than that."

"What?" Kiley turned to him. I was looking too.

He showed his screen to her and then to me. "She's named him."

There was a string of tweets that seemed miles long with Ms. Allen detailing that Dominic Behre was the boy in custody and that she wouldn't be silenced any longer. That she wanted justice for her daughter and wouldn't let the one percent stifle her voice.

And there it was. My brother's name and face splashed all over the internet. And of course people would believe it. Even if the charges were dropped or there was irrefutable proof that he was innocent, this would follow him forever.

Tears slipped down my face, and I brushed them away, but it wasn't helping.

The people in the newsroom added, "There is a group of concerned mothers calling for the Behre family to step down as the
administration of the school and to hire an unbiased board of trust-
ees to handle the affairs of the institution. They're also calling for
justice for their children, whose alleged killer they want to see punished to the full extent of the law and tried as an adult."

Darren was still scrolling through the Twitter thread, and at the
same time, I could see notifications popping up on his phone. They
were filled with death threats, thinly veiled racist comments, and
requests for us to kill ourselves.

"Stop," Kiley said, putting her hand over the phone.

Darren turned and glared at her, and she glared back.

"She's right," I said through my tears. "You should turn your
notifications off."

"We have to know what they're saying about us."

"Do we?" Kiley pushed. "Because we already know it's nothing
good."

There was one more long staring contest before Darren pitched
his phone across the room, where it landed with a dull thud. He
leaned back into the cushions and put his arm across his eyes.

Kiley sighed and reached for her rapidly cooling bowl of pho. She
gestured to me. "Eat."

So I ate.

I needed to tell them. I needed to tell someone what Dom and I
had been doing this whole time. I needed to share what we'd learned
so far so that it could help. But then . . . what did we actually have?
Some haphazard information without any real evidence? The word
of a woman no one but me even knew was dead? Meanwhile, the
police had been building a case against Dom this entire time.

He *had* been there. He had touched the body. He had tampered with evidence. We both had. And we'd slipped up somewhere. The fingerprint that Detective Chambers warned us about. How was what we had supposed to compete against that?

And what if I was wrong? What if I was protecting my brother when all along, he was exactly where he was supposed to be?

At some point we had fallen asleep, because I found myself waking up to the smell of food that now had a more stale than inviting scent. I blinked at the middles, who were sprawled out on the couch, still asleep. And then I noticed that my pocket was vibrating. I pulled out my phone, which said, *Private Caller*, and answered it.

"Hello?" I stood up from the couch and walked away from my sleeping siblings toward the pool room.

"Hey." The voice was muted, but I recognized it as Dom.

"What's happening? Are you okay?"

"What was up with you at the ranch?"

I was thrown off for a second. "What . . . ?"

"I keep thinking about it, so I figured I would just ask. I get a phone call, after all. We were good. But then it's like you closed up. What happened?"

I swallowed. "Nothing," I said, forcing my voice to be bright. "I just—"

"Stop that," he said. "Stop pretending. Stop lying. Stop all that bullshit. Just tell me the truth. I've told you everything. You wanted me to open up, so I did. Did you change your mind? Is it because of what happened with Mack Junior? Did he do something to you?"

"No . . . I just . . ." I could lie, like I always did. But if I wanted him to be honest with me, didn't that mean I should be honest back? "I found a journal from Mom . . . She . . . she had notes on your case . . ."

There was a long silence. It was drawn out, and I didn't fill it. "She thought I did it, didn't she?"

"I . . . I don't know what she thought."

"Stop. Lying. You *do* know. And you believe her, don't you? That's why you don't want to help anymore. You're just going to leave me here. Even when she's dead, you'd rather take her side than mine."

"I don't know what I be—"

"I can never do enough for you! For any of you! No matter how hard I try, you all just see me as this . . . this . . . this *thing* in your house. Am I even human to you?!" His voice was sharp and spitting, but also breathy and broken. "If it were anyone else, if it were Kiley, or Darren, or Karter, you would believe them. But because it's me, you don't."

"Dom—"

The call cut out, and the line went dead.

CHAPTER TWENTY-TWO

The academy was officially a shit show. It was the first day of the new term, and I sat in a purposely nondescript Toyota Yaris with Karter at the wheel, the windows tinted within an inch of their lives. She had insisted on driving me because, and I quote, "You'll get mobbed the second they see you, and you're too annoyingly polite to ignore people, so you can't be left alone." I sat in the back while Dad was in the front with my sister.

Karter drove slowly past the entrance of the school to get a look at the chaos. It'd been a week since Dom's arrest, *and* we were two hours early. It didn't matter. The same group of moms from the news was outside the school with signs held high, fueled by coffee in unbranded cups from the bakery around the corner. Including Marsha Allen.

"Look at her," Karter sneered. "Dom's case had a press hold on it and should have been confidential. Allen violated that order and should be in custody. But here I am, looking at her and her ten-dollar dye job. You think that's a coincidence? That our brother is in jail and she's walking free?"

I didn't answer because I assumed it was rhetorical. I hunched in on myself.

I hadn't heard from Dom again since that initial phone call. I'd contacted the juvenile center where he was being held to request a visit with him, only to be told that he'd declined to meet with me.

It just felt so ridiculous now. Had I really thought my little brother had gone to Pearson Airport in the middle of the night to murder our mom and make it look like she slipped on ice? Could I actually picture Dom, who'd spent his free time watching animated characters with superpowers, drugging his problematic girlfriend who he sincerely seemed to like and letting her drown, or even drowning her himself? More than that, Dom, who'd glowed because Dad patted him on the back, was supposed to be the same boy who'd sliced Duane's throat to the bone and nailed Ziggy to the wall to get revenge on all of us?

He was right. I hadn't given him the benefit of the doubt the way I would have for my other siblings. Mom was gone, but Dom was right here. He'd needed me, and I'd let him down, only realizing after how wrong I'd been. I'd let some words on a page shake my faith in a brother I'd finally gotten to know these last few months. I *knew* Dom. And he wouldn't have done any of those things.

"There won't be a press hold for much longer," Dad said, his voice barely above a whisper. "With this charge, they'll try him as an adult, won't they?"

"It doesn't matter," Karter snapped. "She violated that order when it was supposed to be in effect. If they're so eager to dole out punishment, it should go both ways. But it clearly doesn't. I don't even think they've charged her yet, and Paris is busy with Dom's stuff, but rest assured, she will get to it."

Dad sighed and shrunk in his seat. He didn't look good. His hair was grown out way more than he usually kept it with tufts of curls poking up here and there, and he seemed to exist in a permanent slouch position.

I gathered what little energy I had and asked, "Paris will clear up things with Dom, won't she?"

I met Karter's eyes in the rearview, but she didn't say anything. Just looked away.

The smile on my lips twitched, trying to stay in place.

In an attempt to double down on helping the brother I'd disappointed, I'd finally looked up the kid from the ranch massacre who was charged as an adult and given the maximum sentence of twenty-five years for each of the twenty-nine victims, to be served consecutively. Meaning, he was never going to get out of jail. His name was Jonas Turner, and he'd died in 2013. I'd assumed he was the same Jonas who Dad and Andy were talking about, who was also mentioned in Mom's journal. And if the "Jonas situation" was the massacre, it did nothing but confirm that Mom thought Dom was comparable to a guy who'd murdered a bunch of people when she was my age. Meaning it was not at all helpful in proving that Dom shouldn't be in jail. Another dead end.

I still didn't know how to feel about Mom thinking he'd done this, so I'd chosen to avoid thinking about it at all. My priority was to help Dom.

"At least security is in place," Dad said, looking at the people trying to get the protestors to move to the side of the front steps so they wouldn't block the entrance. Through the glass doors, I could see the two tables set up with security behind each so they could check student bags as they came in.

As Dad scanned the crowd, he froze. I followed his sight line and saw the man right away. He had been at the back of the group, so it was hard to see him at first. But there he was. Mack Feeney Jr. standing with the moms when he had no real reason to be there except for hating us.

My breath started to come faster. Why was he here suddenly? I wondered if he'd somehow figured out that his sister had died at the school. Though the flip side was that he'd killed her.

"What's he doing here?" Dad asked Karter.

My sister immediately glanced back at me and then away. "He's just a rubbernecker."

"Who's that?" I asked, not because I wanted to know, obviously, but because it would have been weird if I didn't ask.

"No one," Karter said. Meaning that she probably also knew about Mack Jr. and his apparent hate for our family.

Karter pulled the car around the block and went behind the school, parking on a residential street, likely planning to hustle us through the park and across the school field. Students were only supposed to enter in the front, but I guess we were bending the rules. The whole undercover operation was pointless in the end because the second we got out of the car, press swarmed.

Dad put his arm around me and hugged me to his side, hunching over to help shield me from the reporters. Karter's expression was steely as she stood in front of us, leading the way through the park.

"Mr. Behre! What do you have to say about the allegations against your son?!"

"What are you doing to protect the students at the school?!"

"What do you have to say about the theory that your wife's death wasn't an accident?!"

I whipped my head around when that final reporter spoke, my eyes wide. A camera flashed in my face. Karter reached back and tugged me forward.

I ducked my head back down and followed my dad and sister onto the school field, where the reporters dutifully stopped. The academy was private property, and they had no right to be on it.

Karter swore and took off toward the building so fast that she left Dad and me behind. He still had his arm around me, clutching me to his side.

He was trembling.

I peeked up at him and almost stumbled away. The look of unbridled fury on his face made the hairs on my arms tug to attention. "Dad? Are you okay?"

He blinked, and his expression smoothed out. "What? Yes. I'm fine." He stopped and pulled me into a proper hug, tucking his chin on top of my head. I could hear more shutters going off. "It's going to be okay. Everything will be okay." He pulled back, his hands on my shoulders, and looked me in the eyes. "Where's that smile, eh?" I ripped my lips into my signature Sunny grin, and Dad smiled back. "That's my girl."

He put his arm back around me, and we continued on our way to the building.

But I couldn't get what that reporter had said out of my mind.

"What do you have to say about the theory that your wife's death wasn't an accident?!"

I knew Dom hadn't done this, but whoever the murderer was, the fact that Mom died on the anniversary of Torri's death kept sticking in my mind. Whoever we were dealing with cared about symbols and ceremony. They were worshipping this Milk Man, but also calling themselves the Milk Man? Or Shirley was calling them that, anyway. But, yes, this was about attacking my family for some reason, but it was also about this entity. It felt like if the symbol was relevant, why not the date, too?

The murderer had made it clear that they didn't like digging, and Mom had dug. She'd been looking into Dom's case. Shirley had mentioned her too. I forced myself to think back and remember what she'd said . . . Wasn't it that she'd tried to get in touch after Mom died? Why had she specifically mentioned that? Why not get in touch before Mom died, considering that this shit had started with Torri when Mom was very much alive? Why wait? The murderer hadn't done anything really but scare me, but that didn't mean they'd never done more to a different Behre. To Mom.

I shook my head. *No.* Hadn't I just said today that I needed to help Dom because he was here, and Mom was gone? I needed to focus on that, not on some random crap a photographer had yelled to get a rise out of us. Besides, if it was all connected, helping Dom would also help me figure out if Mom had been targeted.

Once we were inside the academy, Dad made a beeline for his office. He opened the door and turned to me, but I was looking down the hall where Mom's, now Karter's, office was. Even though he was supposed to be the principal. Typical. "Coming?" he asked.

"Yeah, I just wanted to check on Karter."

Dad nodded and retreated into his safe space. Normally, I would have gone with him, but I needed to know more about what was happening with Dom and his case. If the Crown really had enough evidence to convict him.

I walked down the hall into the main office and went past the desks there to the door near the back of the room. I opened it, and Karter jerked her head up, tears in her eyes.

"Ever heard of knocking?!" she snapped, wiping her face.

"Sorry . . ."

Karter sighed and moved from the desk to collapse onto the couch off to the side of the room. The many windows that Mom had usually left uncovered for the natural light had shades pulled over them. I hadn't been in the room since Karter had taken it over. It was pretty much the same. The big desk in the corner with its array of little plastic, wooden, and clay bears that Mom had been gifted over the years. Her massive leather chair. Even the journals on the desk were the same, like the ones in the tree house. I think Mom had a whole set of blanks. I'd noticed Karter using them too. I thought again of the sticky note I'd found in Mom's office and what it might have been attached to. It must have been a journal of some kind. Like how Mom had put the sticky note in the tree house journal.

It didn't matter. I had to help Dom, not prove that Mom picked me. Especially now that the tree-house journal had made me confused about what exactly she'd wanted me to do.

"It doesn't even make sense." I gestured vaguely like that would explain it. "Dom wouldn't do these murders and endanger our family like that." It was what I should have said to my brother when he called.

Karter shrugged. "Law isn't about motive. It's about evidence. And they've got a bloody fingerprint from Dom. They can place him at the scene. It's a lot more concrete than what they have on him for Torri; it's why they can do first-degree now. Besides, it's not like we were ever the best family to him. Would you blame him if he wanted to destroy us?"

"He wouldn't do that."

"You'd be surprised what people will do."

I swallowed and shook my head. "You can't really think he would."

"That's not what I said. I just said, you couldn't blame him if he had." Her voice dropped lower as she said, "This is a fucked-up family, after all. I know you all hate me."

Well, that was out of left field. "We don't hate you."

Sure, Karter was a bitch, but she'd always been like that. And yeah, I didn't think she was the right leader for the family—she wasn't who Mom had wanted—but she hadn't done terribly. Sometimes she'd even done well. Besides that, she was still my big sister. She'd helped me tie my first wiggly tooth to the door and shut it to get it out. And yes, she'd laughed at me freaking out, but she'd also wiped away my tears and taught me about the tooth fairy. And I knew for a fact that the tube of lipstick that appeared under my pillow along with the money was her contribution. It was the exact shade I'd admired from Mom's collection. She'd stolen it for me and also took the heat when Mom discovered it was missing. She was my sister, and I loved her.

"Don't lie," Karter muttered, and abandoned her spot on the couch to start pacing the room. "Just . . . stay here until class starts." She stopped moving to type furiously on her phone.

Fine by me. I wasn't about to go wandering the halls by myself. "What are you doing?"

"Seeing what Paris is doing about getting the woman who splashed our brother's name all over the internet in a jail cell where she belongs. She promised that Allen wouldn't pull this shit."

While my sister returned to pacing, I sat in Mom's office chair. Against my better judgment, I checked my phone. Most of the group chats I ignored, but I looked at the one with Mercy, Shyanne, and Craig. Just them asking about me. Me not responding. That was bad. I needed to say something. But Karter via Paris told us not to. After all, they might get warrants for our phones, and once that happened, they could twist around anything we had in there.

I stopped at one message.

Shyanne: I really feel some type of way about Allen outing Dom's name like that

Craig: cause Ms. Allen is racist?

Shyanne: yes!

Mercy: how do you know?

Shyanne: him and Torri lived in the same apartment building in middle school, remember?

Craig: yeah

Mercy: I forgot about that!

Craig: we used to hang out sometimes and her mom would say a lot of messed up shit

Mercy: that why you stopped hanging with Torri?

Craig: kind of. She got weird. Goth and stuff

Shyanne: so the alternative fashion is what turned you off? Not the racism? 🫠

Craig: come on, that's not what I meant

I looked over at Karter, who was still texting, her eyes narrowed at the phone. I typed out a private message to Craig:

You knew Torri? You never said anything about it

He texted back immediately, like he'd been waiting for the message.

Are you serious?! Why tf would I say anything about knowing Torri? You didn't tell me your brother got charged with murder!

> It was a private family matter

> You can't be serious. Then why are you asking me questions then? If it's so "private"?

What was his problem? I was so tired of his moodiness. Was I seriously taking this from Craig of all people?

I typed gibberish, then untyped it. Knowing that he was seeing the typing dots come on and off. I typed random letters again, then untyped them. Paused and counted to ten. Then typed and untyped.

Craig broke first.

> I'm sorry. I know you've been having a rough time. I didn't mean to be insensitive or anything. It's just like, I've been texting you all Christmas break, and you didn't respond at all, and then now you finally do, and it's just so you can ask me about this thing connected to your brother? Like, that doesn't make me feel good.

I rolled my eyes. I wanted to feel bad for Craig, I really did. But I didn't. I knew his life wasn't sunshine and daisies—he literally had brothers in jail. Maybe this situation should have been bonding or whatever, but it just felt like he was once again making something in my life all about him. And if he hated me so much, why wouldn't he just break up with me?!

Shouts rang out, and Karter's head jerked up. "What now?"

She rushed out of the office, and I followed behind her. The shouting was coming from the front hall. When we entered it, the group of moms led by Marsha Allen had come inside the school and were arguing with the security guards.

"You cannot be on private school property," Karter said, her voice firm and loud. "You can protest, but you need to stay outside."

"As parents of students at this school, we have a right to be in the building. And since you won't talk to us outside, maybe you'll talk to us inside."

"If you would like to talk, make an appointment."

Ms. Allen gritted her teeth and glared at my sister. "You think that just because you're rich, you can do whatever you want. That boy should never be let out. He's a little beast is what he is. All of you. Monsters with money."

I knew that that was truly how she saw Dom. As less than human. An animal. But she was the one practically foaming at the mouth.

Karter said, her voice measured, "Lucky for you, despite what you think of my family, what we've decided to do with our wealth is try to create a positive space for kids like yours."

"Yeah, and now two of the kids from your 'positive space' school are dead."

Behind her, Duane's and Ziggy's moms flinched. Karter's eyes shifted to them. "Maybe you should be more respectful of the people with you who are mourning. You aren't the only one who's lost a child."

"Don't you talk about my child!"

I saw the exact moment when Ms. Allen lost it. When all that pent-up rage at our family finally exploded and she charged at Karter. The security guards were too busy with the rest of the protestors.

I gasped as Ms. Allen took a wild swing at my sister.

Watched as Karter dodged without any effort.

Then looked on as years of boxing classes and months of frustration and strain brought her arm winding back.

"Don't!" I screamed, just as my sister decked Ms. Allen in the face.

January 13, 1996

It's been a while since I've written in here. My bad. I just haven't felt like it lately. It's like all the energy's been sucked out of everyone. And I'm starting to feel it too.

Still no word from the police, but December was busy because of Christmas and then there was New Year's. I'm sure something will happen soon. It was a quiet Christmas with just me and Dad. Usually the Turners invite us over for dinner, but not this year. ~~I tried not to let it bother me.~~

But Jay and Jonas are more willing to ignore their parents' rules now, so they've been hanging out with me again. Not where their mom can see, though I'm sure she knows. It's better than nothing, I guess.

Me and Jay usually exchange gifts for Christmas too. And since I can't afford multiple things, it always doubles as his birthday present. Nothing big, just little stuff. Andy always gets on us for it. Like, "Ooohhh, what did you get each other this year?" And it wasn't that we didn't do it. We did. It was just . . . different. I got Jay a book because I always get him a book. And Jay got me a bear. A small one that looked hand carved. He said it was to help remind me of how brave I am. I knew it was because he asked me once about all the bear stuff my dad had, and I'd told him.

I don't really buy into Dad's whole thing, but I was really happy about the bear. About Jay thinking I was brave, even though every night I checked out my window, expecting Donald to show up, snapping his jaws at me. And there was something else different about this gift exchange. Usually we just thank each other, me and Jay. But this time we hugged. ~~For a long time.~~ This time, I felt like we were both holding each other up. That if one of us let go at the wrong time, we'd both fall.

I've been thinking about that, and I've been wearing the bear on my key chain.

Today, Shirley invited me to hang out with the maidens. I reminded her that she said I couldn't be one, and she told me it was just logistics. I could still spend time with them if I wanted. That this wasn't Milk Man stuff, they were just going to play a prank on the boys.

I looked at Jay's sister then. I don't know why. I guess 'cause it felt kind of suspect and I wanted to get a read from her. But as usual, she wouldn't look at me. I used to think that Iris didn't like me, but now I think maybe she just doesn't want to be associated with me. We're the only two black girls on the ranch. People always assume we're either related or best friends, even though we're neither. I guess the best way to stop people thinking that is to ignore me.

The whole thing felt weird. I wouldn't put it past Shirley to turn the joke on me. I'm still going, just in case that's not it. I don't want to irritate her and start drama between our families. It'll be easier to just go along with it.

I'll check back in after the meetup.

I'm sorry for this page. ~~I can't stop crying.~~ It's messy. I'm usually a lot neater about it. Jay and Jonas are staying in our house with me until Dad comes home. They didn't want me to be alone after everything. But I need to write this down.

So I'm on our sofa in the corner while the two of them sit at the kitchen table. When I look down to write, I can feel them staring at me. I'm already bleeding through my bandage. And it stings. I want to clutch at my stomach, but I don't want the boys to see and be even more worried.

All of us are quiet. I guess we don't have anything to say to one another.

I was right. The joke was on me after all.

Shirley and the girls showed up to grab me from the house. We were supposed to meet at the tree line. It was kind of strange, but I brushed it off and we left together. They were smiling. Big grins. All of them except for Iris, who kept her eyes on the ground. I kept asking what trick we were gonna play, and Shirley kept saying "You'll see . . ."

We walked through the trees. It was my first time being back in the forest since what happened with Mack and Donald, and I didn't feel great about it. I thought for a moment about turning back but convinced myself that I was being paranoid. Besides, it was the middle of the afternoon, not nighttime. We got into the usual clearing. The streaks of lizard blood on the trees were long gone. Washed away by rain and snow and probably animals licking at it.

Shirley told us to stand in a circle and close our eyes because we needed to listen for instructions from the Milk Man on how to trick the boys, even though she'd initially said this wasn't a Milk Man thing. I only closed my eyes once I saw the other girls doing the same.

But I guess at some point, they opened them. Because I felt arms close around my own, and when I finally snapped my eyes open, two girls were holding my arms steady. One of them was Iris, who still wouldn't look at me. I twisted in their hold, but it's not like I'm used to having to fight people off, and there were two of them.

Shirley was grinning at me. And slowly, from her jeans pocket, she removed a knife. Just a little steak knife. We never had steak, too expensive, but I'd cut chicken with one dozens of times. "You think you're so smart, don't you?" she said.

I didn't say anything in response. Because I <u>am</u> smart. Smarter than her. ~~Smart enough that I shouldn't have fallen for that.~~*

I tried struggling harder against the girls, but that didn't help. At the time, I really thought the whole thing was a prank. That it was just to scare me, and it was working because I couldn't make myself act like it wasn't.

"You think you can ruin my family?" Shirley sneered. "He told me what you were doing. As long as I have him to help me, you'll never touch my family. And now I'm gonna punish you so you know not to ever do something like that again."

That was when I realized she knew about the thermos. Knew that I'd mailed it to the police. And she must have thought it was important, because otherwise why would she be so mad? I'd thought I was careful but apparently not careful enough.

"Get her down!" Shirley said, and the girls started wrestling me to the ground. I fought that, too. Though it didn't matter. ~~I was too weak.~~ It was impossible to get away.

I tried to appeal to Iris, who snapped at me to just be quiet.

Then Shirley came and lifted my shirt, tucking the end into my bra so it would stay put, leaving my stomach exposed.

I saw the glint of the knife as it came down.

---

* I can't help but agree with my younger self. I did so many silly things at that age. I didn't have the guidance that you will. Though I suppose you've never been much of a silly child. You pulled on the responsibility of future leader like a coat and let it guide you in all things. You always adapt.

I remember screaming. I'd never felt anything like that before. She didn't stab. She <u>carved</u>. She dragged the blade through my flesh like she had something to say with it. I bucked and twisted and howled and cried. ~~Begged.~~

It hurt. A lot. It still hurts now.

I can feel the lines there without even touching them because every slice of the serrated blade is etched into my memory as surely as it is my skin.*

Jay and Jonas must have heard me screaming, because they came running through the trees. Jonas knocked his shoulder into Shirley and sent her sprawling on the grass. And Jay ripped me away from the other girls. He was yelling at Iris, asking her what she thought she was doing.

I was stumbling and crying. The girls were hovering around like they didn't know what to do now. But Shirley wasn't done. She ran for me, and Jonas came forward and cracked her across the mouth with an open palm.

Her head snapped to the side. It was audible. Loud. I honestly thought he'd broken her neck. She curled in on herself on the ground, holding her jaw and sobbing.

Now Iris was shouting at Jonas, and Jay was still shouting at Iris.

Jonas had hit her. Had hit this white girl. This white girl who was the daughter of the operations manager.

Shirley turned her face toward us, tears streaking down her cheeks, and she smiled. <u>Smiled</u>. I really don't have a thing about God or whatever, but that smile was like the

---

* I never hid my scars. They reminded me of my failure. That I should have dealt with the situation better. But then pregnancy and stretch marks changed them, along with that little mommy makeover I got after Dom was born. They're so different now. But whenever I run my fingers over them, I remember the way that felt. That total humiliation. And it reminds me to never let myself be fooled like that again.

devil. And she said to Jonas, "Violence suits you, doesn't it?"

Iris tried apologizing to Shirley for her brother. Can you believe that? Apologizing. But Shirley wasn't paying attention. She and Jonas were staring each other down. She said, "Out of all the little calves, why you? Why are you such a good fit?"

Jonas's jaw was clenched so hard that the muscles of his cheeks were straining. His eyes were narrowed and his breathing heavy. I'd never seen him like that before.

I looked at Jay, but he seemed just as confused as I was. And Iris wouldn't stop apologizing. It was sickening, the way she was on her knees, begging Shirley for mercy. Mercy from what? I was still shaking so badly. My teeth were chattering.

But then Jonas suddenly turned away from her and called to Jay, who was helping me off the ground. I didn't even realize that I'd fallen again. Jay hooked my arm around his neck and Jonas patted his back.

"What a good big brother," Shirley drawled behind us. "Always stepping in to save the day."

When Jonas looked back at her, there was something new in his face. I'd thought that moments before I had seen what he looked like mad, but this, it was on another level. It was a fury so potent that I shivered.

I turned to Jay, who was staring at Jonas, and for the first time I had ever seen, he looked afraid of his brother.[*]

---

[*] Adults like to imagine that children aren't capable of great violence. So when they do engage in it, the adults decide that child is some sort of outlier, a monster, not like other children. But I know that all kids are violent. We just forget or we make ourselves forget because children are supposed to be this shining example of innocence. And they are. There is a difference between an innocent sort of physical rage and something purposeful and planned. Something that speaks to a darker inner nature. I thought that was Shirley. She was the beast in the shadows. But I didn't realize the way real monsters can hide. I hope you won't make the same mistake.

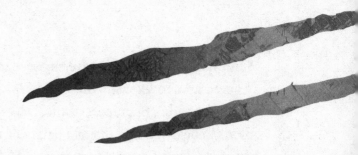

CHAPTER TWENTY-THREE

D ad drove me back home after school. I sat in the front passenger seat, staring out the window at the houses for the small amount of time that it took to get home. The only mercy in the Karter-and–Ms. Allen-situation was that the press hadn't caught it on camera. Though there were witnesses, which wasn't great. And over the course of a short afternoon, Karter had removed herself from school staff and made a promise to stay away from the premises. She hadn't had an official role anyway.

I knew that all the reports would be about how my sister had "brutally" attacked this mourning white woman, and none of them would mention that Ms. Allen was the one who started it, or that she'd called a bunch of Black people animals.

The house was surrounded by more press as we pulled up, and they slowly inched aside as Dad nudged the Yaris forward, their faces clear through the windows. This cheap rental car strategy really hadn't succeeded at helping us fly under the radar. He pulled into the garage, and once the door had closed behind us, let out a deep sigh and dropped his head back against the headrest.

We stayed there silently for the next few moments. Dad staring at nothing and me staring at him. "How are you doing?" I asked. Because obviously he was not okay.

"Your mother would have never messed up like this. She would have known how to fix everything. I don't know what to do anymore. I thought I did. But now it just feels like . . . what's the point?"

I didn't know what Dad thought he'd done to help, because as far as I had seen, it was Karter doing most of the fixing. Though I guess he was supporting her. Maybe that was what he meant.

I knew what I should do now. Encourage him. Lift his spirits. Be Sunny.

Instead, I said, "What did that reporter mean when he said Mom's death might not be an accident?"

"You shouldn't listen to reporters."

"I just didn't know people were saying that."

Dad turned his head to look at me, still leaning on the headrest. "People will say anything." He opened the door of the car and walked toward the house.

I scrambled out and followed him inside, where he retreated upstairs. I went to my own room, changing out of my uniform into something more comfortable and attempting to make progress on my homework. When I heard the sounds of jazz floating up from downstairs, I realized that he was using the pool. It was how he relieved stress usually. He'd do laps or float on the surface for at least an hour.

Which meant I had a chance to take advantage. Now at least I had some names to work with: Mack, Shirley, and Jonas. I made my way up the second flight of stairs and into my parents' bedroom. I was about to go into Mom's office again when I saw Dad's computer open to his email. He must have come up to check it then got distracted and went back downstairs for his swim. I crept toward it and sat in the chair.

The open email was from a concerned alumnus of the academy who regularly donated, asking what exactly was going on at the school. Dad hadn't answered.

I kept the window open and checked in the rest of his email, doing a simple search for the name "Jonas." I didn't know why Mom had compared him and Dom, but maybe something about this guy would reveal some sort of lead. He was dead, so he wasn't the murderer. But there could be something there. After all, how likely was it for our family to be connected to two different sets of murders?

The search brought up no results.

I tried Mack Feeney's name. Nothing. Ranch was too many results.

I was thinking about what to search next when I noticed the tab for starred emails. I clicked on it and started going through what Dad had saved. None were interesting until I got to one that said it was coming from a penitentiary. It noted the sender as inmate #68759. I immediately clicked into it.

Jay,

Usually, I try not to write you. I think it's better if you don't think about me at all. You know that. But things are getting dire, and it can't wait until your visit. It'll be too late by then. The doctors say I don't have long. My burden will be passing soon. I'm sorry that it is passing to you. I never wanted that for you. It was why I took your place all those years ago. I know you never asked that of me. But I wanted to. I had a bad feeling about it all, and I was right. Please know that I've never regretted that decision. Not once. Big brothers are supposed to protect their younger ones. And I was always happy to do that for you.

We still have a chance to fix things. You know that a natural death is worthless. Come today. Please. I'll help however I can.

I'm sorry for everything.

J.

Dad had replied to the email with two words: *I can't.*

I stared at the screen. Who was "J"? My mind immediately leapt to Jonas, but no. Besides, that guy was Jonas Turner, and Dad was a Robinson. Either way, Dad had a brother, just like Mack Feeney Jr. said. He wasn't the liar. My parents were.

I looked up the phone number for the penitentiary and called. When a woman picked up, I said, "I wanted to confirm the name of inmate 68759."

"Sorry, ma'am. We can't disclose private information."

I swallowed and blurted out, "I'm family. I just . . . was trying to sort some things out and needed to make sure that was his number." I was stumbling all over the place, but I willed this woman to believe me.

"And your name?"

"Ainsley Behre." I doubted that my voice could pass for a man, so I couldn't give Dad's name, but he rarely did things without Mom being involved in some way.

"Give me a moment." There was the sound of keys clacking and I stared at the phone screen held out in front of me, clenched between my fingers. "Oh, yes, I see you here. Uh, sister-in-law."

"Yes. So the name noted . . ."

"Jonas Turner."

"Thanks . . ." I hung up as she was asking if there was anything else that she could help me with.

Dad not only had a brother who he'd hidden from us, but his brother was also a mass murderer. Dad must have changed his last name to distance himself.

Was this why Mom thought Dom could turn into another "Jonas situation," because he was our uncle? Did she think homicidal tendencies were genetic?

And what was up with that request Jonas made in the email? A natural death is worthless? Was he asking Dad to kill him?! I knew that sometimes people who were in jail for a long time had suicidal thoughts, but it seemed strange for a man who already thought he was about to die to express that. And it was messed up to ask Dad to do that for him. Especially in a jail, where Dad was more likely to get caught and be locked up himself.

I googled Jonas again, looking for any more information that could help me understand what was going on. Mostly they were just articles reiterating what had happened at the ranch. He'd killed his mother, *my grandmother*, in front of witnesses and was proven to have set the fatal blaze resulting in a total death count of twenty-nine. Jonas had admitted to setting the fire and added that despite having fuzzy memories of the night, he'd "probably" killed his dad and younger sister. His lawyer, however, had insisted that it was physically impossible for him to have murdered that many people by himself. In the end, it hadn't mattered. He'd been charged for all twenty-nine deaths. I paused and swallowed. Dad had had other siblings. He'd never been an only child.

I clicked a link that included photos of the house after the fire. It was mostly ash and soot, but there were a lot of stains that looked bloodlike. Then I paused.

I zoomed into the image as far as it could go, and there . . . there it was. The symbol.

It wasn't mentioned anywhere else. Not in any other articles, but it was there.

Was this why Dad had studied it? Was this how Mom knew it? Why she'd connected it to Dom? And now it was turning up again.

I went back through my searches and found a small local Oro news article on my uncle's death.

Jonas Turner was laid to rest today after serving
seventeen years of his twenty-nine consecutive

twenty-five-year life sentences. He was, statistically, one of Canada's biggest mass murderers but is rarely discussed. Turner was raised on a cattle ranch in Oro-Medonte with his family. One night, he apparently "snapped," leaving only five victims alive. Staff at the penitentiary expressed surprise at the charges against the man who, as an inmate, was a model citizen. No family could be reached for comment.

Dad had put as much distance between himself and his brother as he could. Changing his name not once, but twice. From Turner to Robinson to Behre. And yet that email had suggested that he visited Jonas.

A brother who'd killed Mack Feeney Jr. and Shirley's family.

And then a ranch that Mack Jr. thought he deserved was given to my mother, and by association, to the brother of the boy who'd massacred most of his family, leaving his sister so traumatized that he'd declared her destroyed. And now she was dead too.

No wonder he was outside the school gloating with Marsha Allen.

But it also shed new light on Shirley's warnings. The woman must have known that Dad was Jonas's brother. So why had she warned me? The Milk Man . . . it was his symbol there in the burned ranch house. That suggested that the murderer of those twenty-nine people may not have been Jonas, just like his lawyer had claimed. It might have been this other man, this Milk Man, who was still torturing my family.

Any guy who was an adult back then would be way old by now, though, wouldn't he? In his fifties or sixties. That didn't seem right considering how easily he'd chased me in the school. I didn't know how to explain it, but he'd seemed younger. The thing about a name like the Milk Man was that as long as no one saw your face, you could pass the title on. Maybe the Milk Man torturing us now was really the Milk Man Jr.

And I knew a junior who'd felt wronged by our family and had every reason to come after us. The question was, would he have killed his own sister to do it?

Then again, maybe Jonas had killed them all. In that email to Dad, he'd said that he was going to pass on a burden. What if that burden was the title of Milk Man? But Dad hadn't gone. Or he said he couldn't in the email.

My fingers shook as I clicked out of everything and pushed myself away from the desk.

Had Shirley come to warn me about her family or mine?

I couldn't bring myself to properly look at Dad. After everything I'd found, I'd gone straight to my bedroom and planned to stay there for as long as possible while I thought about how to confront him about his hidden brother. But now, we were sitting together at the dining table with Dad's phone propped up because Karter had arranged an emergency family FaceTime.

The call from Karter came through, and Dad answered it. Another box soon joined with Darren and Kiley squished together, presumably at the house downtown. Darren didn't look good. Actually, he looked like Dad. They had matching bags under their eyes. Kiley wasn't doing much better. Her curls were pulled back into a bun that actually looked messy like she had slept on it, instead of artfully messy.

Karter's eyes were bloodshot and jerky. She wasn't at home with us, but if she were downtown with the middles, she'd be on-screen with them. So I had no idea where she was even calling from. A hotel, maybe, if she wanted to be alone. She was wearing a baggy T-shirt. It didn't even look designer.

"So, clearly we have some issues," Karter started.

Darren snorted. "Understatement."

"Not helpful."

"Honestly," he said, leaning his cheek on his hand. "I'm relieved to know that you can fall flat on your face too. I was starting to feel like the only Behre screwup. But you've really taken the heat off. Truly, the only perfect member of this family is Sunny."

I jerked to attention. Opened my mouth and then snapped it closed. What was I even supposed to say to that?

"That's rich, when you couldn't even be discreet, and now you going in and out of the hospital is all over the news," Karter snapped at Darren. "They're saying our entire family is crazy."

Darren laughed and reeled back. "Are you serious right now?"

Our older sister frowned. "Yes."

"You punched the lights out of the mother of the girl who our brother allegedly murdered, and *I'm* in the wrong because I tried to get help? Are you fucking with me?!"

"That's not what I'm saying. I'm saying that you should have used discretion. I didn't even know you were going that often."

"I should have covered it up, you mean."

I understood suddenly that Darren and Kiley were right to keep this a secret. I knew why they hadn't said anything. Because look what was happening now.

Tears were gathering in my eyes before I could stop them. I was so tired of this shit.

Karter groaned, "What, Sunny?"

"Don't you understand that this is exactly why he couldn't tell you? Aren't you upset that he had to go that much at all? Doesn't that matter more than how the media is using it?"

Dad rested his hand on my shoulder, and I flinched. His eyes went wide, and he blinked at me. I turned away.

Karter actually looked a little guilty. "Sorry," she said to Darren. "I am. I . . . yes, I wish you didn't need to be there at all. And they already know, so . . . no point in rehashing it. I guess."

None of us said anything for a few moments. Darren didn't accept her apology, but he didn't need to.

"Is Dom going to get to come home?" I said finally.

Karter sighed. "No. They had a bail hearing today, and they're not giving it to him. They're saying he's likely to reoffend now. The media exposure is creating pressure for that as well. And the Crown is going to pursue trying him as an adult. Paris says the only thing that could change any of that is to prove a lot of reasonable doubt. Ideally, to show that there's another chief suspect. More evidence than Dom's fingerprint. In that case, we could push for bail. But no guarantees."

That was it then. He was going to sit in juvie until the trial. Unless they had proof otherwise. Unless *I* could supply proof otherwise.

Karter didn't have much else to tell us after. Just to continue to not text people outside the family anything about the case and to keep off social media. That she would update us with any important information.

The call ended, and Dad and I sat there.

"Is everything okay?" he said to me.

I froze. I realized how little my family asked me that question because I was always fine. On the outside, at least. But actually, everything was falling apart, and it was getting harder to cling to the cheery veneer. And it wasn't working like it had every other time. It wasn't fixing anything.

"Why didn't you tell us you had a brother?" Finally I turned to look at Dad, whose face visibly paled.

His upper lip trembled before he spoke. "How . . . ? Who . . . ?"

"Mack Feeney Junior."

Dad sighed, his eyebrows narrowing. "Of course. Junior." He rubbed his hands on his forehead and stared down at the table. "When we were kids, my brother did something terrible. We didn't want you guys to get wrapped up in it. We only visited once a year anyway."

Once a year for seventeen years was a lot. "We? You and Mom?"

"Yes."

"Now Dom is in jail." I didn't know what else to add. That Dom was in jail, but he hadn't done what Jonas had. That Dom was in jail and Mom thought he was like Jonas, that he was a murderer. That all my brother had asked me to do was believe in him and that I had to do it. Because he was my brother and I needed to protect him. I needed to do what Dad hadn't been able to do for his own brother. Not just for Mom, because she'd wanted me to take care of him, but because Dom didn't deserve this.

Dad reached out and took my hands in his. I wanted to rip them away. "I won't let what happened to Jonas happen to Dom. We didn't have enough resources to help my brother back then. The most we could manage was to pay off a few reporters to try to keep it suppressed. It was easier to do that with press in the nineties. But Dom's situation is different. They have less on him, and we have Paris. The press is harder to deal with, but we'll manage."

"And Dom is innocent," I insisted, because it felt important to say. Because he was.

"Yes," Dad agreed. "And Dom is innocent. Please, Sunny. Trust me. We are sparing absolutely nothing to get him out of this situation."

I wanted to believe him. I really did.

But I didn't.

I needed to keep on with the investigation. I needed to keep looking. To find what I could. I had told Dom that we would find the real murderer, and I wasn't going to let my brother down again.

CHAPTER TWENTY-FOUR

I bobbed in the water, the chlorine-filled liquid surrounding me. It was only Thursday, but the whole Monday punching incident had already blown over. In the grand scheme of things, it was almost tame.

The tiles around the pool were clean and shining, as was the wall where Ziggy had been pinned. Someone had repaired the holes where the bolts that attached her had gone in. It was so perfectly done, it was barely noticeable. Not that it mattered. In class, everyone's eyes kept straying to that spot on the wall. Whether they were there when the body was found or not, they all knew where it'd happened.

Shyanne nudged me in the shoulder, and I jerked toward her.

She pointed at Ms. Lorein, our gym teacher, who was giving some sort of instruction that I had missed.

"She numbered us off. We're both twos. We're in the second heat, so we have to get out of the pool," Shyanne said.

I nodded and followed her to the ladder, where I tugged myself out of the water and huddled against the wall with the rest of the number twos.

We were resting our backs against the place where Ziggy had been nailed up.

I made sure to hunch away from the wall.

"It's super messed up," Shyanne whispered. "Harriet said that she only left Ziggy alone for a bit to use the bathroom. The other girls were still getting changed in there. But when they tried to get into the pool again, the door was locked. They tried to get in on the boys' side and it was locked too. They were looking for help when one of the girls tried the boys' door again, and it was suddenly unlocked, and then . . . Ziggy was there."

I knew Karter would probably kill me for saying anything about what happened, but I decided to do it anyway. "There were plainclothes security at the dance. They pretended to be parent chaperones and staff. They should have seen someone unaccounted for." Aka, they should have seen Mack Feeney Jr. if he'd done it. I ignored the way my mind whispered that Dad also had access to the school then. There was no way he was involved. Besides the fact that he was *Dad*, even if Jonas was the original Milk Man, why would Dad decide to pick up where he left off? And say he did and wanted to kill off his family like his brother had, why not just do it? Why wait until now? Why kill all these other kids beforehand? It didn't make sense.

"Oh shit, really?" Shyanne asked, turning to me. "They weren't playing with being undercover. I didn't notice at all."

I nodded. "Yeah. We'd been doing that since . . . since Duane. So I don't know how it kept happening."

"It has to be a student, then. Or a teacher or staff or something, right? Someone allowed to be in the school who could have gotten the door codes and room keys."

It was exactly what I'd been thinking. Could Mack Jr. have a connection to someone who went to the academy? It was a theory I'd already considered before. A student could have found a way to let him in. Maybe even claimed he was their parent or something.

But now I was right back where we'd started, suspecting a student, but having no idea which one.

Even Marsha Allen's kids weren't good suspects, because if Mack Jr. started this setup all the way before Torri's death, they wouldn't have been involved. I had to believe that there weren't that many people willing to murder their sisters.

The whistle blew, and our group returned to the pool. I let out a breath as I slipped back into the water and settled in my lane next to Shyanne.

Trying to guess who it was wasn't working. I needed to find evidence.

The first whistle sounded, and I pulled my goggles over my eyes. The second double whistle went, and I kicked my legs back against the pool wall to help me shoot forward. Doing one stroke after another after another. Losing myself in the motion.

I got back to the wall, tapping it as I surfaced. I looked at the changeroom doors. The boys' side. That was where the killer would have had to come in since all the girls were on their side.

We finished our laps, and at the end of class, I volunteered to help clean up. It was nothing unusual. In fact, it was more my usual than things had been in a while.

I kept waiting for Ms. Lorein to leave me alone, but she wasn't having any of it. I guess given what had happened here, she wasn't going to take her eyes off anyone. Besides, now the teachers had to do head counts before they let students go, and we all had to travel in pairs.

I got changed, watched our teacher do the head count, and waited for everyone to start moving toward their next classes before I exclaimed, "Oh! I forgot my phone!"

Ms. Lorein sighed. "I have a class upstairs in the gym."

I pointed to Shyanne. "We'll stay together. We both have English next anyway."

The teacher sighed once more before nodding and leaving us alone.

Shyanne raised an eyebrow at me. "I literally saw you put your phone in your backpack."

"I know."

This time, I went into the boys' changeroom instead of the girls'.

Shyanne let out a whistle behind me. "Oh my God. First, you lied to a teacher. I didn't even know you could lie. Now we're breaking into the boys' room? Who are you and what have you done with Ms. President Sunny Behre?"

I gawked at her. "Wait, do other people call me that?"

"Ms. President?"

"Yes!"

"Tons of people."

I attempted to look less surprised, but I already knew it was too late. Great. So apparently everyone talked behind my back. "How come no one said anything to me?"

She shrugged. "Your man didn't tell you that? That's foul. I assumed he did. If people were talking shit about Mercy, guaranteed I would tell her."

I shook it off and continued my exploration of the boys' room. I didn't have much time. We couldn't be late for class. I went past the bathroom into the changeroom, and even poked my head into the pool before coming back to the bathroom.

In my frustration, I started looking into the stalls, searching for some sort of clue, when I saw it. One of the drop tile pieces of the ceiling was slightly out of place. If I hadn't been looking for something, I probably wouldn't have noticed it. It was just above the toilet. A perfect position for someone to jump down.

I looked at Shyanne, who looked back at me.

She grinned. "Want a boost?"

Through some extremely awkward maneuvering, I stepped on the toilet and then Shyanne helped hoist me up with her shoulder so I could move the tile aside. I was just about to wonder how I would get up there when I noticed two metal handles attached inside the ceiling. I reached up and gripped them, lifting myself into the space with a grunt.

"Okay, upper-body strength!"

I flushed and was glad that Shyanne couldn't see it when I was up here.

She was talking about how Mercy said upper-body strength was the most necessary in survival situations and how she needed to do pull-ups in the park and stuff because hers was terrible.

I was only half listening as I pulled out my phone and used the flashlight. Around me were drop ceiling pieces, pipes, and wiring, but also ductwork that seemed stronger than usual. They looked like they were there precisely so someone had something solid to crawl on and were wider too. I didn't have to squish my arms at my sides, and Shyanne could have comfortably fit in here alongside me.

I followed the path down a straightaway that split. I sighed and took the one on the left that led to a straight shot upward featuring another ladder. I put my phone in my pocket and started the climb, regretting when it didn't end right away. I had to take a couple breaks but after a while reached a flat plate over my head. When I pressed my hand to it, it was cold. I flipped the latch on the inside and shoved it open. When I popped my head up, wind blew against my face, and while in front of me was ductwork, behind me were rails. More precisely, the rails on the roof.

I swallowed, remembering Shirley being stabbed through the throat. Remembering how the murderer had disappeared, but the only exit was the doors I'd come through. I'd thought so, anyway.

Scrambling to lock the hatch again, I made my way back down

as quickly and carefully as I could and took the right path instead. It turned sharply into a corner, where a giant shaft went downward, lined with metal rungs.

I made my way down the ladder. Toward the end, it stopped, leaving a two-foot drop. I let go and landed on the concrete. I followed the path down a long hallway that turned a corner, around which was a room. The lights flashed on, and I threw my hand over my face. When I put it down, I gasped.

Holy. Shit.

The walls and floors were concrete, but there were automatic lights in the ceiling. In the center of the room was a slab of stone raised from the ground. My mind said the word "altar" and I worked very hard to ignore it. There were straps attached to the slab . . . straps that looked meant for holding someone down, disturbingly close to a drain set into the floor.

I pressed a shaking hand to my mouth.

There were two doors in the room. One with a single code on it next to what looked like a gurney you might see in a morgue, and another with several bolts keeping it shut. There was also what looked like a deep freezer. I tried not to think of all the movies I'd seen where bodies were kept inside those things.

I forced myself toward it. I pulled my sleeve over my hand, because I did not want to leave fingerprints on this thing.

I took a long deep breath. It would be fine. I would just open it. It was probably empty.

I gritted my teeth and tugged it open.

It wasn't empty.

"What . . . ?" I whispered as I looked at the multiple glass bottles filled with . . . milk. I picked one up with my sleeve-covered hand and stared at the liquid inside. Or . . . kind of milk. I was sure that's what it was, but it had a pink tinge to it. Sometimes cows could develop conditions that made them bleed into the milk. I knew because when we raised the calves, that had to be watched out for. We didn't want them drinking that stuff. Which is why it didn't make any sense for it to be stored like this. I put the bottle back and closed the freezer, shivering from the cold air that had streamed out of it.

Maybe this was just a storage room . . . a secret storage room, with a mysterious entrance, an altar, and a disturbingly body-sized gurney. And bloody milk, couldn't forget that.

I went over to the coded door, but none of the combinations I attempted worked. So I went to the other door with the bolts and opened it, revealing a set of stairs leading up.

I shouldn't go up there.

I shouldn't.

But I had to.

The undeniable fact of this room was that it was in our school. Meaning that my family must have built it. Mom had her hand in every aspect of the school's design, just like the house. There was no way she wouldn't have known this was here. Which meant if there was a threat waiting for me at the top of the staircase, it would be from my own family.

Or what if it was because someone else had discovered this room and was using it against us? They had obviously taken advantage of the secret roof access.

It didn't matter.

I had to see where this led. I had to do it for Dom.

I took off one of my shoes and put it inside the door to keep it propped open before making my way up the stairs. They led to yet another bolted door, but when I opened this one, fresh air wound its way down to me.

I swallowed and put my other shoe down to keep that door open. I walked down the long hallway that led outside to a fence covered by a thick leafy hedge. I pushed on it, but it wouldn't budge. A chain rattled.

Buried in the leaves was yet another bolt. But this one had a code on the inside.

You needed it to get both in and out.

Meaning my family created something that could keep someone trapped inside.

My fingers trembled as they hovered over the keypad.

I swallowed and typed in a code that I hoped wouldn't work.

The panel lit up green and the bolt unlatched. I swung open the fence, just the tiniest bit, and peeked out. I could see the school field. Quiet now because everyone was inside in class. It was the hedge that went around the school. I closed the door and leaned my head against it.

The code I'd put in was the day I took my first steps. Dad told me that he'd always remember it because I'd crash-landed into his bowl of ice cream, and the face I'd made, that little grin, had been impossible to forget. Dad used this code all the time.

"What do you have to say about the theory that your wife's death wasn't an accident?!"

No.

I physically shoved the thought away. Dad wouldn't do that. He wouldn't hurt Mom, and he wouldn't do this. Sure, he'd studied the symbol, but probably only because of what he'd discovered about his brother. And he wouldn't be going around murdering people and blaming his son. I couldn't believe that. This was *Dad*.

I didn't want to, but my thoughts went to the email Jonas had sent him.

My burden will be passing soon. I'm sorry that it is passing to you.

This was not my dad.

It wasn't.

I clasped my hands over my mouth and sobbed.

CHAPTER TWENTY-FIVE

t was easy to lie to Shyanne. It was reasonable that I'd wandered around the vents and found nothing, and the truth—that I'd discovered my family had built a secret lair complete with a stone altar, a second secret entrance, and a morgue gurney—was actually the less plausible scenario. Oh, and secret roof access, something that someone had definitely used to murder a woman.

Nevertheless, I'd managed to maintain my Sunny-ness throughout the entire day. And then I'd spent extra time fumbling with my backpack so that I could be the last out of the classroom, snuck into the bathroom, and was now sitting on the toilet bowl, trying to figure out what to do next.

There was still some potential for this to not have anything to do with Dad. After all, why would he purposely ruin our own school and reputation? And so I was sticking to my theory of Mack Jr. working with a student, disregarding whatever that room had been, and assuming Mack had discovered and used the roof access. Which wasn't as far-fetched as it seemed. It was reasonable that Mom had put the room and crawlable vent system in for some sort of utility reason and it had been used in a more sinister way than intended. After all, I had found it too. It was probably in the blueprints for the school, which I hadn't checked, but a murderer making a plan may have thought to steal. Therefore, Mack Jr. was still a viable suspect.

That made the best next step going into the office and looking through student records to see who might be connected to him. They were digital and could only be accessed by the head administrator's computer, which was obstacle number one. Obstacle number two was that I would have to be in the school, after hours, alone.

I gripped my skirt, bunching up the green plaid under my nails. Picturing a hand gripping my hair and pulling me close. I squeezed my eyes shut.

When I opened my eyes again, I did something that I never thought I would.

I texted Jeremy.

Jeremy looked positively overjoyed to be involved in this operation. I only somewhat regretted extending him an invitation. But it was better than the position we'd been in moments before, which had involved finding a way to sneak down into the pool room and hiding in the newly discovered ceiling duct area while security did their safety checks before locking up the school. Because cuddling up to my brother's best friend in an air vent was not something I'd planned to do in my lifetime. He, however, had acted like it was a dream come true. Which it might have been.

Now he waited, shifting from foot to foot as I entered the code for the office door by the light of my phone. The setting to have every light in the school shut off had been changed from six p.m. to four p.m. now that extracurriculars were canceled. The time when, thanks to daylight savings, it also got dark outside.

Jeremy looked up and down the hallway. "Do you think it's a safety hazard that we were able to get past the security that's supposed to be stopping us from being murdered?"

"Can you maybe not mention being murdered right now?"

"Yeah, no, for sure. Probably good not to think about being murdered while we're in a position to be murdered."

I turned to him with narrowed eyes, and he grinned.

With a sigh, I opened the office door, and we stepped into the space. It was pretty basic. A few rows of desks with computers and some filing cabinets against the back wall. I found the one for the lead administrator and sat down, holding out my phone to Jeremy so he could man the flashlight on it.

He found a chair with wheels and rolled himself over with a push, gleefully saying "Whee!" on his way over. Though he did take the phone and angle the light as directed after shrugging off his jacket. Dom's jacket, actually, but Jeremy wore it frequently enough that I thought of it as his. Honestly, they shared clothes so often that I might as well think of their wardrobes as a collective, belonging to both of them.

"Have you heard from Dom?" I asked, trying to sound casual.

Jeremy's usually carefree expression shifted into a frown. "Yeah . . . he said he couldn't say anything about the case, but we talked about an anime we've been watching. New episode dropped on Sunday that he missed." He played with his fingers, tapping the tips of one and then the other. "He seemed really down. Like, I know he's, like, in jail and shit, but before he was, I dunno, optimistic? But now it feels like he just expects that everything is gonna go wrong." He shook his head. "They can't put him in for life, right? He'll be okay?"

I hunched my shoulders. "There's no way my family lets that happen."

"You sure?" Jeremy asked. "Because up until these last few months, you guys didn't seem to care about him at all." My eyes went wide, and Jeremy held his hands up. "No disrespect, Prez. It's just, like, he's your family. Your brother. And you all act like he's some pariah for no reason. You always have. And he pretends like it's nothing, but I know that hurts him. Ms. B. was a real one—like, I'm grateful to be in her school—but it's only now that she's gone that you're giving him the time of day."

I swallowed and didn't know what else to say. For no reason other than Mom's clear dislike of him, we'd ignored my brother all his life. Or used him as a scapegoat. It shouldn't have happened, but it did. Hearing the way Dom had sounded on that one and only phone call we'd had . . . I couldn't help feeling like I was the one who'd crushed that optimism. I'd realized how wrong I was right away, but it was still too late.

"You're right," I said, because that was the sum of it.

Jeremy nodded, then he squinted and leaned forward. "Oh shit, did she really just put the password on a sticky note?" He pointed to a note stuck to the computer monitor that read "student files user: mmabey pass: 0872BehreAcademy." The password was literally the last four digits of the school phone number and then the name. Our digital security really needed an overhaul.

I opened the program and typed in the info. "Okay, any students you can think of with a grudge against Dom or our family?"

"Rachel Higgs," Jeremy said. "She was annoyed that Dom got to do the advanced anatomy course and she didn't. Called it nepotism. Which usually I'd agree with, but honestly Dom's got the grades and she doesn't. I get the jealousy, though. That class is so cool. Dom said there's, like, apparently so many ways you can be stabbed and still live, it's all about placement—"

"Jeremy," I cut in. "Can you think of anyone with, like, . . . a *real* motive to frame Dom? Or just petty stuff?"

"Petty stuff," he announced, voice chipper.

"Okay . . . maybe a different system." I tried looking up Mack Feeney Jr. and Feeney to see if any of the students might have him listed as someone who could pick them up if their parents weren't around. It wasn't exactly easy to moderate with high school students who might just leave the school and go off with anyone, but it was something. No one came up.

It started to become very clear very quickly that this was not going to work.

I looked over to Jeremy, who met my disappointed gaze. "Nothing, eh?"

I shook my head. I didn't know what to do.

Jeremy crossed his arms over his chest. "It's bullshit, man. You know, when me and Dom hang out, it's like someone is always looking for a reason to call the law on us. We're leaning against a lamppost—loitering. We're browsing the shelves—finna take something. We're laughing too loud—disturbing the peace. They're always paying so much attention to us. But at the end of the day, if that was some white dude's girl that drowned, it would have been an open-and-shut-case accident. Look at Duane, even. Had him on the news for all of a day, but now Ziggy's gone and there's protestors and they got her picture up everywhere. And, like, I wish Torri and Ziggy and all of them were alive, I'm not shitting on them. It's just, like, it's not the same for all of us. Dom is my boy, and it's fucked up too that if it were me, without a dime to my name, they'd have already tried me as an adult and locked me up."

I didn't know what to say to him. Nothing he'd said was wrong. Justice wasn't supposed to discriminate, but of course it did. And we were exploiting it too. Using every bit of money and influence to get Dom whatever we could in a way that Black people without the money couldn't.

"And on top of that, she really messed him up, I think, Torri," Jeremy said. "That was why, when he called after meeting up with her and asked if I could come chill at 7-Eleven, I came. Well, also he ordered me an Uber. But, like, I wanted to be there for him."

"Wait, like, the night Torri died?" I didn't realize Dom had called him after meeting Torri. I guess I'd just figured it was a planned hangout. "You guys didn't mention that before."

"Uh, yeah, we did. We said we were hanging out at 7-Eleven."

"Right." I nodded. They had said that, just in a different way. "'Cause they have that footage."

Jeremy frowned. "Footage? Of us at 7-Eleven? Why?"

I wasn't supposed to talk about the case, but this was Jeremy, and he already knew basically everything. Besides, who else could I be real with? No one. "Yeah, Paris says it's good evidence. I think it's our best evidence, actually. Since they have Dom on camera at the 7-Eleven around midnight, which is apparently when they've decided Torri's time of death was."

Jeremy's expression remained confused. I was about to ask him what he wasn't understanding when suddenly his jaw went slack and then he laughed. But it was . . . off, somehow. "Right, right, right. Yeah, that makes sense." He stood up from the chair, bouncing on his toes. "Uh . . . so, like, anything else we're doing? Or should we take off?"

"Everything good?"

"Yeah, I just didn't think they were using the time of death, since before they said it wasn't strong evidence since animals got to her or whatever." He laughed again.

"You're lying," I said, my voice flat. "You never do that. You get mad at me for doing that."

The put-on smile slid off his face. "Don't you think I have a good reason then?"

Goose pimples lifted on the skin of my arms. Jeremy looked down at them, noticing. He always noticed things.

"Can you get me an Uber?" he asked.

I nodded. "Yeah. If I figure something out, I'll update you, I guess." Really, I wanted to know what sort of lightbulb had gone off in Jeremy's head. What had been enough that he'd lied.

But really I needed to concentrate on the fact that this search had led me to nothing. I still had no idea what student might be working with Mack Jr. and no other leads besides that secret room. And the only people who might know about that were my family. I couldn't ask Dad without seeming like I was accusing him of something, and after all the stuff with his brother, I didn't know if anything he said would even be close to the truth. Which left me with one other option.

So I sent Jeremy off in a car and took the streetcar home.

Karter crossed her arms over her chest, holding them so tight that it looked painful. Darren put his head in his hands and left it there. Kiley was just looking off into the distance. I shifted on my bed, carefully watching their expressions on the FaceTime screen as they digested the news that the school had a secret room hidden inside it.

It was the only thing I'd told them. I didn't need them to know how deep I was in this. Especially because part of my involvement had included hiding mine and Dom's interaction with Duane's body and also neglecting to mention a woman whose murder I'd witnessed.

I didn't even want to be sharing this much with them, but we were down to the wire, and Dom needed my help. I couldn't waste time doing bullshit like searching their rooms for clues. And so this was the best method. I'd spun it very much like something that I'd innocently stumbled across, noting that the code in the hedge was a date only Dad would have known and had previously used as a password, and I was sharing with them in confidence and concern, because there was a murderer who had been sneaking in and out of the school undetected. Though technically, Shirley had also managed to do this. But they didn't know that.

"I'll take care of it," Karter said finally.

That was . . . unhelpful.

Darren pulled his hands away from his face. "What does that mean?"

I wanted to ask the same question. Instead, I rearranged my face into an expression of concerned confusion.

"It means I'll take care of it," Karter repeated.

"Why do we have a room like that? It can't actually just be milk storage; that makes no sense. We don't even run a dairy ranch," Kiley said, her voice strained. I had also not mentioned that the milk was bloody. "Did you know about it?"

"No," Karter snapped. "I didn't know we had a storage room in the school."

"Storage room? More like torture chamber," Darren supplied helpfully, and I suppressed a groan. That was not the direction I wanted to go in.

Our older sister glared at the screen, and I suspected it was for Darren. "It's just a room with a freezer."

"Yeah, and an altar, and a fucking gurney." Darren threw her a skeptical look.

"Darren, stop," Kiley said, obviously irritated. "This isn't helping anyone. There's probably a reasonable explanation for this."

But he ignored her, barreling on. "So, like, is the working theory that Mom and Dad had a sex kink room, and the murderer happens to be using it as a base of operations, or are we jumping straight to the 'Is Daddy a serial killer?' angle?"

Christ, it was only getting worse now. And moreover, it was quickly becoming clear that none of them knew about the room. Meaning I was back at square one.

"Why are you doing this?" Karter asked.

Darren raised an eyebrow. "Doing what? Asking reasonable

questions about a murder den that had never been mentioned before?"

I needed to stop this. "I don't think it's anything like—"

Karter cut me off. "Dad is not organized or ballsy enough to kill people." She gnashed the words out between her teeth. "And yes, there's now a room that none of us knew about. All that matters is whether there's evidence down there that could help or harm Dom's case, so I will take care of it, like I said."

Karter, for all her faults, was at least focused on what we needed to be focused on. If only she weren't so vague about what that might involve. Would she even actually share if she'd found anything?

Darren asked, "Is this hiding evidence or collecting evidence?"

Karter didn't get a chance to answer, because our phones all vibrated with a text from Paris.

They've found another body.

CHAPTER TWENTY-SIX

I stood in the entryway of the house with the middles on either side of me. I kept my hands clasped so I would stop fidgeting. We'd already heard the SUV pull in. A few moments later, the side door from the garage opened and Karter walked in, followed by Dad, and then Dom trailed behind them. His eyes were downcast, and he was wearing the same outfit he'd had on when they arrested him eleven days ago.

I couldn't help looking at Dad as he led our younger brother back into the house. Nothing was making sense. Again, I refused to think he was, but if Dad was hypothetically the one behind this, then he was framing Dom. So why do a murder now when Dom was in custody? Unless framing Dom wasn't part of the plan and was more of an accident. Maybe he hadn't expected Dom to stumble upon the body and this recent murder was to get him off the hook.

Either way, now there was enough reasonable doubt that Paris was able to get the bail our brother had previously been denied. No house arrest conditions either, she'd said with a smile, which she was able to push for by arguing that the police were rushing and making wild accusations that had now ruined her client's reputation, and he deserved freedom and normalcy.

As if his life would ever be normal now.

He'd become collateral damage in this whole thing. I just couldn't see the dad I knew and loved hurting people like that. He cried during Disney movies. Last year, his Halloween costume was Steve Harvey. His hobbies included reading and writing essays—*for fun*—on what he'd read.

I met Karter's eyes. She'd promised to take care of things yesterday, but I still had no idea what that meant.

Dom stood for a moment, looking at me and the middles. I didn't know what to do. We hadn't spoken since I had implied that I maybe thought he was a murderer.

"Welcome home," I said, pinning on a smile. "We're happy to have you back."

Dom stared at me, not saying a thing. Then his eyes shifted to the stairs, and he walked straight past me, up to his room.

My shoulders sagged.

"Jesus, what did you do to piss him off?" Darren said, turning to me with a raised brow.

"Leave it," Karter snapped. "Dad and I are going to go meet with Paris. You three can stay here with Dom. He doesn't need to be alone right now. Do you understand?"

Meaning, stay here and watch him. We all nodded.

My older sister glanced at me for a second, then turned and left with Dad. I wondered if they actually had things to do with Paris or if this was just an excuse to get Dad alone and try to find a way to stealth ask about the secret room. Maybe it was both.

Kiley bit her bottom lip and then looked at me. "Do you think she's going to tell him?"

I stiffened. *No.* There was no way Karter would do that. It would heavily suggest that we thought he had something to do with this and was the reason I went to my siblings instead of him in the first place. And in classic fashion for this whole "investigation," they didn't know anything.

And now there was a new victim. Ellis Murray. A Black boy who lived near Eglinton West Station. Freshman. I shivered, thinking of how Jeremy and I had been there, in school, just hours before the body was found. I wondered what sick little rhyme had been pushed into Ellis's hand. His mom and dad had already been on the news, sobbing. The media had turned on the police, and Marsha's protest group had gone silent. I suspected that now most parents would just pull their kids out of the school, forget protesting. We were private, so it's not like the Toronto board could shut us down, but I didn't know how long we could justify keeping the academy open if we couldn't protect the students we had left.

The murderer's plan was working.

I remembered that hand wrapped in my hair. I could feel it now, no longer gentle, tugging the strands tight. Yanking at my scalp. Pulling and pulling, without end.

I swallowed. Well, I'd already involved my siblings. May as well add one more thing.

"Hey . . ." I turned to Kiley. "Can you drive me to Oro?"

The middles both gave me confused looks, and I told them I would explain on the way.

I also told them we'd need to take Dom, and I would go get him.

Darren gave me a look like he maybe didn't think that was my greatest idea, but I ignored him and climbed the stairs to our younger brother's room, knocking on the door.

He didn't answer.

I waited a moment and then knocked again.

When silence greeted me, I opened the door and stepped inside.

Dom was sitting on his bed with his Switch in his hands and his headphones on. "I didn't say you could come in."

"We need to go somewhere," I said.

"Good for you. Go."

I knew that this was my fault. That our relationship had degraded because of me. "I'm sorry," I said. "I believe you. I do. The second I hung up the phone, I knew I'd messed up. I should have always just believed you."

"I don't accept your apology," Dom said, still staring at his video game screen.

Tears pricked at my eyes, but it would feel wrong to cry. He had every right to be mad. He was allowed to not forgive me. Though I wished he would. "I think it's Mack Junior. I need to chase a lead, and you need to come because Karter doesn't want you left alone and neither do I."

"Why's that if you *believe* me now?" He'd rolled his eyes when he said "believe."

"Haven't you been alone enough?" I asked.

That was when Dom looked up. His brow was scrunched and his lips pressed tight, but he still looked like my baby brother. Still looked like a boy who had been treated like a criminal. Not just recently. His whole life. We'd always acted like he was guilty of something even if we didn't know what.

I swallowed and waited.

He said, "I'm bringing my game, and I'm not getting out of the car."

A couple hours later, we pulled up in front of the Wild Pony. The building was tucked away from the country road and had its own dirt parking lot out front. The place had a honey-colored stained log exterior and seemed like it'd been standing for longer than I had been alive. The sign on top was purple and gold and exclaimed the name of the bar. I was honestly shocked that all the lights still worked. Outside, people smoked and laughed with one another, and country music blared from inside the building. It was Friday night, and the place was definitely popular.

It was the closest bar to both ours and Mack Jr.'s ranches and the only place I could think that he might be. I remembered a fair number of empty beer bottles in the guy's house. And at the very least, ranchers nearby must hang out here, so one of them needed to know who Mack Jr. was and if he was around last night when Ellis was killed. I knew it didn't make sense. Why would he commit a murder that would exonerate Dom? But I needed something to look into.

Speaking of Dom, he sat on the left side of the back seat, squished up against the window with his Switch and his headphones, ignoring the rest of us. Darren and Kiley were up front. I'd given them a very abridged version of why we needed to be here, saying only that this Mack Feeney Jr. guy seemed suspicious and had maybe been threatening Dad, and I wanted to see where he was last night. I positioned it as fear for our brother and family. Not as the continuing investigation that it was. Dom had rolled his eyes several times during my telling of the story. It didn't exactly help, and in combination with the secret room stuff, I was starting to wonder how much they would continue to buy when it came to my put-on ignorance.

"So . . . what is it exactly that we're doing here?" Max said, peeking into the front seat. He sat between me and Dom because when we'd grabbed him, Dom had insisted that was the best spot for him. I assumed because my younger brother didn't want to be next to me.

Max, whose name I'd learned today, was the one who'd given us wristbands at the ROM. And he was clearly still *very* interested in Darren, because he'd immediately agreed to come with us despite having almost no information about what we planned to do. Apparently, he was from the Oro-Medonte area, and that was where Darren had originally met him.

My brother turned back and smiled at him. "We need the assistance of a local to help loosen some lips. And I recall you previously saying you knew a fun little country bar you'd love to take me to."

Max flushed and looked around at us. Clearly, he'd wanted that to be a private outing, not one that involved Darren's siblings, but he was taking it in stride. "I meant the Cozy Cowboy, but this one is okay too."

"There are multiple country-themed bars?" Kiley muttered under her breath.

Darren grinned. "See? I knew you were the man for the job. And you know some people here, right?"

"Yeah, a couple girls I went to high school with used to work here. I think one still does? And some of their dads hang out here too."

"Amazing."

Max smiled goofily at my brother.

Kiley rolled her eyes at me while Max was busy staring, and I fought a laugh.

"And . . . how are we supposed to get in?" I asked, gesturing to myself and Dom, who were both underage. Max had snuck us into ROM After Dark, but I didn't think he could get us in wherever he wanted. I could have gotten a fake ID if I'd wanted, because money. I knew Kiley had one. But I hadn't planned ahead for this.

Darren said, "The Wild Pony is also a family-friendly restaurant."

"You're messing with us," Kiley said, turning to our brother.

"Hand to God. They have the bar side and a dining side. I actually googled after our dear sister told us the random place she wanted us to drive her to. We'll get a table at the dining side, where you, my sweet underage siblings, will stay. Meanwhile, Max and I will go to the bar side for a bit. You can observe from afar."

Kiley and I scowled at Darren at the same time. She said, "Yeah, but I have an ID that says I'm nineteen. So I could go."

"And leave Sunny and Dom by themselves?"

"I'm staying in the car," Dom said, as he'd insisted before we left.

"And leave Sunny by herself?" Darren amended.

"Fine," Kiley ground out between her teeth.

Darren tossed our younger brother the key fob, and the rest of us got out of the vehicle. I watched Dom's face through the window, illuminated by his gaming screen, lounged back in the white leather seats.

"Lock the doors," I told him.

He lifted the fob in the air and hit the locks without looking at me.

I sighed and followed the group to the front door of the Wild Pony. Inside, the establishment was split into two sides. The "drinking legality required" half was loud and featured a giant oval-shaped bar with people wrapped around it. There were huge TVs playing some sort of sports game and tables with people chugging beers. The family-friendly side, in terms of decor, was the same wooden tables and log aesthetic, just featuring the addition of booths.

The hostess was a young white girl whose blond hair was tied back in a ponytail. Her uniform featured an incredibly tight T-shirt that said, RIDE 'EM, COWBOY. "Restaurant or bar?" she asked, but she looked at me as if to say, "Don't even try to get into that bar."

"Sally?" Max said, leaning over. "Jenna's sister, right?"

Sally, apparently, squinted, and then her face broke into a big smile. "Oh my God, Max, hey! You live in Toronto now, right? How is it?"

The two of them chatted as Darren walked ahead and picked a booth rather than letting Sally assign us one. Probably because it had a good view of the bar.

More than a few people had already looked at us and then away. Thankfully, there didn't seem to be any hostility. As a family, we never spent much time in the community. We went straight to the ranch and usually brought groceries with us. Maybe sometimes we would go to a local farmer's market, where the vibe was similar to what it was now. Mostly white people who kind of glanced at us and ultimately left us alone. But none of us were sure how this bar experience would go.

Mom had told us countless stories of the sort of shit our grandpa had to deal with when she was younger. And what she and Dad dealt with as kids from Black families in a mostly white area in the nineties. There were places that they just didn't go. Some people might ignore you, and some might even be nice, but others might try to hurt you. And it was hard to tell who was who beforehand. So it was safer to assume that everyone was a danger until proven otherwise.

Sally finished her catch-up with Max and came over to take our drink orders and let us know that she'd be back. The short conversation revealed that she lived in a suburb and therefore probably wasn't up on the ranch gossip.

Darren stood. "Let's try the people at the bar."

"Do you have a plan?" Kiley asked.

He grinned. "Nope!" He nudged Max in the shoulder, and they left us.

Kiley sighed and slouched against the booth. "We'll see if he actually learns anything." She turned to the large glass windows that looked out into the parking lot. The blue-purple wrap of the Mercedes stood out and Dom was illuminated inside the vehicle by his Switch screen. "Well, at least we can see him."

It was what I'd thought when we sat down, but I felt like me and my sister had thought it for very different reasons. I wanted to know that no one could get to him, but it felt like she wanted to make sure *he* couldn't get to anyone.

She looked over at me. "What happened with you two? You were basically attached at the hip, but ever since he got arrested, it's been weird."

I shifted my shoulders inward. "I just got really in my head about everything. And I made it clear that I wasn't sure if he had done it." I shook my head. "Which, like, obviously he didn't. But he didn't feel great thinking that his sister thought he had. Even if it was just for a moment. I don't blame him."

"What else are we supposed to think?" Kiley said, her voice soft. "I know the police suck and all that. But this is his second time catching a murder charge."

"They put charges on the wrong people all the time."

She nodded but still had a frown on her face. I knew Kiley didn't quite believe Dom. Even all the way back to when we'd picked him up from juvie the first time, and I didn't know why.

"Do you think he did it?" I asked.

She chewed on her lip. "He was in jail and a murder happened. That's basically a get-out-of-jail-free card."

I noticed that she hadn't actually said yes or no. "And Torri . . ."

"I don't know . . ." She played with the straw wrapper. "After Mom died, I started watching old home videos."

I blinked. I hadn't even thought about that, but it was true, Mom and Dad had taken videos when we were little. "I forgot about those."

"I did too. I was trying to organize my computer when I saw the Dropbox of them. But, like, when Dom was a toddler, Mom was normal with him. There are videos of her hugging and kissing him and calling him her bear cub."

My eyebrows went right into my hairline.

Kiley nodded, looking at my expression. "I know. 'Cause all I remember was her being weird and distant with him. It was like something changed. But don't you think there must have been a reason for that? Or even if there wasn't, don't you think growing up like that would have some sort of effect? Mom would talk about him like he was . . ."

She trailed off, and unbidden, I thought of Marsha Allen calling my brother a little beast. And that was it. Mom had treated her son like he wasn't a person. She'd loved bears, so it wasn't like she had been shy about claws and teeth, but whatever she'd seen Dom as, it had been different.

Kiley continued, "I know Mom wasn't perfect, but I guess I can't believe she would be terrible for no reason."

I thought of Kiley's ruined sculpture in the shed. Of the way Mom hadn't paid much attention to her either until she started winning awards. I didn't want to think about Mom like that. I was sure that most of the time, she wasn't that way on purpose. But with Dom, there *was* something purposeful about how she treated him.

And now that I knew she hadn't always been like that . . . I wanted to know what had changed. Based on what was in the journal, she'd thought her other children had killed and tortured animals. But Dom hadn't done that. She hadn't had a negative entry for him until he was fourteen. If anything, she should have been weird with everyone *but* me and Dom. So why had he been singled out like that?

I looked at my sister and thought again about Mom's journal entry. I knew now that she had been wrong about Dom. I believed him. But what about the things she'd said my siblings had done? Had she been wrong about those things too?

Kiley said, "Now there's this stuff with Dad. I'm with you. I would rather it was this Mack Junior guy."

"You know Mack?" Sally had come back with our drinks, setting down a chocolate milkshake in front of Kiley and a vanilla one in front of me. "Sorry, I heard you say his name. How's he doing after everything? I really did think you all looked familiar. You have that ranch, don't you?"

Apparently, Sally *did* know about the ranches even if she didn't live on one.

"We do," Kiley said. "What happened to Mack?"

Sally rolled her eyes. "He got into it with some guy. He's got a plot close to you, I think? His name's Andy."

I nodded. I guess Andy had finally hit his limit with Mack.

"Anyway," Sally continued. "They got into an argument and started a whole fistfight. Ridiculous. Police came and grabbed them both, but Mack was worse for wear, so I wondered how he was doing. He's usually in here weekend nights. Friday, Saturday, Sunday, and Thirsty Thursday."

"Wait . . . when did that happen? The fight?"

"Last night."

Kiley and I looked at each other. "About what time?" I asked.

Sally thought for a moment, then said, "Around eleven, I think. He came in and had dinner over here, then went to the bar. Fight broke out later as I was cleaning up the dining area, which is usually around that time. So you haven't seen him?"

"No," Kiley said with a swallow. "Sorry. Don't know how he's doing."

"Oh well," she said with a sigh. "His own fault for getting into a fight." She pointed at the table. "You know what you want to eat?"

We put in our orders, and Sally left again.

I texted Dom to ask if he wanted anything, but he didn't text back.

"Guess that's Mack's alibi," Kiley said.

"Yeah." I already knew it was a long shot. Besides, what would I have done if he didn't have an alibi? This, in terms of solving what happened, was better. Because now we knew that Mack Feeney Jr. hadn't been anywhere near this murder. Which, yeah, maybe the student or whoever he might be working with had done it. But I didn't have anything to confirm that person even existed.

Meanwhile, we still had a secret room in our school.

Kiley sipped on her milkshake and looked over at the bar, where Darren had drawn a few other patrons into some sort of story. "Of course he's found a way to make friends in a country bar."

"And he thought he needed Max for that."

"Well, he's certainly not sad about Max being there."

We had a moment to smile at each other before reality came crashing back in. No matter how I wanted to deny it, all signs were pointing to Dad. He had access to every place in the school and was the most likely to know about that room. And now a murder had, at least temporarily, saved his son. He was, out of everyone, the best suspect. The man who would scream and shout airplane noises while he pushed me on the swings, the man who would crawl on the floor and pretend to be a bear taking me on a ride, the man who pulled me against his side to cry while Mom was lowered into the ground. Sure, he wasn't a perfect responsible adult. But he was a great dad.

And I wasn't ready to lose another parent.

February 10, 1996

Today, the police came to the ranch. I watched the cruiser
pull up right next to the Feeney house. Dad even poked his
head out to look. His fingers shook as he leaned against the
window, which was strange, because it's not like they were
coming for us. The cop got out, and Mack went to meet him. I
was expecting cuffs. That they would go inside and yank out
Donald. That they'd gotten my package and tested the contents
and . . . something! But instead, the two of them laughed and
hugged each other. <u>Hugged.</u>

Then I saw Shirley coming to see the cop. She grinned at
him, and he hugged her, too, picking her up and spinning her
around. When they were all together like that, I could see the
resemblance. The same straight nose and pinched lips.

Was that how Shirley had known what I'd done? Or maybe
she'd just seen me mail the package, and then the cop had
mentioned something? After all, the note had basically said
there was something wrong with the Feeneys. People who I
now know are this cop's own family. Maybe Shirley had put the
pieces together.

All that matters is that no one is going to deal with
whatever is going on over there.

What's the point? Why even go off to school and try to
get somewhere, when white people are always going to be on
top? Are always going to have these sorts of connections? It's

already a miracle that my dad has as much as he does. That Mr. Owens likes us. We're always going to be trying twice as hard just to get close to what they have.

I went over to see Jay and tell him everything, but when I got there, his family was gathered outside, slowly spreading around. From the way their heads were moving, I could tell they were looking for someone. I walked up to Jay and asked what was going on.

"Jonas is missing. He didn't show up to do his work, and there's stuff taken from his room like he's run off."

I said I could help, but then Mr. Turner came over to tell me that it was a family thing. His face was tight. He said my daddy was waiting for me.

And when I turned around, Dad was there, him and Mr. Turner staring at each other a lot more intense than they should have been. Mr. Turner shook his head and said he appreciated Dad, but it was too late. Then he left.

Dad didn't respond when I asked him what that meant. Just steered me toward the house.

He's been strange for a while, but these last few days, it's been more so. He's up at all hours, pacing. Yesterday, Mr. Owens even came by, and they had this secret conversation. When I asked Dad, he just said he'd had to sign some things "just in case," whatever that means.

Jonas is my friend too. I wanted to help, but instead I had to stay at home with Dad.

When I asked him why weren't doing anything, he said they didn't want help from us, and we had to respect that. I thought of when Mrs. Turner was shouting at him. Something had changed between our families, and I couldn't understand what.

~~It made me scared that something might change between me and Jay too.~~*

They still haven't found Jonas. Now more than just Jay's family is searching. Everyone is out there looking for his brother. Even the Feeneys, who have never given a single shit about the Turners. It's hella weird. I even heard one guy complain about why they didn't just "get on with it" without Jonas. And the other replied that they "needed them all." I had no idea what they were talking about. I was even desperate enough to ask Dad what he thought they meant, but he just shrugged.

And so here I am, writing in my journal with Dad sitting at the dining table, sipping on his tea. Not going nowhere.

I asked again to help, because now everyone was, but Dad just repeated the line he had before. They didn't want our help. When I asked why we couldn't give it even if they didn't want it, he said it wasn't our place.

Finally Dad said that it was late and I needed to go to sleep, even though it's a Saturday. That he would be heading to bed too. So I went to my room.

I'm going to wait twenty minutes to be sure he's asleep before I leave.

February 11, 1996

I don't know where to start. But I have to write about this. I <u>have</u> to. Because it's hard to hold on to the reality of it without putting down the words. ~~I wish I didn't have anything to put~~

---

* Change is inevitable when it comes to other people. I learned that eventually. But you can stand firm. Someone has to.

~~down~~. This needs to be recorded somewhere. It's still evidence. Even if I'm the only one who sees it.

So, yesterday . . . I can't believe it was yesterday. It feels like it just happened but also like it happened a long, long time ago.

Anyway, I left the house as quietly as I could to get over near Jay's place because I was going to help. It was strange. Because not that long ago, everyone had been outside with their flashlights searching for Jonas. But now it was quiet. I assumed everyone went home. It was late, after all.

I looked toward the hill where Mr. Owens's house was, and I could see lights on over there, but the lights in everyone else's houses were off. Maybe Mr. Owens was keeping up the search later, was what I'd thought. But I focused on getting to Jay's house, even though their lights were out too.

I took a peek through his window, and there he was. Just Jay. Sitting by himself on the couch in their living room. It was technically leather, but it was scratched up and had tears with stuffing coming out. It was still good enough, so they kept it. I knocked on the window to get his attention. The first few times, he didn't even move. Then finally he looked up and spotted me.

I expected something. Anything. But his face was just blank.

I pointed at the door so he would know that I was coming inside. I left the window and went to open it, but it was locked. It was the first time the Turners' door had ever been locked. So I knocked, hoping that Jay would come.

But for a few moments, nothing happened, and I had to keep knocking, and by the time he came to the door, there were tears streaming down his face.

He told me they took Jonas.

Then he turned around and went back into the house. I

followed because I didn't know what else to do, and he curled up on the couch, not even trying to wipe his face.

I asked Jay to tell me everything. He mentioned that they'd finally found Jonas with his stuff, trying to hitchhike on the road, and that his parents had been angry, dragging him back to the ranch. That Jay didn't understand what was happening. And at Shirley's urging all the families started heading up to Mr. Owens's house. But not everyone. Mrs. Feeney had left Mack Jr. at home, and Andy was told to go home by his parents while his sister and younger brother were taken to the house. And then there was Jay. His parents took Jonas and Iris followed, but his mom told Jay to go home and lock the door.

The surprise must have shown on my face, because suddenly his voice was rising. He'd told me before that his parents were being weird with Jonas. That I'd seen how Shirley had talked to him and how he'd reacted. That I'd known something was wrong but had been too wrapped up in this Feeney revenge shit and trying to leave for my fancy Toronto school. He said I didn't care about him or his family.

I knew then that I'd fucked up. And it wasn't like I could just say "my bad" or whatever and have it be fine. I had known that Jay was worried about Jonas. But I'd cared more about me and Dad, like he said.

Jay was my best friend, and I'd let him down.

I stood up from the couch and told Jay that we were going to get Jonas.

He looked shocked, his mouth hanging open. His dad had told him that he'd get whooped into next Sunday if he left the house. I asked if that was enough to keep him away from his brother.

At that, his expression changed, and I recognized the Jay

that I knew. The one who'd followed me into the forest and helped me hide from Mack and Donald. The one who'd charged at his own sister to rescue me. The one who got me Christmas presents year after year, even though he got teased for it.

We ran up to the Owenses' house. Jay wanted to use the front door, but I told him we should sneak in since we were probably going to have to smuggle Jonas out.

So we went around the side with Jay leading the way and climbed up the trellis to the second-floor balcony that I suspected led to Mr. and Mrs. Owens's bedroom.

Jay got over the balcony first and then helped pulled me in. I was worried about the glass doors because we didn't have anything to break them, but when Jay tried the knob, they opened right up.

It was so quiet. I kept thinking that.

When we got into the hall, I realized why.

I'd only been in Mr. Owens's house a handful of times. But I always remembered the beautiful floral wallpaper, the expensive wood paneling, the plush carpets and rugs, and all the shiny silver and golden objects they had decorating the walls.

But at that moment, there were splatters of red on the floral wall scenes and gouges in the paneling.

Mrs. Owens was lying facedown on the steps leading to the entryway, and on her back were several splotches of red leaking out of her. I reached down and shook her, but she didn't respond. Jay helped me turn her over, and her eyes were wide open and unseeing.

It took almost a full minute for my brain to catch up to the fact that she was dead.

And she was only the first body we saw last night.

CHAPTER TWENTY-SEVEN

I lay in bed staring up at the ceiling after we got home from the Wild Pony. Karter had texted us to say that she and Dad would be staying at the house downtown since they had another meeting with Paris in the morning. Dom had gone straight to his room, and the middles and I had watched some new movie they wanted to see in the theater room before going to bed. Now the house was quiet, but my brain was still working.

I held my phone over my face, scrolling through my messages for something to do. I realized that Craig hadn't texted me since that last conversation we had about him knowing Torri. I wondered if that meant we were finally broken up. Or if we were just continuing in this strange limbo.

Locking my phone, I closed my eyes, making what could barely be called an attempt to sleep.

I couldn't stop thinking about Dad. About how this investigation into protecting the family had devolved into something that now seemed to be implicating my family, just in another way. There had to be some reason for that room and the email from Jonas.

Finally I got up.

I crept out of my room and went up the stairs into Dad's bedroom.

It took me a moment to realize that's what it was now. It wasn't my parents' room anymore. Hadn't been for almost a year.

I sucked in a breath and went inside. I could have turned on the lights since only he and Karter had rooms on this floor and both of them were out, but I didn't. I stayed in the darkness and went back to his computer. It was locked this time, but I guessed the password easily.

Returning to the message from Jonas, I copied the email address and pasted it into the search bar to see if any other emails had come in from his brother. There were none. Which, I guess, made sense. The oldest email was already more than ten years old. The only reason it was still there was because Dad had saved it. If he hadn't saved any others they would be long gone.

I left his computer and went into Mom's office. I booted up hers. She had a more difficult password, but I also knew she kept it on a sticky note somewhere. I turned on the office lights and searched through the drawers until I found one. It was the same yellow as the note given to me at her will reading.

I got into the computer and navigated to her email. I typed in the address and got nothing back.

With a sigh, I leaned back in the chair. When I went to put the Post-it away, I noticed a notebook there. Dom and I found it the first time we came in, but it didn't seem to have any important information. But now that I knew all this stuff with Jonas happened a while ago, I searched through it, looking for his name.

Finally I found something relevant.

Feb 9, 2010

8 a.m.: collect milk from school storage, needs to thaw

If I'd seen this in the journal a few months ago, it would have meant nothing. But now . . . I immediately thought of the freezer in the secret room. That had to be the milk being referenced. Meaning that Mom was the one who put it there if she was planning to collect it. And that was in 2010. And Mom didn't forget to do things. If she put it on that list, she did it. But there was still milk there now. So did she regularly use it for weird bloody milk storage? And why put it in a secret room in the school? Why not just keep it at home? Though in all honesty, if any of us looked in the fridge and saw pink milk, we would have questioned it. And clearly, this wasn't something meant to be discussed at large. But what got me was that Mom hadn't even talked about it with me. Or . . . maybe she had. In whatever she'd left me that had disappeared. I continued to read the entries.

Feb 10, 2010

2 p.m.: visit with Jonas, security id 36 for handoff

That made my eyebrows rise. That sounded like Mom had a specific guard who she planned to give something. Maybe someone who would get something to Jonas? Clearly, this was a bribe situation. But it's not like he'd ever escaped, so it wasn't that. I knew sometimes people snuck cell phones to prisoners. Maybe Jonas had wanted one? But then why would he be emailing Dad through the system if he had a secret phone? So what was being given to him? I also wondered if there was any connection between her visiting Jonas and her going into the secret room the day before. But it's not like she was going to bribe a guard to bring Jonas milk.

I looked at the date again. February tenth.

The same day that Mom—and Torri, too, according to the police—had died. All in different years, but that same day over and over again. And it would be coming up again in just under a month.

"What are you doing?" Dom said from the doorway.

I screamed without meaning to and clapped my hands over my mouth. I paused but nothing happened. The middles were a whole floor down from us. I sighed and pulled my hands away.

"Worried that I'll murder you?" Dom said, narrowing his eyes at me.

Jesus, really? I shook my head. "Of course not. You just surprised me. What are you doing here?"

"Sometimes I walk around the house when I can't sleep. It's supposed to help. I saw the bedroom door was open." He jerked his head at the journal. "What are *you* doing?"

"Looking at Mom's appointments." I quickly summarized for him everything that I had learned about Jonas being our uncle and the secret room. Though I held back the fact that I'd gotten our other siblings involved. I didn't know what he would think about that, and we were already on shaky ground. But I wanted him to know I was still investigating. Still trying to help. "I guess Mom would go for visits. I recognized the date and realized it's the same day that Mom died. But it's probably a coincidence."

"And the last day I saw Torri."

I was glad he'd said it, because I wasn't going to.

Dom looked down at the book, keeping as far away from me as possible. "Isn't that also the day that Jonas killed everybody?"

"What?" I looked down at the date, then scrambled for my phone, going back through my camera roll to the screenshots I had taken of the newspaper articles. He was right. The article itself was dated the next day, but it said the massacre at the ranch had happened the night before. "That's . . . less of a coincidence."

"So who's your prime suspect now? Mack Junior was a bust, right?"

I nodded. I'd said as much on the ride home. As far as suspects, I had Dad in my mind, but didn't want to say it aloud. "I don't know. I thought I would check Mom's stuff again."

Dom shook his head. "Mom's stuff that had you believing I'd done it? Yeah, that'll help. Have you somehow forgotten that Mom was a liar?" He threw his arms up. "Everyone in this family is a liar." He met my eyes. "And yes, I mean you, too, Sunny. That's what you do. You act like everything is sunshine and rainbows all the time, but it's a lie. The only difference is that everyone loves it. Because who doesn't want to pretend the bad things aren't happening? And you're happy to do it every single time."

"And the one time I told you the truth, you threw it back in my face," I snapped at him.

Dom's eyes went wide, and I swallowed, turning away. Shit, shit, shit. I hadn't meant to say anything. But it was true! I'd tried to force down the rising annoyance, but I was so tired of pushing it all down. So fine, if Dom was so desperate to see the real me, he would get it.

I said, "You keep saying that you want the truth, but look at your face right now. Okay, fine, we're a family of liars, but you lie too. I know that I hurt you. I get it. And I'm sorry. I will always be sorry. But you wanted honesty from me and then you didn't like what you got, and suddenly I was your enemy, and yet you're shocked that I pretend to be a different person? With those kinds of rewards, who would want to tell the truth?"

My younger brother crossed his arms over his chest and looked off to the side.

"So what if I only visited you in juvie to look good," I said. "Weren't you happy that I was there? Because no one else was."

Dom's shoulders hunched up, but he said nothing.

"I know I've been a shitty sister. I *know* that. But I'm trying to be better, so don't stand there and pretend you haven't enjoyed the act just as much as everyone else."

I slouched back in the chair and looked away from him. Part of me was screaming to take everything back. I didn't criticize. I didn't get mad. I didn't call people out. I kept my mouth shut and a smile on, and did everything else in the background by myself. That was what Mom had been proud that I could do. I wanted to have done everything the way she wanted.

But it wasn't going the way it was supposed to. And this thing, this Sunny image that she'd loved, wasn't as ironclad as I'd thought. It was one thing for Jeremy to figure things out, but it felt like another thing entirely to have it fall apart like this.

"I was happy that you came," Dom said finally. "But I always knew you never really wanted to be there." I looked over at him and he met my gaze. "You were always the only one who invited me to things, or tried to include me, but you only ever did it when someone else was around to see."

Heat pooled in my cheeks, and I ducked my head like I could hide from the truth of it.

Dom continued, "And the worst part was that I was still glad for it."

"I'm sorry," I said, looking up at him. I tried not to think of how to look genuine. I worked to ignore the thoughts in my head of making my eyes wider, and puffing my cheeks out a bit, and forcing tears. I was so used to pretending. This time I just had to say it and hope he believed me.

"You're right," Dom said. "I asked you for the truth, but I wanted it to be that you believed me. And it wasn't. And I got mad at you. But I'd asked you not to lie, hadn't I? I just . . . I just wanted it to be real. Everyone being nicer to me and feeling like I was finally part of the family, and I thought if you believed me, it would all be real." Tears spilled down Dom's cheeks and he rubbed them away, shoving at his face like he was pissed at it.

All my brother had ever wanted was to be part of our family. And it was the one thing he'd been denied his whole life.

I didn't understand why Mom had done this. Why she'd orchestrated this existence for him. And then she'd died and left nothing behind to explain it. Just that sticky note.

I stood up and reached out for Dom, not knowing what to do, my hand hovering. I didn't want to do something just for the sake of it. He blinked at my arm, lifted and unsure. I ended up settling for patting the top of his head.

"Are you . . . petting me?" he asked, a hint of a laugh sneaking into his voice.

I cringed. "I didn't know what to do, and I panicked."

He started laughing. "Please stop."

"Okay." I pulled my hand back to my chest, my face feeling even more flushed than before, but I was laughing now too.

Once we'd both calmed down, we stood there in Mom's office, saying nothing at all.

"I did actually have one other visitor," Dom said. "But she was super weird, and I told the guards I didn't know her, so she got escorted out."

"You never said anything."

He shrugged. "Seemed too strange to mention. She wanted to warn me about the Milk Man." Dom wriggled his fingers and made spooky sounds until he saw my expression. "What?"

My body felt cold suddenly. Like I was back outside on the rooftop watching a knife get shoved through Shirley's throat. "Tell me everything she told you, right now."

"Okay . . . she said, like, some random stuff about milk maidens. Uh . . . sorry, it was a while ago. Oh, she said, 'A maiden still remains.'"

Then she talked about the Milk Man spoiling the milk and asked if I was rotten, which, like, white woman asking me that shit, that's when I was like, 'I don't know this lady,' and the guard came over. It was super unhinged, so I didn't think anything of it."

It sounded like more of what Shirley had already told me. And I couldn't blame Dom for not mentioning it, because I'd written her off at first too. I took out my phone and showed him the picture I'd taken of Shirley and Mack Jr.'s photo. "Was this her?"

"Yeah," Dom said, surprised. "But her hair was brown. Why does it matter? Who is she?"

And so, finally, I told Dom everything. About how Shirley had approached me, how I'd discovered she was Shirley, and how I'd watched her die.

My brother's eyes got progressively wider as he listened. "Why didn't you say anything?"

I shrugged, hugging my arms around myself. "No body, no crime. I didn't want more trouble for the family."

"You could have told me!"

I shook my head. I knew, objectively, that I could have told Dom, but it went against everything I was supposed to do. It was one thing to not be Sunny when we were already upon a body. And another to share something when I could instead keep it inside, and smile, and let everyone go on happier without knowing.

Dom looked into my eyes and said, "You know that if you suffer just so other people are happy, that's not okay, right?"

I didn't know how to tell my brother that was my strength. That was what Mom had admired about me. Because part of me thought that maybe it wasn't okay either. But also, I wasn't sure how to say that I didn't know how to stop. So instead I said, "Is there anything else Shirley told you?"

"Yeah," Dom said, biting his lip. "She said she was there when

Mom died. That the Milk Man killed her, and he would come for the rest of us." He tucked his hands under his armpits. "Mom's death was in the news, so I just figured she'd seen the reports and it was more bullshit. But now . . ."

But now we knew that Shirley had seen the murderer, tried to warn us, and been killed for her efforts.

CHAPTER TWENTY-EIGHT

The music in the apartment was so loud that I could hear it in the elevator. The woman beside me wrinkled her nose as she assessed my outfit. My jacket hid most of it so you could only see the black tights and chunky-heeled boots on my feet. But I guess that was enough. Though she was at least an equal-opportunity hater, because she gave Dom just as much side-eye for leaning against the elevator wall with his beanie pulled low and arms crossed over his violently neon jacket. When the elevator stopped, she strode out ahead of us.

What I had planned to do this Friday night was stay in and try to figure something out. Dom had already been back home for a week, and we still hadn't figured out what to do with this Shirley information. But I'd at least finally caught him up on letting the rest of the siblings in on the secret room, because it felt safe to tell him everything. Or maybe that wasn't the word. It seemed weird to say "safe" like I needed to calculate the level of danger before sharing things with people, but it was the only thing that fit. Besides, this was about him, and he was the only one helping me. It would work better if he had all the information that I did.

Anyway, that plan was somewhat derailed by Shyanne being

suddenly insistent about me coming to this party that had already started like an hour ago.

"Are you sure it's okay that I'm here?" Dom said for perhaps the tenth time since I'd done my own begging to get him to come with me. I didn't want to be alone, and didn't want him to be alone either. I would just see what Shyanne wanted and then we could leave.

"Yes," I said as I texted Shyanne to let her know I was by the elevator, where she'd told me to wait.

The apartment building was technically in Mimico, but not in the cluster of condos near the water. It was a series of low-rise buildings that had seen better days. The walls were covered in a beige floral-patterned wallpaper. I couldn't tell if that was the original color or if it had faded over time.

Shyanne came around the corner with Mercy hot on her heels. Shyanne had her brow furrowed, and Mercy was speaking quickly under her breath. It seemed . . . heated. They *never* argued.

"Hey . . . ," I said.

Shyanne grimaced. She glanced at Dom but didn't mention him. "Hey. Thanks for coming."

"This is a bad idea," Mercy hissed, looking to me and then to Shyanne. Then she did a double take on Dom, and her eyes practically bugged out of her head.

I shifted, stepping in front of my brother. "What's up?"

Mercy sighed and threw her hands up. "I'm not involved in this." She turned around and walked back toward the sounds of pumping bass.

I focused in on Shyanne. "Is she okay?"

"Yeah." She sighed and rubbed her hands on her head. She was dressed casually in a pair of jeans and a tank top. I guess it was probably hot inside the party even if it was cold outside. "We're . . .

like . . . I know we're not close or anything, but we're friends, right?"

"Of course!" I chimed automatically. But were we? I didn't know. I liked Shyanne, but we weren't friends like Jeremy and Dom were. Which had been my choice. I couldn't really be close with any of my "friends," because I was always trying to act a certain way.

Shyanne crossed her arms. "I get it. You have to be, like, diplomatic and shit with everyone because your family owns the school. But even when you hang out with us outside school, it feels like you're standing apart. I barely know anything about you. Don't know what foods you like or shows you watch or music you listen to." She kind of looked at Dom over my shoulder. "Sorry, are you cool with him hearing this, or . . . ?"

"He's fine," I said at the same time that Dom started to say that he could leave. "What's going on?" Did she seriously make me come out here just to spell out that we weren't friends?

"I'm asking because I don't know you. I really don't. But, like . . . when I see messed-up shit, I need to say something. And I haven't for so long because I didn't know how you would react. That's why Mercy is freaking out. Because she thinks you're super fake."

I kept my posture loose, working hard not to stiffen. "Is that why she doesn't like me?"

"Honestly, yeah. Rich people who smile to your face are usually saying crap behind your back, you know? The way you go around school from group to group makes you look sus. No one wants to share anything with you in case you spread stuff around, but no one wants to be like 'go away' in case you complain to your parents and get us kicked out. No one wants to tell you anything bad people say about you or your family, period, for the same reason."

I wanted to scream.

It wasn't supposed to be like this. I'd been trying to be like Mom. To be the sort of person who could take over. I'd carefully crafted this persona, and meanwhile, everyone could see through it. And worse, they'd made assumptions about what that meant. It wasn't just about not being seen as likable. They actively saw some fake rich girl who could easily get Mommy and Daddy and ruin their lives without a second thought.

"Do you really think that?" I said to her, trying to control the wobble in my voice. "That I would get you kicked out of school?"

She shrugged. "Maybe you wouldn't, but you could if you wanted to, and that's enough. This school, this opportunity, it's everything to us. I'm not commuting for an hour every day for fun. I need this."

"I know you do. That's exactly why I would never do that. We're supposed to be lifting everyone up, sending the elevator back down."

"You say that, but how am I supposed to know that? I don't *know* you, Sunny. None of us do. And you've never known the feeling of standing in the lobby, watching the elevator stuck at the top floor, wondering if it's ever going to come get you or if you're gonna have to make your way up all those stairs alone. *You* don't have to wonder. *You* don't have to walk those stairs. But *we* do."

She was right. Of course she was. Mom did the walking so we could be born as close to the top floor as possible. Even if being Black meant we still came up against a few closed doors. So how could I blame Shyanne for thinking that way? She had to look out for herself.

"Why did you ask me to come to this party?" I kept my voice light, but I didn't bother prettying it up with inflection. It was hard enough to hold back tears.

Dom shifted beside me, and I purposely avoided looking at him. Now that he'd experienced me without the Sunny veneer, I worried that seeing his expression would make it break. Like he was the crack in the mirror reflecting my face, and if my eyes met his,

I would remember it was there, and the whole thing would shatter.

Shyanne sighed. "I need you to see something."

We followed her into the party. The room had a heavy scent to it: sweat mixed with liquor and weed. The apartment was small and open concept. Everyone was crowded in the kitchen and tiny dining room area. While the living room served as a dance floor.

Dom kept his head low, so no one looked twice, which is what I assume he wanted. I shouldn't have made him come. He'd been blasted online as a murderer, and these were kids from school. I was so busy checking on Dom that when I finally looked up, it took me a moment to realize why Shyanne had brought me here.

There, in the middle of the dance floor, was Craig with some girl attached to his front. His hands around her waist, grinding into her with his own hips. Her arms were around his neck, and he was kissing her. Sloppily. So sloppy that I could see his tongue moving in and out of her mouth.

Dom let out a little gasp.

I just stared at them.

This was what I'd wanted, wasn't it? For this relationship to be over?

But not like this.

And in the back of my mind, I couldn't even blame him. It wasn't like I'd been an ideal girlfriend, either. I wasn't brave enough to risk my image to get rid of him, and he wasn't brave enough to tell me he was done. So now here we were.

No one at this party filled with people I went to school with were even watching them. Meaning, they knew about this. Had known.

But no one would tell me. Except this time, they weren't hiding it to protect me. They were hiding it to protect themselves *from* me.

I went into the kitchen and looked at the drink options there, picking up a red Solo cup. I found a bottle of rum and poured some in there.

"Sunny . . . ," Shyanne said from behind me. "You okay?"

"Maybe we should leave," Dom added, tugging on the sleeve of my jacket.

"Mmm-hmm," I hummed, ignoring them both. I looked for the sort of pop that would be best and found an orange Crush. I poured that into the cup too.

"Didn't know you drank," Shyanne said with a bit of a laugh. Her effort to lighten the mood, I could tell.

"She doesn't," Dom said.

Technically, I did. But I liked for people to think I wouldn't touch a drop until I was the legal drinking age. Good-girl stuff.

I checked that the cup was full and then paused to look at my brother. "Hang back by the door."

"Sunny . . ."

"Just do it." I didn't try to make my voice sound chipper. Partially because I didn't need to do that with my brother anymore, but I wasn't really in the headspace for it either. "Please."

Dom nodded and went back toward the entrance of the apartment. Meanwhile, I left the kitchen and headed onto the dance floor. That was when the other partygoers started to clock me walking over to Craig. I saw phones being pulled out, but I didn't care. And I'd already made sure Dom was out of the way.

I waited until Craig turned to me. Until he saw me. Until it registered in his expression.

Then I threw the drink in his face.

He spluttered and stepped back. The girl did too. I knew her from school, but it didn't matter. This wasn't about her. I hadn't been dating her. I had been dating Craig.

"Sunny!" he gasped. "It was— We were—"

He couldn't even form a coherent excuse. I stood there, thinking about what I should say. I could throw out something about him being bad at sex. I could talk about how I would never do something like this to him. I could ask how he would do this to me.

Instead what came out was, "I don't even like you. This could have been over so long ago. This has been such a waste of my time."

That was what it came down to, really.

"Did . . . did your sister tell you?" Craig said, looking around. I realized that Shyanne hadn't followed me over. She was back by the kitchen.

"What?"

He hunched his shoulders. "She . . . she saw us. At the winter dance . . . I thought that's why you hadn't been texting me over the break, but you never said anything about it."

I didn't need him to tell me which sister.

I turned around and walked out of the party, Dom following behind me. No one else came after us. "I'm sorry I brought you here," I said to him.

He shook his head. "I'm sorry about Craig."

I shrugged it off, though I wasn't anywhere near feeling that casually about it yet. I texted Shyanne to say thank you. At the charity event, she and Craig had been arguing. Now I knew that it must have been about this. That was why he was downstairs. Not to "get air" but to meet up with this girl. Which meant this had gone on for months. But still, I was glad she'd finally told me. Even though she'd had no idea how I would react. She'd done more for me than my own flesh and blood.

In the hallway, I FaceTimed my sister.

"Is that a good idea?" Dom asked me, looking at Karter's name on the phone.

I didn't respond, waiting for her to pick up and standing so our brother wouldn't be in the frame. Karter finally answered after five rings. She wasn't at home. Her hair and makeup were done, and her eyes looked glassy. Drunk or high. I couldn't tell which. "Why are you FaceTiming me? I'm out."

"You knew Craig was cheating on me."

She rolled her eyes.

Rolled. Her. Eyes.

"He told you?" she asked.

"No. A friend brought me to a party so I could see firsthand that he was feeling bold enough to make out with a girl in front of everyone. A bunch of students. And no one but this friend wanted to tell me."

She chuckled. "You don't have friends."

"Fuck you," I snapped.

Dom made an audible squeak beside me.

Karter's eyes went wide, and the smile fell clean off her face. She was either too shocked, high, drunk, or all three to have noticed the sound Dom had made. "Excuse me?"

"You should have told me!" I hissed. "You're my sister, and you've known for a month! You could have told me at any time and you didn't!"

My sister's lips peeled back into their own snarl. "Get down off your high horse. You know that if it had been me being cheated on and you found out, you would have sealed your lips shut and done it with a smile. I *protected* you. I *saved* you from realizing your boyfriend was a scumbag." She muttered under her breath, "I'm so tired of being screamed at, fuck."

I didn't care who else had been yelling at Karter. I was busy trying to figure out what I hated more: that Karter was saying this to me or that she was right. "The same way you protected me when we were supposed to be playing hide-and-seek, and you went off to do your own thing, and I got lost and ended up with some dead body?!"

"Don't you fucking blame me for that! How was I supposed to know that would happen?!" Karter shrieked, spit flying onto the screen. "You don't think Mom and Dad have spent my entire life blaming me for that?! You got love, and hugs, and blankets, and all their attention when we found you, and what did I get? It was hard for me, too! That day was torture for me, and *everyone* made it about you. Perfect, special, favorite Sunny! Meanwhile, I was the one they complained to when they had their millions of fights that you were spared from. I have to deal with all their shit! But not you, little miss sunshine. And you don't even realize it. That's the worst part about you."

I was shaking, the phone jittering in my hand, and Karter was still swaying until she hit a wall and leaned against it. She was really trying to make me feel bad about my own childhood trauma. "Mom never wanted you to lead this family," I said. I didn't care that I didn't have proof. "'Karter is rash, impulsive, and lacking empathy.' That was what she said about you. And I knew she didn't want you, but I let you play at being her."

My older sister's face went slack for a moment before it twisted, her nostrils flaring and the veins on her neck bulging. "Why don't you tell the whole family that?" I stayed silent, and she laughed. "That's right, because you know that no one would ever believe you. Because here's the real truth: no one thinks you're the right one for the job. It doesn't matter what Mom wanted. That's why, when I saw her package to you with her cute little sticky note, I took it."

". . . What?" It was the only thing I could say. Karter . . . took it? That was why I hadn't gotten what Mom left me, because Karter had had it the whole time?!

Karter grinned. "You think I was going to let you have what should have been mine? I'm the oldest! She should have wanted me!

And I saw that package nice and neat on Paris's desk, and I lifted it into my purse. And just like I thought, Paris didn't want to lose face and say she'd lost an important part of Mom's will, so she acted like it didn't exist. I've done everything Mom wanted you to do, and I don't think it's a stretch to say that I've done it better than you ever could. And what do you know? Everyone accepted it. Because it's what makes sense. Mom was wrong about you, and she was wrong about me."

The sticky note that I found . . . Karter must have ripped it off. That was why she was in Mom's office that day when Dom and I were investigating. Because she hadn't been able to find where she'd dropped it. And she didn't want me to see it.

And she was right.

No one in the family had contested it.

And if I told them what Mom really wanted, if I pushed back, would they actually prefer me over Karter? Before all this, I would have said yes. But now . . . the way they all saw me. It wasn't as a leader, it was as a child who knew nothing about the real world and needed to be sheltered. They still saw the younger version of me, huddled in that tent, clinging to a dead woman's hand.

Karter said, "Go home, Sunny. Sulk in your room. Cry your eyes out. Eat a tub of ice cream. I don't care. But you slap that smile on your face the way you always do because it's the only positive contribution you make to this family."

She ended the call.

I was still gripping the phone in my hand when I turned and saw Shyanne and Mercy standing there. And from the pitying looks on their faces, I knew they'd heard it all.

I smiled.

It was the only thing I could think to do.

Then my brother's hand slipped into mine and the smile fell away. I looked over at him, and he squeezed my fingers. I squeezed back. I held on like it was the only thing keeping me upright. Because it was.

CHAPTER TWENTY-NINE

The Monday after the incident at the party, I walked into school as usual. The security at the front checked my bag like they did everyone else's, and I went to homeroom on the first floor. I answered that I was here when the teacher did attendance. I stood for the national anthem and sang along in a clear open voice the way the vocal instructor that Mom "treated" us to when we were younger taught us. And then I went to my next class despite the whispers that followed me in the hallways.

In the basement for my chemistry lab, I sat at a table in the front like I always did. Mercy and Shyanne came into the classroom, and instead of going toward the back and taking their seats together, Mercy went to their spot and Shyanne diverted and sat next to me.

I turned to her with a smile that was met with a grimace. "It really isn't necessary for you to sit next to me."

"You'll need a lab partner."

I smiled harder. "I can just work with whoever is left over."

"It's okay. Me and Mercy always work together."

"Get the fuck away from me." I kept the pleasant beaming smile in place even though it hurt. The chatter in the room dropped into complete silence. "Please," I added.

Shyanne slid off the stool and went to the back of the classroom with her girlfriend.

"Thank you!" I chimed, and turned to open my textbook to the appropriate experiment.

I didn't know how to properly express to Shyanne that while I appreciated her, I didn't want to sit and talk with someone who was going to pity me. Or who would want to discuss the multiple ways I had been humiliated on Friday night: first by Craig and then by my own sister.

The only saving grace being that Dom was there with me. He'd spent the whole Uber ride talking inanely about the plot of a video game he'd been playing online with Jeremy. Something about monsters and dancing. I assumed it was to distract me, which I appreciated.

But now I had to deal with school. School where I knew that videos of both Craig cheating and me throwing a drink at him had been making their rounds. The Sunny image was officially destroyed. And there was no point in fixing it. Karter was right. Even without Mom's approval, she was the leader of this family. And I was nothing.

Mom was wrong. Being Sunny hadn't done anything for me. I should have been more like her, because then people would have seen me as strong the way they saw Karter. I could barely recognize Karter last night as the same sister who'd brought me soup when I was sick. But it didn't matter, did it? It was working for her.

Maybe Marsha Allen had a point. Maybe our family was more beast than bear. Not majestic predators but something else. Something twisted and toxic and snarling. I'd spent so much time pretending to be otherwise when I should have just embraced the monster I was meant to be.

At lunch, I picked up my meal from the cafeteria and decided to take advantage of the privilege I had and broke the rule of no food outside the meal area, taking my whole tray downstairs into Mom's office. Another place I technically wasn't supposed to be. I sat at her desk and speared lettuce onto my fork, robotically putting it into my mouth.

Not one person stopped or even questioned me during the entire process. Which I now knew was likely from fear of upsetting me and losing their jobs. Though it could have also just been pity.

There were raised voices outside the door. My first thought was of the protestors, but they were long gone. Ms. Allen had finally been charged for releasing Dom's name and was out on bail with conditions to stay away from our family, which meant she couldn't be at the school. Meanwhile, Paris had neatly wrapped up Karter's assault charge with the Crown, promising community service and no contact with Ms. Allen. While the woman herself was facing serious consequences with a government-assigned lawyer nowhere near Paris's tax bracket. I didn't feel bad for Ms. Allen like I had that first time I'd seen her. I was just glad she was gone. Who I did feel bad for was Duane's, Ziggy's, and Ellis's parents, who had probably quickly realized that Marsha Allen didn't give a shit about them or their kids.

All that meaning the shouting couldn't be the protestors.

I didn't get time to wonder what else might be happening, because there was a series of knocks on the door. I frowned at it, then got up and opened it.

Standing there were Shyanne and Mercy, both holding their lunch trays. "Figured you would be here," Shyanne said with a smile.

"She didn't. We tried your dad's office first, and he said you weren't there," Mercy cut in.

"What . . . are you doing?" I asked, looking between the two of them.

"Thought we could have lunch together."

I narrowed my eyes. "I really felt that I was explicitly clear earlier."

Shyanne nudged her way in, and I stepped aside. Anything else would have required me to shove her, and I wasn't going to do that. Mercy followed behind her, and they shut the door.

I could hear the audible grumble of one of the office ladies on the other side.

The girls came over to Mom's desk and set their trays on the other side, using the two chairs that she always had set up in case she needed to talk to parents.

With a sigh, I went over to my tray and continued eating. If they wanted to stay, they could. That didn't mean that I had to talk to them.

And so we ate. Not in silence, because Shyanne and Mercy were talking to each other like normal. It was like when we usually had lunch except I wasn't having to waste time trying to figure out ways to pleasantly contribute to the conversation while also giving Craig the amount of attention he so pathetically craved.

Mercy paused for a moment to stare at me.

"Staring is rude," I said. Which broke my rule of not speaking, but whatever.

She smiled. "You're kind of bitchy."

"Pot. Kettle."

"Never said I wasn't."

"It's good to be self-aware."

Shyanne watched us go back and forth with a slight smile. Which I couldn't understand, because it wasn't like this was a heartwarming conversation.

"Why rum?" Mercy asked. "Why not throw vodka or gin?"

"Thought rum would burn his eyes more."

"And the orange Crush?"

"Figured it would stain."

She nodded thoughtfully. "Good choices. It definitely ruined some of whatever tanner he puts on his face. It was splotchy after." She cackled to herself.

I narrowed my eyes at the two of them. "Aren't you friends with him?"

"We grew up with him," Shyanne said. "It's not the same. He's like family in some ways. Like a bratty younger brother or something."

"One who you have to repetitively tell not to do things just so he can either get angry about it or ignore it." Mercy shook her head. "When we were kids, it was him suddenly acquiring an 'accent' that he didn't have before. Talking like Toronto mans when we lived in Mimico. Which we corrected. Then we got older, and it was impassioned speeches about the ways Black men are held down that reeked of misogynoir or otherwise had a weird white savior vibe. And we corrected that, too. Now it's this Blackfishing shit. And a conversation where I literally heard him use the words 'side piece,' so yeah, I'm done with the labor. He can make a fool of himself by himself. There's only so long that you can give someone the benefit of the doubt just because you grew up with them."

I couldn't believe that I was seriously going to just permanently deal with Craig to avoid looking bad. That I was going to let him follow me to university and stick to me like a slug. Leaving a trail of shit in my wake. "I should have broken up with him a long time ago."

Mercy snorted. "You think?"

"Mercy," Shyanne said, her tone chiding.

"No," I said. "She's right. I didn't like him. But I cared more about what it would look like to break up with him. He's not getting a pass for cheating. Instead of being terrible to each other, we should have just been done."

Everything I had used to justify the way I lived felt like such bullshit now. It had all backfired on me anyway. I thought my facade was the best thing for everyone. It let me pretend my life was perfect all the time and maintained the Behre standard Mom wanted. But now I knew that it'd never really worked. I'd exhausted myself for nothing. And Karter had taken on the role of leader without any effort.

I'd thought I would feel upset about it. But I was more annoyed with the way Karter had told me than actually losing the title I'd never had. I was already drained without it. I couldn't even understand what Mom had wanted from me, and moreover, I didn't know how I felt about carrying it out knowing that she'd thought Dom was guilty.

"Thanks," I said to Shyanne. "For telling me about Craig. I *am* grateful. I just . . ."

"Didn't want the pity?" Mercy tried, leveling me with a stare.

I was reminded of the conversation I had with Shyanne not that long ago about the way I used my money. How I assumed they didn't have anything and found ways to pay for them. That was pity too. And maybe it would have been hard for them to agree to just have me pay for some things, but it wasn't my call.

"Yeah," I said finally. "And, like . . . I'm not gonna have you two kicked out of school or anything. I wouldn't do that to anyone. So if you don't want to be here, you don't have to. You're good."

Shyanne scowled. "That's not why we're here. Honestly, when you cussed me out in the classroom, I was curious about finally meeting the real Sunny."

Mercy laughed. "I died. I couldn't believe it. I didn't know you could swear."

I smiled to myself, ducking my head.

After school, when I walked into the house, Dom was sitting on the couch watching the news with the middles. It was a weird picture to see. But it was good. I took off my shoes, and as they turned to me, I felt the urge to pull my lips into a smile, but didn't. There was no point.

Darren blinked at me. "You . . . okay?"

"No."

He and Kiley exchanged alarmed looks.

Only Dom took it in stride.

I went to see what they were watching. It was a news report that, once again, featured our school. It was the most coverage we'd ever gotten. But when we were producing alumni who went on to be amazing professionals, the news reports were nowhere to be found.

The white woman on-screen was wearing a bright pink blazer that matched her nail color. "No further leads regarding the series of grisly murders committed at Behre Academy. The police are now facing criticism due to the fact that the killings continued despite their prime suspect being in custody. That individual has now been released on bail that was previously denied, and the investigation seems to have stalled as the authorities scramble to acquire more information."

"They haven't dropped the charges?" I asked, looking at my siblings.

Dom shook his head. "Paris said they already look bad and dropping the charges will make it worse. That they'll probably try to find a new suspect with more evidence before doing anything about my charges."

I looked back at the TV, where the woman continued, "The public, however, is skeptical and has been criticizing the way this investigation is being handled, suggesting that authorities made the charge to try to 'kill two birds with one stone' and close two active murder cases at once. This has also called into question the legitimacy of the initial second-degree charge made against this suspect for a case that was previously ruled an accident. Meanwhile, concerned citizens are questioning what the police are actually doing to get the real murderer off the streets. More on this at eleven."

The news report then changed to a shooting that had happened downtown.

"This is good, right?" Darren said. "If they're being questioned about the legitimacy of Dom's first charge."

It was. And sure, they definitely had more on the stuff with Torri, but still, not enough. Knowing what I did about the incident with Jonas at the ranch, I realized Mom was probably left paranoid and traumatized by what had happened. She was looking for patterns where none existed. That was why she'd drawn that symbol on Torri's autopsy report. My brother was innocent. And now people were finally starting to understand that.

"Did Paris say anything about the first charge?" Kiley asked Dom, and there was something . . . off in her voice. I looked at her, but her face was neutral.

"She's pushing to get that one dropped. Threatening to sue the police for their own negligence and bias, proven by how long it took them to deal with Ms. Allen. But if they won't drop it, she said she can probably get it from second-degree to something lesser. Plea to criminal negligence. Doesn't come with an automatic life sentence like first- and second-degree, it won't put a murderer label on me, and it'll help us avoid a trial. Then it'll get locked away when I turn eighteen." Dom said this all with a sort of detachment.

I thought of what Jeremy had said, about him having lost hope. That even now when things were going his way, he still seemed to be expecting the worst.

Meanwhile, I was finally starting to feel like everything was going to work out. Dom and I didn't even need to try to find the real murderer at this point because it seemed like the police were actually going to do that instead of just blaming him. And Paris would handle the rest. We just needed to stick together and stay safe.

But then I thought of the room in the school.

There was something more to this that I was missing.

Even if everything went Dom's way, this wouldn't be done. Not while I knew that place existed. That Mom had created and used it. That Dad had password-protected it. But maybe it would just become one of the many unsettling things about this family that I learned to ignore.

February 12, 1996

Everyone keeps asking if I'm okay. I'm not. But I say I am. I had
a psychological evaluation today. They seem happy with my
results, which is what matters the most.

I thought that if I broke the night up into separate entries
like this, it would be easier to tell the whole story. Honestly,
yesterday when I sat down and started writing, I thought I
would write it all. But I kept stopping.

The psychologist has noticed it. My writing. She's
complimented me on it. Said that writing everything down
is a great way to keep a record for yourself. And to have a
conversation with yourself too. To work through your thoughts
and feelings. She said that it doesn't even need to be complete
entries. That it can be schedules or dates, or to-do lists, or
drawings or poems, or pictures.

I wonder if she thinks I'm traumatized.

Maybe I am.

Shirley definitely is. She was screaming when they brought
her in, and kept at it for hours. Earlier today, we were both in
the dining area for breakfast but at different tables. I think
they're trying to keep us separated. Though when I saw her
going to the bathroom, I followed. Just to see how she was. And
she was there, waiting for me.

She told me the maidens hadn't needed to be at Mr. Owens's
house that night and she'd made them come anyway. She'd

wanted the audience. It was supposed to be her moment of glory. She was going to save all the little calves just like she'd saved the ranch. The Milk Man was going to heal their ailments.

I wanted to ask her more, but someone else came into the bathroom then, so I left.

Someone's screaming now even as I write this. And I wonder if it's Shirley.

They let me keep the bear Jay gave me, though they took the key chain part. I like to hold on to it. I think of Jay and what he said about me being strong. Of what Dad says about bears. About us and our family.

I'm keeping it close to me now to remind me of that because I need to finish writing about what happened.

We were staring at the dead body of Mrs. Owens.

Jay looked at me then and told me that I had to leave. That something was wrong and I needed to get out of the house. I challenged whether he would come with me, and he looked away. I knew he would stay to find Jonas.

So I refused to go. I told him I wasn't going to leave him. Not then, not ever.

I meant it too. We needed each other. I should have been there for him, and I wasn't, but I wouldn't make that mistake again.

Dad and Jay are both my family. And you don't leave your family behind.*

We continued down the stairs, shouting for Jonas. I was shaking, though I tried to ignore it. Because I knew that

---

* Your father and I very much took this to heart. I'm sure it's confusing to you, given everything, but family is complicated. It's important for you to know that no matter how you and your siblings get along, you have to keep the family together. And you have to be willing to do whatever it takes to make that happen.

someone had killed Mrs. Owens and we were in the house with that person, and maybe they would kill us, too. I thought of Donald with that cat and the way he'd bitten his dad.

In the entryway, there were more bodies.

They were all families from the ranch. Mrs. Miller, who helped weigh the cows, had a slash across her throat. It was jagged and ugly. She was holding the hand of her daughter, Kansas, who was fourteen. Her eyes bulged, and there was a telephone cord wrapped around her throat. The weird thing was that there was also a knife in Mrs. Miller's hand. And some of the telephone cord was in her fingers, too.

I stumbled away from them to keep following Jay, who was getting too far ahead.

We got into the main ballroom. It was the pride of the house for Mr. Owens. This huge space where he and his wife would hold events for their friends.

It was filled with corpses.

People with their throats cut, resting in pools of blood that seemed to stretch on endlessly. Others with various stab wounds, the knives still sticking out of their bodies. One person had a meat tenderizer stuck in their eye socket. Parents, and kids, and all the girls from Shirley's group, though I couldn't see Shirley herself. And the smell . . . that smell is what I won't forget. It was thick and heavy. Once, Dad had to go to the slaughterhouse we sent the cows to, and I went along with him. Their operations manager was in the main butchering room, and when I got in there, I immediately had to run out. The scent of blood was suffocating. It felt like what I imagined biting into a raw steak would be like.

And there, among the carnage, I finally spotted Mr. Turner and Iris. Both of their bodies littered with stab wounds.

I threw up on the floor. And that made the stink worse.

Then we heard our names being whispered softly. So quiet we almost missed it. And there was Jonas, peeking his head out of a closet. There was something about the way he looked. I can't explain it. But when Jay went to run to his brother, I held him back. He struggled. I knew he'd seen his dad and sister lying there, dead. I didn't know where Mrs. Turner was, but I figured she was gone too. And here was his brother, <u>alive</u>.

I asked for Jonas to show us his hands, and he did, slowly peeling his body out of the space. His palms were covered with blood. It was smeared on his clothes, too.

Jay made a choking sound and asked his brother what he'd done.

Jonas didn't say anything. He just kept staring at Jay.

I was searching the room, my grip on Jay getting harder as I attempted to tug him back. Though his older brother wasn't moving toward us.

Jay was crying by then. Sobbing about his brother being blamed. After all, he was the only one still alive. What else were they going to think?

That was when I started to notice the smell of smoke.

I didn't know who'd set it. If it was Jonas or someone else, but the place was burning, and it was going fast. It felt like we'd only just noticed the smoke when flames started licking at the wood.

We stumbled out of the house together, the fire behind us. Jay had turned to check on Jonas, who was moving slower than we were. And so I saw her first. Mrs. Turner, running toward the house.

She must have gotten away at some point, probably to go find Jay. I was relieved in that moment. Relieved for Jay. But she was shouting at us. She kept saying to "stay away!" But it was only when she got closer that I could hear what she was really saying.

Stay away <u>from him</u>.

I twisted around and saw the glint of the knife in Jonas's hand before Jay did. I ran without thinking, barreling into Jay's side and taking him down to the ground, away from his brother. I scrambled onto my butt, rushing to defend us, but Jonas had already moved on.

He'd turned his gaze to his mom and was sprinting after her. She'd stopped coming toward us and started to run in the opposite direction.

But Jonas was so much faster than her.

And so we watched as Jonas plunged the knife deep into his mom's back.

Jay screamed and tried to go after them, but I clung to him and kept him down. I needed him to stay safe with me. He shoved me away and rose to his feet, screaming at his brother.

He was standing between me and Jonas. A few feet separating all of us from one another.

Just then Jonas turned to face us. And I swear, what was looking our way wasn't Jonas.

I froze in place staring into those eyes. They went on and on and on and on. Dark and deep and endless.

Then I saw Dad, creeping out from behind a nearby house with a shotgun in his hands. Jay was saying something. Several somethings to Jonas. He was completely focused on his brother. He didn't see my dad. Mrs. Turner was on the grass, twitching and moaning.

Dad put a finger to his lips and raised the gun.

Jonas was walking toward us, was raising the knife, was looking at Jay.

And I knew in that moment that Dad was going to kill Jonas. And I knew that Jay would hate me forever for not saving his brother. But I wasn't going to lose him to keep Jonas.

So I squeezed my eyes shut, and the shot rang loud in the air.

Jonas cried out.

I pictured him in my mind, because I thought it would help prepare me. I imagined him laid out on the grass, his eyes wide, blood pouring from a bullet wound in his head.

Except when I opened my eyes again, Jonas was clutching at a bleeding leg, very much alive, and Dad was hitting him on the head with the rifle. Jonas went down, and Dad pulled out a rope, binding his limbs together. He called out to Jay to take off his shirt and press it against his brother's wounds.*

The police and fire department showed up a while after. It was too late for the blaze, but not for Shirley. She'd used some sort of blanket to cover herself with, and had been saved while attempting to drag out Donald's lifeless body, screaming the entire time. I hadn't even realized that she was inside.

Everyone else was dead except for us, Andy, and Mack Feeney Jr. Every other family on the ranch had been at that meeting in Mr. Owens's house. They found him in his son's bedroom, hanging from a ceiling beam. His son was on the floor with a knife sticking out of his chest.

When we got to the police station and Dad was inside talking with the cops, Jay asked me how I knew my dad was going to shoot Jonas in the leg, not the back. I made a face

---

* My father was as soft as soft could be. He gave chances to everyone. I should have known that he would have gone for the nonfatal shot. If the gun had been in my hands, Jonas would have died, and things would be very different. Sometimes, I'm glad I wasn't the one with the gun. And sometimes, I think of this moment, and wish more than anything that my father had killed him.

at him, and he dropped it. I was too afraid to tell him that I hadn't known.

All I'd been sure of was that I couldn't lose him.

February 19, 1996

We're on the way back home now. I'm in the back seat with Jay, who isn't speaking and just keeps staring out the window. Dad is driving but keeps looking at us in the rearview mirror.

I've had my journal returned to me.

At first, I hadn't thought anyone would care that I wrote in one, until the psychologist had pointed it out. I don't think she lied. I think she really liked that I was using it to deal with everything. But once I realized that she'd noticed, I also understood that other people might care that I was keeping a record. So it wasn't a surprise when the police showed up and asked about it. Dad said it was good to be cooperative, so I handed the book over. They took it to photocopy. Though Jonas had already confessed.

And now we were finally getting to go home together, just like <u>he'd</u> promised.

I hadn't heard the Milk Man's voice in a long time.

The first time, I'd ignored him.

And he hadn't come again. Not until a few nights ago after everything that happened.

That time I knew better.

No one had ever cared what I'd put down in my journal before. So I'd never had to be careful. But I'm glad now that he told me to be.

CHAPTER THIRTY

I couldn't help but think of today as cursed as the middles and I got out of the car and walked to the doors of the Cineplex theater. The building was a massive structure that I was used to seeing from the Gardiner Expressway with its movie posters declaring the latest releases. It was split into the regular theater and the VIP experience, where they brought the food to your seats and you could buy cocktails. The middles were chatting excitedly about the movie while I was thinking about the fact that Mom had died a year ago today.

In the close to three weeks since that news report I'd watched with Dom and the middles, Paris had, according to her, made significant progress with the Crown for Torri's case. Which was great. And I hadn't seen any black-clad figures hanging around. But on the flip side, the police continued to have no leads on the school murders.

And now we'd come to the day I'd been dreading. I knew from experience that the murderer didn't calm down without plans to resurface. And now felt like the perfect time. The day of the fire at the ranch all those years ago, and of Mom's and Torri's deaths. It was also the date that my parents had chosen to visit Jonas in jail and give something to him that required bribing a security guard.

I didn't know how any of it connected, and I didn't need to know anymore. Things were being handled the way they always should have been, by our legal representation.

I texted Dom to see if he was feeling any better. The middles had actually invited him, but he'd been feeling off since dinner.

He replied, I'm not throwing up anymore, so there's that.

I cracked a little grin.

"Wow, a rare smile from Ms. Debbie Downer," Darren said.

I scowled at him. I think it was still weird for my siblings to get used to a Sunny who wasn't constantly "on." Though Darren and Kiley seemed to be taking it mostly in stride. Karter was another thing altogether. She was the most irritated at my supposed change in attitude. I didn't know what Dad thought. He was spending more and more time on his own in his bedroom.

I didn't know how to feel about it. He was still my dad. And the longer we went without a new murder, the easier it was to think that room in the school really was just unnecessarily secretive milk storage, that maybe he didn't know anything, and it'd been a secret that Mom had kept to herself. Maybe she was the one who made the password about my first steps. She was there too when it happened. That passcode originally didn't seem like one of hers—she never used important dates. But she could have been in a sentimental mood.

We walked into the theater, where our tickets were scanned, and headed to our seats tucked in the upper right corner. We looked over the menus, and the middles discussed which cocktails they were going to get. I had been automatically designated as DD since my license was valid as long as there was an experienced driver in the car with me.

I texted Dom again. Did Dad and Karter say anything about the case?

Technically, we weren't supposed to be talking about this via text, but they'd already taken our phone records, and this wasn't anything that Paris wasn't going to say anyway. Besides, before we'd left, Dad and Karter had been doing this long conference call in Mom's office with Paris. Which I hoped meant that things were wrapping up.

He texted back:

> They said that Paris thinks the Crown is prepping to hand me a plea deal for criminal negligence instead of second-degree. They wanted manslaughter, but they also don't want a trial, so she's pretty sure they'll say yes.

> And it'll be scrubbed when you turn eighteen, right?

> Yeah, since they're not trying me as an adult. But I won't be able to go back to the academy, so I'll have to be homeschooled. Then I can do whatever after.

> And what exactly do they want you to admit to for criminal negligence?

> I guess we'll see

I bit my lip. Meaning that Paris and the Crown would decide together what he was meant to say, and he would be forced to say it.

But according to Paris, settling out of court was always better than a trial. And for Dom, skipping a trial would also avoid scrutiny and media attention. Beyond the case being dropped, this was the best outcome.

He sent another message.

> Dad brought me some medicine. He said it'll probably make me sleepy, so I guess I'll be out for a while. I hear the movie you're seeing isn't complete trash, so enjoy it.

> Thanks. Feel better.

I leaned back into the seat and attempted to enjoy the movie. Like Dom said, it wasn't terrible, though I also didn't know if I thought it was good. But I got to eat cheesecake, so it was enough of a win.

As we left the building, Kiley said, "You know what we should do? Get ice cream!"

I scowled and looked at my phone. It was already ten past eleven, which wasn't that late for a Saturday, but I didn't like the idea of not being home with Dom at night while the murderer was still out there. The middles had actually wanted to go to an even later showing, and I'd had to argue to get this one. "We have ice cream at home," I said.

"It's not the same as fresh ice cream," Darren said. "We should go downtown. Get something expensive."

"Yesssss," Kiley said, grinning at me. "You down?"

"You guys can if you want. Just drop me off at home."

My sister's smile fell off her face. "For fuck's sake, Sunny! It's Saturday night. Live a little."

I hoped that the full weight of the incredulity of my expression was coming across. Why was she getting mad at me over ice cream of all things? "I want to check on Dom."

"He's fine," Darren said with a laugh. "He's in a medicated sleep right now."

I stopped and blinked at my brother. "How do you know?"

"What?"

"How do you know that he's in a medicated sleep?" Dom had texted me that he'd gotten medicine from Dad, but it's not like he was texting updates to all of us.

Darren crossed his arms over his chest. "Because Dad gives us all the same thing when we're sick?"

Did he? I shook the thought away. What was I even accusing Darren of? I was being paranoid, and I knew it. "I just want to go home," I said. "You two can Uber downtown if you want, and I'll drive your car back. But I'm going home."

"You know," Darren ground out, "you used to be so agreeable. Easy. Now you're such an annoying little—"

"Let's just go home," Kiley cut in, her voice firm. She met Darren's eyes. "She wants to go home. So let's go home."

I looked between the two of them, trying to figure out what was going on. They were so on edge. Was it because of Mom? That was the only thing that made sense. I didn't want to think about her being gone either. But I also needed to think of our brother. He could easily be a target, and I would just feel better if we were all together right now.

I got behind the wheel and drove home. The middles were silent for the entire trip.

When we walked into the house, it was quiet. Which wasn't unusual since it was past eleven on a Saturday night. Dad was probably in his room, and Karter must have gone out. Darren and Kiley trailed behind me as I went to Dom's room and looked in. There was a lump bundled up in the sheets.

"See?" Darren said. "He's fine."

I squinted and moved forward to check on him when my sister's hand suddenly locked onto my arm. I turned to Kiley.

"You should let him sleep," she said, her voice clipped.

I shook her off, and she let me go with a soft sigh.

It took me only moments to realize that the lump was just sheets and a duvet. I threw them aside, but Dom wasn't there. My fingers curled into fists in the cloth.

"Maybe the basement?" Darren suggested, though he didn't make any move to go there himself.

I went down into the basement and checked the gaming and theater rooms, but he wasn't there. I even checked the storage room. Nothing.

"Dad!" I shouted as I got to the top floor. "Where's Dom?"

Not today. This could not be happening today of all days.

"Karter?!" I tried.

I knocked on her door, but she didn't answer. I tried the knob, which I expected to be locked, but it wasn't. The door swung open.

The room was empty.

Okay . . . that was fine. She was just out.

I went across the hall to Dad's room.

Empty.

By the time I came back down to the second floor, the middles were waiting there. Just standing by the stairs. Not looking. Almost . . . as if they knew . . . our brother wouldn't be here.

"Where's Dom?" I asked.

Darren shook his head and ground his teeth together. "Should have just come with us to get ice cream."

"Where. Is. Dom?"

Kiley sighed again and turned to Darren. "What now?"

"How should I know?" he snapped, throwing his arms up. "Lock her in her room, I guess."

What? I looked between the two of them. I didn't understand what was happening. I didn't even move as they came toward me because I was so confused.

Then Kiley's fingers closed around my arm again, and this time when I jerked back, she didn't let go. Darren clasped onto my other arm. "Just come with us," he said. "Don't force us to make you go. This is for his own good."

"Let go of me," I said, but my voice was too small. I was still in disbelief about what was happening.

The two of them began to pull me toward my room. And my brain started to work again. Dom wasn't here. Dom was gone. The middles knew. The theater trip was just to keep me out of the way.

Finally my body responded, and I ripped my hand back. I got free of Kiley, but Darren grasped onto my other arm, pulling me back and locking his elbows around my own. He tugged me toward my room.

"Stop it!" I screamed, kicking out my legs and thrashing. But it didn't matter. Sure, Darren was skinny, but he wasn't weak. He had the gym selfies to prove it. "Let me go! Kiley!"

My sister hung her head and walked in front of us, opening the door to my bedroom.

Darren shoved me in, and I fell onto my knees. By the time I scrambled up and turned, the door was already closed. I shoved against it and met pressure. The two of them holding it shut, probably. I rammed my entire body up against the door again and again, but couldn't get it open.

"Stop!" Darren shouted. "Just stay in your room and chill."

I stopped trying and stumbled away from the door. There wasn't any point. I wasn't going to get out that way. Why were they doing this? For Dom's own good? What did that mean?

I looked around the room and spotted the glass doors leading to the balcony. The balcony that was right over the pool room. If I got over the railing, I could get to the next floor. It wasn't even that high a drop. I knew because the middles used to sneak down to that space to smoke without Mom knowing. It was easy. And from there, I could jump onto the grass outside and sprint to the school.

Because that must be where they were. In that fucking room. The room that I told Karter about, and she'd said she would handle it, but clearly she was in on whatever Dad was doing. Of course she was. She'd seen me in his office that night when I'd found the paper with the symbol, and then later it was gone. She would have told him. And the winter dance when Shirley was murdered, the two of them had gone off together and hadn't reappeared until after the scene was cleaned up. It was Dad after all, and Karter had been helping him cover it up. The middles, too. They should all be actors, because they'd really sold that they had no idea what was happening.

I clasped my hand over my mouth to fight the sob that tried to come out.

No. I didn't have time to mourn who Dad had become or think about him killing Mom or any of that.

They had Dom. I didn't understand why they would take him or what they were going to do with him, but obviously, it wasn't good if they were working so hard to keep me out of the way.

Slowly I moved toward the balcony, and as quietly as possible, slid the door open.

Not quiet enough, because I heard Kiley scream, "The balcony!"

I rushed toward the railing and hastily threw one leg over just as the hallway door was ripped open. Between trying to get over the ledge and Darren running at me, I lost my balance, and instead of slowly lowering myself down, in my panic to get my other leg over, my hand slipped off the rail.

And I fell head first toward the concrete platform below.

CHAPTER THIRTY-ONE

My skull was going to smash like a watermelon on concrete. *Messy,* I thought. Mom had always cut ours up so precisely into bite-sized chunks.

Fingers grasped my legs, and I screamed as nails dug into my skin and my body slapped against the side of the balcony glass. A second pair of hands got around my ankles and tugged. Up, and up, and up, slowly, Darren and Kiley got me over the railing.

Darren immediately pulled me into his arms. He was shaking. And crying. "Why would you do that?!" he yelled.

"Have . . . have to help . . . Dom." I was panting between words. I was trembling, too. And somehow still picturing my head bursting into a flourish of red flesh and black seeds, even though that wasn't going to happen anymore. I wanted to stand but didn't think I was strong enough to yet.

"I hate this," Darren said. "I *hate* this. Why couldn't you just listen to me and stop digging into everything?! How many creepy bear messages do you have to get to make you leave things alone?!"

It hit me harder than smashing against the railing. I remembered the figure that had stalked me. The way they'd used that distorted computer voice. It was strange, but I'd just thought it was part of the scary act. But of course . . . it was really because he didn't want me to recognize his voice.

"It's been *you*?!" That made the least sense of anything I had thought of. "*You've* been killing people?"

"No!" Darren shouted, tears spilling down his face. "Just the stuff messing with you. I'm so sorry. I didn't want to do it, but Karter said we had to scare you off of investigating, and I knew that if I let her handle it, she would take it too far. I figured I could be a little gentler, like I was at the Halloween store. But then you just wouldn't stop, and Karter kept saying if I couldn't manage things, she would. So then I . . . I chased you at school . . . and then you fell . . . I'm so sorry."

My brain was rapidly trying to catch up and sort out that the person in black had apparently been two people: Darren and Dad. "How did Karter even know I was investigating?"

"Let's go inside," Kiley said, wrapping her arms around herself. It was February and not exactly hang-around-outside-with-no-jacket weather. Though I couldn't even feel it; adrenaline was heating my entire body.

I got to my feet with Darren's help and we walked back into the hallway. My brother waved his hands around. "Karter has cameras everywhere. In the house, and at school, and at the ranch."

Kiley muttered, "She used to update us on everything you were doing, but she hasn't since we put our foot down after what went down at school with you and Darren. We figured you were freaked out enough, and Karter seemed too busy to keep up with all the surveillance anymore. Besides, it's not like you were making any real progress. No shade, just, like, you weren't."

"Sorry that I didn't want to believe that Dad was a murderer," I snapped.

The middles' eyes both went wide.

"You don't even know how wrong you are," Kiley breathed. "Is that what you think?"

I looked between the two of them, not even sure what I should trust anymore. Was that the truth, that it wasn't Dad? Or was this just another move to protect him?

Darren shook his head, his voice flat, picking viciously at his nails. "Karter is so full of shit. We should have just left you alone. You have no idea what's happening."

"Then *tell me*! What's happening?" I tugged myself away from Darren. "Where is Dom?"

"Dom is sick," Kiley said, pacing the length of the hallway. "He needs help. Karter and Dad are trying to help him. That's what they said. And Mom said . . ." She cut herself off, pressing a fist to her mouth, clearly fighting tears.

"Mom left us notes at the will reading," Darren said.

I cut him off. "You told me all you got was money."

He rolled his eyes. "We *lied*. The notes told us to take care of Dom. We thought it was weird and just ignored it at first, but then Karter and Dad said this is what we need to do to take care of him. And he deserves that, doesn't he? After how we treated him year after year."

I felt like I was over the railing again, floating in the air. She hadn't just left them notes, she left them the *same* note that she'd left me.

Kiley slouched against the hallway wall. "Karter said that . . . that he's not okay, and we'll have to do something about it. Mom left her this whole, like, I don't know, manual or journal all about it."

No. Mom left *me* a journal. That was what that note I'd found meant when she said it would explain everything. It apparently had told Karter what was going on, and if this was the result, she was obviously messing up Mom's instructions. But then again, hadn't

Mom thought that Dom killed Torri? So maybe Karter was actually following them.

I massaged my temples and finally said, "What are you talking about? How is Dom sick?"

Kiley sucked back a sob. "It's *him*! Don't you get it?! He's the murderer."

"No." I shook my head. She was wrong. They were wrong. Our brother was innocent.

Darren sighed and ran his hand over his shaved head. "No one wanted you to worry. And it's . . . it's not his fault. He doesn't even know he's doing it." There was something almost wistful about my older brother's voice. "He's lucky in that way. That he doesn't remember."

Protecting me again. Sheltering me from everything. Except I had gotten that note too. But the way I'd interpreted the instructions and the way my siblings had were very different. "Where is Dom?" Unless I saw Dom holding a knife to a throat, I wasn't going to buy into this.

"At the school," Kiley said, wringing her fingers. I wondered if this was the real reason for her sudden inability to make art. For the shattered sculpture. Just like it was for the sudden decline in Darren's mental health. Or maybe it was the combination of this, Mom's death, and being forced to torment me. "They just want to keep an eye on him. That's all. They think he's going to have another episode."

I laughed. I couldn't help it. "They just want to keep an eye on him, but you two have to physically attack me to keep me away? Not to mention that he's supposedly killed three people—one when he was in *jail*, because that makes sense—and now all of a sudden Dad and Karter can predict when he's going to murder?"

Darren hunched his shoulders and glanced at Kiley. "I told you it was bullshit."

"You're the one who said to grab her!"

"Because *you* said we should just do what Karter and Dad told us. That they would know what Mom wanted. But we knew there were holes in their story. Like Sunny said, Dom was in jail, and someone *still* died."

"Copycats! Just like Karter said."

"Do you seriously believe that?"

Kiley bit her lip. It was obvious that was a hard sell, but she insisted on doubling down anyway. "He's dangerous! That's why they have that room in the first place, to help keep him under control, when really they should have just let the police lock him up. But no, because we can't have a Behre behind bars, can we?" She crossed her arms over her chest and started pacing again.

"They didn't even mention the room to us until Sunny discovered it," Darren hissed back.

I blinked. "Wait, you really didn't know about it?"

Kiley looked away and Darren laughed. "Of course we didn't! Just like we didn't know about the cameras until we saw one, then suddenly Karter told us about it." He pointed at Kiley. "This is what I've been talking about. We're not getting the whole story, but we're expected to participate. The only—and I mean the *only*—reason I've done any of this was to protect Sunny, but you and I both know that they're lying to us."

I scowled. "I didn't ask you to protect me."

"Too bad," Darren snapped.

"We need to go," I said, finally standing up. "Let's go together. I just want to see that Dom's okay. You can show me that I was wrong, and we'll come back home, and Karter and Dad won't know a thing."

The middles looked at each other. Darren raised an eyebrow, and Kiley stopped pacing. "Just to look," she said. "Right?"

"Yes," I breathed.

My siblings exchanged one last look, but I knew that they were going to agree. Because Darren didn't quite believe in what they were doing, even as he helped, and because Kiley seemed to desperately want me to believe Dom was the problem. And for that to happen, we needed to go.

I led the middles to the hedge where I'd come out of the secret room before. I didn't have a ton of hope that Karter wouldn't have changed the passcode since I'd told her about discovering the hidden room, but I at least had to try. We snuck around the edge, and I found the buried keypad. I typed in the same code as last time, the screen flashed red, and the lock remained closed.

"Fuck," I muttered. "We have to get inside."

We walked to the back doors, and as I went to punch in the code for it, Kiley waved me away. "Karter changed them. I didn't realize why you were going to that hedge earlier, or that there was an entrance there, or I would have told you that whatever code you had was probably wrong by now. She only gave us the password in case we needed to come get her for some reason." My sister entered the correct code, and I led the way down to the boys' changeroom at the pool.

"How exactly are Dad and Karter helping Dom?" I asked the middles as we made our way down the hall.

Darren shook his head. "They didn't say specifics. Just that he's got some sort of genetic illness and that sometimes they can tell an episode is coming on, so they 'deal with it.' But it hasn't been working lately. Or they haven't been able to predict the episodes correctly? Some bullshit like that." He bit his lip. "Anyway, he blocks it all out after. Dad said his brother had the same problem. Oh yeah, apparently Dad had a brother."

"I know," I said.

"Wow, you actually found out some stuff?"

I ignored the comment on my investigative skills and looked at Kiley to see if she would add anything, but she stayed quiet.

I wondered how much Dad had really shared about Jonas. Not to mention, even with those details, the story still didn't make any sense. If this was hereditary, why didn't the Turners have some long line of murderers? And why had Jonas not done anything until he was seventeen, but Dom had allegedly killed someone at fourteen? Not to mention, Jonas had said the burden was passing to *Dad*, not to Dom.

"What is it with you and Dom?" I asked Kiley. "Right from the time he came home, you were so reluctant to give him the benefit of the doubt. Why?" There was something feverish about the way she was convinced that Dom was a murderer, whereas Darren was more on the fence. Whatever this was about, she hadn't shared it with him. Confirmed by the way he stopped to look expectantly at her.

"That night . . . when they say Dom was with that girl . . ." Kiley rubbed at her arms. "I had cramps and felt shitty, so I stayed in and went to bed early. Everyone else was out. But then something woke me up, and I couldn't get back to sleep, so I went downstairs to watch a movie. And Dom was already there. In the dark. Just . . . sitting."

"Okay . . . ," Darren said.

"This is exactly why I didn't want to tell you," she snapped. "I knew you would act like it wasn't anything." She adopted a mocking tone. "Oh, Kiley is so free-spirited and fanciful and she doesn't know shit."

I'd never actually given much thought to how my sister assumed we perceived her. I definitely didn't expect that she and Darren, who were so close, didn't have a perfect relationship. That she might hide things from him. She was Kiley. She was gorgeous and artistic and just . . . there.

Darren's eyes softened. "I would never—"

"Whatever! I know Mom thought I was an airhead. The only time I ever impressed her was when I won something, so I entered every contest I could find. And I tried to do it again after she'd died, but there isn't any point, is there?"

"Kiley—" I started.

She cut me off. "I know what I saw."

Our brother cringed. "Sorry, I just . . . I'm trying to understand."

Kiley scowled. "When I asked Dom what he was doing down there, he said he'd accidentally sat on some juice or something earlier. He was washing his clothes."

"I'm . . . confused," Darren said, and I could tell he was trying to be delicate.

"So either he was telling the truth, and for some reason decided he needed to wait around for his laundry at half past midnight," Kiley said. "Or . . . his clothes were wet, and for some reason he didn't want anyone to know they'd been wet." She looked right at me, and I knew what she was saying. If Dom had wet clothes, it was proof that he'd been in the water with Torri.

"He was on video at the 7-Eleven at the time of her death. He was dry then. How could he have been in both places at once?"

Kiley turned away and crossed her arms over her chest. "Have you seen that footage? It's not exactly 1080p. And people are racist. They could have mixed him up with someone. Besides, they used to be unsure about her time of death, remember?"

"Or he was telling the truth," I said. And yeah, it was weird for him to do laundry that late, but Dom often had trouble sleeping. Maybe he'd decided to just wash his stuff since he was up.

My sister shook her head and kept shaking it. "You don't understand. You don't get it because you don't know what it feels like. Something is wrong with our family. Something . . . invades us. Crawls inside us. It makes you do things . . ."

I was about to ask what Kiley was talking about when I thought of Mom's journal entries. "The tongues . . . ," I mumbled.

Kiley's eyes went wide, and tears sprang to them. Darren visibly winced. She said, "I remember sawing them out. And I was happy to do it. It was a hobby. Every time after, I would hate myself. But when I was doing it, I never thought it was wrong." She bit her trembling lip.

I looked at Darren. "The thing you drowned."

He hunched his shoulders. "How do you know about this stuff? Mom said we couldn't talk about it. Not in therapy, not anywhere. Karter said it's part of this genetic thing, but it's stronger in Dom. That's why he forgets and we don't. How it affects him is, like, more complete, she said. It happened to Karter, too . . . you're the only one of us who's never been affected." The corner of his lip tugged into a strained smile. "The only good one."

That was why they believed in what Karter had told them. Why they'd banded together but left me out. This cruelty that lived inside them but had skipped over me somehow. Or maybe it hadn't. I wasn't torturing animals, but I wasn't anywhere near perfect, or good. But I guess comparatively, they saw me as better. As worth protecting and sheltering.

I thought again of Mom's journal and the entry that was dated the same day I'd gone missing. She'd put it on the same page as what my siblings had done but then crossed it out. They were saying that Dom had forgotten what he'd done. Had . . . had I done something to that woman and forgotten? Did I have the same version of this genetic thing that he did? I was the favorite, I knew that. Had Mom decided to pretend I hadn't done something that I had? No. *No.* I was letting their bullshit get into my head.

"This is unhinged," I hissed. "And it's still a leap to go from what you did as kids to murder."

"Animal torture is a precursor to killing people," Kiley said.

"Then why aren't you running around stabbing people?!" I snapped back. "They're lying to us. And I'm not going to just look away this time. He's my brother. He's *our* brother."

Kiley sighed. "Let's just go. You'll see that it's fine."

We continued into the bathroom, and I showed them the secret entrance. We climbed through the vents and dropped down into the hallway, quietly inching our way over, pressed against the wall. When we got to the corner that led to the room, I stopped and peeked around it.

It was dark. The auto lights had been turned off. And instead, only candlelight lit the space. Which was good because it helped hide us in the shadows.

And in that room, on the concrete slab, Dom was unconscious and tied down, and on the gurney in the corner was Lauren Pierce, a senior like me. Her dark skin looked ashen, and she had tears running down her face and her mouth was gagged. Meanwhile, Dad was by the freezer, shaking a thawed bottle of pink milk. Karter stood off to the side, a massive blade in her hand that looked almost two feet long—the sort of thing you'd see actors in action movies use to cut through the jungle.

I pulled away and gestured for the middles to have a turn looking.

When they came back, Darren sunk to the floor and buried his head in his hands. And Kiley looked at me, mouth agape.

The girl in there was alive. And Dom was clearly incapacitated.

Meaning something was very off with the story the middles had been told.

Before I could even begin to think of a plan, Karter spoke. "I know you're back there. Good fucking job, Darren and Kiley. When I saw you leave the house on the cameras, I had hoped it was to keep stalling, but instead you made a tremendous amount of noise coming down here because, shock and surprise, you're not good at sneaking around." Her voice dropped lower. "Now, come over here. I guess this is going to be a full family affair."

Turns out that Karter had been keeping up with the surveillance after all. Or, at least, she had for tonight.

"*Now*," Karter snarled. "Don't make me come get you."

With a trembling breath, I came out into the main room with the middles following close behind me.

February 20, 1996

In the end, I got my wish. Just not how I wanted it. Mr. Owens
left the entire ranch to Dad. The Owenses' house burned down,
but we're rebuilding it. Dad wants it to be more of a family
home than the glamorous mansion that Mr. Owens had. He's
using the extra money from the insurance to give bonuses
to anyone who wants to work on the ranch. People think it's
cursed now.

I don't blame them.

Shirley told me he'd ruined us. We were passing each other
in the hallway as they were letting me out of the facility, and
she was surprisingly quiet. I didn't look at her. And she didn't
look at me. But I heard her whisper those words. <u>The Milk Man
has ruined us.</u>

I'd known, hadn't I? That her little game would eventually
get out of hand. I thought that when I saw her.

At least now I can write down what really happened that
night.

I had to be careful while I was in the hospital with them
watching me, but I don't need to now. Jonas's lawyer is going
to try, but even he knows it's a losing case. They already have
enough evidence to put him away. They won't be checking in on
my journals again.

Everything I wrote was what happened, right up until
we saw Jonas standing there in Mr. Owens's house. I knew

Jonas had done something bad. It was obvious by then. But looking around at the bodies, it did feel impossible that he had murdered them all. Though I knew that didn't actually matter. He still looked hella guilty.

It wasn't fair. This had started with the Feeneys. With Shirley and Donald, but in the end, Jonas would be the one taking the blame.

The scars on my stomach seemed to burn then. I remembered that Jonas had come to help me. Him and Jay. They'd looked after me.

But when this all shook out, the Feeneys would be the victims.

That was when I remembered the jerricans. Mr. Owens always kept a bunch in his basement because he had a few gas generators in case his house ever lost power. A fire could burn the bodies. Burn the evidence.

If we got Jonas out and cleaned him up, we could be his alibi. There was no one else in the house to see us.

Once, Jay had asked me how far I would go for family. At that moment, I knew.

I told Jay about the jerricans.

At first he said no.

But then he looked at his brother, covered in blood, still tucked into the closet, and something changed in his face. He didn't say anything. He only moved ahead of me toward the basement.

There were six cans down there, and we grabbed them all, carrying them up the stairs and putting them by the landing. The idea being to spread the gas everywhere first and then light the match once we were ready to leave.

I let Jay go upstairs while I rushed around the basement,

splashing the gas all over the floor. I was about to leave the area when I heard a choked sob. I froze. And it cut itself off.

I looked back to where Jay had been, though he didn't reappear. I crept toward where I'd heard the sound, looked around a corner, and spotted Shirley. Her golden hair was matted, and she had a body in her lap.

I thought that maybe it was Donald. I couldn't tell because half his head was missing. It was like she was cradling raw meat with a torso, legs, and arms attached. Mack, her dad, was lying barely a foot away, facedown with a shotgun in his right hand. A pool of blood around his own mangled head.

I meant to call out to her. To tell her to leave. To get out.

But another part of me realized that then she'd know about our plan and about Jonas.

Then she looked up at me. Met my eyes.

She was pitiful. Pathetic, really. Not like me. Not like how I could be.

And a pain rolled over my shoulders, pressing down hard enough to make me gasp. It was one I'd felt before but never acknowledged. It'd happened at the beginning of all this when Shirley had burned that lizard.

She looked at me and mouthed a word that I couldn't hear. But I suppose I knew what she was asking. Begging.

She wanted me to help her. How, I don't know. Help drag her brother out, maybe. I couldn't be sure.

I'd begged her too once.

I left the basement without saying a word.

I kept thinking, I'll tell Jay once we've spread all the gasoline. But we emptied the cans without me saying anything.

I thought I would do it before we set the fires.

But I lit the match and tossed it into the basement, shutting the door.

I thought that before we left, definitely by then, I would say something. I would do something. I wouldn't just leave her down there.

And then all the fires were blazing, and we were rushing out the back door of the mansion with Jonas trailing behind us.

Everything else happened the way I wrote it. Jonas tried to attack Jay. Mrs. Turner showed up. I saw Dad with the gun. I mentally practiced how I would look shocked and anguished so Jay would never know that I'd seen what was coming.

The pain in my shoulders became a soft caress.*

And somehow Shirley got out anyway.

But she was wrong in the hospital. We weren't ruined. We were rebuilding it better. What she'd really meant was that her time, her family, her legacy was ruined. But ours was finally getting a chance. Dad even says that he thinks we'll be able to get more black families on the ranch.

There are none now.

Jay's entire family is gone.

They played "One Sweet Day" as we stood in the church, me holding Jay's hand while his parents and sister burned in an incinerator somewhere, and the only family he had left sat in a cell. He gripped my hand hard and stared up at the ceiling, tears slipping down his face, as if he were trying to see them smiling down at him from heaven like the song said.

---

* Maybe this will make you think badly of me. Maybe this entire entry will horrify you, but I've included it anyway. Know that I could have just shown you the sanitized entries meant for the police, but I didn't. I know that you of all people are used to having a public persona, which is necessary, and you do have a special gift for it, but you need to have space to be honest with yourself at some point. Otherwise, the cracks will start to show when you don't want them to.

Now we're his family.

I told him that when we got home. I'd put his little bear carving back on my key chain, and I knew I would keep it forever.

I said that I would always be his family, no matter what. I would never leave him. And I meant that. When I finished speaking, my voice was trembling. And that was when he kissed me.

Put his palms on either side of my face and brought my lips to his. And we stayed like that for a long while.

We could remake what he'd lost. Someday we'll be the mom and dad, and we'll have kids, and they will live the sort of lives we always wanted.*

Especially now that Dad is sending us both to university in Toronto once we finish up school.

Jonas is still awaiting trial. But we all know he's going to lose. And when he does, they'll put him away for as long as possible. And he seems to be fine with it.

He'll die in jail.

I haven't asked Jay how he feels about it.

February 10, 1997

I made an important decision today. I made it for the family.

The ranch is on the verge of bankruptcy. Dad has been late

---

* I hope you know we did this for you. That was all the two of us ever wanted. For you to have the lives we wished we could. You won't know, not until you have your own, what it's like to carry a life inside you and fill it with your hopes and dreams before it even comes out. I wanted the best for you. For all of you. But anything can be corrupted. Even children. You can look at someone who came from your body and feel like you're staring at a stranger. I think of the way Jonas's eyes looked that night. That deep, empty blackness. How can you fix something like that? That's why you have to want the best for the family. For the unit. And you let go of what's already been ruined to save the rest.

paying tuition for me and Jay, and we've both gotten letters saying we will not be accepted for next semester without payment. Our checks for rent in the city have been bouncing. And it seems like no matter what jobs the two of us apply for, we lose them.

I could hear Shirley's voice in my head. Her saying we were ruined.

But she was wrong then, and she's still wrong now.

Her little games ended, but what she started never stopped.

I remembered the first time I'd felt the Milk Man. The sensation of a pushing between my shoulder blades, a pinching of my skin, and the sting of a slap on my face. He wanted inside. I was supposed to let him into my heart.

Instead, I'd ignored him.

I hadn't wanted to believe in Shirley's silly game.

And then it stopped. I told myself that I'd imagined it. This thing that I was too afraid to record in my own journal.

But then I'd stood in that basement looking down at her. And he'd come to me. Just like the first time, he'd said no words, but I understood that I needed to open myself up to him. I hadn't until I was in that hospital, alone, worried about what would happen with me, and Jay, and Dad. Finally I'd let him in, and I heard his voice for the first time.

All the girls in her group were maidens, but Shirley was special. It was why her dad became so suddenly beloved. She'd had a deeper connection to the Milk Man, but then she'd failed.

By the time Dad finally broke down in front of me and Jay, I already knew the whole story, but I let him explain. He told us why they were gathered in that house that day. How they'd been trying to fix the children who'd gone wrong. What they'd done to make the kids end up that way in the first place. How he'd managed to refuse to participate but hadn't stopped it.

They'd wanted to make the ranch better. I understand why that was the directive, because it was in trouble and it would help us all. But it wasn't *really* supposed to help us all, was it? Just those at the very top, like Shirley's family. And because of what they'd done, we all suffered.

But now . . . now this is our ranch. This is our family. Me, and Jay, and Dad.

And so yesterday, I went back home. I took the bolt gun out back and I shot a cow. I cut the milk free, letting it mingle with the blood, and collected it in a thermos. Screwing the lid tight. Today, Jay and I took it to Jonas. On the anniversary of the massacre. The same day our ranch made him a promise that they couldn't keep. All they had to do was keep the little calves fed once a year on this special night, and they couldn't even do that much. I used everything I'd saved from part-time jobs to make sure the guard would deliver it to Jonas with plenty of time for him to do what needed to be done.

I knew Jay didn't want to do it, but Jonas understood. He wanted this for his brother. For us.

His life was already ruined, but ours didn't have to be.

The Milk Man always collects his dues. And I have no plans to be late like Shirley was. To see my family punished.

The power should have always been used to protect us. Not a plot of land. The family.

Because that's what bears do. They'll risk their lives, even fight to the death to protect their own.

And our family is no different.

You should be able to feel it by now. How he presses into your shoulders and grips without letting go. The way he whispers between your ears without speaking a word and you just know what he wants. It can be scary. I was afraid too. But you must understand that this is how our family thrives. I know you have the strength to bear this, the way I did, and put on a brave face for everyone. I'm confident that the role of maiden will fall to you when I pass.

One maiden for one little calf. All you need to do is care for him. To take care of Dom.

Once a year, one bottle of milk. The hardest part is the timing. But it's a simple price. Your father can explain the method. I don't think he'll like the idea of you leading, or of you being involved in this, but I'll tell him when the time is right.

The greatest cost of this exchange has been my children. But I've been willing to pay it, and I hope you will too when your time comes.

The ruination of one need not mean the destruction of all.

—Mom

CHAPTER THIRTY-TWO

Lauren immediately started to struggle against her restraints when she saw us. Maybe she thought we were going to save her, though I had no idea how that would happen now. Dom, meanwhile, was still unconscious.

Dad turned sad eyes to me, and I forced myself to look back. "We really wanted to keep you out of this."

So then he *had* known about this room. It was part of something unexplained that he and Mom and Jonas were all wrapped up in. Though I didn't understand how Dom was involved or why they'd made up this shit about him being a murderer. Or why Karter, who was skeptical and questioning of everything, was going along with it. Either way, it didn't seem good.

"Please don't hurt him," I said, looking at Dom. "He's your son."

Dad's eyes watered. "I would never hurt him. I would never hurt any of you." He looked away and up to keep the tears from falling. "Your mom and I did this to protect this family."

"By killing Dom?!"

"No one is killing him," Karter snapped at me. "This is *for* him."

Darren snorted. "I'm sorry, did our baby brother ask to be knocked out?"

Karter took her phone from her pocket and frowned at the screen.

"Twenty minutes until midnight. We don't have time for this."

"You can't take five minutes to explain why our brother is on an *altar*?" Darren asked.

I shuffled close to Dom, pulling his limp hand into my own. I waited for Karter and Dad to look at Darren before slipping my keys into my hand and slowly stabbing the tip into the underside of Dom's palm. I needed him to wake up. *Now.*

"Okay," I said. "So you're not killing him, but why is he here like this?"

Dad wrung his hands together. "This is why your mom had this room made. Every year, we give him the bloody milk, and we keep what's inside of him appeased."

I could have laughed in his face. "What's 'inside of him'? Are you talking about the genetics bullshit you've been feeding the middles?"

He flinched when I swore, I guess not used to hearing that language from my mouth. "No. You're right. It's not genetic. But in our family, it is, unfortunately, something that gets passed down."

Karter snapped her eyes to our dad. "We're on a deadline!"

"How do you expect them to accept this if they don't understand what's happening?" he said back, voice suddenly loud, gesturing around the room. "We are in a secret basement room, with a girl strapped to a gurney, and their brother restrained on an altar, and you're holding a knife. You think they're just going to be okay with that?"

Karter crossed her arms over her chest. "Fine. But be fast. You've already screwed this up twice. We can't fail him again."

I homed in on my sister's words. We can't fail *him* again. "Him? You mean the Milk Man . . . you're working for him?!" Even as I said it, it made no sense. "Why?! He's been targeting our family. He killed Mom!"

Karter reared back like I'd slapped her. "Um, no, Mom slipped on ice and died." But even as she said it, her brow furrowed, and I watched her lips move without sound, mumbling to herself.

"Sunny, I can tell you're confused," Dad said, and he nodded to Dom. "The Milk Man, he's inside your brother. As he was once inside my own brother. I assume Shirley told you about the Milk Man? I don't know if she fed you that lie about Ainsley's death. What happened to your mom was tragic, but trust me, if there was foul play, we would know. Dom is one of the little calves. Your mother used to be our family's maiden."

Dom said that Shirley told him there was still a maiden remaining . . . but Mom was dead. And I didn't even understand what that title meant. "Shirley didn't get to say much of anything to me because you stabbed her in the throat," I snarled.

"Wait," Kiley said, looking between me and Dad. "Dad did what now?!"

"I too would like to understand who Sunny thinks you stabbed in the throat," Darren added.

"Shirley Feeney." Dad shook his head. "She shouldn't have tried to involve you. She dyed her hair, and I hadn't seen her in so long, I didn't realize who she was right away. When we saw she'd left that note in your locker about meeting up . . . something had to be done. She was the one who started this. She named him. The Milk Man, and his maidens who listen, and the little calves whose skin he slips under for warmth. He promised to help our ranch for these small sacrifices, burning lizards. But then he wanted more, larger animals. And then Shirley said all the families needed to do was feed their children some bloody milk. They were uneasy, but they agreed. After all, it was such a little thing. You have to understand, they didn't really know what they were agreeing to. It attached him to their bloodlines, to ours, too. And the only way to separate the line from the Milk Man . . . is to cut off the connection. To slaughter the little calf he resides in."

I thought immediately of Jonas's email to Dad. He'd asked for

Dad to kill him . . . Was this why? Because he believed in this thing? This wasn't the Milk Man as a real person. Dad was talking about him like the stuff Jeremy had found about people worshipping the Yew Man, who gave them gifts in exchange for sacrifices.

Was this what Shirley had meant the entire time she'd been trying to warn me? Not of a real man. But this thing Dad thought was hiding beneath Dom's skin. "You think the Milk Man . . . is controlling Dom? Making him kill people?" I asked, my voice every bit as incredulous as the situation demanded.

"Is . . . is that what happened to us, too?" Kiley said, her voice shaky. "The tongues, and the drowning, and all that . . ."

"You can't be serious," I said to her. She couldn't be buying into this. But my sister was looking at our dad for an answer. To Dad I said, "Your brother murdered people, and I'm sorry he did that, but he did. Dom isn't like that."

Dad looked at me with these soft eyes. Like he was so sorry I didn't understand this collective delusion that he and Karter and Shirley were all under. That, if I was honest with myself, Mom had also suffered under. They'd had this traumatic experience, and none of them had dealt with it, and this was the result. And they'd taken whatever my siblings had suffered with that made them hurt animals when they were younger and joined it to this. Not allowing any of them to see someone to get help. Using their fear of what they'd done to keep them silent.

I loved my parents, but they were severely fucked up, and I hadn't realized how much until now.

"I'm sorry," I said to Dad, my eyes filling with tears. "I'm sorry for what your brother did to your family. What he did to that ranch. That you and Mom suffered like that. But what you've done . . . killing Torri, and Shirley, and Ziggy, and—"

"You don't get it," Karter said, shaking her head. "You don't know what it feels like to have him inside you. You don't understand what it's like to do bad things, horrible things, and enjoy it. Only to find yourself with blood on your hands, remembering it all, being horrified, and not knowing what's wrong with you. He spoils us. Turns us. Infects us." She looked over at Darren and Kiley then, and the middles looked anywhere but at me. I didn't blame them. Because this freed them. If they'd done those things only because they were being influenced, then they didn't have to face why they'd done it. But that didn't change the fact that the Milk Man wasn't real.

Karter pointed at Dom on the altar. "He holds the Milk Man better than any of us ever did. Something about him just fits with it. He's never dealt with the sort of corruption that we had. When it was our turn, it was like we were driving with the Milk Man in the back seat whispering in our ears. But Dom is a perfect innocent calf. No backseat driver for him. That is, unless he isn't fed on the ritual day at the right time. You see, that's a very different case. Because on that day, if you miss your payment, the Milk Man comes to collect, and his charge is blood. He takes over. That's why Dom never remembers. Because when that happens, he's fast asleep in the back seat, and the Milk Man takes the wheel."

Our Christmas family ritual that Mom started, that she'd done with her own dad. It wasn't to teach us where our money came from. It was for this purpose. A simple way to weave this act of collecting the liquid needed for this ritual into our lives. Mom always had us drain the milk as soon as possible. Just flushing. And of course, blood would get in it, but it was supposed to be thrown away, so what did it matter? She said it was part of the process, but I'd never actually checked if that was true. Why would I?

And every year, she collected the milk from the freezer and fed it to Jonas, just as she did to Dom. Because she'd believed in this sacrifice. She'd believed in the Milk Man.

Dad said it passed through the bloodline. I looked at him. According to that logic it should have gone to him, but he'd also said the Milk Man had wanted the little calves. Children. I asked Dad, "Based on what you're saying, you passed the Milk Man from child to child—your *own* children . . . assuming any of this is real, why would you be okay with that?"

Dad wrapped his arms around himself. "I was willing to receive the Milk Man only because I thought we might end it. But as you suspected, I was too old. Though he offered Ainsley the choice to pass him around, try him out, so to speak, in all our children to find the best fit. So we did, from oldest to youngest."

I rolled my eyes. How convenient that this imaginary figure was so accommodating. "And if none of us fit?"

Dad let his arms drop. "We would have dealt with it."

But I'd never done anything like what my siblings had. I still refused to believe in this, but their delusion did actually seem to have rules. Based on what they were saying, I would have remembered if I'd hurt anything. If I was special like Jonas, considering our birth order, the Milk Man wouldn't have been passed to Dom in the first place. They would have kept him in me if the fit was right. I made a guess and asked, "I was never tried out as a little calf, was I?"

"No. You weren't. Mom didn't want you to be, apparently." Karter gritted her teeth as she said it. I wondered if this was what she thought of every time she called me out for not knowing anything and being sheltered.

Mom had skipped me. Because I was supposed to lead the family. I was supposed to fulfill her role. I knew that was the reason. She . . . she'd really believed in this. And if she did, what was in that journal she'd left for me? What had Karter been reading?

Darren said, "Can we get to the part that explains why people have been dying left and right?"

Dad sighed and hung his head.

"He wanted more, didn't he? The Milk Man?" I asked him, and he looked up at me, his eyes pained. It was exactly as Shirley had said. He always wanted more. And even knowing that, they kept doing what he'd supposedly said.

"Yes, as penance for the last two failed rituals. Silly mistakes. It's a simple task, but it's hard to get just right," he said, licking his lips. "He wanted bodies. Placed publicly in the school so he could . . . so he could see them. We suggested private viewings down here for the sake of keeping everything under control but were denied."

That was why Duane didn't have more blood around him. They killed people down here, then moved them later. Or they'd tried to, anyway. Ziggy and Shirley had clearly been rush jobs.

I dug the keys so hard into Dom's palm that wetness started to pool in my fingers. I felt him twitch, and his expression twisted for a moment.

I was thinking of finding Dom with Duane's body. Of the way he'd seemed to know exactly where to go when Ziggy was killed.

No. There was no way. I was not going to get wrapped up in their bullshit. Dad was mourning Mom, and he'd pushed the delusion so he could give himself permission to murder away his grief. And Karter was supporting it because she desperately wanted to do what Mom wanted. I'd wanted to too. But now . . . was this really what Mom had hoped for? It was one thing to feed Dom some milk and another to kill in his name.

I looked over at Lauren. "And so you plan to just keep doing this forever?"

"No." Dad's voice was firm. "This is the last one. Four sacrifices for the four points where his symbol intersects."

"Are you sure?" I taunted, sarcasm coating my words. "Or is he going to want more later?"

Dad shifted in place, and Karter cut in, "This is the last one. He's promised."

"And how does that work?" Darren said, looking between our sister and dad. "How's he talking to you?"

"One maiden for at least one calf. And one calf per family. The maiden listens, and the calf hosts." My sister looked pointedly at me. "You hear that? He chose me. *Me*. He told me everything I needed to know."

"Then why take Mom's journal from me?" I shot back.

Karter grinned. "Because it should have been mine. You couldn't have done this. That was what Mom never understood. That day, I tried to get her to see how strong I really was."

My siblings and Dad turned to look at Karter. I looked at her too. *Really* looked at her. There were bags under her eyes; I knew because the foundation was caked there. She wasn't her usual skinny. She was underweight. And she was less holding the giant knife in her hands than leaning on it. Karter was exhausted. But I could tell that she'd been building up to saying this to me. It was like when I'd called her. She had held back then, but now, what was the point? I was already seeing the worst possible version of her.

Karter's voice got louder. "I stayed in the trees while I sobbed and threw up. So that when I came to Mom with blood on my hands, she would know that I'd tried my best to be strong. But all she'd done was make me wash up and ask where you were. And when I went to finally look for you, you were gone. I'd lost you and she never forgave me for it."

"That's not true," Dad said, moving toward her.

"It is!" Karter shrieked. "You both blamed me. You have never stopped blaming me. And then she had the fucking gall to say that *Sunny* was who she wanted to lead this family? Are you kidding me? But *he* knew. So when Mom was gone, he chose me."

Kiley said, "Wait, Mom wanted Sunny to be in charge of us?"

Darren and Dad were both giving Karter confused looks, but she didn't care. She was looking at me.

And I was processing what she'd said. Karter had ditched me. And I'd come across that woman. Her body was so fresh. They never caught who did it. And Mom had listed that date in her book, along with her other children's atrocities. In 2013, the year Jonas died. Oldest to youngest, Dad had said.

"You killed the woman in the tent," I whispered, knowing it was true. "That was why Mom blamed you. Not just because you lost me but because she knew what you did."

Karter's eyes shone with tears, though she didn't let any fall, blinking them away instead. "You don't understand what it's like to be a little calf. I would have never done that. But I was the first one. I was terrified. I pulled myself together to show Mom I could handle myself, and it didn't matter. She still picked you."

Mom had crossed the date out. She'd decided to pretend she didn't know what my sister was capable of, even as she shunned Dom. She held on to her delusion and kept him at arm's length because she believed that they'd put a monster inside him, and it was happy there. And what did that say about my little brother? Apparently, Mom thought it said something worse than her other children. Even though one was already a murderer. I guess because she believed it wasn't Karter's fault, and it was easier to ignore because none of them were calves anymore. Not like Dom apparently was.

There was something very wrong with this family. And it wasn't the "Milk Man," but it was something. I could understand why Mom and Dad preferred the supernatural explanation. If my parents could blame this figure, they never had to examine if they were the problem. They didn't have to try to help my siblings, either. They could bury themselves in imaginary rituals and claim they were doing everything they could.

It was tragic.

And it made my sister's role in the rest of this sad story obvious.

"Dad hasn't been doing the killing," I said to Karter. "You have. You killed Shirley, and Duane, and Ziggy, and Ellis, and Torri, even!"

Darren made a choking sound in the back of his throat, and Kiley stumbled over to the wall, sinking her side into it.

But Karter remained unmoved. "Someone had to do it."

Dad at least had the decency to look down at his shoes.

"Why the creepy notes?" I asked. "Did the Milk Man want that, too?"

"No. I wrote those to make sure we were seen as the victims. I even suggested some to Darren so when he made his very pathetic attempts to scare you, it would be consistent," Karter said like it should have been obvious. "But of course the police never see Black people as victims, do they? So that didn't work out so well."

"The victims are the people you killed," I insisted.

"Don't be so sanctimonious, Sunny," Karter snapped. "You think I don't know about you helping Dom clean up after you found him with Duane's body?"

I froze.

Karter grinned. "Yeah, those school cameras? I set them up after all. Because I knew Dom would be drawn to the bodies and wanted to make sure he didn't incriminate himself. But you did that work for me. Then you watched me stab Shirley in the throat and didn't say shit. You're not on the moral high ground here. And if it makes you feel better, I didn't kill Torri."

I snorted and Karter glared at me.

"I didn't! That was Dom. The result of Dad's first fuckup when Mom had to be away for business. He couldn't find Dom to knock him out, spent all night looking for him, and Dom had already killed her by the time Dad found out he was at 7-Eleven with his little friend. For fuckup number two, Dom was already down here, restrained, but Dad was freaking out over not hearing from Mom, so he missed his time."

Delusions aside, Karter didn't know anything about this stuff until after Mom died. So if Dad was down here with Dom, then Mom . . . she really did just slip and die. It was like he'd said. A tragedy. And Shirley was just as affected by this as the rest of them. She'd probably watched Mom fall and assumed that somehow the Milk Man was responsible.

And even after admitting all of this, Karter was still lying. I shook my head at her, the disgust plain on my face. "I can't believe you're trying to act like Dom was involved in any of this."

"Don't pretend you ever cared," Karter said, her voice flat. "None of us gave a shit about Dom. Mom was understandably cautious with him. And what she did is why this family has everything it does. We appease the Milk Man, and in return he's given us the houses, the cars, the school, the clothes, the fancy galas. Dom can't even remember what he does. He got off easy! I remember everything! I get to remember kids begging and screaming for their lives, but I'm doing it for this family. Dom is *lucky*."

"Lucky?!" I actually did laugh then. "You *chose* to do this. Dom was treated terribly because of some imaginary figure and this bullshit that Mom and Dad projected onto him."

Mom thought she was protecting us, but she wasn't. She'd ruined our brother's childhood, and for what? She could have just loved him. That was all she'd ever had to do. But because of this Milk Man delusion, she hadn't.

Dad cut in sharply, "We both made the decision to make your brother a calf. Which we thought was better than killing one of our own children."

"Oh yeah, completely altruistic," Darren drawled, his face still pale. "Not at all to do with this supposed money and power you were promised."

"Money and power that your privileged ass has benefitted from your entire life," Karter snapped. "We do not have time for this. Lauren needs to be sacrificed and taken somewhere in the school to dump, and I still have to draw this symbol and feed Dom the milk."

Lauren, upon hearing my sister's plans for her, started to struggle and scream against her gag in earnest. The muffled cries felt like they were being sobbed directly in my ear. I needed to help her and get Dom out of this situation.

"I'm taking Dom and Lauren out of here," I said.

"You can't take Lauren," Karter said, eyes narrowed. "She'll talk. You're really going to have the whole family go down for this?"

I swallowed, shaking. I couldn't just let her die, but this . . . this would destroy everything. All that Mom had built. But now, what *had* my mom built? This worshipping of a disembodied voice that demanded blood, and milk, and sacrifices, and ruination?

I squeezed my eyes shut, tears spilling out of them. This wasn't the family it should be, and if that meant destroying it, then maybe that was what needed to happen.

When I opened my eyes, ready to say as much, Karter was already walking toward a screaming Lauren. I tried to move, but it was as if I were frozen, forced to watch as she raised the knife high and brought it down hard on the girl's neck. Blood gushed from the wound. I clutched at my stomach and turned, emptying it next to the altar.

Kiley was screaming, and Darren was saying, "Oh shit, oh shit, oh shit." Over and over again.

My ears felt clogged. Like I was drowning, I swayed in place, watching the blood from Lauren's neck run toward the drain in the middle of the room.

I stumbled back over to Dom just as his eyes were opening.

Karter sighed, her face marked by a splatter of blood running down her cheek and sinking into the silk of her peach-colored top. "Great. Now he's awake."

CHAPTER THIRTY-THREE

om's eyes widened as he took in Lauren's body, limp and bleeding out on a metal gurney while our older sister held a knife and was covered in blood. Karter stared up at the ceiling, as if taking a moment to compose herself. "Well, Lauren is taken care of, and the silver lining is that Dom was awake to witness it. But *he* still wants the public placing of her body, so I'll roll her off." Her voice was empty. It almost seemed to have its own echo. Like she hadn't just killed a seventeen-year-old girl. She gestured to Dad. "You can do the milk thing. Don't mess up the timing and make sure to hold his nose so he swallows."

"No," I said, shaking my head. "You're not feeding him anything. I'm taking him."

Karter let out a long, exhausted groan that was on the edge of a whine. "Sunny, *please*."

Kiley stepped up beside me, her legs shaking, alongside Darren, who had remnants of vomit in the corner of his mouth. "You heard her," Kiley said. "We're taking our brother away from you and your Milk Man cult."

Darren gestured to the two of us. "What they said."

I looked at the middles, fighting another onslaught of tears. I hadn't been sure if they would actually help me. They had bought into this whole thing. But they'd also not known the full scope of it. Which had made a big difference in their decision about who to stand with.

Our older sister said nothing for a moment, then pursed her lips, and her expression changed, hardening into something tight and compact. She looked at us, raising her knife. "You sure about that?"

Dad made a strangled sound in the back of his throat that Karter ignored.

"Yes," I said, though my voice came out as a tremble. She wouldn't hurt any of us. She wouldn't. She *wouldn't*.

"Sunny," Darren said quietly. "Get Dom unstrapped."

Before I could even start, he let out a scream and rushed at Karter. She obviously hadn't been expecting it, because she dropped the knife to fend him off. And then Kiley joined in with a cry of her own, prompting Dad to get involved in trying to unlatch them.

Leaving me to tackle Dom's restraints.

"Sunny . . . ," he slurred, his voice heavy. "What's . . . what's . . . happening? That girl . . ."

"It's okay," I said, shushing him. "It's going to be okay. Let's just get you off this thing."

With the straps unbuckled, I helped maneuver him off the altar and onto the ground. I put his arm around my shoulders and tugged him after me. "Move, you need to move! We need to run!"

"The middles . . ."

"They'll be okay, let's go."

He wasn't exactly walking in a straight line, but he was moving. I shoved him in front of me and made him climb up into the air ducts in the ceiling. He swayed on the ladder, making slow progress, and I kept looking behind us.

I had said the middles would be fine, but I didn't actually know that. I didn't know anything anymore. I'd just watched my sister murder a girl in front of us. I had no idea what she and Dad were capable of.

Finally we got into the ducts, and I urged him forward, muttering, "We have to go. We have to go. We have to go."

We made it to the spot over the toilet, and Dom dropped down with all the grace of a newborn kitten. His foot went straight into the toilet, and he fell forward, only just catching himself with his hands so he didn't smash his face.

I jumped down after him and helped him up. "Let's go. We need to go."

"Yeah, I figured that out," he said, leaning on me for a moment, panting heavily before he stepped away. "I can walk. I'm fine."

I made him go first out the door so I could keep watch behind us in case Karter or Dad came. But there weren't any sounds up there. The middles were still succeeding at holding them back.

We ran together out into the hall and up the stairs to the main floor. But before we could leave the stairwell, the door was wrenched open, and Karter stood there grinning, her face still bloody, holding the knife.

I yanked Dom back by his shirt to keep him away from our sister, but he lost his footing and fell back into me. I screamed as we tumbled down the stairs. My head hit the ground, and I gasped, my vision going white and then black.

I was still on the floor, too in shock to move, watching Karter come down the stairs. Dad was behind her. He was saying something, but his voice was so quiet.

"Dom," I choked out.

He was lying on his side but facing me, squeezing his eyes shut. His forehead was bleeding.

I forced myself to turn and get on my hands and knees. To push myself up. I walked in front of him. "Leave him ... alone," I gasped. I tried to tug him up, and after a few tries, we made it.

But Karter had already closed in on us, and we were backed into a wall. I pressed my brother behind me. I wasn't going to let them involve him in whatever their messed-up plan was. I wasn't going to let this keep happening.

Karter's lip curled. "Get out of the way. We are in a time crunch. Move! This is for *you*. For all of us!" She gestured at him. "All he has to do is drink some milk." She laughed, her voice filled with disbelief. "That's all! Which he could have done unaware, but you've changed that now, haven't you?"

"This isn't normal. How can you not see that?"

"See, this is why she should have chosen me!" Karter screamed, spit landing on my face. "You don't have what it takes." There were tears in my sister's eyes. "You of all people should know how important it is for us to carry on Mom's legacy. If we don't do this, everything will fall apart. This is our last chance. Displease him one more time and things are going to get bad. We already lost Mom. How much more do you want us to lose? This is what she wanted for us. To do this the right way!"

"You don't know what Mom wanted!" I screamed, clinging to Dom behind me. Because Karter was right, I couldn't have done all this. I *wouldn't* have done it. And maybe that was what Mom really wanted. I couldn't know because Karter had stolen what she'd left for me. Now I was just getting my sister's interpretation.

Tears streamed down my face. I loved Mom so much, but Dom wasn't the only one she'd kept at arm's length. She'd done it to us all, just in different ways.

Karter said, "Mom wanted us to survive. And this is how we do it. Time is running out. Give him to me, or I'll take him."

"Sunny . . . ," Dom whispered behind me. "I think she's serious . . . You should just let me go."

I jerked my head toward him.

He was staring at the knife in our sister's hand. "I don't want you to get hurt. Not because of me." He hung his head. "I'll just do what she wants."

"No," I said, my voice firm.

He started, "Sunny—"

"*No!* You are my little brother, and I'm going to take care of you. We're not doing this anymore." I looked at Karter when I said it.

Dad gripped his head in his hands behind her. "Sunny, we aren't going to hurt him. Karter, calm down."

"She doesn't want to listen," Karter said, her voice low. I couldn't even tell if she'd heard Dad. She raised the knife and snarled, "Move!"

I flinched and pressed myself farther into Dom.

Dad leapt into action and shoved her away from me. "Enough!" he screamed.

I watched as my sister fell.

It felt like a moment that should have been in slow motion. But it wasn't.

It was fast.

The arc of the knife as Karter brought it down wasn't gentle. She had put force into it. But when Dad pushed her, he threw the trajectory off. And the knife came down on her leg as she fell, slicing right through her thigh.

Karter shrieked. Blood exploded from the wound upon contact.

All I could do was stare.

Dad gasped and scrambled over to her. The knife was on the floor, blood flowing from her leg at a speed that felt unreal. He was saying, "No, no, no, no, no, no," as he pulled off his shirt and tried to staunch the bleeding.

I was frozen against the wall. Trembling.

Karter was sobbing now. "Fuck," she cried. She looked at our dad. "I was aiming for the air in front of her. It was j-j-just to scare her." She was shaking, and blood wouldn't stop pouring from the wound. It was happening so, so fast. "I wouldn't have killed her! I would have never done that. Did you really think I would? Is that . . . what you think . . . of me?" Her breathing was getting heavier now, and the blood pool was getting bigger. Dad's shirt wasn't doing anything to stop it. "She's . . . my . . . favorite . . . too." She looked up at me then through hazy, tear-filled eyes. "Sorry . . . I didn't . . . tell you . . . about . . . the Craig . . . thing . . . sorry . . . I'm . . ."

She didn't finish the sentence. Karter stopped talking, and her eyes drooped closed.

Dad called 911.

But when they finally got to the school, she was gone.

The time of her death was 12:01 a.m.

On Sunday, a week after she'd died, we watched as Karter's casket was lowered into the ground, and I thought again of Mom's favorite nursery rhyme. She always counted up. One bear cub, then two, and so on. But there was a version that counted down, too.

> *Five bear cubs*
> *Had to tango with a boar*
> *One ran away*
> *Now mama has four*

I learned recently that bears grieve too. Cubs suffer when separated from their mothers. Crying and moaning. Apparently, bears care a lot about families. I wondered if Mom knew that. If that was why she'd had so many around us all the time.

We walked one by one—me, Dom, Darren, and Kiley—and threw dirt onto Karter's coffin. I paused an extra moment to gently toss a teddy bear down and tried not to wince as I bent over. I'd had a persistent ache in my back and headaches since the day of Karter's death thanks to my fall down the stairs. I ignored the pain, as I had been, and watched as my eldest sister was buried.

Karter was laid to rest next to Mom.

Dad had been denied bail, so he wasn't there to see his child buried. I didn't know if that was for the best or not.

None of us spoke. We hired someone nondenominational to read a poem. I only noticed the irony later when I thought about the bastardized nursery rhymes Karter had written as the killer.

I fought tears as they came. Not because I didn't want to be seen crying but because I didn't know how to feel. I had loved my sister. And I'd known she was under pressure, that she was unraveling, and now I knew why. She'd acted like it was nothing. Killing people. But that was how Karter was. She always pretended she was tough and untouchable. But she'd cried when we'd been here saying goodbye to Mom, because she'd felt just as deeply as the rest of us. She'd been so desperate to fulfill what she thought were Mom's last wishes that she'd taken lives. To prove that Mom should have chosen her to lead. And Dad had let her. Our parents were not the same parents to all of us. I got the best of them. But Karter . . . Karter had gotten a very different version. And she'd thought we hated her, and still, she was doing something she believed would help us all. My sister loved us so, so much. And she didn't know how to tell us, so she'd done this instead.

I wanted to say to her that I loved her exactly as she was. I wanted her to know that I hadn't really believed she would hurt any of us. I wanted to share that she didn't need to do all this alone. That she could have been honest with us. We could have figured it out together. I wanted to scream that she wasn't responsible for protecting us all by herself. No one should have been. Mom shouldn't have made *anyone* leader. Normal families didn't have leaders. The pressure of our success and survival should have never been put on one person.

I loved my sister, and I missed her, and the worst part was that I didn't know if she'd known that when she died.

I didn't believe in the Milk Man, but real or not, he *had* brought ruination to our family.

There was no additional service after. We just buried Karter and went home. Though it wouldn't be home for much longer. The family finances had been suffering, and they'd only gotten worse since Karter's death. Paris had already advised us to sell the family home. The house downtown was up in the air, but we would probably need to sell that, too. Soon, the academy would be under new ownership as well. Not by a family, but a board of directors. Some of the parents of the victims would be on it too—notably, Duane's mother. I would never be a fan of Marsha Allen, but she was right about who should control the school. Our family had abused the authority we'd had. It would be better this way.

Everything would take time, but it would happen. And we would make it through together.

CHAPTER THIRTY-FOUR

The penitentiary was cleaner than I thought it would be. It had plain tiled floors in a sort of faded yellow and drop ceilings. The walls were rough cement painted white. Uninspired but not dirty. The staff were friendly, giving me a badge that said VISITOR in big block letters and handing me off to a guard, who led me down the hall.

And thankfully, I hadn't been followed. Initially any visit I'd made to Dad was accompanied by reporters trying to grab footage of me. Anywhere our family went, really. The media circus had been intense. Lots of requests from true-crime people, too, wanting to do interviews with us. We'd said no to all of them. Though we'd been tempted by one offer from a woman whose show we'd watched about forgotten Black girls a while back, when Mom was still around. I remembered because Mom had immediately hired one of the people featured in the documentary to decorate inside the house with a bunch of plants.

I'd liked the woman's pitch because she'd wanted to focus on the victims, who deserved the coverage: Duane, Ziggy, Ellis, and Lauren. Shirley and Torri, too, though my personal feelings about them were complicated. I was glad that Dad had led the police to Shirley's body and that she'd be laid to rest. It just wasn't easy to let her off the hook because she'd tried to help, when she'd likely only done it to ease her own guilt. Similarly, I appreciated that Dad had stopped blaming Dom for Torri's death, even as I firmly believed she'd been a negative influence on my younger brother and shouldn't have been with him. But at least the victims would have been the focus of the documentary instead of some juicy pitch about our family being rich and murderous where the dead were barely a consideration. And I actually trusted her to give as much screen time and focus to the victims who were Black as the ones who weren't. But in the end, we'd said no.

It had been almost a year since Karter died. Nearly two since Mom. We wanted to move on. And doing interviews talking about the past was the opposite of that.

It was busy in the visitation area. Lots of people seeing their loved ones, and big open windows so lots of sunlight came in. There were vending machines on either side, and even a small cafeteria area if you wanted to have an actual meal.

Dad was already waiting at a table for me with a box in front of him. He was dressed in a gray shirt and matching pants, with his name and ID number on a plain metal badge pinned to his lapel. He smiled at me. He'd grown a salt-and-pepper beard.

It was hard to look at him and realize he was never going to leave this place. Charged for murder in the first degree for six victims. Even though Karter had carried out most of them, he'd helped plan, which made him just as guilty. He'd admitted to Torri's death as well, noting her as a first sacrifice, even though Karter had insisted that it was Dom. Dad had known all the relevant details about her death, including the symbol he said he'd notched on her headboard. He'd be serving six consecutive life sentences. I hadn't seen Detective Chambers again since she'd crashed Dad's birthday breakfast, but I imagined she was happy to have all her cases closed.

I hugged Dad, burying my head into his neck. He smelled different now. Scentless. No rich cologne or organic soap scents. We pulled away from each other and sat down.

I looked at the box between us, but he didn't mention it. "How is school?"

"Good. I like my classes." I'd gotten into the University of Toronto, as expected. And so had Shyanne, Mercy, and Craig. I actually still hung out with the girls. They'd taken the whole my-sister-was-a-murderer-and-my-dad-cosigned-it thing very much in stride. I was grateful for them. Craig, I'd seen on campus a few times, though I didn't talk to him. He was still walking around with his tan, which I guess worked for him.

"What about Darren and Kiley? And Dom?" Dad asked. His voice changed. I knew he was trying to seem casual and failing.

"Darren and Kiley are good. Dom, too. He's doing his home-schooling, and he joined an intramural basketball team at the YMCA. It's nice since we're all at the house together, so we see each other every day."

We did get to keep the downtown Toronto house after all. Thanks to hiring a financial advisor, who pulled us out of our debts and brought on someone to manage the ranch who was actually doing well with it. And in light of Dad's confession, both cases against Dom were dropped, though we'd decided not to reenroll him in the academy anyway. Which Jeremy hated, but he did get to take Dom's place in that anatomy class, so he was happy about that. Though I never forgot what he'd said that day. That if it were him, he'd have already been tried as an adult and sentenced.

Because things were different when you had money. After all, we'd bounced back. Even though we didn't have as much as before, we still had more than enough. Mom had us in the academy trying to act like we were the same as those kids when we weren't. I knew now, more than ever, that pretending nothing was wrong wasn't how you protected people. My friends hadn't wanted me to act like I was like them. They'd just wanted me to take a minute to understand how their lives might be different and actually listen when they told me.

I expected Dad to look relieved that Dom was fine, but he didn't. His lips pulled into a frown. "Did you . . . did you find the journal?"

Dad asked me about this every visit. The journal hidden in Karter's bedroom that he'd wanted me to retrieve. And I had. It took only seconds for me to realize it was the one Mom left for me. The one Karter had stolen.

I still loved Dad. But he was the one with clean hands. Karter was the one who was made to slice into bodies. She was the one losing sleep. Losing her grip. Suffering. All by herself, because not even the middles understood the extent of what carrying out our parents' instructions meant.

And then at the end . . . *she'd* tried to apologize to *me*. Over Craig. Over that bullshit that I got so mad at her about when she was just trying to protect me. And yeah, it was fucked up. But so was she. That was how we'd been taught to live. We'd been taught to look out for one another no matter the cost to ourselves. And I had no doubt that my sister was only trying to help me. Even if she was doing it the wrong way.

Every visit since I'd found the journal, I'd lied to Dad and said I hadn't read it yet.

I didn't want to talk about the words in there. Those entries with all Mom's notes. The toxic shit she'd spewed just for me.

Because I knew that if it had been given to me at the time it was supposed to, I might have believed it.

But it wasn't. So I saw it for what it was. Trauma that Mom and Dad had never dealt with and had instead passed down to us.

I was starting to finally accept that Mom hadn't left anything concrete, not to be purposely cryptic, but more likely because she hadn't expected to die this early. I guessed that was why I'd found that one journal in the tree house—she'd meant to include it with the one in the will but had never gotten the chance. She'd probably thought she would be running the show that was our family much longer. We'd all thought that. Our notes to take care of Dom had probably been something she'd thrown in years and years before, when she'd first written the will. And we'd all desperately read into it because, once again, we'd wanted to be led by her the same way we had been our entire lives.

But she was gone.

And she had been wrong. Wrong about so many things. But she'd never wanted to admit that.

"I read it," I said finally.

Dad's face lit up. I pressed my lips into a thin line. "Then you understand now, right? It's not over. We're only a couple weeks away from the tenth." He reached for my hands. I jerked them away and put them in my lap. I ignored the way his face fell. "He's been left unsatisfied. All these curses that happen in the fallout, the failing crops and businesses, are child's play compared to what he can do if you don't appease him. You have to watch Dom. He's susceptible on that day to the Milk Man's influence in a way that he isn't usually. The Milk Man will start to steer your brother without him even knowing. Like Dom agreeing to meet that girl at night. When midnight hits, if you haven't succeeded, the full possession takes hold. If he can possess Dom, that gives him real power in the world, and directly or indirectly, it can destroy us. He punishes the bloodline. He always does." Dad's breathing was heavier now and his expression feverish. "I've been thinking, and maybe you were right before. That he'd come for your mother. It was an accident, but he has the power to do things like that on that day. To delay flights. To shut down elevators and force her to take the stairs. To steer her in a certain direction. Like, with my brother and the others at the ranch, it came for all their families. And last year, he took Karter. She died a minute after midnight—only one minute after we failed to appease him, and he killed again. He'll come for you, too. Sunny—"

"You are the only one afraid of this shit," I muttered under my breath. And *he* was the one who'd killed Karter. He was the reason she'd died. Not the Milk Man. But even now, I didn't want to say that to his face. Because just like he hadn't wanted to believe his brother was a killer, I knew he couldn't accept that he'd taken his child's life, even if it was by accident.

Dom was fine. He hadn't done anything on the eleventh last year after this supposed midnight deadline. We'd all been in the hospital together being treated for shock. He hadn't been possessed and gone out and killed someone.

I wished that Dad wouldn't do this. He refused to budge from this delusion. He was also completely uncooperative in therapy. He wasn't changing or improving. This was the reason that I was the only one who actually visited him.

He narrowed his eyes at me. "You should be afraid."

"Well, I'm not."

"If you can't please him . . . you'll have to stop him."

I remembered very clearly that the only way to "stop him" was to kill Dom, which I would obviously not be doing. I stood from the table. "Why don't I come see you again next month?" I told him. "It'll be after the tenth, so we can have a nice lunch and skip all this, okay?"

"Sunny, please," he said. "You need to be careful. It's not safe to be around Dom on the tenth. At least knock him out. That helps. Then he can't run around and cause damage."

"I love you," I said, and I turned around and left my dad sitting by himself.

CHAPTER THIRTY-FIVE

Everyone at our table cheered as multiple giant platters of Sneaky Dee's famous fully loaded nachos were set down. I had to admit that they were pretty impressive as far as tortilla chips and cheese went. There was even a big pile of guacamole with an additional dollop of sour cream on top.

Most of the group were more Mercy and Shyanne's friends than mine, but I was friendly enough with them to not mind hanging out. And I'd stopped attempting to be "sunny," which had greatly improved my interactions with people.

Shyanne unabashedly leaned over and stuck a candle in the middle of the mess, and I held the base steady so it wouldn't fall as she prepped her lighter. She threw me a little grin. Once the candle was lit, everyone started a loud chorus of "Happy Birthday" that some of the other guests at the restaurant joined in on, stumbling when it came to the name, so our table shouted "Mercy" loudly and then finished.

The almost-birthday girl in question leaned against her girlfriend and adjusted the party hat we'd forced her to wear. She blew out the single candle, and we all cheered again and started reaching for the nachos.

I carefully slipped the candle out and set it aside before it got lost in reaching hands and cheese.

"May I never see Professor Sullivan again for as long as I live," Mercy said, finishing off a nacho.

I shook my head. "That's great for you since you dropped the course, but the rest of us are stuck with him."

Mom and I had always talked about business as a major. But instead, I found myself taking an odd mismatch of courses from psychology to history to biology and more. I wanted an answer for what my family had gone through, and didn't know where to find it, so I'd sought as many sources as I could. When I found the best fit, that would be my major. But you couldn't take more psychology courses without doing the introduction course, which meant I'd have to deal with Sullivan and his convoluted rambling lectures and inconvenient Monday night 6:00 p.m. to 9:00 p.m. class slot.

My original plan for today had been to head straight to the ranch after Sullivan's class. It was the tenth again. Not that we believed in Dad's bullshit, but it was technically the anniversary of both Mom's and Karter's deaths. We thought it might be nice to get out of the city and go to the farm for a couple of days. The middles and Dom were already at the ranch since they'd just skipped class and left earlier.

But Sullivan docked points for attendance, because of course he did, and this was the only day that worked for everyone to celebrate Mercy's birthday. So I'd promised to come out for a few hours before I left. We wouldn't actually be doing anything tonight anyway. Especially given the tradition our parents had on this day. It was better to remember them on the eleventh.

Honestly, I was glad for this. For the distraction. I could hear Dad's voice in my head warning me. I needed this to help drown it out.

It was already eleven fifteen by the time I'd said my goodbyes to Shy-anne and Mercy and gotten back to my car. I didn't normally drive to campus, because it was a waste of time—finding parking was hell and transit worked fine. But I'd done it this time so I could leave straight from the restaurant.

At least I had my own car and finally a license that let me drive by myself. It was just a compact. A Yaris, actually, which I knew Karter would have been appalled by. Me, in a budget vehicle, and not just for temporarily attempting to be stealthy.

I texted the middles that I was on my way and headed off. The good thing about leaving so late on a Monday was that the Don Valley Parkway was basically empty. I could probably get to the ranch in under an hour at this speed.

I merged onto the 401 highway and then made my way to the 400, which would take me straight to the ranch. I passed an Esca-lade, sleek and black. I immediately thought of both Mom and Karter. Of how, for so many years, seeing that SUV pull up made me stop whatever I was doing knowing it was Mom. And how different it was when my older sister took it over. I didn't know how it wasn't torture for her to be in it. We'd sold it last year.

At first, I just glanced at the one on the highway. The way you do when you drive.

And then I froze.

Because inside the vehicle, Mom was at the wheel. The back of her head was bleeding onto the leather seats, and she turned to me with empty eyes. Karter, meanwhile, was in the passenger seat, so, so pale, as pale as she'd been when I'd watched her die. They both met my gaze and smiled.

I slammed on the brakes and swerved onto the shoulder. A car blared its horn at me. I squeezed my eyes shut.

I gripped the steering wheel and forced myself to take deep, long breaths. My shoulders and back cracked, and I winced, twisting the way I usually did to try to shake off the pain. Every doctor I went to said it was from the time I fell down the stairs. They promised I would recover in a couple months. After all, Dom had fallen too, and he was fine right away. But the pain had persisted. It pressed down on me. I saw a physical therapist every week, which helped a little. I reached into my purse and popped a Tylenol into my mouth. I had stronger, but didn't think I should drive on it.

I pulled back onto the road and tried to calm down.

Despite my desire not to, I looked at the time.

12:03.

The phone rang, and I answered it through the car Bluetooth, trying to act as if I hadn't almost killed myself driving. "Yeah?" I looked at the caller ID. Kiley. "I'm on the 400. I should be there soon."

"Sunny . . ." My sister's voice was low and breathy.

My heartbeat started to speed up. "What?"

"Dom . . . I think . . . something's wrong. He's . . . he's in the barn, and he's just standing there."

Okay . . . strange, but not completely off. "Where's Darren?"

"I don't know . . . they were together. Dom thought he saw something weird on the cameras for the barn, so Darren went with him to check it out. But then . . . they didn't come back."

"Where are you?!" I pressed my foot harder on the gas pedal and went into the fast lane. I kept hearing Dad in my head and shook it off. No. I'd avoided getting caught up in his bullshit, and I wasn't going to start now.

"I'm outside the barn. I'm just being paranoid, right? Just 'cause of the day. I'm sorry. I'm gonna go talk to him. I'll call you back after."

"Kiley, wait!"

"Oh, he's waving." She let out a small laugh. "Sorry, I don't know why I freaked out like that. It's—"

There was a sound. A scuffle.

And then my sister screamed.

"Kiley?!"

There was no sound for a moment. It cut off completely. Like someone had muted the phone.

I kept screaming my sister's name, pushing the car faster and faster. Trying to get closer to the ranch.

Finally Dom's voice came on the phone. "I think I scared her."

"Dom . . . I want to talk to Kiley."

"Oh, Kiley can't come to the phone right now."

"Dom!"

"See you soon." The line clicked off, filling the car with the weight of its silence. I tried calling back. But no one answered. I shoved my foot harder against the gas pedal.

When my phone rang again, I jumped to answer. "Kiley?!"

"What? No. It's Jeremy."

I sighed. "I don't have time to talk right now."

"Okay, but wait, Prez, something is up with Dom. He texted me this really weird message."

I ignored his persistent use of that nickname despite the fact that I was in university now. "I know something is up with him. I'm trying to get to the ranch right now. That's why I can't talk."

"Yeah, cool, good, but, um . . ."

"Spit it out," I snapped, switching lanes to get around a car that was going too slow.

"I didn't say anything before because he's my boy, and in the end, your dad said it was him, so—"

"Jeremy!"

"It was me! On the video. At the 7-Eleven. You guys said it was proof that Dom wasn't with Torri 'cause he was there when she died, but he wasn't. He came *after* he saw her. Like, *way after*. I was pissed, honestly, 'cause he called me out and then he was late."

"What are you talking a—" And then it hit me. The security footage from the day Torri died. The evidence hadn't been used in the end, but it had been our best bet. Except Jeremy and my brother shared clothes. Dom had cut his hair in juvie, but before then, he'd had locs, just like Jeremy did. My brother hadn't been at the 7-Eleven when Torri died. "Jeremy, what did Dom text you?"

"He said, 'Milk isn't enough. Bears taste better.'"

I hung up.

I had barely parked the car before I was stumbling out, throwing myself onto the frozen grass of the ranch and sprinting to the barn. The entire rest of the ride, I wrestled with whether or not to call the police and decided against it. Not when it involved my brother, who they seemed to love throwing charges at.

I threw open the barn door—

And fell to my knees, pressing my hands over my mouth.

Darren and Kiley lay against hay bales with their eyes closed. Their chests were littered with stab wounds, their clothes slowly soaking through with blood. And on the floor, the stray hay had been arranged in a design. Into a giant rendition of the symbol. The same symbol that had haunted this family for years.

And there was Dom. Huddled against the calf pen, shaking, a discarded paring knife next to him. I recognized it from our kitchen set. His hands and chest were bloody too. But not from wounds.

He looked over at me, his eyes wide. "I didn't do it. I swear. I didn't do it. I didn't!"

I wondered if this was what Dad had felt like when he'd watched his brother stab his mom. This perfect moment of anguish, confusion, and betrayal.

I swallowed and pulled myself to my feet, shuffling over to where

Dom was. I crouched down and gathered him into my arms. Pulling him close. He cried against me. He was shaking so hard. And he kept saying, "I didn't do it. I didn't do it. I didn't do it." Over and over and over. Like a mantra or a prayer. A desperate hope.

"It's okay," I said, pressing my lips to the top of his head.

I looked up to where I knew the cattle bolt would be waiting, hanging. I reached up for it, tipping it off its perch into my hands. Feeling the cool metal touch of it.

Everything was so simple, so evident, right from the start.

Take care of Dom.

Mom was nothing if not pragmatic. She'd known it would come to this, and so she had stopped loving this child a long time ago. He was a means to an end. And maybe it was all in her head. Hers, and Dad's, and Karter's, but none of that changed the facts. My brother was a murderer.

I didn't know why she'd asked this of me. She'd had years to do this herself but she hadn't. Maybe she'd hoped she wouldn't need to. Or maybe she just hadn't been able to and had simply passed the burden to me, just like everything else she'd wanted of me as the future leader of this family.

My bottom lip trembled.

Sunny Behre. The favorite child. Always kept safe, always protected. And Dom. The little calf sent to slaughter. The boy who no one protected. Who instead was shoved forward at every turn, thrown to the beast in the dark so we could keep going. So we could be the Behres: rich and powerful.

My shoulders shuddered and cracked, and I let out a sob, swallowed by the tiny curls on my brother's head. I understood suddenly how this all played out. There was still time. There were so many nearby ranches. Mack Feeney Jr., for one, and that man, Dad's friend, Andy, and his wife. If I was fast and I took the knife from Dom, I could get there. I could slice their throats wide open. And we already had a cow ready. That could come last. I could pour the milk down Dom's throat. I could restore everything. I could keep using him the way he was meant to be used. As long as I did it *right now*.

What was it Mom said? *The ruination of one need not mean the destruction of all.*

But the voice wasn't my voice.

They sounded like my thoughts, but I knew they weren't.

They were *his*.

I clenched the muscles in my neck, fighting against the plan that was so clear in my mind. My spine compressed, and I cried out, biting down on my lip. It felt like it was going to snap if I didn't move. If I didn't do what I needed to do.

I pressed the barrel of the cattle bolt to my brother's forehead, unclicked the safety, and rested my finger on the trigger. Pain flared across my shoulder blades, and sweat broke out on my brow.

Take care of Dom.

When I looked down at him, he was looking back at me. He stared at the bolt in my hand and then swallowed. He cast his eyes down and stayed in place.

"It's okay," he whispered. "I get it."

"What?" The word slipped out, accompanied by spit and blood. I'd bitten through my lip fighting the pain.

He shook his head, tears slipping down his bloodstained cheeks. "No matter what I do, it just . . . it doesn't get better." He lifted his hands up, holding the bolt in place against his head. "This family would have been better off without me. We've always known that."

Take care of Dom.

Another vertebrae in my spine crunched and snapped. It wanted me to get up. To go and fix this. And didn't I want my brother to live? And then there was Mom's note. There was Dad sitting at that table in jail. If I did this, maybe somehow I could help Dad, get his sentence reduced and set him free. And then there was Dom, holding the bolt steady on his head. And I knew that I could end it all if I just pulled the trigger.

I ground my teeth together, and with a cry, threw the cattle bolt away and hugged my brother close. "I won't," I sobbed. "I won't do that to you. You're not dying. You're not drinking dead cow milk. You'll be okay. We'll be okay. Don't worry. I'll protect you."

Dom was incoherent. I couldn't understand anything through his cries, and I wasn't even sure if he was trying to say something, so I just kept holding him.

My brother would not be a tool. Would not be a sacrifice.

Fuck Mom, and fuck what she'd wanted, and fuck her for trying to make me do something that she couldn't even do herself.

I didn't care about her note or journal. I didn't care about the pressing, pressing, pressing down on my shoulders. Dom was my baby brother, and I would keep him safe.

A cough ripped my gaze away from Dom toward Darren. He opened his eyes wearily and coughed again, blood slipping through his lips.

He was *alive*.

CHAPTER THIRTY-SIX

Dom's anatomy class, it turned out, had very good practical applications. Like knowing that there are a lot of places where you can stab a person without killing them. The doctor had smiled when he'd told us how lucky they were that every vital spot had been missed.

I didn't think luck had much to do with it.

Now Dom and I sat in chairs that technically had cushions but weren't very comfortable, in a private room where our siblings lay on hospital beds.

"You should have killed me," he whispered, staring at his hands.

I sighed. "Please don't say things like that."

"Torri—"

"No names." I didn't know how secure this hospital was or who was listening. I would have preferred that we didn't speak about it at all right now. It could wait until we were home.

He scrubbed the palms of his hands against his eyes. "You shouldn't help me. You should stay far, far away from me. Mom understood that. Did I want to be raised like that? No. But she was right. I . . . I did a terrible thing. It doesn't matter if I don't remember. Now I know." He pulled his hands away from his face and looked up at the ceiling. "My whole life, all I wanted was for this family to love me." He choked and swallowed, trying to regain his composure. "Now I know that you were right not to. I should be punished just as much as Karter or Dad."

"No, they weren't right to do that to you. We weren't. But I do love you. And it was horrible that Karter and Dad went after those kids our school was supposed to protect, and they paid for it. So why do you need to pay for it too? You didn't choose this. They did."

Dom stared at me with wide tear-filled eyes.

I knew that he'd done wrong. I hadn't believed Karter then, but I believed her now. She'd come clean about the other murders but insisted Torri wasn't one of hers. And knowing what I knew now, I understood that Dom had killed Torri. She hadn't deserved it. No matter what I thought about her or what she was actually like, and regardless of the sort of person her mother was, she should still be alive. And he'd taken that from her. But he also hadn't.

"What about Mom?" Dom croaked. "Did I kill Mo—"

"No," I said firmly. "Dad said he had you restrained that night, remember?"

My brother relaxed a bit, nodding.

"You didn't do this," I added. "This was done *to* you." I could feel my voice rising even as I tried to stop it. "They should have protected you. You were their child. They should have never done that to you. And I know there wasn't any easy way to stop what had already been started, but they knew what they'd done, and they treated you like a pariah, and now you're here, you're only sixteen, and you're telling me I should have killed you? Do you realize how messed up that is?"

Dom looked down at his hands. "Don't you think it means something that I'm the only one whose body the Milk Man likes?" When he clocked my shocked expression, he said, "I heard some of what Karter and Dad were saying that day. In that room. She said something about me just fitting with him."

"Or maybe you fight him in a way other people can't. Maybe it's not about him being comfortable in your body as much as it is about you refusing to be corrupted. That's his thing, right? Spoiling innocence. Making kids do horrible things."

He shook his head, a wry smile forming on his lips. "No one's ever thought I was innocent."

His words make me freeze. I think immediately of Jeremy. The way he talked about how whenever he and Dom hung out, people automatically assumed they were up to no good. Had Jonas thought that about himself too? I wondered about the difference it might make to be a child who was innocent but who felt they were already ruined somehow. Because people looked at boys like my brother and they assumed things. Darren had struggled with that too, but he'd always been charismatic. Likable. And that ridiculous word they never said, but you knew they were thinking: nonthreatening. Because the default, of course, was the opposite. Dom hadn't been like Darren. He'd been quiet and shy. How early in life would my brother have picked up on those signals? I couldn't say.

I didn't really know what made Dom the ideal calf. I could only guess. But it didn't matter either way. "Hosting a monster doesn't make you a monster."

Dom said nothing, but he refused to look at me.

I reached out and held on to his face, gently directing him to meet my eyes. "You should have been protected regardless. Yes, something terrible happened to me when I was a kid, but something terrible happened to you, too. Mom and Dad should have protected us, *all of us*, because that's what parents are supposed to do. Now we're all we have, okay? And we're not going to do the same thing they did."

Continuing with our parents' tradition would mean more than just feeding Dom some tainted dairy—it would demand lives. The Milk Man had made that much clear. He'd asked for slit throats, the same way I assumed he had with Karter. And even if we gave him that, it wouldn't end. He would always want more. So I refused to give him anything.

I watched the way my younger brother's eyes darted away, like he didn't want to believe that things might be different. And I couldn't blame him. I couldn't, in a single night, undo years of him being treated like he was nothing. I couldn't fix the realization that this thing was living inside of him. All I could do was try to convince him that I wasn't going anywhere, that I would be here for him.

Slowly he nodded, and I let go of his face.

There was a brief knock on the door before it opened, and Detective Chambers stepped in. I wondered if she'd been listening behind the door. If she'd been noting it down. I needed to call Paris.

She adjusted the lapel of her dress shirt and said, "Sorry to have to see you like this again."

I didn't give an answer, nor did I question why a woman who worked for the Toronto Metropolitan Police force was coming to talk to us about a crime that had been committed in the Oro-Medonte area.

The detective, perhaps picking up on how little interest I had in talking, said, "They thought it might be best to have me come in, given our existing rapport." I wanted to laugh at that. She pulled over a chair and sat down, facing me and Dom. "Can you tell me what happened?"

"I was driving over from the city. I met Dom at the house. He said that Darren and Kiley were in the barn looking after a calf. They were taking a long time, so we went to see what was keeping them, and we found them like that."

"Kind of late to be checking on the livestock, isn't it?"

"Calves need extra care round the clock."

"Did you see the weapon used?"

I shook my head.

"Hmmm."

"Hmmm?" I mimicked.

"Just . . . we can't find the weapon used to attack them. Seems like it might have been a small knife. Something from the kitchen, or even a pocketknife? Any of that jog your memory?"

"Are you saying that you have no evidence?"

"Unfortunately, no. You have cameras on your property, don't you?"

I shook my head again. "We're in the process of changing providers. So they're out of service." There were benefits to having enough money to use your own closed security system. Just like the ones in the school and at home that Karter had used, the company provided the equipment, but we controlled whether or not they remained active and had exclusive access to the footage.

"You deactivated them before you canceled with your provider?"

"Shouldn't you be out there finding the person who did this instead of questioning my sister about our security systems?" Darren's weary voice said as he tried to sit up. I jumped to my feet to help adjust his bed and realized that Kiley was awake too. But she wasn't saying anything. Was just lying silently against the pillows.

Detective Chambers cleared her throat. "So you remember being attacked?"

"Kind of hard to forget," Darren said, deadpan. "Didn't get a good look at the face 'cause of a mask. Maybe my height."

"Man or woman?"

"You can't tell gender from body shape."

The detective smiled in a way that looked strained. "Slight build, medium build, heavy build?"

"Medium. Had muscles."

Chambers turned and looked over at Kiley, who wasn't saying anything. "What about you? What did you see?"

The room hung in silence as my sister stared out at nothing. I willed myself not to look at Dom, but that's exactly where Kiley's eyes went. They stared at each other. The detective looked between them, her brow furrowing.

"Are you okay?" Kiley said finally.

Dom's eyes filled with tears again. "I'm . . . I'm trying to be. I don't know . . . I *want* to be."

Our sister held her gaze with him. Finally she said, "Me too."

"Ms. Behre?" Detective Chambers pushed.

Kiley looked at the detective. "I couldn't see. 'Cause of the mask. But you can figure out who it was if you find the knife, right? I know it was a knife."

Chambers swallowed and nodded. "Yes. We're looking for it now."

"We'll leave you to it, then."

Detective Chambers gave us another tight smile, reminded us that we knew how to reach her, and left the room.

Dom shuffled over to the middles. He opened his mouth, and Kiley shushed him, holding out her hand for him to grasp. He held on to her. "It's okay," she said. "It's okay. It's not your fault."

I joined my siblings, putting my hand over Kiley's and Dom's joined fingers, and Darren reached out too, until we were all connected. Something we could have never been with Mom here.

I didn't know what to do with the knowledge I had now. The Milk Man was real. What I'd seen as delusion was something more, and this was the only explanation that fit. And somehow, it didn't change anything. It didn't make me see Mom in a different light. It didn't make me want to take up the mantle she'd tried to force on me. All it did was make me furious at her. It was unfair to be angrier at her than Dad, but I couldn't help it. Because I'd loved her the most. And she'd loved me the most. And she was my superhero. But she'd been my brother's villain. I couldn't ever think of her the same way.

She and Dad had passed this monster on to us, with its blood-lust and curdled milk scent, and it had made beasts of us all. We'd snapped and clawed and bitten at one another. We'd left deep, gaping wounds.

I felt the pressure on my shoulders and back. Pressing down. Pushing into me. But I would fight it because I knew that Dom was fighting too. We all would. We would take care of one another until the day we could escape it.

Because how could we call ourselves a family if we were only able to be that by leaving someone behind? Maybe that was how Mom and Dad survived. But it didn't need to be how we did it.

We weren't beasts anymore.

EPILOGUE

One year later . . .

It was simple enough to clear a space in the middle of the living room. Our downtown Toronto home had changed a lot in the last year. The baseboards and crown molding used to be a perfect brilliant white, but we couldn't afford cleaners anymore and hadn't quite gotten used to handling all the upkeep ourselves, so instead they were covered in a thin film of dust slowly turning them yellow. We'd pulled the curtains closed. They'd previously let a ton of light into the room and looked out onto the beautiful tree-lined street. The windows both specially made and tinted so we could see out but others couldn't see in. Though we'd had the misfortune of being targeted by a thief that smashed one of the three panes. We'd had a lot of misfortunes in the past year, to be honest. We covered it with a slab of wood and got a quote for fixing it. It was more than what the middles and I made combined in our part-time jobs. The first jobs we'd had our entire lives that were now necessary.

It was all very poor little rich kids. This year I'd spent more time feeling sorry for myself than I ever had. I remembered how, in that secret room exactly two years ago, Karter had tried to impress upon us the level of privilege we had. I was so ready to talk about checking my privilege at the door and all that shit, but it was a lot different to be up close to it.

The Milk Man collected his dues. Last year had only been the beginning. This year, we'd learned just how bad things could get. The ranch was on the brink of bankruptcy, and the overdue bills were piling up at our door. Before, I'd been shielded from all that, but now it was very much out in the open.

Once we'd cleared the space, I turned to the middles. "Can you grab the buckets?" We'd put them in the garage because of the smell. Though I also suspected that none of us wanted to look at them as we walked around the house.

Darren groaned, but walked out of the room toward the garage to collect them. I raised an eyebrow at Kiley. "Not going to help?"

"It's two buckets. He can manage." She stared at the middle of the room, where we weren't supposed to look. "Besides, I don't want to leave you alone."

"I tied the knots myself. They're good."

"Still."

I pulled out my phone and checked the time, gnawing on my lip. Eleven forty-five p.m. We were easily ahead of schedule for a twelve a.m. ritual, but I knew from our family's past that being on time could quickly become complicated. Dad had been blamed for their previous failures, but now I suspected that their struggles were by design. The same way the Milk Man just happened to find those who were the most desperate for his help. My parents' and Karter's problem was that they thought like people when the trick was to think like the monster.

Darren returned to the room with two sloshing buckets filled with thick crimson liquid. He wrinkled his nose as he set them down beside us.

Each of us grabbed a brush, one of the many the middles owned, and dunked them into the buckets. The cow's blood spread onto the bristles but struggled to stick the way paint might have. There wasn't anything else for it. So we moved around the room, creating a large circle with two diagonal lines slashing through it.

When we finished, we stepped back to survey our work. I noticed that once again, the middles were letting their eyes stray to the center of the room. The place we were supposed to be ignoring. We'd decided that would be best in the lead-up to the ritual. No communication. It would make it easier to do what we needed to.

"Stop looking," I said, and they snapped their eyes away.

Kiley shifted in place. "It's hard, sorry. I don't know how you can—" She cut herself off, shaking her head. "Never mind."

She avoided my gaze, but I knew exactly what she was saying. "I can do it because it needs to be done."

"Sunny's right," Darren said, picking at his nails. His cuticles were flaked and bloody, though he didn't seem to care. "And we're wasting time."

I pulled my hair back into a bun, securing it tightly so nothing could be grabbed, and suggested that Kiley do the same. She gave me a long look before complying.

Once we were all ready, I picked up the first bottle of milk. It was pink, just like the ones Mom had used. But there was a distinct yellowish sheen to it, and when I turned the bottle in my hands, the chunks floating in it became obvious. We'd had to leave several in the sunroom upstairs over the last couple weeks to get them to this state.

Finally I faced the middle of the room.

Dom was lying there with a gag over his mouth, hog-tied to keep him in place. I'd added the blindfold later as an extra precaution. Not because I didn't want him to see me. But because I didn't want to look into his eyes while we did this.

I gestured to the middles, who flanked me on either side.

"Kiley, you let us know when it's time," I said.

"I know," she muttered, staring at her phone.

In the end, I didn't need Kiley to feel when the Milk Man came. It was obvious. As if he'd walked through the front door. Veins popped into life on my little brother's neck, and his limbs flexed against the ropes.

"Now!" Kiley said.

I clasped onto Dom's jaw, pressing my fingers to force his lips to pucker. Though he fought, gnashing and attempting to bite me. I understood now why our parents used to knock him out for this. But everything we'd researched had said that this would work best if he was conscious.

I nodded to Darren. He yanked down the gag, and I shoved the glass bottle into Dom's mouth, pressing on the back of it so he couldn't spit it out. Kiley held his nose closed to make him swallow. He struggled in our grasp but eventually was forced to ingest the clumping liquid. The stench of the spoiled milk invaded my nose, and I fought the nausea rolling over me. But I kept the bottle pressed up against his mouth, forcing his head to tilt back until it was empty.

"The next one," I said, and Darren rushed to grab another bottle. I replaced it with the empty one, moving as fast as possible. But not fast enough. Dom's teeth clamped around my fingers, and I screamed. I set down the bottle and forced his teeth open, ignoring the way my fingers throbbed and bled, crimson slipping down his chin. Darren shoved the bottle in, and we pushed his head back again.

Dom bucked and thrashed, though the middles were keeping him as still as they could. My hands trembled.

At some point Kiley had started crying. But she obediently got up and retrieved another bottle when the one we were pouring was empty.

Two more. Four bottles in all for the four intersecting points of the yew branches.

"Does he seem kind of pale to you?" Darren said, looking from me to Dom and back.

I'd noticed, though I hadn't said anything. The third bottle was done. We stuck the fourth in. Dom was crying too. The blindfold was damp. Tears and snot rolled down his face. Two of my fingers were turning purple.

"I can't," Kiley said suddenly, twisting her head from side to side. "I can't do this. What if he dies?!"

"We're almost done!" I snapped at her. The final bits of the fourth bottle disappeared into Dom's throat. I tore it away, throwing it behind me, the sound of shattering glass loud in my ears. I clamped his lips shut, forcing him to keep the liquid down.

Darren was looking between me and Kiley, but I ignored him, too. We just needed to wait a little bit to make sure everything had gone down and stayed down.

"We're doing this for his benefit," Darren said finally.

Kiley curled her lip. "That's exactly what Dad and Karter said."

Dom's body started to thrash violently. "Shit!" I struggled to hold him down. I could tell he was still keeping some of the milk in his cheeks, but I couldn't squeeze them to make him swallow while I fought to keep him still. "Kiley, we need you!"

My sister hesitated for a moment before she dove forward, pushing her weight down along with Darren. I pressed against his cheeks. In the scuffle, the blindfold had slipped, and I could see one eye peeking out at me. I was worried about having to look into them, but when I stared back, I saw nothing of my brother in there.

Only the Milk Man looked back at me.

"Now!" I shouted, and released Dom, sprinting to get out of the circle while my siblings followed. Each of us was breathing hard, sweat coursing down our faces. My fingers had gone completely numb. And in the middle of the circle, Dom began to projectile vomit. The sickly white liquid splashed against the original hardwood. I stared at it and felt my shoulders slump.

I ran to the couch, flipping open the rare book I'd found. The one that cost a lot of money we didn't have and had required selling a lot of stocks we couldn't afford to sell. We could barely pay the property tax on the house as it was.

I read over the words again and again, but they said very clearly that a successful purge of the entity would yield red vomit.

"Well?" Kiley said, looking over at me. "Did we do it?"

I shook my head and tossed the book back on the couch, going to the other side of the room to collect my phone. Fighting tears, I slumped on the floor, cradling my injured hand to my chest. The middles came over and sat beside me.

"Fuck," Darren moaned. "What now?"

Before I could answer, Dom, his lips coated with sick and snot, suddenly ripped free of his bonds. Knots that he absolutely shouldn't have been able to break. The middles swore beside me, and we all scrambled to our feet, but it was too late. He was already upon us.

But as soon as his foot touched the blood on the floor, the entire symbol lit up red and he slammed into an invisible barrier.

"Holy shit," Darren breathed. "It actually worked." He was clutching Kiley, whose mouth was wide open.

That was when I finally let myself cry.

We hadn't done it, but we'd made progress.

I fumbled with my phone and played the video that Dom had recorded and sent to me just before we'd come to the living room to tie him up. Now that he was aware, he could ignore the sudden urges he'd had to leave the house. He was able to push against that suggestibility to the Milk Man that came on the tenth. But what we really needed to deal with was the possession. That was what this ritual was for.

Dom had told me to play the video if I ever doubted what we were doing today.

But I hadn't. Though I played it now because I wanted to hear his voice.

It was Dom sitting in his bedroom in yet another of his anime hoodies. He said, "Hey, so . . . I know that I'm going to be different after midnight. He's going to take control, and it's scary, even if I know that's the plan. But it's worse thinking of me hurting people again. So just remember that if he tries to tempt you into stopping. We decided together to end this curse. To get rid of him. It's a family effort, and I'm happy to play my part as long as you all play yours. I . . ." He paused and looked down and away, his throat bobbing as he swallowed. "I love you. See you tomorrow."

I brushed at the tears slipping down my face. This was why we were doing this. To help Dom. I looked at my siblings, who looked back at me.

"We'll do it next year," Kiley said, nodding at the two of us. "Right?"

Darren nodded. "Next year."

"Next year," I repeated.

I could tell that the Milk Man was screaming, but you couldn't hear it outside the circle. He thrust Dom's body against the barrier to no avail. When he finally stopped to stare into my eyes, I felt the rough shove against my spine, the heavy weight on my shoulders, the sting of scraping on my skin. I gritted my teeth and stared him down. A challenge.

Poor little rich kids. Yeah. We were. I would never pretend that I didn't miss how easy money had made everything. That I didn't still want it someday. We all did. But not at the cost of our brother.

The Milk Man could keep destroying crops, and tanking businesses, and spreading bad luck to us, but we wouldn't let him ruin our family anymore.

If he wanted to be in Dom's body so badly, then fine, it would be his prison until we found a way to get him out.

But my brother would live free someday.

We would make sure of it.

The Milk Man might be a monster, but we were Behres.

And he would come to learn that we had claws too.

ACKNOWLEDGMENTS

Thank you for following me into the depths of this novel about unseen beasts and the weight of what we pass on. It brings me just as much joy now as it did with my first book to see my words reaching people.

I would love to thank my superstar literary agent, Kristy Hunter, who I've come to think of as my coach in the corner of the boxing ring, always there to spur me on even when I'm not sure I can make it through, and to help pick me back up when I have a loss. Thank you to my fantastic editor, Sarah McCabe, who never fails to impress me with her thoughtful insights and understanding of my stories. And an enormous thank you to the Simon & Schuster teams in both the US and Canada, whose hard work I always appreciate, from editorial to marketing, publicity, copyediting, proofreading, design, education and library, sales, and more. Thank you to Elena Masci for the hauntingly beautiful illustration of the cover and to Greg Stadnyk for another fantastic cover design.

Many thanks as always to my friend of over a decade, Cassie Spires, for being an early reader and constant cheerleader of my work. And I would also love to thank Kashay Warren, Laura Fussell, Lindsay Puckett, and Kevin Savoie for their early reads and wonderful comments, suggestions, and support. So much of what

I've come to love about the writing community is the friends I've made, and all these people have been so invaluable in the positive experiences I've had as an author. I often say this, and it's still true: I would not have kept going in this industry as long as I have without the friendships I made along the way.

Last but never least, thank you to my always supportive partner and my little beagle coworker.